I0599744

when the wind is right

ALEXANDRA AYRES

When the Wind is Right
Copyright © 2025 by Alexandra Ayres

All rights reserved.

No part of this publication may be reproduced, stored in a retrieval system, or transmitted in any form or by any means, electronic, mechanical, photocopying, recording, or otherwise, without the prior written permission from the author, except in the case of brief quotations embodied in critical reviews and certain other noncommercial uses permitted by copyright law.

This is a work of fiction. Names, characters, places, and incidents either are the product of the author's imagination or are used fictitiously. Any resemblance to actual persons, living or dead, events, or locales is entirely coincidental.

First Edition: August 2025

Published by Northern Creek Press LLC

979-8-9919800-0-5 (Paperback)
979-8-9919800-1-2 (Ebook)

Cover Design by Books and Moods
Editing by Simply Write
Proofreading by Chloe, English Proper Editing Services

To everyone who believed in this book before I did.
You're the reason I finished it.
Also, kilts. Kilts were a motivator.
Slàinte, you saucy enablers.

JULIETTE

Running was never supposed to become my thing.

I'm not talking about the good kind of running either, where you buy expensive sneakers and track every mile. No, my specialty is the other kind. The messy, heart in your throat, bad decision kind of running. The *flight* half of fight-or-flight.

It started seven years ago during my senior year of high school. Mom sat me down at our old wobbly kitchen table, her hands shaking, her voice thinner than I'd ever heard it. It was the first time I bolted.

"I'm so sorry, Juliette," she whispered back then, as if the words would shatter me if she said them any louder.

One second I was sitting there, staring at the woman who was supposed to be unbreakable, and the next, I wasn't. My feet moved before my brain could catch up. I ran out the door. Down the porch steps. Away from the house. And as far from those words as my feet could carry me.

I didn't have a plan or a destination. I definitely didn't have the first clue of what the hell I was doing. All I knew was that staying felt impossible.

It was spineless of me to flee when *she* needed *me*, but I didn't know how to be strong. So, I ran.

I ran until my lungs burned and my legs gave out. Until I found myself in a clearing I didn't recognize, surrounded by nothing but the quiet wilderness and sky and the distant hush of wind through the trees.

And for a minute, I could almost pretend none of it was real. *Almost.*

As it turned out, I got pretty good at running. It was the stopping that proved to be difficult.

one

JULIETTE

I pull into my driveway on my lunch break, already running through the plan—run inside, grab my bag of art supplies, and get back to work before anyone notices I'm gone. My usual spot is already taken by a car I don't recognize.

It's black and sleek, its exterior gleaming with a high-gloss shine that catches the sunlight in a way that's almost blinding. Everything about the vehicle is unsettling. It's too pristine, too perfect.

I can't explain this uneasiness coursing through me. Maybe it's the way the car looks out of place, or maybe it's the nagging feeling that something's off. I've been jumpy for weeks now, ever since I noticed a change in James, with his late nights out and quiet phone calls he likes to take in private. Still, I shake it off and tell myself I'm being ridiculous. That I'm tired. Paranoid. That it's nothing.

He wouldn't do anything to hurt me. Would he?

I swallow hard, but the question refuses to loosen its grip on my thoughts. *Get out of the car, Juliette Miller. You're spiraling.*

It's just a bag. The one I left smack in the middle of the dining room table during my usual morning circus act that consists of half a cup of forgotten coffee, keys nowhere to be found, hair still wet as I ran out the door muttering promises to myself about "getting it together."

And now here I am, back in the driveway I already left once today, stewing in my own unease because my over-worked brain forgot a stupid tote full of worksheets and markers.

My fingers close around the door handle, but my body... stalls. It's like it knows something my brain hasn't caught up to yet. I force myself out of the car, the weight of each step so heavy that my feet drag behind me. The air has an edge to it, too cool for spring but too warm for winter. It sneaks through my sweater and settles deep into my skin.

I climb the front steps on autopilot, push the front door open, and that's when I hear it.

A laugh.

Light, musical, feminine, and *devastating*. It slices through the silence and cracks me wide open with it.

Time stops as I step into the living room, each second drag-ging like molasses as I take in the scene before me. There, on *our* couch, is my fiancé. He's sprawled out, one arm slung casu-ally behind his head, the other resting on the thigh of the woman currently draped over him like a sheet. She giggles as her nails trail down his chest with a familiarity that makes my stomach churn.

She's bare. Glowing. Her platinum hair is tangled in a halo of sin with that messy, ruined look people wear when they think no one's watching.

Except I am, and I can't tear my gaze away from the disarray of the throw pillows tossed carelessly on the floor or the wine glass teetering dangerously close to the edge of the coffee table. All these little things make this moment painfully real.

James's eyes aren't on me. They're fixed on her, locked in a way that tells me everything I need to know. It's as if I never mattered, never existed at all. Just like that. I'm...erased.

My chest burns as I try to push through the hammering of my heart, each beat loud enough to drown out her giggle that seems to mock me from across the room.

This isn't real. It can't be...but my engagement ring biting into my clenched palm tells me otherwise.

"Are you serious, James? In our house? While your ring is still on my finger?" My voice cracks, splitting the air like a gunshot. I barely recognize the sound. It's like someone else is speaking in my place as I take in the wreckage unfolding before me.

The woman's eyes flash wide with panic, her shame painted across her face. She scrambles, her hands moving in desperate, frantic motions, grabbing at the discarded fabric on the floor as if she can somehow undo what's been done.

From a distance, I can tell she's pretty. Long blonde hair, symmetrical features, and smooth skin. There's also more. *Way* more. She's got curves in all the places I don't with an obvious and unfair advantage in the chest department.

Was I not enough for him? Not delicate enough, not striking enough, not the kind of woman who stops a man dead in his tracks and makes him forget everything else?

James jolts upright the second he sees me and clambers to his feet...but when he steps forward it's not towards me.

It's towards *her*. He plants himself between us, his stance rigid and defensive. His arm rises instinctively, a shield to block her, to protect her from me, as if *I'm* the threat.

As if his loyalties lie with her now.

"Juliette, I—"

5

He says my name like he forgot I still lived here. Like my name tastes sour in his mouth.

His eyes flicker toward me for a second, then dart away. He shifts on his feet, looking anywhere but at me.

I stare at him and for a second, I wonder if this is what heartbreak actually looks like. If it always comes wrapped in soft lighting and bare skin and laughter that isn't yours.

I should be angry, right? How dare he look at me—or not look at me—like I'm the thing causing his pain? But instead, I feel small, almost hollow. I feel invisible in a way that's deeper than just being ignored. It's like the person I used to be to him doesn't exist anymore.

A six-year relationship, gone in the blink of an eye. Just... over. I don't even want to know the details of whatever mess I've been blind to or the lies he's spun that have woven them- selves into everything I thought was real.

I can't fix this. I don't even *want* to.

"Don't." I cut off whatever pathetic excuse he's about to offer. "There's nothing you can say that changes what I just saw."

The truth burns as it leaves my mouth, but I won't let the tears behind my eyes spill. I refuse to give these two the satis- faction of seeing me break.

I walk past them without another word. Their eyes follow me, wide and startled, like *I'm* the one who's shattered some- thing delicate.

The bag is right where I left it, perched on the corner of the dining room table. God, that was just this morning. It feels like another lifetime.

My fingers close tight around the strap, knuckles white and pleading with the canvas for an ounce of steadiness. It doesn't work. My hand still shakes.

I glance down at my left hand and the ring I've twirled

absentmindedly a thousand times. I've worn it like a second skin. Now it's cold. Heavy. Wrong.

I tug it free. It slides off with unsettling ease, and I let it fall onto the hall table on my way to the door.

I don't look down. Don't look back.

I just go.

Behind me, there's a frantic rustle of denim against skin, the clumsy thud of feet hitting the floor. James swears under his breath, fumbling to pull himself together as he races after me.

"Juliette, wait!"

My name rips out of him as the door swings open, but I don't turn around. I don't have it in me, and yet, I catch him out of the corner of my eye anyway. His gaze wild, hair a chaotic mess from where *my* hands were in it hours ago. *Hours.* Jesus.

My legs keep moving because stopping might just kill me. There's no plan, just the mindless push of feet on concrete. Down the steps. Across the driveway. The world around me fades, everything wrapped in a suffocating fog as the rest of my heart splinters into a thousand scattered pieces.

I press a hand to my chest, as if holding myself together will somehow stop the unraveling. But it's no use. The image of James's body tangled with hers on the same couch where we used to whisper about forever is etched into my brain like a burn I'll never heal from.

His laugh, once warm, once *mine*, is now a weapon that slices through every memory I have of him.

I wrench open the car door, collapsing into the driver's seat and slamming it shut behind me. My hands shake as I fumble for the keys, tears streaking down my cheeks and blurring the world beyond the windshield. The car is too small, too stifling. A metal box that traps me in the moment I became someone who knows what betrayal tastes like.

But the world doesn't care. It doesn't stutter or pause,

doesn't tilt sideways to acknowledge that I just walked in on my future going up in smoke. The sky stays blue. The breeze keeps blowing. Somewhere, someone laughs like hearts don't break in real time.

I start the engine and slam my foot down like the road might offer absolution. The tires screech against the asphalt, but the sound fades quickly, swallowed by the blur of the highway and the scenery whipping by in smudged streaks of green and gray. My hands are locked on the steering wheel so tightly my palms burn.

How am I supposed to walk into a classroom like this? Smile at the kids? Make small talk in the break room like I didn't just watch my entire life detonate in my living room?

The pressure behind my eyes threatens to burst, but I keep my foot down, pushing harder on the accelerator. Maybe speed can outrun the mess clawing at my insides. Maybe if I go fast enough, I won't have to feel it quite yet.

By the time I pull into the school parking lot, the raging wildfire of hurt fizzles down to something newly kindled. My emotions switch from *set everything on fire* to *congratulations, you're just a hollowed-out human shell now*.

Progress, I guess.

I cut the engine and sit there for a second, staring out at the same cracked pavement and faded parking lines, like maybe they'll offer some kind of answer. They don't.

Of course they don't.

I blow out a breath and square my shoulders. Fake it 'til you make it, right? Or at least until the final bell rings, and I can crawl into bed.

One step at a time.

The hallways are loud with the cheerful havoc of students, their laughter and chatter bouncing off the walls. I move through the crowd like a ghost, disconnected and untouchable.

It's all just noise that attempts to drown out the echo of James's laugh, the cruel sight of his face, and that wide-eyed panic when he noticed me.

I make my way past bulletin boards dressed for spring and the faint scent of crayons clinging to the air. My classroom door comes into view, construction paper letters spelling out *Ms. Miller's Room* in a rainbow of bright and happy colors. Pausing just outside, my hand hovering over the doorknob, I take a breath. Then another. No more stalling. Time to plaster on a smile and lie through my teeth.

I turn the knob and push the door open, the familiar creak stretching down the empty hallway like it's announcing my arrival. Here she is, folks. Emotionally unstable but still showing up to work.

The classroom is still and oddly peaceful. It won't last long, though. I'm on borrowed time until twenty-four pairs of sneakers come thundering back from music class.

They spill through the door a little while later, their energy vibrant and carefree, unaware of the storm swirling just beneath my skin. Little feet thud against the floor as the air buzzes with the innocent mayhem of their day-to-day lives.

I paste on a smile, or, at least, I'm pretty sure it's a smile. When one of the kids clambers up to me with a concerned expression, I question if I've failed at hiding my emotions entirely.

"Are you okay, Ms. Miller?"

One of my students, Lily, stands before me with her little face tipped up like I might actually have answers. Her brow is pinched and she's frowning. It's the kind of concerned look kids get when something feels off but they can't quite name it. And apparently, today, that *something* is me.

Cue the lump in my throat.

Her voice is impossibly soft with that gentle, unfiltered

sweetness kids have before the world teaches them to keep their tenderness to themselves. It cracks something in me wide open, loosening the iron grip I've had around my heart since I left that godforsaken driveway.

I swallow hard and force a smile. "I'm fine," I manage. "Just a long morning, that's all."

She stares at me for a second longer, but then she nods. And just like that, she skips away, ponytail swinging, already chatting with her friends like she didn't just unknowingly throw me a life preserver.

Everything's a mess. James, the lies, the way my life split open in the middle of a Wednesday. Except, then there's Lily checking up on me. Proof that not *everything* breaks your heart.

I MAKE IT THROUGH WORK, but the illusion of a perfect afternoon taunts me. The air is crisp, thick with the scent of blooming dogwoods and magnolias, the entire world buzzing with this relentless and almost obnoxious kind of hope. It's everywhere, daring me to feel it.

I don't.

So instead, I sit here in the grass, staring at the horizon, silently begging for even a sliver of peace.

I was supposed to be walking down an aisle in an over-priced dress next month, staring at the man I thought was my forever. The thought hits like a sucker punch, but the sting of it barely scrapes the surface compared to the scars I already carry. As gutting as James's betrayal is, this isn't my first or worst heartbreak.

I pull my knees to my chest, curling in on myself like I can make my body small enough to dodge the next wave of hurt.

For a second, I almost convince myself it's better to push the memories down and shove them back where I keep all the other things I don't feel like dealing with.

But they're already there. Funny thing about memories... They don't ask for permission.

I'm taken back to my senior year. Nearly a decade ago now. The day my mom got her cancer diagnosis, I thought that was it. Rock bottom. The lowest of lows. But grief's got trapdoors you don't see coming until the floor's already given out beneath you.

Turns out, that day was just the beginning.

Everything that came after unraveled so fast. The appointments, the quiet looks from doctors who'd already made up their minds, the way Mom's laugh got quieter while my fears got louder.

Helpless doesn't even cover it. There's nothing quite like watching someone you love fight a battle you both know they're going to lose.

When it got too loud in my own head, I used to come to this clearing. I still do. It's not much to look at. Just grass and trees and sky, but it's mine.

Tucked deep in the hills, hidden behind a winding trail that snakes through trees older than god, it's the one place nobody ever looks for me. Which is probably for the best, considering I'm completely unhinged right now.

At twenty-seven years old, I'm sitting here like some freshly dumped prom queen, still in my work dress and heels. Mascara is streaked down to my chin. My eyes are puffy. The very picture of *she's not doing well.*

If anyone stumbled across me, I'm pretty sure they'd slowly back away. Maybe even whisper a little prayer for me on the way out.

Right now, with nothing but the hush of the wind through

the trees and the low hum of cicadas settling into dusk, I don't have to care. Here, in this quiet little nowhere, I can fall apart without having to explain myself to anyone.

I don't doubt that James loved me once upon a time, but I'm realizing that he never really knew how to love someone who didn't fit into the mold he was so comfortable with. Looking back, it's clear. We were both clinging to the hope that the other would change, holding on to different versions of what we thought we could be. We were doomed from the start. We just hadn't figured it out yet.

Or I guess, *I* hadn't figured it out.

We met during my senior year of college, when the only thing that existed was that weird, empty space after I lost my mom. I was barely human. Just...existing. Floating through my classes like a ghost in leggings and oversized hoodies, surviving on caffeine and autopilot.

And then there was him.

He had that kind of confidence that didn't just turn heads but rearranged entire rooms. He was the sun and the rest of us were just caught in his orbit.

And yeah, I got pulled in. How could I not? That easy grin, his jet-black hair that always seemed perfectly, artfully tousled, and those warm brown eyes that made it dangerously easy to forget how broken I was. I didn't have anything left to give, but I convinced myself that standing close enough to him would trick the universe into letting me borrow a little of his light.

It happened on a random Tuesday. On one of those blurry, gray afternoons not long after midterms when I was just trying to breathe without falling apart. He walked up to me, all charm and smirks, knowing exactly what kind of impression he was making.

"Are you a parking ticket?" he asked, his voice smooth,

confident, and completely unbothered by how ridiculous he sounded. *"Because you've got fine written all over you."*

I remember rolling my eyes, torn between secondhand embarrassment and the amusement I hadn't felt in months. But I laughed.

God help me, I loved that line.

I fell hard. I let myself get caught up in the idea of us. I convinced myself that it was real. That *we* were real.

two

JULIETTE

I 'm still sitting in the grass when the faint sound of footsteps comes from behind me. I don't need to turn around to know who it is. There's only one person who always knows where to find me when I vanish. No matter how far I retreat, she finds me every single time.

Then again, I also sent a frantic text before I left work, unloading everything like she would have the power to fix it.

When I glance up, Bree's stormy blue eyes are already on me. "Do you want me to give you some more time alone?"

There's no judgment in her words, no pressure. Bree's always known when to stay and when to give me space, when to let me have my silence and when to fill it. She doesn't try to fix me, but somehow, being around her makes it easier to want better for myself. She offers soft words when the world is harsh and a shoulder that doesn't flinch when I lean a little too hard.

She watches me, patient as ever, and gives me the space I need to decide. "No," I say. "There's nothing left for me to do here."

She stands and extends a perfectly manicured hand,

pulling me up with no hesitation. Bits of old leaves and soil fall away from my clothes.

"Where can I take you?" she asks. "Do you want to go home and grab some stuff?"

I huff out a bitter laugh. "You mean James's house? No thanks. Anything I left there can stay."

I swipe at the dirt on my dress, but the movements are too fast. It's almost like I'm trying to scrub away more than just a few pieces of dried mud and lingering blades of grass. Each brush of my hand feels less like cleaning and more like a desperate attempt to erase the day.

"Can we just go to your place for now?"

Her head tilts, eyes searching mine. "Yeah, of course. Let's go."

I loop my arm through hers, letting her strength steady me as we start the walk to her parked sedan. Bree's been my person since second grade when she came up to me with her wild blonde hair and gap-toothed grin. All it took was, *"Hey, you wanna be friends?"* for me to claim her as my best friend.

Twenty years later, she's still the one who shows up, no matter how wrecked I am. She's the sister I never had. The one who knows how to gather my pieces and hold them until I remember how to breathe again.

I don't know who I'd be without her. I hope I never have to find out.

When we finally reach the car, I open the passenger door, slipping inside with quiet relief. My fingers move to pull down the sun visor. I catch my reflection in the mirror a second later. Bloodshot hazel eyes stare back at me, wide and weary. My dark brunette hair is still pinned in place, and my lashes are spidery and mascara streaked, but for the first time in hours, they're not wet.

"You're sure you want to go to my place, yeah?" she asks. "You can absolutely stay as long as you need to."

"Mmhm, your place. And I appreciate that, but I won't stay too long. I just need some time to get my old place set back up."

I lean back against the headrest, watching the sun dip below the horizon, the light fading in a slow exhale. Time slips through my fingers, and no matter how hard I try to hold on, it just keeps moving. I can't get a grasp on where it's going or if I even want to follow it anymore.

She gives a gentle nod and pulls out of the parking lot. My mind drifts, and before I realize it, we're in her garage. How did I zone out that hard?

She puts the car into park, the soft click of the gear shift breaking the silence. I look over, and she's already watching me. Her eyes are gentle, threaded with worry, but she doesn't speak. She just reaches across the console and wraps her fingers around mine.

We finally climb out of the car, and I follow her up the two wooden steps as she pushes open the door to the mudroom. The second my foot crosses the threshold, a tail-wagging tornado hurtles toward us.

"Hey there, Nugget." I crouch down, greeting the enthusiastic German shepherd with a scratch behind the ears. He lets out a soft whine of approval as he presses closer to my hand.

"I think he missed you," Bree muses.

Inside, I kick off my heels with a sigh of relief and drift into the kitchen. My fingertips graze the cool quartz countertops. It's something steady in my storm of thoughts.

Bree tosses her oversized purse onto the bench by the door. "It's just the two of us tonight. Dillon's on duty."

Dillon is her boyfriend of nearly a decade. He's a patrol officer, and though she never says it, I know she worries every time he walks out the door. I've seen the tight smile she wears whenever she talks about his job.

"You want something to eat?" she asks, cracking open the pantry door. "You know I'm always stocked up on the good stuff."

Her pantry is a masterpiece in its own right, stuffed to the brim with every snack and ingredient imaginable. It's organized chaos, but in that Bree kind of way—precise, thoughtful, and just a little bit over the top. Each shelf is meticulously sorted by category, each item placed just so, glass containers neatly labeled in her uniform handwriting. Baskets are arranged in perfect rows, each one holding a specific snack.

"I'm okay for now. I wouldn't want to ruin your perfectly symmetrical setup."

She shoots me a look, lips twitching. Then, she gently says, "Do you want to talk? Or do you want me to leave you alone? Oh! Maybe some music? I can totally sing for you, but you know I sound like a cat in a blender."

A laugh escapes me, small and surprised, but real. It's the first one in... I don't know how long. "I love you, but I'll pass on the song this time."

"Suit yourself." Her teasing smile falters just enough for the concern beneath to show. She's holding back a dozen questions I'm not ready to answer.

Suddenly, my dress feels too tight, too *much*, and I can't stand the way it clings to me. I loved how airy and free I felt when I slipped it on his morning, but now it's all wrong. Too tight across my ribs, too heavy on my shoulders. The neckline scratches and I swear I can feel every seam pressing against me like it's mocking the girl who thought she could keep it together.

"Hey, can I borrow something to wear? I need to get this off immediately."

And then throw it in the trash.

I don't say that part out loud, but I really do need to get rid of it. I don't want any lingering reminders of what I saw today.

"For sure," she replies, leaning casually on the counter. "You know where my comfy clothes are. Matching sets are in the—"

"Bottom drawer on the left. I know," I interrupt with a smirk, heading toward the stairwell as she waves me off.

In the bedroom, I rummage through her drawer, fingers brushing over fabric until they land on a baby blue cashmere sweatsuit. I swear I can almost feel heaven in its softness.

I shed the dress, sliding into the sweatsuit with a sigh that could almost pass for relief. The fabric drapes over me like a cloud, its comfort stealing the edge off the tightness in my chest. Bree knows what she's doing with clothes. I make a mental note to find out where she got this because I need a set of my own.

I glance at my reflection in the mirror and force a weak smile, but it hardly softens the emptiness staring back at me. Could be worse, I guess.

The sudden sound of a cork popping echoes up the stairwell, dragging me back downstairs.

"You know me oh so well," I say, stepping back into the kitchen and spotting the bottle of white wine and long-stemmed glasses waiting on the island. "The only thing that could make this day better is if that was a bottle of whiskey."

Bree scrunches her nose. "You know I can't stomach that stuff, but we can at least agree the events of the day warrant at least one bottle of wine, if not five."

I take a long sip after she pours us some and settle into the white-upholstered couch. Just as I start to relax, Nugget's high-pitched whining cuts through the quiet at the back door. Bree doesn't miss a beat, swinging the door open just enough for him

18

to dart through, his body a blur of excitement as he bolts into the fenced yard.

I let out a sigh as I tug the checkered linen blanket over my lap. "What do I do now?"

The question is rhetorical, but I get a response anyway.

"You keep going, just like you always have," she says. "This sucks. There's no other way to say it. And I'm so sorry this is happening. Of all the people in the world, you are the least deserving of this."

Tears sting at the corners of my eyes again, but I'm so tired of crying. "You know, I saw this coming. I changed so much about myself to make sure it was going to work. He didn't even ask me to, but I was convinced it was the only way we'd make it."

"I know," she replies softly. "I didn't know how to bring it up. I just...wanted to be there to support you however you needed it."

I glance out the living room windows, a smile tugging at my lips as I watch Nugget prance around the backyard, completely carefree. He's chasing a butterfly, snapping at the wind, totally lost in his own little world.

"Yeah, well, next time you see me spiraling over a guy and his snobby family, smack me." I say it with a half laugh, but I mean it. Someone really should've whacked some sense into me years ago.

She snorts. "Noted. But seriously, I'm here for you. Anything you need, just let me know."

I take a sip of wine, letting the warmth of it spread through me. "I need to get my car from work at some point. I left it there when I walked to the park. And I need to drive by my old place to check things out before I move back in."

After graduating college, I bought the cutest little craftsman bungalow on a quiet street lined with sycamore trees.

It was perfect for me. I lived there for a few years before moving in with James after we got engaged. My place was "too small" for his liking, his being "more suitable" for a future family.

Ugh.

He wanted me to sell it. I talked him into renting it out, playing the money card because it was the only thing that ever worked with him. Not that I ever followed through. I kept it, slipping in to check on it every now and then, always careful not to let him catch wind. He never noticed. Didn't care enough to.

"You want to do all that tomorrow?" Bree asks. "I'm not working, so I can come with you."

It's rare for her to get a Saturday off. As a nurse, her week-ends are usually spent at the hospital, running on caffeine and too little sleep. When she gets a free day, she's all about squeezing every bit of life out of it.

"Yeah," I reply. "That would be good."

We sit in comfortable silence, the kind that only happens with someone who knows you inside and out. It's one of those moments where you almost forget everything's falling apart. *Almost.*

Just as I close my eyes and start to exhale away the stress of the day, Bree's voice slices through the fragile peace. "I'm going to ask one last time... Are you okay?"

I blink, opening my eyes to meet her gaze, but she doesn't stop there.

"Because, honestly, I expected uncontrollable tears or something."

I snort. If anyone knows the routine of my breakdowns, it's her. They usually involve crying, disappearing for a bit, and then dragging myself back up out of the hole I fell in. But this time?

"What's the point?" I finally say. "It doesn't change anything. I'm just so furious I wasted years of my life on him."

If we were talking about the stages of grief, I'd say I skipped straight past the denial and anger and dove headfirst into hopelessness. It's hard to deny what you've seen unfold in front of you like a bad soap opera, with every lie and betrayal laid out so perfectly it could've been scripted by a team of writers trying to make it as painful as possible.

Bree tilts her head slightly, her gaze drifting to the side as her brows knit together, a faint furrow appearing between them as she thinks. "I wouldn't call it wasted. Love is never wasted, Jules. It's just...sometimes we give it to the wrong person."

She pauses for a moment, giving me time for her words to sink in. She offers a casual shrug, and there's a glint of mischief in her eye when she says, "That being said, screw that guy."

And just like that, I burst out laughing. A real, unfiltered laugh that's been trapped inside for too long. "God, this is why I love you."

She's got this gift of being a therapist one second, and the person who'll grab a pitchfork in the next. Equal parts heart and fire, all wrapped up in one incredibly kickass package.

By the time I drag myself upstairs to the guest room, it's well past midnight. I collapse onto the mattress and stare up at the ceiling, moonlight casting silver shadows across the room.

The memories that come first are the ones I wish I could cling to forever. I remember the way his hand fit in mine when we'd walk downtown on lazy Sunday afternoons. Then there was the time he surprised me with the weekend getaway to the cabin. We spent the weekend in a fog of laughter, talking about everything and nothing, about our future, about our dreams. I had no idea then that it was all a lie.

Soon enough, the painful flashbacks filter in, each one cutting deeper than the last. They twist and tear until the tears

I've been holding back spill over. I cry until I'm gasping for air, my sobs slowly losing their strength. Everything feels hollow now—my chest, my limbs, my heart. Empty.

Exhaustion settles in, dragging me down until there's nothing left but the numbness that follows a good, hard cry. Sleep doesn't come easily, but it creeps up on me, a slow, inevitable pull. I let myself slip into that strange in-between where the world feels miles away and nothing can hurt. At least for a little while.

three

JULIETTE

T he next morning, I shuffle downstairs, the weight of the night still hanging heavy in my bones. Bree's perched on the couch while Dillon's standing in the kitchen, elbows propped on the counter.

"Morning, Sunshine," Bree chirps, a little too chipper for the hour.

"Hey." I nod at both of them, accepting the mug Dillon offers with a quiet thanks. His gaze lingers on Bree for half a beat too long before shifting to me.

"You sleep okay?" he asks.

"Sure." It's mostly true.

The silence hangs there, stretching just enough to settle awkwardly between us. Bree's fingers tap restlessly against her cup. Dillon watches her with a look I can't read. It's not soft, not hard, just...stuck.

"What's the plan today?" he finally questions.

"Gonna grab her car," Bree answers without looking at him.

Another pause comes after.

Cool.

No one says anything, and it's starting to feel a lot like Mom and Dad are fighting.

I clear my throat in hopes of shattering the tension. Dillon finally pulls his gaze from Bree with a resigned sigh, though the shift in the air feels less like resolution and more like a pause.

"C'mon," Bree says with forced cheer, standing too fast. "Bring your coffee upstairs and let's get you dressed."

Upstairs, away from Dillon's stare, the silence follows us like an unwelcome shadow. Bree hands me a handful of clothing without meeting my eye.

I hesitate. "You and Dillon okay?"

She shrugs. "Yeah, everything's fine. Just the usual stuff."

That, coming from Bree, feels a lot like saying *not even a little bit fine*. I don't believe her. It's not like them to be so tense around each other. They've always been the picture-perfect couple that makes you believe in love even when your own heart is broken.

"I'll meet you downstairs," she says softly, squeezing my hand before turning to leave.

I slip on the borrowed jeans and sweater and head back down. Bree's already waiting at the bottom step, blonde curls pulled into one of those infuriatingly perfect ponytails that looks effortless but somehow never is. She gives me a bright, practiced smile.

"Ready?"

I offer a nod, and we slip out to the car. My brain, traitorous as ever, starts putting together a grocery list that consists mostly of comfort food and bad decisions. Chips. Ice cream. Cheap wine. Whatever will get me through.

As we pull into the school's parking lot, I spot my black SUV parked squarely in the middle.

"I can come with you if you need to run any errands?" Bree offers.

I shake my head. "You know what? No, that's okay. Spend some time with Dillon. You two rarely get a day off together."

For half a second, she doesn't answer. Just bites the edge of her thumbnail, a nervous habit I've started noticing more recently. She drops her hand as soon as she catches me watching, pressing her palm to her jeans like she wasn't just in her head.

"You wound me. Chicks before dicks. Sisters before misters. I want to tag along if you want me there."

And then it hits me. I can't remember the last time Bree talked about Dillon the way she used to. Something's definitely wrong.

"But in all seriousness," she continues. "I know you need your space sometimes. You won't be a bother either way. Whatever you need."

I stare at her for a moment, struck by how much she gets me, even when I don't get myself. I give her a small, grateful smile, hoping she knows I appreciate her more than anything.

"Honestly, I need to go home to take inventory and clean first. I'll give you a call later when I'm settled back in?"

As if on cue, my phone starts ringing in my hand. My stomach drops when I see the caller ID. *James.* As if seeing his name isn't bad enough, the photo of us that pops up feels like a slap to the face.

Our smiles are bright, his brown eyes even brighter. I suppress a groan, my thumb quickly swiping the screen to decline the call. I add *block his number* to my mental to-do list with a heavy sigh.

Bree grimaces along with me. "You planning on talking to him?"

I shrug. "I don't know. I guess I should at some point. All my stuff is still at his place."

She hums in response. "I think you need to consider what you actually want from a conversation with him before you decide." She shifts in her seat to face me fully. "Is it just about your belongings? Because if that's all, I can go grab them. I'll even wear my scariest heels and stare him down until he hands it all over. I'm very intimidating when provoked. Just ask the poor barista who gave me whole milk last week."

I smile at the mental image, but it fades quickly. "It's not just about my stuff."

Her voice softens. "I didn't think so."

"I want to know *why*," I admit, my voice barely audible. "Why he cheated. Why he thought I wasn't enough."

Bree's eyes flicker with understanding, and she reaches over to take my hand. "Jules, his cheating had *nothing* to do with you not being enough. Just because that was his narrative doesn't mean it's the truth."

"But then why—"

"Because some people are just broken in ways that have nothing to do with the people who love them," she interrupts. "James didn't cheat because you lacked something. He cheated because *he* lacks something."

Sometimes, I genuinely wonder where she stores this wisdom. Like, does she have a secret stash of emotional clarity next to her dry shampoo and endless supply of snacks? It always comes out of nowhere and hits like a freight train wrapped in a warm hug.

I consider her words as the silence stretches between us. She's right. She has this uncanny ability to cut through the bullshit and get right to the heart of matters.

"Still," I say finally. "I think I need to hear it from him. For closure or whatever."

She nods, her lips pressed together in a tight line, her eyes narrowing just slightly as if weighing her next words. "Just promise me you'll remember your worth when you talk to him. Don't let him twist things around."

"I won't," I say, though I'm not entirely convinced I can keep that promise.

I lean over and pull her into a tight hug. "Thank you for everything, Bree. Seriously."

"Anytime." She pulls back and quirks a brow. "All right. Love you. Call me if you need anything."

"Love you back. Talk to you later," I say, shutting the passenger door with a firm push.

The drive home is quick, but the final turn onto my street slows time. My neighborhood has that old charm—houses with wraparound porches and crooked mailboxes that somehow add to the appeal.

Pulling into my driveway, I take in the deep teal siding, the dark oak front door, and the cozy front porch with a swinging bench. It's the same as I left it, but sitting here now, staring through my windshield, I realize just how much I missed it. Not only the house, but the version of me that lived inside it.

The porch steps groan under my feet. I catch a glimpse of the once bright and colorful flower beds, now mostly crunchy and beige. I sigh, turning the key in the door and stepping inside.

I spent so much time making this place *mine*. Painting the walls sage green. Picking out deep brown furniture, then adding pops of yellow like sunshine I could rearrange. The bookshelves across from the fireplace are crammed full, sagging under the weight of well-worn novels. Dust clings to everything now, a thin veil of neglect.

I roll up my sleeves and get to work. The place isn't a complete disaster, but the urge to clean feels a little like survival. Scrubbing away grime and swiping away dust always does the trick. *Control what you can, wipe away what you can't.*

I wipe the countertops like they personally offended me while thinking about James. Not even his betrayal—oddly enough—but all the tiny ways I made myself smaller over the years. The way I used to triple-check his calendar so he wouldn't be *inconvenienced* by anything I had planned. How I stopped buying garlic because he claimed it made everything taste like feet, even though I *love* garlic.

I scrub harder.

I think about how I used to rearrange my own needs around his moods, and how I thought that was normal. That if I kept everything just right—me, the house, the wine selection— maybe it would mean something.

My phone buzzes somewhere in the distance, but I ignore it. If it's James, I'm not ready. If it's Bree, she'll know I'm spiraling.

Time slips by without me noticing. It isn't until my stomach rumbles that it hits me...oh, right. I haven't eaten today.

I scan the room one last time. It's starting to look less like desertion and more like a life I recognize, so I slip on my flats, grab my keys, and head for the door.

I expect it to hit me on the drive to the grocery store now that I'm not distracted. The heartbreak, the fury. But mostly, I just feel...hollow. Almost like I'm stretched thin and weirdly detached, as if my body's here but the rest of me hasn't caught up yet.

It's not peaceful. Not even close. But it *is* quiet. And after the way yesterday shattered my entire world with every ugly little truth I didn't want to see, the tranquility almost feels like mercy.

I don't want to poke at the bruises while they're still form- ing, so I tighten my grip on the wheel, shake off the weight threatening to press down again, and ease into the grocery store parking lot.

Once I'm inside and steering my cart toward the junk food aisle, a little bag of Scottish cookies catches my eye, immediately making me think of my Aunt Rose. She's the only family I've got left now, my mom's twin, with the same sunshine smile and the same eyes that saw straight through you, but that's where the similarities end. My mom wore her heart on the outside, gentle in a way that made people lean in. Aunt Rose is all grit, keeping her softness buried deep under layers of dry humor and stubborn pride.

Either way, I like to think I inherited that same smile and warmth, despite never knowing what my father looked like. Mom never said much about him, except once, when she told me he didn't deserve to know me. That was all I needed. Her silence told me more than his story ever could.

My aunt's probably tucked away in her cozy cottage, somewhere in the folds of the Scottish countryside. It's mid-evening over there, which means she's likely nursing a glass of something strong.

I dial her number with one hand and start scavenging the shelves for anything loaded with salt, sugar, or both. I could really use a dose of her wildly inappropriate life advice right about now.

She picks up just as I chuck a family-size bag of sour cream and onion chips into the cart.

"Juliette, baby! How the heck are you?"

"Oh, you know, just living the dream. If that dream were to include infidelity and hunger."

It comes out lighter than it should, but that's the only way I can get the words out without crumbling in the middle of aisle five.

The silence on the other end of the line is deafening, a rare thing for her before she whispers, "Wait...what?"

I take a shallow breath and go for casual, even if my insides are still doing that slow churn of disbelief. "Short story even shorter? I walked in on James and his secret lover yesterday." I toss a pack of cookies into the cart. "And I haven't had lunch."

There's a pause, just long enough for me to brace. Then I hear that sharp inhale she only ever makes when she's about to go into full-blown auntie mode. "That absolute muppet—"

I cut her off before she can really get going. "Don't worry, I'm handling it. Mostly by stress-buying junk food and garlic, but still."

I eye the produce section. I should probably balance out my diet so I won't hate myself later. A few apples and some lettuce should do it, right? Maybe I'll throw in a couple of bananas for good measure. There's a rustling sound on her end of the line, like she's shifting the phone against her shoulder, followed by a deep male voice that has a casual Scottish lilt to it. Who was *that?*

"Sorry," she says quickly. "I'm still at work helping my boss."

"Your boss sounds suspiciously hot," I say before I can stop myself, mostly to fill the silence in an awkward attempt to break the tension. It's not a lie, though. Something about that easy drawl hints at trouble wrapped in charm.

She laughs. "You think so? I'll be sure to tell him he's got a fan."

"I didn't say I was a fan," I protest. "I just...appreciate good acoustics."

I may not be totally interested in men at the moment thanks to James, but I'm not dead. I know when to appreciate the low timbre of a man's voice, and that one practically came with a warning label and a jawline I could easily imagine.

"Sure, sure. Back to you," she says before I can deflect more. "Is James actually brain dead? Are you okay? What do you need? You want me to come stay with you for a while? You need me to kick his ass? Hide a body? I've watched enough true crime documentaries to make it look like a tragic accident."

Her rapid-fire questions pull a small laugh from me. "Easy there. He's not worth an elaborate cover-up. But I'll keep those last few offers in my back pocket, just in case. Right now, I'm okay. Ask me again in an hour, and I'll probably be sobbing. But no need to book a flight just yet."

She exhales sharply. "Fine, I won't pry. But I need to know you're actually okay. I'm so sorry, Juliette."

"Honestly, I'm...managing. Distraction seems to be the name of the game. I didn't call you to freak you out," I reassure her. "I just wanted to hear your voice."

"Oh, sweetheart. You're strong just like your mama was. Life goes on, but you already know that," she says softly. "Hey, why don't you come visit me soon? You still haven't been out here."

I pause for a moment, balancing the phone between my shoulder and ear while I fumble for my wallet. I never made it to Scotland to visit because James and his family always had my schedule packed, leaving little room for anything else.

"I do have the summer off in a few weeks—perks of being a teacher. Let me think about it?"

"Of course! You know I'd love to have you for as long as I can. Just tell me when."

We chat for a few more minutes, the conversation light and easy, a welcome break from the mess swirling in my head. By the time I load the last of the groceries into my trunk, I'm a little steadier. Maybe I won't completely unravel today.

I skip turning on the radio as I pull out of the lot. My thoughts are already loud enough without adding a soundtrack.

Instead, I focus on the soft rustling from the trunk, the sound of my impulsive grocery haul shifting with every turn. I really should've eaten before shopping. At this point, I have no clue what I even bought. Bananas? Pickles? A chaotic mix of regret and desperation?

Then my phone rings, and for some inexplicable reason, I just *know* it's James.

KNOX

The still is running hot, the scent of malt and oak is thick in the air, and Callan's already pacing like a man on a mission to ruin my morning.

"Shipment's late again," he groans, waving his phone in my direction. "That's the third time this month. I swear—"

"Callan," I interrupt, calmly. "Breathe. It's eight in the bloody morning."

My brother tosses me a glare that would hold more weight if I didn't know him better. The lines etched between his brows are deep, aging him beyond his mere twenty-seven years. Most days, he's easygoing to the point of reckless. Always the first to take the leap, the risk, the shot. But when it comes to the family business, he tightens up and wears the worry like a second skin.

He runs a hand through his mess of hair, leaving it sticking up in wild directions. Morning light spills through the distillery windows, catching on the copper stills and rows of tasting glasses. Normally, I'd find the whole scene peaceful, but today it reminds me of how far behind we are with the festival prep.

My phone buzzes in my pocket, and I don't want to look. I already know who it is, but my hand moves anyway.

Hallie.

She always had a gift for timing, waiting until I'm buried in the thick of work and barely breathing through deadlines. Then she strikes.

I stare at it for a second longer than I should, then I flip the damn thing face down on the counter like that might shut her out.

It never does.

"Not going to answer that?" Callan asks, his irritation momentarily redirected.

I shake my head. "Nothing worth hearing."

The phone stops, then immediately starts again. *Persistent as always.*

"Hallie again?" His voice softens slightly. For all his bluster, my brother knows when to tread carefully.

I nod once, picking up the phone and jabbing at the screen to silence it.

"Two years of this." He shakes his head. "You'd think she'd have found someone else to torment by now. She already took enough of your money to live like a damn queen. What more does she want?"

"A stake in the distillery," I answer flatly.

His head snaps toward me, eyes wide. "She wouldn't."

"She would. She's been circling this place ever since I uttered the word *divorce*."

He mutters a curse and starts pacing again. If she ever got her claws on this place, it wouldn't just ruin me. It would wreck him, too. I won't let that happen.

"This place, our name, it means something," I say, quieter now. "It's the only thing Dad left us. I'm not letting her take that, too."

He stops parading back and forth, hearing the steel in my words before he says, "You'd burn the whole place down first."

Dragging a hand across the back of my neck, I let my gaze wander over the space our dad tried to pour his life into. Weathered wooden beams hang overhead, the copper equipment gleams in the light, and there are barrels stacked against the far wall waiting to cradle our whisky for years to come. This place is more than a business. It's our legacy. Our home.

"I'd rebuild it with my bare hands if I had to," I finally say.

"You've done a fine job with this place, aye?" Callan says, voice low. "He'd be proud."

I glance over, a little caught off guard. He's never been the sentimental type, but he's got the same serious look he used to wear when he was three years old, stomping into Dad's office in his muddy wellies, declaring himself the boss. Little spitfire could barely reach the desk, but he'd slap his tiny hand down on the surface and bark out orders like he was running a damn empire.

Even back then, he had that fire in him. All piss and vinegar and too much heart for his own good.

"Not just me," I say. "You kept the lights on more than once."

He huffs. "And kept you from tossing your phone through the wall every time Hallie called."

A dry laugh pulls from my chest. "Close calls."

"Understatement."

JULIETTE

I regret this. I never should have answered the phone when James called.

I told him to give me some time before we actually met up, and now here we are, a couple days later, with plans for him to come to *my* house. The one that hasn't been tainted by him.

I told him he could drop off my things. Just the essentials. I should've been more specific, though, because now I'm spiraling and wondering if he'll bring the sweatshirt I left in his drawer. The one that always smelled like him. Musky and warm, familiar in a way I don't want anymore.

I smooth the throw blanket on the couch, then immediately mess it up again. Fluff a pillow. Unfluff it. I know it's stupid, but my hands need something to do or I might chew through my lip. I don't want him back, *god* no. I don't even want his apologies. I only want my stuff, my space, and maybe my dignity.

I suck in a slow breath, tug my sleeves down over my hands, and remind myself that I survived the worst part already. I caught him. I walked away.

36

Today's just logistics. A clean exchange. Closure, if I'm lucky. A migraine, if I'm not.

The doorbell rings, and I nearly jump out of my skin. I take another deep breath and move to the door.

When I swing it open, James is standing there with a cardboard box balanced on his hip. He looks good. *Damn him.* His dark hair is freshly cut, his jaw cleanly shaven, and he's wearing that blue button-down I always loved. The one that brings out the flecks of amber in his eyes.

I step aside without saying a word, letting him walk into the house while trying not to flinch as his cologne drifts past me. The scent hits like a memory I don't ask for. Movie nights. Sunday mornings. *Lies.*

I trail behind him into the living room where he sets the box down on the coffee table.

Nope. I change my mind. I don't want to talk. I don't want closure or an apology or whatever self-serving confession he thinks he needs to unload so he can sleep better at night. I just want him to leave, because I can't.

This is my house. My living room. My sanctuary. He's stolen my trust and invaded my peace, but this space is mine. The longer he stands here, the more it feels like he's stealing that, too. So maybe he looks good. Maybe some small, bruised part of me still aches for him when I take him in, but I don't want him here.

I want him gone. Now.

He clears his throat. "I didn't know if you wanted your old sweatshirts or not, so I brought them anyway."

I stare at him. That's his lead? Not *I'm sorry* or *I was a complete coward?* Just an update about hoodies?

"I figured I'd just...drop this off and let you get on with your day," he says, like he's doing me a favor.

I nod once. "That would be great."

But of course, he lingers. Hands shoved in his pockets, rocking on his heels.

"Look, Juliette..." he starts, and my stomach sinks. Here it comes. "I never meant for things to get so complicated."

A bitter laugh bubbles in my throat, but I keep it down. "Complicated? That's what we're calling it now?"

His jaw tightens. "You know what I mean."

"Oh, I do. I remember hearing that same line when your mom first met me and couldn't hide the fact that I wasn't up to par with the Montgomery pedigree."

Color rises in his cheeks. "That's not fair."

"Not fair?" My voice stays calm. "James, I didn't even meet your parents until a year in. And when I finally did, your mother opened the door to her mansion—sorry, *estate*—wearing pearls while judging my department store flats before I even said hello."

The thing about anger is that I don't wear it well. Anger is messy and unproductive, and I'm really not the yelling type.

But this anger feels earned, even though I hate that I'm feeling it. Hate that I *have* to feel it. Confrontation has never been my weapon of choice. I'd rather retreat, fold myself into pieces and let things pass like weather.

But not this time.

He flinches, most likely surprised by my directness, but I'm not done.

"You stood there and let me walk into that house completely unprepared. No warning, no heads-up. Just a polite, '*My mom has certain expectations,*' afterwards."

There was always going to be a chasm between us. His world was one of horse farms and country clubs, soft linens, and crystal glassware. Mine was peanut butter sandwiches and thrift store finds. And the truth is, I spent more time trying to blend into his life than I ever did feeling like I belonged in it.

The first time I stepped into his family's sprawling mansion, it was like walking onto a movie set. Everything was polished to a shine. Marble floors. Art probably costing more than my college tuition. His mother's perfectly clipped voice floating through the air like she owned every ounce of oxygen in the room.

I should've realized then that I didn't fit in and was never going to.

But I loved him.

"I was trying to protect you," he mutters.

I blink. "By what? Keeping me in the dark? Making me feel small so I wouldn't realize how much I was giving up just to stand beside you?"

The words spill out before I can stop them, not in rage, but exhaustion. A bone-deep weariness from pretending for too long. The worst part isn't even the cheating. It's that I bent myself backward for someone who never reached out a hand to meet me halfway.

"I changed everything for you, James. I lost pieces of myself trying to fit into a life that never really had room for me. And you still cheated."

He looks away.

"Wasn't I already miserable enough for you?" I say with a sad, humorless laugh. "Or was that the problem?"

Silence stretches between us, thick and heavy.

"Juliette..."

"Don't." I lift a hand. "I really don't want an explanation. I just want you to leave."

He's already taken enough of me, and I'm finally starting to realize how much I want it back.

He stands there, blinking at me like I've spoken in a language he can't understand. His mouth opens then closes. For once in our relationship, James Montgomery is speechless.

"I'll text you if anything's missing," I say, nodding toward the door.

His shoulders drop a fraction, and he gives a stiff nod. Mechanical. Defeated.

"Right. I should..." he trails off.

He crosses the threshold with slow steps, his posture no longer pulled upright by pride or pretense. It's the first genuine thing I've seen from him in a while.

Then, he hesitates, his back still to me before he glances over his shoulder. "For what it's worth, Jules..." His voice is lower, rougher than before. "I did love you."

The nickname catches me off guard. *Jules.* It doesn't sound right coming out of his mouth anymore.

"I know," I say softly.

He doesn't ask for forgiveness or try to explain his choices. Maybe he finally understands there's nothing left to salvage.

And then he's gone.

My breath catches somewhere in my chest. My throat burns from the sheer force it took to say what needed to be said.

I *never* do that.

I've always been the one who smooths over the rough edges, who bites her tongue so no one else has to feel uncomfortable. I can't believe I just stood there, spine straight and voice steady, and I told him the truth. I just wish it didn't hurt so damn much.

My knees give the tiniest wobble as I close the door and press my forehead against it. The tears come slowly at first, just a sting behind my eyes, but then they fall hard, ungraceful and hot, as they run down my cheeks. No sobs. No gasps. Just tears.

There's grief for the love I poured into someone who didn't know how to hold it, though beneath it, there's also a small flicker of pride.

I wipe my face with the sleeve of my sweatshirt, sniffling

before letting out a mirthless laugh. For the first time in a long time, I didn't disappear to make someone else comfortable.

I'm just beginning to notice the calm take over when there's a sudden knock on the door. It better not be James coming back to drag this out any longer.

But when I open the door, it's not James.

One of my neighbors, Mrs. Boone, is standing there looking like she's been waiting for this exact moment, a bottle of wine in hand. She lives a few doors down and knows everything that grows, wilts, or misbehaves on this street. She also owns a garden center. When I first moved in, she showed up on my doorstep with a potted succulent and the kind of smile that made me feel right at home.

"Hey, darling," she says, that unfiltered, boisterous tone of hers filling the doorway. "I thought you might need this."

"I'm glad you came by," I say, stepping aside to let her in.

"I figured you might be in need of some serious hydration and a good old-fashioned dose of unasked-for advice," she tells me. "Have you been sitting in this house, waiting for him to show up, looking like a wilted fern for the last hour?"

"I wasn't looking like a wilted fern," I quip with a small laugh, but there's truth in her words. I'm drained and worn down.

She shoves the wine into my hands, then points at the corner of the room where one of her overgrown monstera plants sits. "See that? That monstera's been sitting in that spot for years. Same pot, same light, same space. You think it's been happy? Hell no. It's not thriving, it's surviving. You need to move that plant. Get it some new soil, some new light. It might scream, it might sulk for a bit, but it'll thrive. Same as you. You've been standing still too long, darlin'."

She makes her way to the kitchen, pulls out a chair at the table, and sits down. "Sometimes we need to rip up the roots, toss 'em out, and find a new patch of soil. Don't be afraid to leave something behind if it means you can finally grow. Maybe you've been too scared to move. I get it. But trust me, you don't want to be a sorrow-ridden, crumpled mess stuck in the same old spot."

I stand there, holding the wine bottle in my hands, staring at her. I didn't expect a lesson on plant care, let alone a life lesson.

"You've been so busy looking after everyone else's needs, you forget about your own. That's gonna stop. Right now, you're gonna take a deep breath and ask yourself...do I want to sit here and mope, or do I want to *live*?"

I blink, caught off guard by the whiplash of her no-nonsense wisdom wrapped in affection and collapse into the chair across from her. "You're something else."

"Damn straight," she says. "And you're gonna thank me when you've got a new pot to plant yourself in."

six

JULIETTE

I t's been two weeks since my conversation with James, and I still haven't quite figured out how I'm supposed to feel. I tell myself I'm fine, that I've processed it. In reality, I might just be a little numb. But I like to think I'm actually making progress toward being *me* again, and that it wasn't detachment that fueled my spur-of-the-moment decision to book a one-way ticket to Scotland last night.

My second graders file out of the classroom for the last time, their excited voices fading as they bolt toward summer freedom. I look around at the marker-streaked whiteboard and the crooked line of tiny chairs tucked beneath little desks. A swell of gratitude hits me, but there's sadness, too. And a bit of terror, because this is real. I'm actually doing this.

I pull out my phone, fingers hovering over the screen. I still need to tell my aunt.

ME

So... I booked a flight.

I stare at my phone, my finger tapping restlessly against the side of it. Her reply bursts onto the screen like confetti a second later.

AUNT ROSE

You're actually coming?!

ME

Ticket purchased, bag half packed, and classroom officially closed for the summer.

AUNT ROSE

The room's yours. The kettle will be on.

ME

Tell that sexy-voiced boss of yours to behave himself. I'm emotionally fragile.

AUNT ROSE

He's single...

ME

Stop it.

Okay, that's on me. I opened the door with that comment, but that doesn't mean I'm ready to waltz into a candlelit dinner and a rebound situation. Besides, her boss is probably twenty years older than me. And while I can appreciate a good voice and a strong set of forearms, I'm not about to become the plot of someone else's midlife crisis.

JUST BEFORE THE PLANE LANDED, I pressed my forehead to the window and got my first look at the Scottish countryside. Rolling hills, stone buildings, and wild greenery as far as my eye could see. It was the kind of beauty that didn't ask for attention. It just existed, unapologetically stunning.

I don't know if the jet lag will catch up to me later, but for now, I'm running on pure adrenaline and a ridiculous amount of caffeine. It only makes the scenery that much better.

Once I'm through the airport, I find the nearest bathroom and slip inside. I run a hairbrush through my long, loose waves, the bristles smoothing out some of the travel-induced frizz, and swipe on a little mascara. Nothing dramatic, just enough to make me feel like I've got it together.

Feeling a little more like myself, I head out, following the signs toward baggage claim. I try to slow my thoughts, to let the excitement settle just a little, but it's hard when everything seems so *new*.

Just as I round the corner, I spot Aunt Rose rushing toward me, her face lit up with the biggest smile. Her energy sweeps over me, and before I can even process it, she wraps me in a tight hug. I melt into her embrace, the familiar sensation of home blanketing me in a way that makes the traveling and exhaustion worth it.

She pulls back just enough to cup my face in her hands, like she used to when I was little, and something inside me stirs. It's a mix of relief, longing, and the kind of grief I don't know how to manage yet. I didn't realize how much I needed this, how much I needed her, until this very moment.

"Oh, sweetheart. You have no idea how glad I am that you're here."

"Ditto," I reply, giving her the best smile I can muster.

It's been years since I've seen her, but her beauty hasn't faded a smidge. If anything, she's more striking than ever. Her silver-streaked brunette hair is pulled back loosely. Her hazel eyes, the same as mine, still have that familiar lively spark, and the lines around her mouth are evidence of a lifetime of laughter

My thoughts drift to my mom, and a tightness settles in my chest. It's that recurring ache, the one that always hits when I'm reminded of what could have been. I can't help but wonder if she would have looked like Aunt Rose if she was still here.

The thought lingers, but I blink away the sudden sting of tears.

We weave our way through the crowd, dragging my bags behind us, the buzz of travel chatter and rolling suitcases fading as we break out into the cool, open air. Aunt Rose pops the trunk, and together we wrestle my overstuffed luggage inside.

Without thinking, I veer toward the right side of the car.

"Other side, love," Aunt Rose calls, a teasing lilt in her voice. "That's the driver's seat in this neck of the woods."

I pause midstep. "Right. Okay. This is fine. I'm totally fine," I mutter, pivoting around in the most awkward little shuffle that has her outright grinning.

"Give it a week," she says, chuckling. "You'll be opening the wrong door like a local in no time."

When I climb into the passenger's side, the seat belt gives me hassle, because of course it does, before I'm able to wrangle it into place with a victorious click.

"How long's the drive to your place?" I ask, settling back against the seat, already bracing myself for how wildly out of my depth I am.

"About forty minutes, give or take. I'll take the scenic route so you can see why I decided to call this place home."

"Oh, I'd love that. Best taxi driver ever. Ten out of ten," I tease.

"Yeah, well, don't tip me just yet. I'm a talker."

Twenty minutes into the drive, I'm completely in awe. She wasn't kidding when she said scenic. Scotland is every bit as breathtaking as I imagined, maybe even more. The green hills stretch endlessly in every direction, dotted with grazing sheep, like something plucked straight from a painting. The winding roads curl around hillsides, leading to cozy little cottages, and a river appears now and then, winding through the landscape, its surface shimmering under the soft sunlight.

The moment we drive up the dirt road to her house, I'm practically itching to hop out of the car. The cottage comes into view from behind a grove of towering birch and oak trees, its rustic charm greeting me with open arms.

I push open the door and step out of the car. "Well, I hope you know you're never getting rid of me now," I say with a laugh, falling into step behind her as we head up the path to the door.

She shoots me a sly grin. "Then my plan is working. Let's give you the grand tour before we haul your bags in."

She guides me up the short stone staircase leading to the front door, then waves me inside. The space is exactly what I expected. Eclectic, full of character, and brimming with warmth, just like my aunt herself.

We enter a cozy living room where well-loved furniture is arranged around a wood-burning fireplace. To the right, I catch a glimpse of the kitchen through a small dining room, and to the left, there's a hallway that I'm guessing leads to the bedrooms.

Aunt Rose looks around with her hands on her hips. "It's small but it's home."

I glance around appreciatively. "It's wonderful. How long have you been here?"

"A couple years now," she replies. "I bought it shortly after I started working at the local distillery. I handle their marketing but work here a lot of the time. Hence, the desk in the corner of the dining room." She gestures to the small piece of furniture cluttered with papers, computer monitors, and a few scattered pens.

"Do you go into the office much?"

"A couple times a week, mostly by choice. I work with a great group of folks." She clasps her hands together as she leads me down the hallway. "Now, let me show you to your room. There are two bedrooms and two bathrooms down here."

We reach my bedroom at the front of the house. The walls are painted a soft blue, and there's a sunlit bed. It's the view beyond the windows that steals my breath. More rolling green hills scattered with wildflowers, framed perfectly by glass panes that Aunt Rose keeps meticulously clean.

I curl into the corner chair, legs tucked beneath me, already picturing lazy afternoons.

"Let me grab your bags so you can get comfortable," she offers.

I grab the armrests to pull myself up. "I'll come out with you."

"No, you sit! You have to be exhausted. I'll get your things."

I drop back into the chair, letting out a quiet sigh, though I'm far from tired. The truth is, my body's still running on adrenaline. This is the first moment of peace I've had in over twenty-four hours. No rushing, no packing, no hopping between airports.

Being here with my aunt makes me miss Mom. She used to make everything feel...*safe*. I haven't felt that since she's been gone. I'm afraid I lost home the moment I lost her.

I tried to find home in James after she passed away, but we all know how that turned out.

The breeze drifts in through the open windows, crisp and clean, carrying the scent of something new. I exhale through my lingering sadness. There are no expectations here. Just...me.

I can't decide if it's exhilarating or terrifying. Maybe both. But I guess that's the point, right?

seven

JULIETTE

B linding light pours in from the window. The sky outside is a flawless blue, not a cloud in sight. I peel myself out of bed, my feet dragging across the old wood floors in slow, clumsy steps. Everything aches in that soft, heavy way that only sleeping in a strange bed can give you. But then...salvation.

Coffee.

The scent winds through the little cottage like a thread pulling me toward the kitchen. I follow it blindly with bleary eyes and wild hair and pour myself a mug like it's the most sacred thing I'll do all day.

The first sip? Bliss. Hot and bitter and alive. My brain slowly starts the uphill climb, breaking through the fog.

Behind me, a creak sounds from the doorway. A second later, Aunt Rose pops her head into the room. "Well, look at you," she says, grinning like she just caught a rare animal in its natural habitat. "Bright-eyed and bushy-tailed."

I snort quietly into my mug. "Sure," I say, my voice still rough with sleep, "something like that."

She breezes in, already dressed and ready for the day like

she's been up since dawn, which, knowing her, she probably has been.

"Have you had your coffee yet?" I ask.

"Nope, just brewed it. You can put it in one of the travel mugs for me, please."

I fill the mug, casually leaning against the counter as I hand it to her. She takes a sip and lets out a content hum. "What are your plans for today? I do need to head into the office, but you can drop me off if you'd like to use my car for the day."

I shrug. "I hadn't really thought about it yet. I might just hang out here, but I wouldn't mind having the car, just in case. As long as you trust me to drive on the right side of the road," I add, raising a brow.

"Oh, you," she chuckles. "I have faith."

"Are you ready to head out soon? I can get ready pretty quick."

"Ready when you are. Did you want to drive over to the distillery?"

I shake my head. "I'll let you drive first. I need to watch you again to make sure I've got the hang of the whole wrong side of the road thing. Maybe take some notes," I tease.

She rolls her eyes but doesn't argue, and a few minutes later, we're coasting down a narrow road with the windows cracked just enough to let the crisp air in. The drive there is smooth, but it's the building that really stops me. I don't know what I pictured exactly. Something rustic, maybe. A little rough around the edges like the distilleries I've seen in documentaries or splashed across whiskey ads. But this? This is something else entirely.

I take in the stone walls weathered smooth by wind and rain. Tall, arched windows frame intricate ironwork that catches the morning light just right. The oak doors appear heavy enough to withstand almost anything. It's beautiful in that intimidating, old money, deeply Scottish kind of way.

Aunt Rose pulls up directly in front of the doors, leaving the car running as she turns to face me. "I'm not sure how long I'll be here today, but I can give you a call when I'm wrapping up?"

I nod. "Works for me."

I make my way around to the driver's side, feeling oddly like I'm gearing up for battle.

I take my time, settling into the seat slowly and adjusting it forward a few notches to account for the fact that I'm only five-two. I go as far as angling the mirrors until they give me a fighting chance of survival and make sure I know where all the buttons are that I might need.

As I pull out of the lot, my breath comes faster than it should. For about thirty whole seconds, I almost convince myself that I've got this. I can totally do something as simple as drive a car in a different country.

I take it easy, softly pressing my foot on the gas as I hyper fixate on the lines of the road. I squeeze my eyes shut, but just briefly, and then settle my gaze back in front of me, even if I am tempted to look at the passing greenery, which is exactly when I see it.

A massive pickup truck barreling straight toward me. My heart stops.

Wait.

Oh, god.

Wait.

My eyes go wide as the pieces fall together in slow, horrible clarity.

Wrong side.

I'm on the *wrong* side.

Every nerve ending lights up like a fire alarm. For one

terrible beat, I just sit there, frozen stupid, hands clenched tight around the steering wheel like maybe I can will myself invisible.

"Shit!" I wrench the wheel hard and swerve onto the gravel shoulder like my life depends on it. Because...it does. I slam on the brakes, hard enough that the seat belt digs into my shoulder and my whole body jolts forward before snapping back. The car shudders to a stop. My heart does not.

The only thing I can hear is the frantic pounding of my pulse in my ears. And then, because the universe has apparently decided I haven't suffered enough today, the pickup truck slows to a stop beside me.

The driver's face is barely visible through his window. With a groan, I roll mine down, preparing for whatever lecture is coming my way.

I'm already gearing up for the worst. An angry rant, a possible horn blast, maybe even a sarcastic little clap for the dumb American who can't tell left from right.

Honestly, all of it would be fair.

I swallow hard, palms slick on the wheel and wait for the inevitable confrontation. The person rolls down their window, but my eyes stay glued to the dashboard, too mortified to look at them. My cheeks are on fire. *Please, sunglasses, do your job.*

"You all right, lassie?"

The voice throws me for a loop. It's deep. Steady. Rich enough to roll right through me and knock the air out of my lungs.

Oh no. Absolutely not. I am not that girl.

Except, apparently, I *am* that girl. Because for a second, the near miss, the terror, the deeply unflattering sweat happening under my jacket, all of it just...disappears.

All I can hear is *him.* And worse?

It sounds familiar.

My heart gives a traitorous little stutter as I slowly drag my gaze upward and regret every life choice that brought me to this exact moment.

Because *of course* he's beautiful.

He's got the sharp features that look like they were carved by the same wind that weathered every stone on land. His beard is trimmed close, and his hair, that soft, chestnut brown mess that practically begs for fingers to sink into it, is wildly at odds with the stern line of his mouth.

It's his eyes that really do me in.

They're green. Not the soft, hazy kind. No, these are clear and cutting. Keen enough to see straight through every flustered, flailing thought in my extremely frenzied brain.

What is wrong with me?

I nearly killed us both, and here I am, staring at him like a lovesick fool. Did the near accident knock a few brain cells loose? Adrenaline is clearly not my friend.

"Lass?" he says again, and I swear I hear the faintest hint of concern in his voice. He's probably trying to figure out how to ask if I've recently hit my head and wandered off without supervision.

When his gaze drops to my lips, it's like a switch. That small, fleeting glance feels like a charge running straight through me, and before I can stop myself, the panic spills out. "I'm so sorry! Honestly, I'm so embarrassed right now. I'm obviously not from here, and I told myself a million times before I got in the car that I needed to drive on the other side of the road. Sorry. So, so sorry."

Oh my god. Someone, please help me make the rambling stop.

He doesn't speak right away, just studies me. His head tilts slightly, brows raised in curiosity and amusement. I'm still bracing for the worst—him snapping, calling me reckless, reporting me, *something*.

Instead, his lips twitch into a smirk.

"Is that so?" His voice drops half an octave lower and something inside me melts. "First time driving here, then?"

I nod, my throat suddenly dry. "First full day in Scotland, actually."

"Well..." he says, leaning slightly out his window, his forearm resting casually on the sill. The muscles in his arm shift as he moves, and for a split second, I catch myself staring, way too aware of how damn attractive those forearms are. I tear my eyes away, but it's too late. He notices. "Welcome to Scotland. Nearly getting yourself killed is certainly one way to make an entrance."

My breath catches, not because I'm still panicking, but because he's smiling now. *Really* smiling, all slow and relaxed, with just enough mischief to make me forget I almost ran him down.

"American?"

"From Kentucky," I confirm, finally finding my normal voice. "Land of bourbon, horses, and people who don't drive on the left side of the road."

"Bourbon country? Well now, that's a topic worth exploring." He lets his engine idle as he shifts his body to face me more. "Pity we can't have this conversation over a proper dram."

My heart skips. Is he flirting with me?

But before I can respond with something coherent, a car horn blares behind him. The spell breaks, and suddenly, I'm acutely aware we're having this conversation in the middle of the road.

The handsome stranger glances in his rearview mirror and sighs, running a hand through that perfectly disheveled hair.

"Seems we're causing a bit of a traffic jam. I should probably get a move on."

"Of course. Again, I'm so sorry," I apologize, my voice steadier than I feel. "I'll, uh...make sure I'm on the correct side this time."

His eyes linger on mine for a moment longer than necessary. "Mmm, that would be advisable, though I'm not opposed to seeing you again under less...precarious circumstances."

Another horn blasts, blaring longer this time, followed by a muffled Scottish curse from one of the waiting drivers.

"I think that's my cue," he says with a smirk. "Left side. Remember that."

He gives me a quick two-fingered salute before rolling up his window and pulling away, leaving me to sit there with my mouth ajar and my brain scrambling to process what just happened.

I watch his truck disappear down the road, my heart still racing, though I'm not sure if it's from my poor driving skills or the encounter itself. Did a gorgeous Scottish man just flirt with me after I almost crashed into him? And did I actually try to flirt back?

Well, I definitely won't be telling Aunt Rose about that. She left me alone for less than a minute and I nearly turned her car into scrap metal. Niece of the year. Someone get me a trophy.

I let out a shaky breath, my fingers still gripping the steering wheel like my life depends on it. My heart is pounding so hard I can practically hear it, the adrenaline slowly fading but leaving behind a lingering sense of unease and a little nausea. Who knew driving on the wrong side of the road would be this intense? I'm clearly not cut out for this whole spontaneous exploration thing.

I take another deep breath, forcing my pulse to slow, and

decide right then and there that today isn't the day for adventures. Nope. Not happening. I'll head back to the cottage slowly, carefully, and on the *correct* side of the road. No more mishaps. No more near-death experiences. Just me, some hot tea, and the safety of four walls.

As I ease back onto the road, I mutter a new mantra to myself, "Left side, left side, left side." I repeat the words over and over again so I don't forget them. At this point, I'm not taking any chances.

KNOX

The troubled American woman seemed pretty shaken up. Can't say I blame her. Almost flattening a stranger with your car would rattle anyone. Though, in her defense, these roads aren't exactly forgiving. Not the kind of place you just show up and wing it.

Something about her stuck with me, though. Maybe it was the way she gripped the steering wheel like it was the only thing keeping her tethered to the earth. Or the way she stumbled through her apology, flustered and breathless, that soft American drawl sounding like a melody despite her panic.

Then there was the way her wisps of brunette hair caught the breeze, escaping from her ponytail to dance across her face. She brushed them away with slender fingers, and for some stupid reason, it created this strange little ache that curled low in my chest.

Shaking my head, I pull into the distillery lot, gravel crunching under the tires. First one in, or so I think, right up until I reach the door and find it already unlocked.

"Hey, Boss." Rose's bubbly voice echoes through the lobby, catching me off guard. Interesting. She's already here.

"Hey, Rose," I greet her with a nod. "What's up? I didn't see your car in the lot."

A smile stretches across her face. "Oh, I didn't tell you. My niece is visiting from the US. I had her drop me off this morning so she could go sightseeing for a bit."

Hell. The American in the car that almost ran me down is her niece. I didn't even clock the car at first, but thinking back, it was the same beat-up old thing Rose has been driving since I've known her.

Guess I was too busy staring at the girl behind the wheel to notice anything else.

I clear my throat, trying not to laugh at the coincidence when Rose catches my eye with a knowing lift of her brow.

"That makes sense," I say, clearing my throat. "I think I just passed her on my way in. What's her name?"

"Juliette." Her face practically glows as she says it. "She just got in yesterday."

Juliette. That fits the woman I saw, with her stubborn hands on the wheel, messy brown hair stuck to her cheeks, and panic written all over her in a way that managed to make her look...well, beautiful.

"Right." I nod, already flipping through the day in my head. "I'll make the team meeting quick. You should spend some time with her."

Rose gives me that big, grateful grin. The one that's gotten her out of trouble more times than I can count. "You don't need to do that, but I appreciate it."

I shrug like it's nothing, but the truth is, she's earned it. Earned a hell of a lot more than I probably let on. She's sharp. Creative. The reason half our new business exists in the first place.

Besides, seeing her light up like that makes the whole near-death experience a little less heavy. Still, some devil on my shoulder pipes up before I can think better of it.

"Actually, why don't you invite her for lunch? You two can eat in the café, on the house. We'll give her the tour afterward."

Callan would be proud. I can already hear him giving me hell for suggesting something on a whim, just for fun. *Look at you, finally loosening up.* Maybe I am. But I'd also be lying if I said I wasn't curious to see the look on Juliette's face when she walks in and realizes she's about to spend the afternoon with yours truly.

"That's a great idea! I'll give her a call in a few to see if she's up for it."

As she pulls her phone from her pocket, it rings. "I need to grab this. It's our contact at the magazine." Without missing a beat, she answers and heads for her workspace, her voice morphing into business mode.

I make my way to the back and the hours slip by in a blur of numbers and noise while I try to wrestle the latest batch of spreadsheets into submission. Not exactly the glamorous part of running the place, but somebody's gotta do it.

Somewhere out in the front, I catch Rose's voice calling out a cheerful, "Hey, you made it!"

Juliette. Right on time for round two.

I'll give them space for a bit and let them catch up over lunch. No need to go terrifying the woman twice in one day so close together.

Less than an hour later, a knock on the doorframe of my office pulls me from my work. Rose leans against it. "We're ready if you are, Boss."

I stretch, rolling the tension from my shoulders. "Sure thing."

I follow her down the hall, my boots echoing in time with

hers. As we round the corner, I spot Juliette. She's standing with her back to us, completely absorbed by the wall of black-and-white photographs. Snapshots of the distillery through the years, generations caught mid laugh or mid work.

She's small. That's the first thing I notice as she stands in front of me. Petite, but not fragile. There's something about her posture, about the way her head tilts like she's cataloging every detail, that pulls at me.

Rose grins, cutting through the moment. "Jules! Meet the boss man. He's gonna take us around for what we call the *MacKenzie Experience*."

She spins around at the sound of her name, all smiles and polite curiosity. Right up until her eyes land on me.

For half a heartbeat, her smile falters. Most people wouldn't have caught it, but I'm not like most people.

And up close? *Christ.*

Whatever flustered impression I had of her through the car window doesn't hold a candle to this. She's damn stunning.

She has wide, hazel eyes that catch the light and me right along with them. There's gold threaded through them, little flecks of amber sparking when she moves. I'm too busy staring like an idiot to comment on or question the tiny frowns tugging at the corners of her lips.

She recovers fast, though. That polished smile snaps back into place, the kind people wear when they've had no other choice but to. And then she's holding out her hand like we didn't just share a moment of mutual surprise.

I need to get a grip.

I let a grin slip onto my lips as I take her hand, so delicate and soft in mine. "Juliette, nice to meet you. I'm Knox MacKenzie."

A faint blush tints her cheeks as she glances between Rose and me, clearly unsure of how to handle the situation. I shake my head with subtle ease, offering a smile that I hope tells her I'm not here to make this complicated. When she exhales, I notice the shift in her posture. She's more relaxed, but there's still a measure of caution, as if she's carefully sizing me up.

"Very nice to meet you too, Mr. MacKenzie. And thanks so much for having me."

I can't help but tease her a little, to break the ice and ease the tension between us. "Knox, please. Or Boss Man, if that suits you better." It's an invitation. A dare that I wait to see if she'll take.

Rose snorts out a laugh. "Well, we're ready!"

Except fate, or whatever cosmic force that keeps screwing with my day, has other plans. Rose's phone starts blaring from somewhere in her pocket, and I watch her grimace when she checks the screen.

"The magazine again," she groans. "Go on without me. I'll catch up in a bit."

Just like that, she's gone, retreating toward the offices and leaving me standing in the lobby with Juliette. Alone.

Brilliant.

I glance over to find her shifting from side to side, like she's debating between bolting for the door or toughing it out. To her credit, she stays. Straightens her shoulders. Meets my gaze head-on.

"Hi again," she offers, a little wry. "I'm so sorry. I—"

"Juliette," I cut in, shaking my head. "No apology necessary. No harm done, aye?"

That earns me a look. She quirks her eyebrow and the corner of her lip curves in a way that tells me she's not quite buying my forgiveness.

"Aye aye, captain," she fires back.

The smirk I've been fighting tugs loose and a deep, genuine

laugh rumbles out of me before I can stop it. She's trouble, I can tell. But it's refreshing. Unexpected.

I watch as the tension in her shoulders dissipates completely, the guarded edge in her expression disappearing. That spark in her eyes returns, and for the first time since she walked in, she looks like she's finally found her footing.

Good. Because seeing her unsettled earlier had me feeling something I don't usually let myself dwell on.

"I have a question for you," she says, her voice light. "Why doesn't whisky have an 'e' in it here? I was browsing your selection and honestly thought you had a typo on everything."

"Ah, the 'e' debate." My fingers brush the edge of my jaw before I tuck my hand into my pocket, like I need somewhere to put the energy she stirs up just by looking at me. "That's actually a great question. Whiskey, with an 'e', is distilled in Ireland or the United States. Whisky, without an 'e', is mostly Scottish, Canadian, or Japanese. It's all about where it's made."

She tilts her head slightly, her hazel eyes twinkling with curiosity. "Well, that's an interesting tidbit. I'm glad I asked. For a second, I was nervous for you."

I arch a brow, playing along. "I've got two questions for you now. Do you like whisky, and do you like history?"

She falls into step beside me as I start walking toward the distillery, answering without hesitation, "Yes, to both."

Interesting. I figured she'd be more of a wine-and-cheese kind of girl, not someone who drinks whisky neat.

She catches the look on my face, and her eyebrows shoot up, lips twitching as she holds back a laugh. "What? Not what you were expecting?"

She's trouble. No doubt about it. That glint in her eye, the knowing curve of her smile. She's enjoying this. And me? I already know we're going to have some fun.

Her gentle appearance might make her seem reserved, but

the sharpness in her words, the way she meets me head-on, tells a completely different story. There's fire beneath that calm, and damn if I don't want to see more of it.

"I didn't take you for a whisky-loving lass, but I suppose I should know better. I do work with your aunt, after all."

She grins, her love for her aunt written all over her face. "She's something else, isn't she? One hundred percent the fun aunt everyone wishes they had. I'd be lost without her."

I step up to the railing overlooking the heart of the distillery, palms curling around the cool metal rail. Below us, the copper stills rise, catching the light, all heat and history.

"This," I start, gesturing to the tangle of pipes, vats, and valves, "is where the magic happens."

And then I'm off, explaining the process like I've done a hundred times before. Fermentation. Distillation. The quiet patience of aging. It's muscle memory by now, the words coming easy enough that I've learned to watch for that telltale glaze in a visitor's eyes when I've lost them.

But when I risk a glance at Juliette, expecting polite endurance at best, what I find makes me pause.

She's...listening. Really listening.

Head tipped, eyes bright, following every word like it matters. And hell, if that doesn't throw me just a little.

"This really is fascinating," she says, scanning the space like she's trying to memorize it. "You mentioned something about history, too?"

That sparks something warm in my chest. A good kind of surprise.

I nod, leaning a little heavier on the railing.

"Aye, I did. The place has been in the family for five generations now," I tell her, glancing out over the still house. I've looked at it a thousand times and cursed its quirks, but standing here next to her, watching her take it in with wide, curious eyes,

I see it differently. "Started with my great-great-grandfather more than a hundred and thirty years ago. Passed down to my great-grandfather, then my grandfather, then my dad...and now, me and my brother."

Legacy. It's in the walls here. In the whisky. In my blood, whether I like it or not.

Standing here with Juliette while she looks at me like none of this is ordinary makes it feel a little less like a weight and a little more like pride.

"That's incredible. Has it always been successful?"

My gaze sweeps over the worn brick walls and copper bones, all of it held together by generations of stubbornness and sweat. Perseverance layered over failure, year after year. The kind of work you don't do for glory. The kind you do because it's yours.

"No," I tell her honestly. "Far from it." My thumb brushes absently along the railing, lost in the memory of lean years and late nights. "There were some tough stretches. Years where it could've gone either way. But we fought for it, and now, we're in a damn good place."

When I glance back, she doesn't look away. Doesn't even flinch. Just holds my gaze like she's flipping through pages I didn't mean to leave open. Her brow's slightly pinched, like she's puzzling me out, but there's a softness there, too, that makes it weirdly hard to swallow.

I clear my throat, glancing away before I let myself get caught up in it. "There's more to see, if you're interested?"

"Absolutely," she beams. "Lead the way, Captain."

The nickname makes me smirk. I could get used to hearing her call me that.

Our next stop is the tasting room, which is Callan's domain. This is where my brother thrives, right here in the thick of it.

I catch sight of him mid tour, standing at the head of the

crowd, glass in hand, voice as smooth as the whisky he's pouring.

"Swirl your glass gently," Callan instructs, "take in the aroma, really let it hit you. Notice the color. Sip slow and let it roll over your palate. Let it change on your tongue."

Juliette slows beside me, watching him work like she's stumbled upon some kind of magic show. I've spent my whole life watching him hold court like this, spinning stories and tasting notes until strangers start looking at a dram of whisky like it's holy.

It's a gift, I'll give him that.

His gaze snags on us then, his charming grin pulling at his lips as he lifts his glass in a casual salute.

"Feel free to ask questions as you go," he wraps up, voice carrying effortlessly through the room. "And most importantly —enjoy. Slàinte Mhath!"

The room fills with the clink of glasses, blending with the soft murmur of conversation. We linger near the door as Callan makes his rounds, answering questions and cracking a few jokes before finally making his way over.

"Hiya," he greets, clapping me on the back. His gaze shifts to Juliette, and a slow grin spreads across his face. "And who is this bonnie lass?"

She steps a little closer to my side, and just like that, her scent wraps around me, all sunshine and citrus. It catches me off guard, how easily it pulls me in. I've never paid much attention to things like that before, but with her, it's impossible to ignore for some reason.

Focus. This isn't the time to be noticing how good she smells or how she's slipped into my space like she belongs there.

I nod toward Callan, keeping my voice even. "Juliette, this is my brother, Callan."

I fight the urge to roll my eyes as he takes Juliette's hand, ever the showman, and presses a light kiss to the back of it, all charm and theatrics. The foolish flirt. It's a wonder his ego still fits in the room.

Looking at him is like seeing a slightly younger version of myself. We have the same build, same height, though his hair is lighter and more golden blond to my lighter brown. The biggest difference is our eyes. Mum always says mine are as green as a spring meadow and his are blue as a glacial lake. She has a knack for sayings, always tossing them around like bread-crumbs. When we got too rowdy as kids, she called us *squirrels on espresso*.

Juliette's sweet laughter spills out, and the sound hits deep in my chest.

"Quite the gentleman," she muses, dipping into a playful curtsey. "It's nice to meet you, Callan."

He clutches his chest like he's been struck by a mortal blow. "A lass after my own heart! Tell me my brother hasn't already whisked you away. Get it? Whisked. Whisky."

I roll my eyes. "Not quite," I reply, basking in the melody of her laugh again. "Juliette is Rose's niece. She's visiting for a while."

His brows shoot up, his eyes lighting with recognition. "You don't say! I see the resemblance now. Rose's family around here, which means you are, too. Hopefully, Knox here is treating you well."

"No complaints so far. It's a really great place you guys have here. Honestly, impressive."

"Ah, that's good to hear. You sitting for a tasting?"

I shake my head. "I was thinking about taking Juliette over to the lounge for a more intimate experience." The words slip out before I can process what I say.

Juliette and Callan freeze, eyes locking for a split second before they burst into laughter.

My face heats up as I realize the connotation behind my words. "Obviously not what I meant. Get your heads out of the gutter," I scold, trying to maintain some semblance of dignity. "What I meant to say was, I can show you our whisky lounge, and you can taste some there if you'd like. It's a bit quieter in there."

The two of them are practically doubled over, tears streaming down their faces as they giggle like a pair of schoolgirls. I stand there, trying to look serious, but my lips twitch. Before I know it, I'm caught in the same infectious fit of laughter.

"I'd love to see the lounge," she replies, still catching her breath. She glances around the room, her brow furrowing a little. "I wonder where Aunt Rose is? I thought she would've caught up by now."

"We can go find her if you want." Before I can finish the thought, she shakes her head, her lips curving into a reassuring smile.

"No, that's okay. I'm sure she's busy," she says, her voice softening, the faintest hesitation in the way her eyes flick up to meet mine. "I don't want to take up all your time, though. I'm sure you're busy."

I hold her gaze a second longer, letting the reassurance linger in my tone. "I've got all the time you need."

Before I can say anything else, one of the guests waves Callan over, calling him back into the crowd. He's quick to respond, flashing a smile in our direction before jogging toward the table, his voice carrying back to us. "Duty calls. I'll catch up with you guys later."

I turn my attention back to Juliette. "My schedule is pretty open today. It's no problem at all."

The change in her expression is immediate. Her face lights up, that radiant smile of hers sweeping away any trace of indecision. I swear the room brightens along with her.

JULIETTE

I t turns out my aunt's boss is most definitely not some sixty-year-old man. In fact, he's none other than the annoyingly handsome guy I almost ran over with her car. Funny how life works out like that. I nearly sent him straight to the ER, and yet, he stood in front of me as if nothing had happened. He either has nerves of steel, or he's just really, really good at pretending.

I managed to exhale a breath I didn't even know I was holding when he finally spoke. He was relaxed, wearing a pair of faded jeans and a flannel shirt with the sleeves rolled up, giving me a clear view of forearms that had no business looking so good.

The next thing I noticed was his height. Towering, really. He stood at least a foot taller than me, and it should've been intimidating, but instead, it made me feel small in a way that wasn't entirely uncomfortable. He's definitely the kind of person who doesn't need to shout to be heard. Weirdly enough, all that authority didn't make me want to run. And that was...unexpected.

Now, here I am, following him to the lounge. I can't focus on anything other than his spicy, woodsy scent. Cinnamon and oak with just a hint of something I can't place. The aroma alone wraps itself around my thoughts, making it impossible to concentrate on anything but him. And, god, every time he speaks, my face practically bursts into flames. That accent. The way he says my name like he's savoring it. It's enough to turn my insides into a puddle.

I'd like to think I could keep my cool if he wasn't so damn attractive. The quiet confidence he carries with him, the steady stride. Everything about him was made to be admired. Honestly? He should work on being a little less attractive.

My eyes are drawn to the wooden beams that stretch across the ceiling as we step into the lounge. They frame the room, guiding your gaze to the plush leather seats that practically beg you to sink into them. The muted lighting is, dare I say, *intimate*, as it casts a muted glow over everything. It gives the space an air of sophistication.

I can't help but admire the design of the room as we settle into one of the rounded booths. "It's beautiful in here," I comment, my fingers tracing the smooth edge of the table. "It's so relaxing. Refined."

Knox flashes me a grin, the pride in his voice unmistakable. "I appreciate that. I had a hand in designing the lounge. It was one of my more recent projects."

"Well, you know what you're doing, that's for sure."

He raises an eyebrow, leaning a little closer as his gaze shifts to the shelves above the bar that are full of bottles that sparkle in the low light. "You mentioned you're a whisky fan. What would you like to try?"

My eyes follow his, taking in the treasure trove of bottles. But it's not the whisky that has my attention. It's the subtle glint in his eye that's daring me to trust him, to let go and let him decide.

"Surprise me." It's just a drink, right? But the way he's looking at me, like this small decision actually matters, makes me want to get it right.

He stands, and it's impossible to ignore the shift in the room. The few women still talking fall quiet, and I can't blame them. The man is all broad shoulders and a powerful frame. It's distracting. I tell myself to look away, to focus on literally anything else, but my eyes have other plans.

The man is a walking ad for everything I've sworn off. My brain is firing warning shots, but it's still not enough to convince myself to look away.

I really can't afford another wrong choice. Not when I'm still trying to piece myself back together after the last mess. So, why does my heart *not* listen? Why is it still pounding in my chest as if he's already a part of my story?

A minute later, he's back, holding two tulip-shaped glasses filled with a dark amber liquid that glimmers like liquid gold. He sets one in front of me, his gaze still intense as he gestures for me to try it.

I follow Callan's earlier advice and swirl it gently, letting the aroma fill my senses. It's spicy, a little smoky. I take a small, tentative sip. Knox's eyes are on me, and there's an almost predatory focus to his gaze, waiting for my reaction.

The whisky is smooth and rich, a slow unraveling of oak and caramel. As it slides down, the heat lingers, curling low in my stomach. It takes a second for me to remember exactly who's watching, exactly how fast my heart is beating, and exactly how much I should ignore both.

He brings his own glass to his lips. My eyes trace the way his throat moves as he swallows, the deliberate control in every action. My pulse jumps, my thoughts scrambling to catch up with the sudden rush of heat.

Knox's lips twitch, just a ghost of a smile, but his focus doesn't shift. His eyes are still locked on me, watching every flicker of my expression as if it's something worth noting.

"Wow." The word slips out before I can filter it. "That's really great."

His grin widens. "That's our single malt scotch. Fan favorite."

"My new favorite, too, I think." I take another sip, letting the rich heat settle deep.

I clear my throat, needing something to fill the space between us. "So, Callan is your brother?"

As if there could be any doubt about it. Callan has that same easygoing charm, that same mischievous glint in his eyes. Knox, though...he's all rugged intensity, a man who doesn't waste words or movement.

Maybe that's what's pulling me in—the way he carries himself, like he's got layers no one's ever fully uncovered. Like there's more to him beneath the controlled exterior, something deeper, something worthy. And damn it, I want to know what it is.

He nods, a hint of fondness in his expression. "Aye. We're five years apart, and I swear, he's made it his mission to keep me young."

I can't help but laugh. "He's a character. You can't be too ancient, though. Hardly an old man."

It's almost too bad he *isn't* an old man. If he was sixty-five with a limp and a penchant for birdwatching, maybe my heart wouldn't be trying to do flips in my chest.

A deep, rumbling laugh spills from his lips, and the sound is enough to send a jolt through me. It's rich, effortless, and completely disarming. "I'm thirty-two. So, no, not ancient, I hope."

Of course, he's only five years older than me. And obviously so much more mature than the guys my age who still have the emotional depth of a kiddie pool. Maybe that's why I'm noticing him more than I should.

I need to knock it off. He's just a guy, right? I don't know why I'm trying to justify my interest in him.

"I'm not too ancient myself, but I don't have any siblings to keep me young. Your brother reminds me a lot of my best friend back home. She's also quite the character."

"Ah, so you know what it's like then."

"I do." I smile, making a mental note to give Bree a call later.

Just as the conversation starts to pick up again, Aunt Rose's voice cuts through the air. "I am so sorry about that! That took longer than I expected, but I'm all yours now," she says, settling in next to me.

I nudge her with my elbow. "You're an important woman, I understand. Knox was the perfect tour guide, and I met Callan as well."

She huffs out a laugh. "Oh, you poor thing. Did you come out unscathed?"

I shrug before shooting a wink in Knox's direction. "Mostly."

Knox stands, and for a second, the space between us is oddly too big. "I'll leave you ladies to it," he says, looking at Aunt Rose with that confidence I'm still trying to wrap my head around. "Rose, I'll call you tomorrow to go over the plans for the event?"

"Sounds good," she replies, her tone professional. "I'll make sure to get the details together before then."

His gaze settles on me again, and for a split second, there's a shift. That perfect smile softens, and the intensity in his eyes eases.

"Juliette, it was very nice to meet you. I'm sure I'll see you around before you head back to the States."

I return his smile, but there's a faint tug in my chest. One I haven't felt in a very long time. We just met, but something about him makes me want more time, more conversation, more...something.

"You sure will. Thanks again for showing me around today. You've got a truly incredible place here."

He gives an appreciative nod before turning to walk away. With each step, the muscles in his back shift beneath his shirt, a motion that's entirely too mesmerizing. I tell myself to look away, to reclaim some dignity, but my gaze lingers a beat too long. By the time I finally tear myself free, he's gone.

I turn back to Aunt Rose, who's watching me with a grin that says she knows exactly what's going on inside my head. "Earth to Juliette. That man is a human being, not a snack."

"I beg to differ," I joke, completely unashamed by my perusing. "He's...intriguing. But I'm not here for that. I'm here to clear my head and figure out my next steps. I've got my heart on hiatus. I was simply appreciating the view."

And what a view it was.

"If you say so," she quips.

I'm not fooling her. Not one bit.

I take another sip from my glass, the whisky suddenly a bit too warm as Knox's comment about the event starts to simmer in my mind. Funny how something so simple can trigger a flood of memories. The galas I used to attend with James flash through my mind—the stiff conversations, the forced smiles, the way everything felt like a performance. I have to bite back a cringe. Been there, done that, and I've got the emotional hangover to prove it. Curiosity tugs at me, despite the mental warning.

"What's this event you're planning?"

"Oh, it's so exciting!" she exclaims, slapping her hands down on the table with such force I nearly jump out of my seat. "We were voted the number one distillery in Scotland by the most popular whisky magazine. There's going to be a feature on Knox and Callan in the next issue. We're throwing a big party to celebrate."

I can't help but grin at her enthusiasm. It's contagious. "How neat. Are you guys hosting it here?"

"We are. It'll be the first event held here in the new space. I'd love it if you could come, if you're still here in July."

That's...almost two months from now.

Her fingers squeeze around mine. I don't think she even realizes she's doing it. How long *am* I staying? When I booked my ticket, I wasn't really thinking that far ahead. But the idea of still being here in a couple months doesn't seem so far-fetched.

"Maybe I could. Do you need any help with anything?"

"I don't want to put you to work, but we'll see," she concedes. "Are you ready to head out? Anywhere you want to go?"

"Honestly, I think the jet lag is catching up with me," I admit with a slight yawn. "I'm fine if you just want to head home."

She offers her hand to help me slide out of the booth. "Works for me. Let's hit the road."

The drive back is uneventful. We spend the rest of the day on the back deck, enjoying the fresh air. I could sit there for hours, but my stomach grumbles, reminding me food is needed.

Aunt Rose takes charge of dinner, and I'm grateful. The day's exhaustion catches up with me. After we eat, all I want to do is crawl into bed, pull the covers over my head, and sleep for a solid twelve hours.

"I think I'm going to call it a night," I say, my voice thick with fatigue as I start clearing the dishes. "I feel like I could sleep for a month."

"Leave those, hun. I'll take care of it," she says, shooing me from the kitchen.

I give her a quick hug, squeezing just a little longer than usual before heading to bed. After brushing my teeth and washing my face, I crawl into the softness of the sheets. The night air drifts in, carrying the sound of crickets and rustling leaves.

But sleep doesn't come quietly. It arrives wrapped in the shape of a tall, broad, devastatingly beautiful man. His dark green eyes, like the heart of a forest after a storm, pull me in, whispering secrets I know I'm not ready to hear. And yet, in the dream, I lean in anyway.

JULIETTE

The next day rolls in overcast and quiet, the sky a wash of gray that's more comforting than gloomy. We're heading to my aunt's favorite café, Thistle & Spoon, and while I'm mostly in it for the caffeine, I'm really looking forward to the slowness of an easy afternoon. Maybe it's just the novelty of a life with no set agenda.

"I hope Lucy's working today," Aunt Rose says, cutting a glance my way.

"Lucy?"

Her lips curl into a smile that can only be described as mischievous. There's something about the way her eyes sparkle, a little too innocently, that immediately puts me on high alert.

"Lucy MacKenzie," she says, drawing out the last name. "She owns the place. Makes the most divine scones you've ever tasted. Little bits of heaven."

I slow my pace along the cobblestone sidewalk, watching as she pretends not to notice my hesitation.

"MacKenzie," I repeat carefully. "As in..."

"Knox and Callan's sister," she confirms. "The youngest of the bunch. Sweet as honey and twice as warm."

Another MacKenzie establishment? Interesting.

The café comes into view just as the first raindrops begin to fall. It's barely enough to be considered a drizzle. When we step inside, it all hits me at once—sweet vanilla and butter, the bite of fresh coffee, followed by a wave of conversation and laughter. The café is bustling but not crowded, filled with mismatched furniture that works perfectly together.

"Rose!" A woman's voice calls out, and I turn to see someone weaving between tables and making their way over to us.

I know right off the bat she's Knox's sister by her unmistakable green eyes. She has the same auburn hair, though hers falls in loose waves above her shoulders.

"I was hoping you'd stop by today!" She embraces my aunt with genuine affection, then turns those striking eyes toward me. "I'm Lucy, and you must be Juliette. I've heard so much about you."

"You have?"

Her smile is kind. "All good things, I promise. Rose sings your praises."

My shoulders relax a little, soothed by her bubbly energy. "Well then," I say with a small laugh, "I guess I'll try to live up to the hype."

"I've got a good feeling you will. Come, let me show you to my favorite table."

She leads us to a cozy corner by the front window with overstuffed armchairs and a small round table. "This is the best spot for watching the rain."

I settle in, shrugging off my jacket as the cinnamon-laced air wraps around me. Lucy grabs our drink orders and heads back behind the counter.

She returns a few minutes later with them, carrying a tray with expert balance. "Here we are. A latte for you, Juliette. I added a hint of vanilla, hope that's okay. And Rose's usual. Earl Grey with a splash of milk."

Between us, she arranges a small plate of scones that look as divine as promised.

"Fresh from the oven," she says with a hint of pride. "Blackberry and white chocolate today. We're experimenting in the kitchen, but I think we've got a winner."

She hovers for a moment, tucking a strand of hair behind her ear. "So, I'm actually doing something new next week that I've been meaning to tell you about, Rose. We're hosting our first local author night."

Aunt Rose perks up immediately, setting down her cup with a soft clink. "Ooh, that sounds like so much fun. What's the plan?"

Lucy leans against the edge of a nearby shelf, her excitement sparking beneath the surface. "We're keeping it casual. Just a few authors reading excerpts from their work, maybe a Q&A. I'm trying to make the café feel even more like a community space, you know?"

"That sounds incredible," I say before I can stop myself. "Exactly the kind of thing that makes a town feel like home."

Her eyes light up. "Right? That's exactly what I'm going for."

"If you need help with anything, let me know. I've found myself with quite a bit of time on my hands."

The truth is, I *love* to write. I always have. Not professionally or anything, but in the margins of notebooks, on napkins, in the notes app on my phone at two in the morning when I can't sleep. It's the one thing that's always been mine, especially when everything else felt like it belonged to someone else.

So, helping out at an event like this? With authors and cozy lighting and people who care about words the way I do? It sounds like heaven.

"Really? Oh, that would be amazing. I need all the help I can get. I won't take up any of your time now, but stop by any day, and we'll chat, aye?"

And just like that, I volunteer myself for a community event in a town I barely know, surrounded by people I've only just met. It doesn't feel overwhelming. It feels *right*.

THE NEXT FEW days fly by in a blur of exploration. My aunt's busy with work, leaving me to wander on my own now that I've gotten the lay of the land. I've learned the twists and turns of the village well enough now to no longer feel like a tourist, though its charm still sneaks up on me when I least expect it.

Evenings have become a ritual of cooking dinner together, followed by long chats on the back deck as the sun dips below the horizon. It's simple. Uncomplicated. And in those quiet conversations, in the way she talks about my mom with such tenderness and mischief, I feel something in me start to settle.

The thought of leaving all this behind sits heavy on my mind. Part of me wants to hit pause, to hold onto these moments where the air is lighter, the days slower, and life a little more easygoing. It's strange how quickly a place can feel like home. How the right people, the right pace, can make you want to hold onto every last second. I know reality will eventually call me back, and I'll have to face whatever it is that's waiting for me, but for now, this is enough.

It's almost June, and while the weather has mostly been gray and moody, today is an exception. It's bright and breezy with no sign of the infamous Scottish rain. I'm out at the nature reserve, trying to soak in as much of this rare sunshine as I can. The paths seem endless, twisting and turning into new surprises at every corner. Waterfalls spill down hidden slopes, quiet streams mirror the sunlight, and birds fill the air with their songs. The place is alive, almost vibrating with energy.

I check the time—mid-afternoon already. Perfect for a detour to the café. I need to catch up with Lucy and see if there's anything I can do to pitch in. Maybe I'll give Bree a call, too.

By the time I'm settling into the same cozy corner of the café with my latte, my phone is buzzing on the table. Speak of the devil.

"Hey, you."

"Don't *hey you* me. You've been gone for almost a week, and this is the first time you've picked up. You're grounded."

I roll my eyes, even though she can't see me. "Okay, Mom. It's not like we haven't texted each other a thousand times since I've been gone," I joke. "I miss you, too, by the way."

"Yeah, yeah. You better." I can hear the smile in her voice. "Tell me what you've been up to today."

I settle into the chair as I start recounting my day.

Bree sighs. "It sounds amazing." There's a pause, then her voice lights up with a new thought. "But I am seriously disappointed in the lack of pictures. Specifically, the ones of burly Scottish men."

I can't hold back my laugh, not even caring when a few people glance my way. "I'm not going to be a creep, and I'm definitely not on the hunt for one of those."

"Well, you should be."

"A creep?"

"Well, no. But maybe? Scratch that. No to that, but yes to the hunt."

I shake my head, a laugh escaping me. "You're impossible."

"Don't be silly. You love me madly."

I can't argue with that. I'm about to ask her when she'll be making her trip out here as the door chimes, cutting me off. A commanding presence fills the room, and I don't even need to look up to know exactly who it is. That hair, those worn boots, and the way he stands just a little taller than everyone else, owning the space the moment he steps in.

I lose track of my conversation with Bree, my attention shifting to him as he strides toward the counter. His sister's face lights up when she sees him, and she hands him a drink that's already waiting for him along with a small treat wrapped in brown paper.

My pulse quickens when he catches my eye from across the room, a slow, knowing smile tugging at the corners of his lips.

"Hello? Juliette, are you there?"

Shit. I forgot I was on the phone. "Sorry, I think we had bad connection for a second."

"No, we didn't. I could hear all the background noise. What are you hiding from me?"

Busted.

"Nothing, but I do need to run. I'll call you later. Love you, bye!" The words come out in a rush, cutting off her protests not to hang up on her when I do, indeed, hang up on her.

eleven

KNOX

I don't need to search for her. Juliette's impossible to miss, and as soon as I step into the café, there's an invisible current that pulls me in her direction.

She's sitting at a corner table, head tilted, lips curved around something that probably isn't meant to be seductive, but Christ, it is. That sun-warmed skin, dark hair falling in waves over her shoulders, the flush in her cheeks like she's just come in from a long walk through the hills.

My eyes stick to her like they've found their home, and when hers meet mine, a little unsure but not backing down, I know I'm not the only one caught in whatever this is.

I walk over to her, my voice low and teasing. "This seat taken?"

Her soft chuckle lands like a shot of adrenaline. "Come on now. I'm sure you have a better pickup line than that."

Challenge accepted.

"Ah, lassie, don't flatter yourself. You just looked a bit lonely, and I figured you could use the company."

Her eyes sparkle with amusement as she nods, clearly satisfied with the answer. "That's better. Permission granted. Take a seat."

I don't need any more encouragement. I grin and slide into the chair with a bit more confidence than I should have, but hell, she makes it easy.

"Must be my lucky day," I tease.

She goes quiet for a second. Not awkward, just...somewhere else. Like her thoughts aren't meant for sharing.

She glances over, her eyes a little softer, a little distant. "You're just lucky I'm trying to do things differently these days."

I tilt my head. "Different how?"

She lets out this slow, almost reluctant breath. Then comes a little shrug. "Got tired of playing it small," she says quietly. "Living small. Showing up for everybody but me."

I feel that. Right in the center of my chest. I've been walking that same damn line so long it's almost second nature.

"Funny," I say, meeting her eyes as a grin tugs at the corner of my mouth. "Thought I was the only one daft enough to do that."

Her gaze snaps up, startled, possibly. Or maybe just seen.

For a second, neither of us says anything. Then she huffs a laugh. "Daft, huh?"

"Aye," I say, my grin tugging a little wider. "But in good company, apparently."

She clears her throat, her fingers tapping on the edge of her mug as she gestures toward the counter where Lucy's busy organizing pastries and the small crowd is going about their day.

"So, tell me," she says, a mischievous glint igniting her eye, "is there anything the MacKenzie family can't do?"

I lean back in my seat, folding my arms across my chest. "Mm, you're aware Lucy's my sister?"

"I was here with Aunt Rose a few days ago. She looped me in on the secret. Besides, I think I would have figured it out eventually. The similarities are striking."

"Aye, well, Lucy's much better looking."

Her eyes narrow just slightly, assessing me. "Your sister's gorgeous, but I have to admit, you're more my type."

I catch the flush climbing her neck, barely there. I don't say a word. Just let my eyes linger, soaking in the way she fidgets slightly, pretending I'm not grinning on the inside like a damn idiot.

She clears her throat, quickly shifting her gaze away from me, like she's pretending she didn't just let something slip. Damn, if it isn't adorable how easily she sparks up with fire one second, then tuck it away the next. It makes me want to close the space between us just to see if she'll light up again.

"You know what?" I lean in, dropping my voice to a more intimate level. "I'm going to take that as a compliment and run with it."

"You should," she says, the corner of her mouth lifting. "It was meant as one."

I rest my elbows on the table. "So, Juliette from Kentucky, how are you finding our little corner of Scotland?"

"I love it. I'm fully immersing myself. I'm even helping your sister with her local author night next week."

"I didn't realize my sister was recruiting beautiful Americans for her literary endeavors."

I didn't expect that to come out of my mouth. It's not like me. I'm usually the type to keep my thoughts to myself, but with her, the words seem to slip out before I can stop them.

And there's that blush creeping up her neck again. I can't help but find it oddly satisfying.

"She wasn't. I sort of volunteered myself." She tucks a strand of hair behind her ear, a gesture that catches my attention more than it should. "I've always loved books, and I figured it would be a good way to meet people while I'm here."

"And how long do you plan on being here exactly?" I ask, trying to sound casual, though I'm very invested in her answer.

She shrugs. "Not sure yet."

I should leave it there. I know I should. She's barely unpacked her suitcase, and here I am, mentally rolling out reasons for her to stay—good coffee, better whisky, my sister's community events, me.

Jesus.

She's not some local woman I'll see again at the pub or passing by church on Sundays. I shouldn't be letting anyone mess with the steady life I've carefully built over the past couple years. One I've spent too long convincing myself is enough.

I'll back off and be polite. Be the reliable guy with a light-hearted tone and no emotional investment. That would be smart. That would be safe.

"Well," I say, tapping a knuckle on the table, "I'm glad to see you again. I was hoping I would."

There.

That was gentle. Friendly. No invitation, no ask, no reason for her to second-guess my intentions.

I offer her a nod before pushing myself up from my chair, but then, she smirks.

"Glad I got to see you, too, *Captain*."

This was supposed to be easy. A quick hello, a polite retreat.

But simple doesn't smirk like that. Simple doesn't make my pulse kick up, doesn't stir heat low over nothing more than a look and a few words.

Simple shouldn't make me want to lean in just to watch her lips move when she speaks.

I steel myself and step away, refusing to glance back. Because if I look at her now, I might just forget why I ever stood up in the first place.

I've just kicked back on the couch for the night when my phone buzzes next to me. I shake my head. I knew this call was coming.

"Hiya, dear sister," I answer, settling deeper into the cushions.

"Mm, hello, brother."

I can practically hear the shit-eating grin in her voice.

"Ask away. I know it's been gnawing at you since I left the café," I taunt, propping my feet on the coffee table.

"Well, is there something specific I should be asking? You were looking very comfortable with Rose's niece, aye?"

"Now you wouldn't be getting nosy now, would you, Lou?"

"Me? Never," she teases. "Just curious, is all. The few times I looked over it seemed you were having a grand time."

"I was, for the most part. Rose invited her to the distillery earlier in the week, so I met her then."

"She's lovely."

"That she is," I agree, my voice lowering just a little, but not enough to reveal how much I'm actually enjoying the idea of seeing her more.

"Now that the questions are out of the way, yes. I was being nosy."

"I'm well aware, Lou. You're worse than Callan when it comes to sticking your nose where it doesn't belong."

"It's different when I do it. I'm the youngest. I've got privileges."

"Is that so?" I shift, propping the phone between my ear and shoulder as I reach for my glass of whisky on the side table. "And what privileges might those be?"

"The privilege of making sure my big brother doesn't scare off a perfectly nice woman before she even gets a chance to know what she's missing."

I roll my eyes. "Christ, Lou, we've barely spoken three times. I'm not planning our wedding."

"No one said anything about a wedding." She lets her voice lose some of its edge. "But, Knox, when was the last time you did something just for yourself? Something that wasn't about the distillery or helping one of us out of a jam?"

I take a slow sip of my whisky, letting the familiar burn settle before answering, "I do plenty for myself."

"Like what? Working sixteen-hour days? Taking on extra shifts when Callan needs time off? Spending your weekends helping Mum?"

"That's different," I mutter, though the argument sounds weak.

"Is it?" she challenges. "When was the last time you took a proper holiday? Or went on a date that wasn't arranged by someone else?"

The silence stretches between us, heavy with truths I don't particularly want to face.

"That's what I thought," she says, but there's no triumph in her voice. "You're always taking care of everyone else. The responsible one. The steady one. When do you get to just be Knox?"

Fuck, when she says it, I feel the sting of it. What does it say about me that when I try to think back, to recall the last time I did something for myself, just because I wanted to... there's nothing. Not a damn thing.

I don't have an answer for her.

"I'm fine, Lou," I finally manage.

"You're always fine," she sighs. "That's the problem."

"What do you want me to say? That I'm lonely? That I've spent so long making sure everything runs smoothly for everyone else that I've forgotten how to want things for myself?"

"That would be a start."

"What the hell," I mumble, running a hand through my hair. "When did my little sister get so bloody wise?"

"Around the same time my big brother started forgetting he deserves to be happy, too."

The last time I chased after something for my own *happiness*, it bit me in the ass and tried to drain my bank account in the process. So yeah, happiness isn't exactly a priority for me these days.

We wrap up the call and say our goodbyes, but the weight of her words lingers. Every decision in my life has been filtered through the lens of responsibility to my family and to the distillery.

I exhale, rubbing a hand over my face. I need to focus. I planned on going through the menu options Rose sent over from the caterer. With a resigned breath, I grab my laptop off the coffee table and pull up the document.

"Christ," I mutter under my breath. She should've sent me this menu without the pricing. I'd rather be clueless if I'm going to enjoy any part of this. I quickly shoot her an email, telling her she can pick whatever fits the budget. I make sure to underline that last part.

90

JULIETTE

Every Friday night, Aunt Rose flits off to the local brewery to meet up with her friends, a true social butterfly. She invited me along, but after the day I've had, a quiet night at her place sounded a lot more appealing.

The rain's stopped, leaving behind that damp, earthy smell and a sky still streaked with clouds. It's taken real effort to shake off the lingering tension from my conversation with Knox earlier. That's three times now I've been caught zoning out around him. It's completely absurd. I barely know the man.

As if that wasn't enough, I've also landed myself in the doghouse for hanging up on Bree. The strongly worded text she sent me afterward made that much clear. With a sigh, I settle into one of the old wooden chairs on the back deck with a blanket draped over my legs. I pull up my contacts, my finger hesitating over her name before I give in and hit call. I barely get a chance to brace myself before she picks up, ready to let me have it.

"Juliette Skye Miller. Who do you think you are, hanging up on me?"

Yep, there it is.

I wince. "I'm sorry. I panicked. I was in the middle of a... situation."

Bree huffs dramatically. "Uh-huh. And what kind of *situation* are we talking about?"

I think about the way my stomach flipped when Knox's grin met my gaze from across the room. The deep timbre of his voice. The way he read my nerves like an open book and eased them without a second thought.

"Oh, Bree," I mutter. "I'm doomed. I don't know what I'm doing here."

The shift in my tone catches her attention. "What's going on?"

I exhale and start from the top. "Okay, so first of all, I may or may not have almost run a man off the road—"

Her laughter explodes through the phone before I can finish. "You, what?"

I roll my eyes, waiting for her to settle down. "Yeah, yeah, get it out of your system. Anyway, that happened. I panicked, nearly crashed, and then had to endure the most awkward interaction of my life while he remained completely unbothered and flirted with me. Then, somehow, I ended up on a whisky tour with him because he's my aunt's boss, which was interesting in its own right. And now? I can't stop thinking about him, no matter how hard I try." I sigh. "His name's Knox, by the way."

Another pause, but this time it's not for her to laugh. It's for me to catch my breath.

"Then today," I continue, "we had this chat in the café, and I swear, every time he smiles at me, I feel like I've been hit by a truck. But...in a good way. Does that make sense?"

Okay, I'm rambling. "Anyway, that's the week in a nutshell. So, you can imagine how my head's been spinning."

Bree's silence is troubling. She's either about to say something incredibly insightful or utterly ridiculous. Not being able to see her expression makes it hard to tell where this is going. Then, just as I'm about to open my mouth, the ping of a video call request comes through the speaker. Apparently, she had the same thought.

I swipe and my best friend's face lights up the screen.

Her tone is serious. "This requires a face-to-face conversation."

"Agreed. Lay it on me."

"Are you telling me you're in a full-fledged, head-over-heels, butterflies-in-your-stomach spiral over a Scottish man named Knox?"

I groan, dragging a hand down my face. "No. Maybe. I don't know."

She snorts. "Oh, babe. You're done for."

I throw myself back against the chair. "That's what I'm saying! It's ridiculous. I've barely spent any time with him. And don't even get me started on my heart rate. It's embarrassing."

Bree hums knowingly. "Sounds like a textbook case of instant attraction to me."

I scoff. "Yeah, well, attraction is one thing, but this? This feels...dangerous."

"Dangerous as in, abort mission, or dangerous as in, this could actually be something and I'm terrified?"

I hesitate, chewing my lip. "The second one."

Her eyes narrow. "You're spiraling, but I can't figure out why."

It appears we have insightful Bree this evening.

"Gee, I don't know. Maybe because I just admitted I'm having borderline heart-palpitating feelings for a man I've known for a grand total of *seven days* and have spoken to, oh, *three times?*" The words tumble out in a frantic rush, too fast, too revealing.

Bree, naturally, is unfazed. She just lifts a perfectly arched brow. "And?"

I blink. "And? *And?* You seriously think any of this is a good idea?"

"What makes it a bad one? From what you've told me, you're having the time of your life. And, might I add, you got exactly what you wished for—your very own brooding Scottish man."

There's *ridiculous* Bree. I knew she was hiding in there somewhere.

"I'm kidding...kind of. Let me ask a different question," she says. "I know you can give me a thousand reasons why getting involved with this guy is a bad idea, but forget all that for a second. What do *you* want? Not regarding him but in general."

Her question catches me off guard. I've spent the last few weeks untangling my thoughts, replaying my past, and trying to make sense of where I'm headed. But somehow, I've never stopped to ask myself *that*.

I shift, my fingers tracing absent patterns against the fabric of my sweater as I glance toward the horizon. The sun is slipping lower, its golden light threading through the trees, stretching shadows across the ground. My chest tightens, not in panic, but in realization.

"I want to wake up every day in a life that feels *peaceful*, one that's built with love." The words come slowly at first, then with more certainty. "I want more time outside, to breathe fresh air and feel the sun on my skin. I want a home that feels like *home*. Not just a place to sleep, but a place to *be*."

Bree stays quiet for a beat, then murmurs, "Go on."

"I just want to be present. To stop overthinking, to stop worrying about expectations, and just live."

She pounces on that. "Okay, last one, and don't overthink it. Would you say yes if he asked you out?"

"Yeah," I admit quietly. "I think I would."

"See? Easy."

I groan. "It's not, though. Bree, I don't *live* here. What's the point of starting something when it's got an expiration date? Besides, this could be totally one-sided."

She rolls her eyes. "You just gave me this whole heartfelt monologue about wanting a life built on love and peace, and now you're trying to logic your way out of it?"

I open my mouth to argue, but she steamrolls ahead.

"Do something for *yourself*," she says. "But if you genuinely feel like you're putting yourself at risk, that's a different story."

I squint at the camera, making sure she feels the full weight of my gaze. "Wait a second, am I talking to Bree here? How exactly did you become a licensed therapist in the week I've been gone?"

A spark of mischief sparkles in her eyes as she leans closer to the camera, clearly enjoying my discomfort. "Cute."

I can't help but laugh, the sound a little lighter than it was a second ago, the tight knot in my chest loosening just enough to let me breathe. A minute ago, I was drowning in self-doubt, ready to let it consume me. Now? I'm still uncertain, but it's funny how one conversation can pull me from the edge of a pity party to something that feels...hopeful.

We stay on the phone for another hour, slipping into that easy flow we always have. We talk about everything and nothing, catching up on life, making plans for when she visits, talking about where we'll stay. The distance between us cuts in half with each laugh.

I lean back, tilting my head to the sky. The stars are scattered above, so bright and endless. For a moment, I just stare, feeling like a tiny speck in the vastness of it all. It's like I'm woven into something much larger and part of a bigger story. It's strangely peaceful.

Then, a rustling breaks the silence. My heart jumps, my body going rigid. *What the hell was that?*

I scan the darkening landscape, eyes darting through the shadows. There's no way I'm sticking around to find out. My pulse spikes as I hurry back inside. I'm not sure what kind of creatures lurk around here after dark, but I don't plan on becoming part of their nightly routine.

thirteen

KNOX

I told myself it was a coincidence that I just happened to wander past Rose's office around lunchtime when she was meeting Juliette a few days after our run in at the café.

But that was a lie.

And now, here I am at my sister's coffee shop again to help set up. It's not because I'm deeply passionate about folding tablecloths or stringing fairy lights. And it's definitely not because I give a damn about whether the mic stand is positioned at the optimal angle.

No. I'm here for Juliette. I haven't even tried to convince myself otherwise.

The door chimes, and my eyes snap up before I can stop them. I'm ridiculous. Like some half-grown idiot circling the schoolyard crush he swore he didn't like.

Except I do like her. Too much for someone I barely know. Too much for someone who's here temporarily.

Juliette walks in, arms stacked high with books. Her focus is entirely on the task, a determined furrow in her brow, her lip caught between her teeth in that innocent way that makes my mind wander to dirty places. I imagine the gentle pressure of those same teeth grazing my bottom lip, the satisfying sting that would follow if she bit down just hard enough. What would she taste like? Something sweet and intoxicating, I'm sure. Something that would have me coming back for more, again and again.

I imagine her mouth trailing down my neck, my chest, my stomach, moving lower with each kiss. Those hands of hers, the ones now clutching books so carefully, would they be gentle or demanding when they touched me? Would she whisper what she wanted, or would she show me? Christ, the thought of her naked beneath me, those hazel eyes dark with want, her hair spread across my pillow—

Damn it. I need to get a grip. I shouldn't be noticing how her deep blue sweater clings just right, or how her dark hair's pulled into a loose braid that reveals the elegant curve of her neck.

Before my thoughts get too carried away, Lucy rushes over, relieving her of half the stack. "Oh my goodness, Juliette! I didn't expect you to bring so many!"

"I got carried away at the bookshop," she says with a laugh. "The owner kept recommending Scottish authors I absolutely had to read, and well, here we are."

I stay where I am, watching as she sets the books down on a table. She arranges them by size, her fingers moving with careful precision. Her movements are graceful and unhurried. I try, but it's damn near impossible to remember why I ever thought keeping my distance was a good idea.

I can't stand here all night like a brooding statue in work boots, pretending I'm not itching to close the space between us. So, I do what any rational, emotionally mature man would do.

I walk over.

"Careful," I say, nodding at the stack of books. "If you

alphabetize them, Rose might start expecting that kind of organization from the rest of us."

"Knox!" she exclaims, nearly dropping one of the books. "I didn't expect to see you here."

I run a hand through my hair. "Actually, I'll be honest. I may have asked Lucy what time you'd be here."

"May have?"

I just shrug.

She laughs, the sound warming something in me that's been cold for longer than I care to admit. "And here I thought our meeting was serendipitous."

"I'm not above a bit of reconnaissance when necessary."

I have a hard time believing I'm the only one feeling this crackling thing between us that seems to live in the air whenever we're within a few feet of each other. It's not just in my head. It can't be.

The way she looks at me says she feels it, too. Her cheeks flush, just enough to make my pulse pick up speed.

Her mouth opens like she's going to say something, then closes again. She presses her lips together and glances down at the books like they suddenly need more rearranging, like looking at them is safer than looking at me.

I watch the curve of her mouth. The way she tucks a stray hair behind her ear again, fingers a bit too fidgety. The slight sway of her body as she shifts her weight from one foot to the other. Not nervous, exactly, just aware. Of me.

And damn if that awareness doesn't stir something reckless in me.

If I reached out and touched her cheek, would she lean into it? Would her breath catch the way mine just did?

I clear my throat, forcing my gaze away before my thoughts go too far. Before I let myself imagine things I have no business wanting.

"What are your plans for the rest of the week?" I ask.

She exhales a breath she's clearly been holding, her shoulders relaxing just enough for me to see the tension slip away.

"Nothing much, honestly. I've been raiding my aunt's pantry since I got here, so I need to make a grocery run to replace everything I've eaten. I promised her I'd restock the tea biscuits she pretends not to hoard in the tin above the fridge."

"Just groceries?" I ask, not bothering to hide my amusement.

"Just groceries," she confirms with a small laugh. "It's my turn to plan our dinners this week."

"Do you like to cook?"

She lets out a chuckle, the sound lifting the heaviness off my chest. "Honestly, I do enjoy it but I'm not very good. Aunt Rose does most of the work while I supervise. I've proven myself untrustworthy when it comes to handling sharp knives."

She gestures toward her left hand, which I now see has a bandage wrapped around her index finger. "No stitches," she adds with a wry smile. "Hurt my pride more than anything else."

"Christ, lass. I've seen grown men lose fingers that way. You should take a knife skills course."

"Are you offering, Captain?" she quips.

"Aye, I suppose I am if it means saving those delicate fingers," I reply, letting the teasing tone slip in, though there's a hint of seriousness beneath it.

She quirks her head, considering it for a second. "I assume these lessons come at a cost?"

"I think having dinner with me would cover it."

Did I just say that? The words are barely out of my mouth, but there they are, hanging in the air between us, bold and reckless and completely unplanned.

I asked her out in exchange for teaching her knife safety. Romantic. What the hell am I doing?

She's not a fling. She deserves more than flirtation wrapped in sarcasm. She deserves patience. Clarity.

I get the sense she's definitely not looking for someone to complicate things, especially not someone with a tangled past. It's the perfect reason to stay far, far away from whatever this is.

But then again...she did ask if I was offering.

"Very bold assumption that I'd want to have dinner with you," she teases, but I catch the slight tremor in her voice. "But, um, just so I'm clear, is that a real offer? Dinner?"

The question gives me a chance to backpedal and pretend I didn't mean it, or perhaps to retreat before things get messy. But I don't hesitate. Not for a second.

I step closer, letting the space between us shrink, because the distance feels all wrong now.

"Juliette, I'd really like it if you'd have dinner with me sometime."

She looks at me, really looks at me. I swear the whole world stills. She blinks, just once, her breath catching ever so slightly, and that's when I know for a fact she feels it, too. That moment when everything stops being a question and just becomes what it is.

There's no retreat, no laughter to deflect. She doesn't pull back, doesn't break eye contact. For a moment, I want to stay there and try to decipher every flicker of emotion crossing her face.

"I'd like that, too," she finally says, her voice softer than before. "But I need to think about it, if that's okay?"

"Of course that's okay, lass."

She gives a subtle nod, her gaze lingering just a moment longer. I think we're both on the same page, even if we don't know exactly what the story is yet.

"I just want to make sure it's a good idea," she adds.

I always joke about Callan being the foolish flirt, but it looks like I've taken the crown. I'm not the type to jump into my feelings. Hell, I barely like *acknowledging* I have them most days. For the past two years, I've kept my head down, handled my shit, and didn't complicate things. That's been the whole playbook.

But then Lucy went and said that throwaway comment that landed harder than it should've.

When do you get to be just Knox?

Never.

It might've been a little reckless to ask her out, but that wasn't my intention. Either way, I'm going to chase this feeling with Juliette *carefully* from now on.

I let out a breath. "I get it. And...sorry if I made things awkward. Here's the deal, though. If you want to take me up on the offer, reach out whenever. If you're just after the lesson, no worries. I'm happy to give that to you. No charge." I flash her a wink, though it's more for show than anything else.

Her melodic laughter rings out. When her eyes light up, that spark flickering back, I can't fight the grin that spreads across my face.

"You've got a deal."

It's LATE when I get home, and I'm just about to sink into the couch cushions. The house is still. Silent. Everything's in its place, just how I like it.

But then, a high-pitched screech slices through the air, followed by a blur of gray darting past the window outside. I freeze, the calm moment instantly shattered by the chaos. A little pulse of irritation rises in me because I *like* my peace.

I should ignore it. Whatever it is can figure itself out, but I find myself moving toward the front door, too curious to let it go. I ease the door open just enough to see what's happening on the other side.

In an instant, a small creature races past me, and before I can fully process what's happening, it's inside.

I slam the door shut and turn around, reluctantly taking in the scene before me. A kitten is perched on the armrest of my couch, its bright copper eyes locked on mine.

Well, this is interesting.

I move slowly toward the couch, keeping my eyes locked on the tiny intruder. The kitten watches me approach, tail swishing with what looks suspiciously like enjoyment. When I'm close enough to grab it, I lunge forward, but the little beast is quicker than I anticipate. It leaps from the armrest, landing gracefully on the floor, and darts under the coffee table.

"Seriously?" I mutter, dropping to my knees.

The kitten peers out at me from its new hiding spot, whiskers twitching. There's something almost mocking in its gaze, like it's enjoying this little game. I reach under the table, fingers stretching toward the gray fur, but it skitters away at the last second, seeking refuge behind the bookshelf.

I spend the next five minutes chasing the damn thing around my living room, behind the curtains, under the side table, between my legs. Finally, I corner it in the kitchen.

"Got you," I say triumphantly, scooping it up. It's lighter than I expected, all bones and fluff. Those copper eyes stare up at me, unblinking, as if to say, "And what exactly do you plan to do now?"

Good question.

The kitten makes a pitiful mewing sound that *almost* makes

me hesitate. I've lived alone for years now, and a plant is one thing, but a cat? Absolutely not.

I cradle it awkwardly against my chest and head for the front door. "All right, little one. Time to go back to...wherever you came from." I set the kitten down on the porch and give it a gentle nudge. It doesn't move.

A frustrated sigh leaves me, and I turn to head back inside, figuring that it'll wander off on its own. Before I even get my hand on the door, a blur of gray zips past me, darting through the crack in the door, straight back into the house.

I freeze.

Again.

It's inside *again*.

JULIETTE

This really is a great little town. The atmosphere, the people, it's all got a certain charm that makes it hard to resist. Helping Lucy at the café last night was...fun, actually. Everyone who showed up brought that small-town charisma you can't fake. Not once did I feel like I had to explain myself or shrink to fit in. I didn't have to try so hard. I could just *be*.

And then there was Knox. I wasn't expecting him to ask me out. But he did, and when he said it again without any of the joking or the teasing, it made my breath catch. I couldn't help but wonder what going out with him would be like.

It wasn't the usual pressure that made me hesitate. It was the way he'd said it, like he was giving me space to decide, not rushing me, just curious if I'd say yes. Part of me wanted to, more than I cared to admit, especially with the way the tension between us was practically crackling in the air. But I didn't, and I immediately regretted it. Not because I'm trying to rebound or prove something to myself. But because, for one tiny second, it felt like it could be *easy* to say yes to him. It was something I wanted, plain and simple.

And yet, I wonder...is it too soon?

I mean, James hasn't even fully faded from my life. Not because I'm still tangled up in him. I'm absolutely *not*. That chapter closed long before either of us admitted it. And maybe it's crazy to even be standing here, heart skittering at the idea of starting something new, when the dust hasn't fully settled yet. But I want this.

Wasn't that the whole point of coming to Scotland? Not to be reckless, exactly, but to stop living like every decision needed a pros and cons list. To stop holding myself hostage to things that didn't fit anymore.

I want to spend time with Knox.

No overthinking. No grand scheme. No rules to follow.

Just because I want to.

"I know the perfect spot for lunch. You're going to love it."

I blink, snapping out of my thoughts, only to realize I've been staring blankly out the car window for...god, who knows how long? Long enough that Aunt Rose hasn't said a word. She's let me sit here and stew in my overthinking silence. She's been driving for...what, two hours now?

We pull up to a stone building with a cream-colored exterior that blends into the rugged landscape. Its slate roof and wooden awning give it a laid-back, rustic vibe.

The host greets us with a friendly smile and leads us to a table in the back. The space is cozy in that carefully curated way, with dim lighting, jazz playing low. Modern, but not cold.

And then there's the view.

Rolling emerald fields give way to towering, blue-shadowed mountains that look almost unreal. I sink back in my seat, exhaling a slow, happy sigh that feels like it's been trapped in my chest for months.

"If you told me we were just going to sit here all day,

soaking in this view," I murmur, feeling every last knot in my body begin to loosen, "I'd be all in."

Aunt Rose takes a moment to appreciate the expanse of beauty beyond the window. She lets out a contented sigh. "You should see it here in the winter. It's even more stunning."

"I can imagine. Maybe I'll come back during the winter holiday break this year."

I haven't even left yet, and I'm already planning on coming back.

The waitress arrives to take our drink orders. We both opt for water. Once she's out of earshot, I clear my throat to get my aunt's attention. "So, there's something I need to talk to you about."

Her eyes widen, her lips parting as she gasps. "Oh god, are you pregnant?"

I laugh, shaking my head. "No! Although now that you thought I was dropping that kind of bomb, this conversation just got a lot easier."

She raises an eyebrow, her lips curling into a smirk, and gestures for me to continue.

"Well, I ran into Knox at his sister's café yesterday. We chatted for a bit, and he asked if I'd have dinner with him sometime."

"Mm, go on."

"I told him I needed to think about it. He really doesn't know much about me or what I'm going through. I don't even know how long I'm going to be here. I guess...I just want to know what you think."

She looks at me for a moment, then asks, "Can you tell me what you know about Knox?"

"Honestly? Just the basics. Where he works, how many siblings he has. Our conversations haven't gotten too personal, but what I do know, I like."

She leans back in her chair, taking a thoughtful sip of her water. "I see. Well, I'm not going to tell you what you should or shouldn't do. Are you asking me because you're having the same thoughts as I am?"

I chew on my bottom lip, turning her question over in my mind. "Would those thoughts be that I just had my heart broken and explicitly said I *wasn't* going to jump into something new with another guy?"

Her lips twitch into a smirk. "You said it, not me." She pauses, watching me carefully when she says, "I've known Knox for years now, and I know you. Both of you are easy to love. That can either be wonderful or painful, Jules."

I fiddle with my napkin. I know I'm not supposed to get attached. I'm not supposed to feel *anything* after what happened back home. Still, there's something about being around Knox that quiets all the noise in my head. It's not just that, though. It's this overwhelming sense of comfort that comes with him, like the universe has decided to cut me a break and show me that maybe I can have something good again.

And besides, no one said anything about *love*.

"Yeah, but it's different here," I say. "It doesn't feel like I'm forcing anything. More like I'm just...letting it happen."

She doesn't say anything for a moment, then lets out a laugh. "You've got the heart of a poet, you know that? Just like your mom. That doesn't mean you won't get hurt."

Yeah, I already thought that, too. Hearing her say it makes it much more real, though.

"Follow your heart, hun. Just be careful and make sure you have all the facts before making any decisions." Her tone is light, but there's something in the way she says it that sends an uneasy chill down my spine. Like she knows something I don't.

I've already made up my mind, though. I just needed

someone to reassure me that I'm not completely alone when the inevitable heartbreak comes knocking.

People move on. People change. Some disappear because of life circumstances, others by choice.

"Stop it." My aunt's voice slices through the gloom in my head. "I see your mind doing bad things. You're going to be fine, no matter what you decide."

I let out a relieved laugh. "Well, that's creepy that you knew what I was thinking. Does the twin telepathy thing work on me, too? Show me your ways."

Her laugh rings out, bright and contagious.

I take a deep breath, trying to sound as casual as possible when I ask, "Does that mean you'll give me Knox's number?"

She rolls her eyes, clearly seeing right through me, but still, she reaches for her phone without missing a beat and hands it over. "I don't know what I'm going to do with you."

Later that evening, Aunt Rose disappears down the hall with a yawn, and the house settles into its usual hush. I curl into the corner of the living room couch, tucking my knees up and wrapping the throw tighter around me. Before I let myself think too hard, I grab my phone and hit the call button after finding Knox's name. My heart kicks up, and my stomach does that ridiculous fluttery thing as it rings.

"Hello?"

Knox's voice rumbles through the phone, and I swear my cheeks heat up in response. A slow burn spreads across my skin, and suddenly, I'm acutely aware of how flustered I am. How is it possible for a voice to do such a thing?

"Hi, it's Juliette."

"Juliette, how are you?" His voice slides over the words with that effortless ease, making me forget how to breathe for a moment. I swear I'm about to melt right into the phone.

"I'm great. Spent the day with Aunt Rose in Glencoe. Lots of dramatic skies and sheep. Very scenic. Very moody."

He chuckles. "Aye, Glencoe's good for that."

God, even his laugh makes me want to say and do things I definitely shouldn't.

"So," I clear my throat, shifting to the edge of the couch, "I thought maybe I'd take you up on those lessons."

The second the words leave my mouth, my stomach flips. I don't just cross the line. I leap straight over it. When he doesn't answer right away, I start second-guessing myself. This is what happens when I do something for me.

His voice is softer when he speaks again. "Sure, just let me know when's a good time."

"Well, I thought maybe we could use our dinner plans for the lesson, too? You know, two birds, one stone."

I can almost picture the slow curve of his lips as he replies, his voice a little playful, a little dangerous. "Ah, are you accepting my request for a date as well, lass?"

The heat in my cheeks spikes again. "Aye, *Captain,* I am."

He chuckles, and the sound ripples through me, sending a little flutter straight to my heart. "Okay, then. What are you doing tomorrow night?"

I hesitate for a moment, caught off guard by how easy it is to hold a conversation with him. Like this is no big deal. Except...this *is* a big deal. "Well, nothing. My schedule's wide open."

"Can you be ready around four?"

"I can do that." My voice comes out steadier than I feel. "Do you want me to meet you somewhere?"

"I'll pick you up if you're comfortable with coming over to my place for dinner?"

"Of course," I reply. "That would be great. I'm really looking forward to it."

I'm pretty sure I sound like a giddy schoolgirl with a massive crush.

His rich, hearty laugh rumbles through the phone, shattering the silence and sending another thrill straight through me. "Me too, lass. I'll talk to you tomorrow."

"Sure thing! Talk to you then."

Yeah, I'm definitely not playing it cool.

Another chuckle. "Goodnight, Juliette."

Dizziness sweeps over me, tumbling around inside like I'm fifteen again. I'm too old for this teenage-level flailing. Too smart to let a goodnight send me spinning.

But here I am anyway, grinning like an idiot in the dark.

Yep. I am so screwed.

KNOX

Juliette's call last night threw me, but in a good way. Sundays are about the only day I get to myself, so tonight seemed like the perfect chance to spend time with her.

Her suggestion of combining the lesson and dinner on the same night was kind of genius. I've already got an idea for something we can make together at my place. Everything is falling into place...until I remember one small problem, the same one that is currently glaring at me from the corner of my living room.

I've tried to put the damn cat back outside five times now. Each time, it manages to slip past me, darting back in before I can shut the door. And now, it's just sitting there all smug, like it knows I've lost the battle.

I think it's safe to say I have a cat now.

I have to grab groceries and, apparently, cat supplies, but there's no way I'm leaving the creature alone in the house. Plus, it needs a vet check before I can let it near anyone else. I pull up Callan's number, half expecting him to ignore me. Just as I'm about to hang up and send a text, he finally picks up.

"Why in god's name are you calling me this early?" he grumbles.

"Good morning to you, too," I muse. "I have a situation. I need your help."

"Knox needs me? This ought to be good."

I drag a hand down my face with a sigh. "Long story short, I have a date and a cat."

"I'm sorry, what? You have a date...with a cat?"

I pinch the bridge of my nose. "You know that's not what I said. I have a date tonight with Juliette, but I've also ended up with a semi-feral beast that I can't get rid of. Damn thing got in last night and won't leave."

"Hold the phone! A date with the American, aye? Good for you, brother!"

I let out a frustrated sigh. "I need your help with the cat, Cal. Can you bring over some cat stuff and sit with it while I get groceries?"

"On my way, brother. I can't wait to meet my new niece or nephew."

I should have called Lucy.

Less than an hour later, the sound of Cal's truck rumbling up the gravel drive signals his arrival. Behind me, the kitten trots along, somehow always right underfoot. I glance down just as it stops beside me, gives Cal's approaching truck a slow, suspicious look, and flicks its tail like it already knows this guy's about to mess up whatever calm it had going. Smart little thing.

Sure enough, the second Cal's boots hit the ground, that tiny scrap of fur puffs itself up like a lion in a housecat's body. It plants its feet, squints, and lets out a hiss.

Yeah, this one's got spirit. Definitely keeping it.

Cal slows mid step on the porch, raising a brow. "You've gotta be kidding me," he mutters. "It's already protective of you?"

I reach down, letting my fingers glide through velvety-soft fur. The kitten practically melts against my ankle, its whole body vibrating from its purrs. Fierce little thing.

"Can't blame him," I say, trying not to smile. "He's got good instincts."

Amusement flickers across Cal's face. "Well, this is an interesting sight—you taking care of a cat."

I step back into the house, giving Cal just enough space to slip in sideways. He avoids the kitten with the same level of carefulness as someone trying not to step on a landmine. I watch him, stifling a chuckle.

"It's probably safe now," I tease. "I don't think he sees you as a threat anymore. Besides, he's smaller than your foot."

Cal sets the bags on the floor with a soft thud and bends down to pull off his shoes, all while giving the kitten a wary glance. Before I get a chance to dig through the supplies, I catch a glimpse of him out of the corner of my eye.

He's somehow already got the kitten scooped up in his arms, cradling it like a newborn. He sits down on the couch, the little ball of fur tucked close against his chest.

"Well, that didn't take long," I mutter under my breath, fighting a smile.

Cal coos at the kitten. "Look at you, you little fluff ball. Who's a sweet baby? I could squish you all day." His voice morphs into that ridiculous tone parents get when they talk to their baby, and I can't help but laugh. "Aw, are you purring?" he continues. "Best nephew ever."

Ridiculous.

"Hey, Cal. Is your friend still a vet? Would she be able to check him out for me?"

He glances up, already reaching for his phone. "Jamie? Aye, she still is. Makes house calls, too. I'll give her a ring and see if she's free to swing by this morning."

"That would be great. I'll pay extra if she can."

Cal sets the kitten down and straightens, already dialing.

While he talks, I yank open the fridge and swear under my breath. Bare shelves.

Cooking has always been something I enjoy, but when I'm on my own, it's never a priority. The state of my fridge is a clear reflection of that.

I grab a notebook from the drawer, flipping it open just as Cal finishes his call and drops onto a barstool.

"You know there's an app for that," he says, nodding at my pen.

I shoot him a look. "Paper doesn't die when you forget to charge it. What'd Jamie say?"

"It's your lucky day. She was already coming out this way for another house call, so she's going to stop by in a bit to check the little guy out."

I nod, relieved. "I owe her one then." I pause for a moment, eyeing the fridge once more before glancing back at him. "Would you mind hanging back, so I can make a quick trip to the grocery store?"

"Aye, no problem." He waves me off. "Hey, what's my nephew's name?"

I roll my eyes. "I haven't decided yet."

"Figure it out before your date tonight." His tone is all serious. It's hilarious when he thinks he can boss me around. "You can't tell a woman you own a kitten and then say it doesn't have a name. Red flag," he adds.

"Okay, coming from the guy who burns through flings like kindling."

He just grins. Smug as hell. "Exactly. I would know."

I shake my head and let out a laugh. "Noted."

"You'll thank me later," he says. "Go ahead and get out of here. My sweet nephew and I will be fine."

I grab my list and keys, slip on my boots, and double-check that my wallet is tucked safely in my back pocket.

"I won't be long," I call back to Cal, who's already snatched the kitten off the floor.

He waves me off, barely looking up from the TV. "Take your time."

The instant I'm outside, I'm hit with a wall of rain. It's coming down in sheets, the kind of downpour that soaks you to the bone in seconds. I make a mad dash for my truck, my boots splashing through the rapidly forming puddles. By the time I wrench the truck door open and haul myself inside, I'm completely drenched. *Great.*

After a quick trip to the store, I head back home, steering through the rain-slicked streets. Pulling into the driveway, I spot an unfamiliar SUV, its tires caked in mud. Looks like the vet's already here. Perfect timing. Now I get to find out what's going on with the nameless kitten, though if Cal has any say in the matter, it's most likely already named.

I grab as many bags as I can from the back of the truck because no way am I making more than one trip. Carefully dodging puddles, I climb my way up the porch steps, the weight of my shopping spree threatening to cut off the circulation in my fingers.

Shifting the bags to one arm, I push the door open and step inside. It's quiet...suspiciously so. No rustling, no tiny paws tapping across the floor.

I can just barely see Cal and Jamie posted up on opposite sides of the kitchen island from my spot in the foyer, gazes locked. Their mouths move as they talk a little too closely, but I can't make out what they're saying.

Not that it matters. In the next breath, the squeak of my boots on the hardwood cuts through their conversation.

Cal is the first to pull away. "Knox! This is Jamie. Jamie, Knox."

I shrug off my soaked jacket and hang it by the door, water dripping in streaks onto the floor. As I head into the kitchen, I catch my first real look at her. Jamie's tall, with red hair pulled into a sleek ponytail, freckles across her nose, no makeup. She looks like someone who knows how to handle herself in a barn full of half-ton animals or a bar full of rowdy locals. Exactly the kind of woman Callan might end up arguing with just to flirt.

"Jamie, hey. Appreciate you coming out this morning," I say, dropping the grocery bags with a dull thud and brushing rain from my sleeve.

"No trouble at all. I already did the exam. He's feisty, healthy, and full of attitude. Gave him a flea treatment and his vaccinations, so he's good to go for a while."

I nod. "Sounds perfect." Then, without missing a beat, I add, "And what about the cat?"

Jamie bursts out laughing. Cal, on the other hand, levels me with a flat look, clearly less amused. That only makes the joke better.

"In all seriousness, thank you. How much do I owe you?"

Jamie waves a dismissive hand. "Don't worry about it. Just call it a favor. I have a feeling you'll need me again at some point, so just keep me in mind."

"Deal. If there's ever anything I can do to help you out, just say the word."

She nods, slinging her bag over her shoulder. "I'll hold you to that. I've got another stop, so I should get going. Nice meeting you, Knox."

Her gaze drifts to Cal as she gives him a once-over that's anything but subtle. "Good seeing you again, Callan."

I lean against the counter, arms crossed, watching Cal with

barely concealed amusement. The smirk on my face? Completely involuntary. He waits while Jamie gathers the rest of her things, then walks her to the door. When it latches shut behind her, the soft click rings out like the final note in whatever the hell that just was.

The second he turns and sees me standing there, he jabs a finger in my direction. "Don't."

I hold up my hands. "I didn't say anything."

His eyes narrow. "I won't tell Mum about Juliette if you don't say a word about Jamie."

That does it. A full, booming laugh rips out of me as I push off the counter. "You've got a deal, brother."

sixteen

JULIETTE

It's been raining all day, but somehow, it only makes everything feel more alive. The gray sky hangs heavy as the rain falls steady. All I want to do is capture the scent of rain and the hush of the world to take with me.

I glance in the bathroom mirror again, swiping a final coat of mascara over my lashes as the bathroom door creaks open. My aunt's face pops around the edge of it.

"You look beautiful," she says, a genuine smile tugging at her lips.

I raise an eyebrow, meeting her gaze through the mirror, and return her words with a little smirk. "You're the beautiful one, but thanks."

I brush a hand through my hair, the soft waves falling past my shoulders. I didn't want to try too hard, so I kept the makeup light, just enough to feel put together. My outfit's a little more polished, though. I went with my oversized sand-colored sweater and a pair of slim jeans, but the touch that really gets me is the necklace.

My mom's. The one she wore all the time when I was a

child. It's gold and delicate; the chain is so fine it practically disappears against my skin. At the center, a tiny oval locket sways gently with every movement. The edges are scalloped, worn smooth in spots from years of my mom's touch. I used to watch it catch the light when she bent to kiss my forehead, that glint of gold pressed warm against my cheek.

"What time is Knox coming to get you?"

I glance at my phone. "He's supposed to be here around four. So any minute now, really."

She nods, giving my arm a soft squeeze. "I'll let you finish up, then."

I take one last look in the mirror, smoothing a hand down the front of my sweater, then reach for the bottle on the vanity. One quick spritz, and the scent unfurls in the air—citrus at first, followed by a trace of sandalwood. With a quiet snap, I close my makeup bag.

As I'm zipping up my boots a few minutes later, the low rumble of a truck rolls in like a heartbeat in the distance. The sound gets louder, then fades, signaling that it's stopped.

My heart leaps. Why am I nervous? I've seen Knox multiple times now. Our first encounter was way more nerve-racking than this, so why do I feel like a teenager getting picked up for prom while her parents are glaring at her from the front window?

With a deep breath, I straighten my shoulders and head to the living room, determined to get to the door before Aunt Rose. The absolute last thing I need is for her to answer it for me. That would crank the awkwardness up to about a hundred real quick. Nope. Not happening.

When I catch sight of Knox, the hills framing him like a perfect backdrop, I'm speechless. I can't even blame it on the rain anymore. He hasn't done anything but flash that perfect smile before heat curls low in my stomach and my breath stumbles right along with my common sense.

I've got it so bad.

For a moment, I just stare. I let my gaze linger on him, soaking in every detail, marveling at how effortlessly he pulls off looking so damn good. He's wearing a flannel button-up again, sleeves casually rolled up to his elbows. His jeans are faded just enough at the edges, worn-in and perfect. And, of course, my heart decides to skip again, trying to remind me how hopeless I am.

"Hi," I manage to say, my voice betraying just a hint of the nerves I'm trying to hide.

His grin spreads wider, like he's been waiting for this moment all day. "Hi. You look beautiful."

A dimple pops up on one of his cheeks, and how did I not see that before? Now it's all I can see.

"So do you." I say it before I can stop myself, not bothering to pretend I'm not a little awkward. My aunt's snort from the couch yanks me back to reality. Oh, right, she's still here. Wonderful.

Knox doesn't seem phased, though. He extends his hand, the other holding up an umbrella to shield us from the relentless rain. "Shall we?"

I don't hesitate. "Yes, please. Bye, Aunt Rose!" I call out behind me.

"Bye, Rose. I'll have her back by curfew," Knox teases.

She waves but I barely notice, because the second I step outside, he takes my hand without hesitation, his fingers wrapping around mine like it's the most natural thing in the world. My heart stumbles. Just once. Maybe twice.

He walks me to his truck and opens the passenger door. I climb in, and before I can even reach for the seatbelt, he's leaning in close enough for his cologne to wrap around me. His hand brushes against my ribs as he buckles me in, his jaw ticking like he's trying not to look at my mouth. The buckle clicks into place, and then he steps back, shutting the door with a gentleness that doesn't match the strength in his frame.

I blink, momentarily stunned. This is a first. No one has ever thought to make sure I'm settled in before shutting the door, let alone buckling me in. It's so unexpectedly sweet.

If his goal was to make me fall hard for him, he could've just handed me a snack and called it a day. But no, he had to go full chivalrous gentleman on me.

He sprints through the rain to the driver's side, shaking the umbrella before tossing it into the backseat.

"Ready?" he asks.

I don't answer right away. Instead, I take in the spark in his eyes, the way the rain's glistening on his skin. When I'm ready, I nod. "Take it away, Captain."

His grin widens, that mischievous glint flickering in his eyes. He shifts the truck into gear, his palm landing casually on the center console. He doesn't say a word, doesn't push, but the invitation to hold his hand again is there. It's up to me.

Like there was ever a choice.

Without a second of hesitation, I slide my hand into his. The instant our fingers tangle together again, there's a sigh inside me, like a long-held breath finally released. His hand is warm and rough in all the right places, but it fits perfectly against mine. The way his thumb strokes lightly over the back of my hand is intimate in a way that has nothing to do with lust and everything to do with connection.

I swear, nothing has ever felt more natural. More right.

After a winding drive that seems to stretch on forever, we finally round a bend and Knox's mountain home comes into view. It's something straight out of a storybook. Nestled against a wild expanse of towering pines, it looks less like it was recently built and more like it's always existed. The dark timber logs and solid stone blend seamlessly with the landscape, like the house itself was carved from earth.

My gaze drifts to the wide wooden porch stretching across the front, practically begging for slow mornings with coffee in hand and late nights wrapped in a blanket. Beyond the house, the mountains rise up, bold and unyielding. It's breathtaking. So perfectly still that it seems too unreal to be true.

A little slice of heaven.

I can't help the awe that spreads through me. "This is your place?"

"Aye, it is," he says.

I shake my head, still taking it all in. "It's remarkable. Truly."

He nods, the pride in his expression unmistakable. "Thank you. This was another one of my projects. Had it built a few years ago. I love it out here."

His thumb brushes the back of my hand one last time before he shuts off the engine. "Let's head inside. We've got dinner plans."

Before I can even think about reaching for the door handle, he's already moving, swift and sure, jogging around to my side of the truck with the umbrella in hand. I let him help me out of the truck, his hand steady on mine and guiding me as I step onto the soggy ground.

His touch lingers just a little longer than necessary as he leads me up the porch steps. The whole scene unfolds in slow motion, and with each step, I draw closer to him, more aware of his presence than ever before. His large hand rests on the small of my back, sending little flutters through me. It's a calm kind of touch, but there's a buzz in the air, too.

He unlocks the door, his hand falling away from me just as

he gestures for me to step inside. I hesitate for a moment, my breath caught in my chest. I was wrong before. *This* is heaven.

As I step into the entryway, my gaze is immediately captured by the floor-to-ceiling windows. They frame the view flawlessly, the mountains stretching out in the distance, their peaks brushed by the soft light, while a shimmering lake nestles between them. The room feels alive with the golden light spilling across the polished wooden floors, casting everything in a soft, inviting glow.

From here, I catch a glimpse of the kitchen. It's filled with wooden cabinetry and natural stone countertops that scream rustic charm. The sleek, stainless-steel appliances positioned throughout keep things modern. It's a beautiful balance of old and new.

Without warning, a small, gray furball comes bounding toward us from the living room.

"Oh my goodness, you have a kitten!" I exclaim, barely able to contain my surprise as the tiny creature zooms up to our feet, demanding attention.

The kitten flops onto the doormat next to Knox's boot-clad feet, its tiny body a stark contrast to his towering presence. The sight of him, all rugged masculinity, standing next to this helpless little ball of fluff is almost more than I can take. I take a mental snapshot, locking the moment away in my mind.

"What's his name?"

"*Uile-Bhèist,*" he replies. There's a serious expression on his face that's far too amusing given the situation. He pauses before attempting to spell it out for me.

"Um, I'm sorry, what?" I ask, sure I didn't hear him right.

"It's pronounced like oo-luh-vesht. *Uile-Bhèist.* Scottish Gaelic for monster."

I blink at him, then at the kitten, then back again. The tiny fluffball just stares up at me, eyes slowly blinking like I'm the one being ridiculous.

"Right," I say slowly. "I was thinking something more along the lines of Stormy. Smoky. Maybe even Ash. But...sure. That works?"

He lifts a shoulder, casual, like naming a kitten something ninety percent of the population can't pronounce is the most normal thing in the world.

The sheer absurdity of it all hits me, and I can't help it. I burst into laughter. Actual, tears in my eyes, laughter. "You're something else. We're going to get along just fine."

A smile tugs at the corner of his lips, and I'm instantly riveted. It's that dimple. It's downright hypnotizing.

"Come on, lass," he says, his voice all rich and velvety as he nods toward the back of the house. "Let me show you around the kitchen."

He leads the way, and I follow. At this point, he could've said, *Come on, lass, let me lead you straight to your demise*, and I would've trailed after him.

He pulls out a barstool, gesturing for me to sit. I slide onto the seat, feeling oddly at home as he moves to the other side of the island. He rests his hands on the counter, his gaze steady on me.

"You don't actually need to help if you don't want to. I'm more than happy to do the cooking as long as I've got your company."

His words come out with indifference, but it's the way his muscles flex as he turns to pull ingredients from the fridge that steals my attention. The way his shirt stretches across his back is borderline unfair. My eyes have completely abandoned my control, shamelessly locked onto the show he's putting on.

Am I drooling? No. Definitely not.

I clear my throat, forcing my gaze away before I embarrass

myself. "Honestly, I'd love to learn. I'll do whatever you decide to trust me with." I pause, trying to sound like a normal human being and not someone fighting for their life against the distraction that are his glorious muscles. "What are we making?"

"Ever had cullen skink?"

I tilt my head, furrowing my brow and mentally digging through any possible memory of those words. "I'm going to say no, considering I have no idea what that is."

"I figured," he says with a smirk. "It's a soup made with smoked haddock. I hope that's okay. Rose told me you eat fish."

If he wasn't already swimming in brownie points, he just dove straight into the deep end.

"Sounds great. Where do we start?"

He tells me about the recipe as he moves around the kitchen with ease, gathering the rest of the ingredients along with the pots and utensils.

"All right," he says, his voice steady and inviting, "you want to come over here and help me chop some of this up?"

I hop down from the barstool like it's nothing, but inside, I've got a full-on adrenaline rush happening from such close proximity. My pulse quickens as I move to stand beside him. "Show me what to do, Chef."

"I'll dice the potatoes if you can do the onion?"

"You got it. Which knife should I use?"

Without a second thought, he pulls one from the block and places it into my hand. "We'll use a chef's knife for that. Make sure you've got a good grip on it."

I wrap my fingers around the handle, adjusting my grip like he suggested. The weight of the knife is surprisingly natural in my hand, but it's hard to focus when he's hovering and watching me. His closeness does nothing to help my nerves.

I place the onion on the cutting board, the pungent odor hitting me like a punch to the face. *Onions.* There's absolutely nothing sexy about them. Nothing romantic about the sting that immediately starts crawling up my nose or the way my eyes water before I begin. This is not the sultry cooking scene I had envisioned. This is a tear fest.

"Now," he continues, "keep the knife angled down just slightly so it doesn't slip."

It's impossible to ignore how his voice seems to resonate with me so well in the quiet kitchen, or the way the space suddenly feels a bit too small with him so close.

I glance at the blade, trying to mimic his instructions. "Like this?"

He moves just a fraction closer. "Mm, not quite. Here."

I freeze when he moves in behind me, his breath warm against the back of my neck as he leans in. The heat from his touch lingers as he gently adjusts my grip on the knife, guiding it with a steady and reassuring pressure.

"Like this," he murmurs softly. "And then you'll want to take the onion with your other hand and grip it firmly before you start dicing."

My thoughts take an unexpected detour. I can't help but think about gripping something else, something a lot less...*culinary* in nature. A flush creeps up my neck as my thoughts veer into dangerous territory.

Shit.

Has Bree taken over my mind, planting these dirty thoughts?

I try to refocus, but my brain is on a loop, running through every thought except what I *should* be doing. Like paying attention to the task at hand. The second he leans in again, I'm overwhelmed in the best way. I hear the sharp intake of his breath before he speaks.

"Ah, make sure you keep your fingers tucked on that hand or you'll have another incident."

It's a reminder I definitely don't need, but his voice is so low—so close—that my body forgets how to function. His hands guide mine again, but it's the way he's standing behind me that undoes me. His broad chest brushes against my back, all heat and muscle, and I swear I can feel every inch of him.

The space between us is nonexistent, and when his mouth presses close to my ear, everything inside me tunes into his proximity. It's dizzying.

If I turned my head slightly in his direction right now...

"Juliette?"

His voice cuts through the haze of my thoughts, snapping me back to reality. I blink a few times, trying to clear the fog.

"I'm sorry, what were you saying?"

He moves to stand beside me. The absence of his warmth leaves behind a lingering chill.

"I just said your positioning looks good now. I think you're ready to give it a try."

I nod and get to work. Every now and then, I catch him watching me. Not in a calculating way, but like he's genuinely curious about my abilities, or lack thereof.

"So," I start. "How long have you been cooking like this?"

He smiles, his attention momentarily shifting to me. "Since I was a wee lad. My grandmother wouldn't let any of us leave her kitchen without knowing how to feed ourselves properly."

"That's really sweet."

"It was something," he says dryly. "Although, the first thing I ever tried to cook without her supervision was an absolute disaster."

"Oh, now this I need to hear."

He groans. "I was maybe ten? Thought I'd surprise my mum with breakfast. Figured eggs were easy enough." He shakes his head, grinning at the memory. "I didn't take the shells off before I scrambled them."

My laugh bursts out before I can stop it. "No."

"Aye." He winces. "She bit down, heard the crunch, and just...paused."

"That's incredible." I'm still laughing, picturing tiny, earnest Knox serving up crunchy eggs like it was fine dining. "Honestly, I respect the confidence."

"What about you? Any tragic kitchen disasters I should know about?"

"Oh, mine aren't in the kitchen," I say, shaking my head. "I grew up with a mom who could turn basically anything into comfort food. It was like a love language for her. Homemade bread, soups that could fix just about anything, pies cooling on the windowsill. Safe to say I steered clear of competing with that."

The words slip out easy enough, but there's that familiar pinch that comes right after. The hollow ache that sneaks in when I'm not paying attention. Funny how grief works like that. It doesn't always show up loud. Sometimes it's just a little echo in the space where somebody used to be.

I can still picture her barefoot in the kitchen, flour smudged on her cheek, humming off-key to whatever tune was playing on the radio. Always humming. Always home.

God, I miss her.

I clear my throat, forcing a smile because that pang could swallow me whole if I let it. And tonight, with Knox standing there looking at me like I'm not half as complicated as I am, I don't really want to drown in it.

"Anyway," I add, shaking it off, "my most embarrassing story? It didn't happen in the kitchen but in the driver's seat."

That gets his attention, and the irony isn't lost on me. He leans a hip against the counter, arms crossed.

"I failed my driver's test because I hit a cone. Like...obliterated it. Full speed. The instructor didn't even yell. He just sighed as if he'd seen it a thousand times before."

Knox laughs, *really* laughs, and it does ridiculous things to my heart. "Poor man. How many attempts did it take you to pass?"

"Three. The second time I almost ran a stop sign. The third time was the charm."

He chuckles under his breath, shaking his head.

I set my knife down carefully. "Is there something else I can do?"

"Sit. Relax. I'll make us something to drink after I finish up."

I slip onto one of the stools at the island, tucking my feet on the rung as I watch him move through his space with confidence.

If you would have told me three months ago I'd be in the Highlands at the beautiful home of a handsome man while he cooked me dinner, I would've laughed in your face. Hell, I certainly wouldn't have believed you. I mean, James never even asked to help me when I attempted to cook. Never offered to wash the dishes. All those duties fell to me.

But now? Sitting here, watching Knox and listening to the sound of the rain tapping gently against the windows, it feels like a dream. I have absolutely no complaints.

He wipes his hands on a towel, his forest-green eyes locking onto mine. "All right. That's going to need to cook on the stove for a bit. Ready for a drink?"

"I sure am. Are you playing the role of bartender now?"

"I wear many hats. I thought I'd make us some Scotch mists. Seems fitting, given the weather."

He reaches for two highball glasses, filling them with ice before he starts pouring, explaining as he works. "Scotch, lemon juice, simple syrup, and soda water." The ice clinks softly as he stirs each drink.

He slides one glass across the counter toward me. "Tell me what you think."

I wrap my fingers around the cool glass, lifting it to my lips, the citrusy sweetness filling my senses before I take a sip. The smooth whisky rolls over my tongue, and I can't tell if the warmth spreading through my body is from the alcohol or the heat in his gaze. I'm thinking it's the latter.

"Well," I say with a smirk. "I think bartender just became my favorite hat of yours."

His gaze shifts from my lips to my eyes. "It's good, aye?"

"*Aye*, it is."

"Careful, lass. Keep complimenting me like that and I might start thinking you're sweet on me."

I laugh, taking another sip to hide the blush creeping up my neck. "Would that be so terrible?"

He shakes his head, that maddeningly perfect dimple carving into his cheek as he smiles. "Not terrible at all."

I feel myself tipping into that dangerous territory where every look seems loaded. It makes me nervous. I need a breath. A reset. Something a little safer.

"So," I clear my throat. "What made you decide to build out here away from everything?"

He leans against the counter, taking a slow sip of his drink. "The quiet," he says simply. "After years of traveling for work, hotel rooms, and constant noise, I wanted somewhere that felt like mine." His eyes drift to the window. "Plus, you can't beat that view."

"I can't argue with that logic." I follow his gaze. "It's breathtaking."

"What about you?" he asks, his voice softer now. "What's your perfect place look like?"

I consider the question, swirling my drink thoughtfully. "I guess I've always imagined somewhere with big windows, lots of natural light, and maybe a little reading nook where I can curl up during rainstorms."

"Like this one?" He gestures toward a seat tucked into a bay window between the kitchen and living room.

My heart does a little flip. "Exactly like that, actually."

"You should try it out sometime. It's the perfect spot to watch a storm roll through."

"That sounds an awful lot like an invitation, Knox."

He chuckles before his expression shifts. It's subtle, but just enough for me to notice. The glint in his eyes softens, his tone more serious. "Maybe it was."

I swallow hard, suddenly aware of how fast my heart's beating. Damn it, I'm blushing again.

The timer on the stove dings, saving me from my own racing thoughts.

"So," I say, sliding off the barstool and following him back to the stove, "what's the verdict on my onion chopping skills? Am I hired as your sous chef?"

Knox lifts the lid, releasing a cloud of fragrant steam that immediately makes my mouth water. "I'd say you're qualified for a probationary period, though you did get a bit distracted during orientation."

Ah, so he noticed.

"I wonder what could have possibly distracted me."

He stirs the contents inside the pot slowly, not looking up, but I catch the smirk playing at his lips. "Complete mystery."

"I blame the teacher. Very hands-on approach."

He laughs, a deep rumbling sound that reverberates through the kitchen. "Is that so?" He reaches past me for two bowls from the cabinet, his arm brushing mine. "And what would you prefer? Verbal instructions only?"

I bite my lower lip, gathering courage. "I didn't say that."

His eyes darken slightly as they meet mine. "Noted for next time."

Next time.

The promise in those two words makes my heart race.

"Would you mind grabbing the bread from the counter?" he asks.

I nod, grabbing it before following him to a beautiful wooden table positioned perfectly beneath a large window.

He sets our bowls down and pulls out a chair for me. "Your dinner awaits."

"Such service," I tease, sliding into the seat. "I'm impressed."

"I aim to please." He takes the spot next to me at the head of the table, close enough that our knees brush.

The soup is *heavenly*. Creamy and rich with a smoky depth that warms me from the inside out.

"This might be the best thing I've ever tasted."

"High praise."

"Well-deserved praise." I take another bite, letting out an involuntary hum of appreciation.

"Glad you like it. It's a staple around these parts."

The little gray *uile-bhèist* weaves around our feet, darting between the chair legs in search of something. I chuckle, watching him with amusement. "I think he finally caught scent of the fish," I muse. "Does little Beastie want some fishies?"

"Beastie?" Knox raises an eyebrow.

I cross my arms over my chest. "You don't think I'm going to call him that dreadful name you gave him, right? Beastie is much cuter."

He gives a quiet exhale, something caught between disbelief and amusement and runs a hand along his jaw. We talk for a bit longer, conversation easy, unhurried, before it fades into a quiet stretch of stillness, the kind that feels like settling in.

Leaning back in my seat, I take a sip of my drink, letting out a satisfied sigh. "I can't take another bite. I'm stuffed. Thank you for this. It was wonderful."

"Anytime, lass. I mean it."

I try to fight the blush that creeps up my neck but it's no use. It spreads across my cheeks, hot and undeniable. I drop my gaze, hoping he doesn't notice, though I'm pretty sure he does.

"So...tell me about Lucy and Callan. I know you mentioned Callan was a bit younger."

"Aye, Lucy's the youngest of the bunch. I had to threaten many people on her behalf growing up." There's a tenderness in his gaze as he talks about her. "She's so innocent. I've always felt like she needed a little more protection than Cal. He's just a nut."

"I never had any siblings. I do have Bree, though. She's as close as I've got to one and has had to step in for me on more than one occasion as well." I pause, fingers toying with the edge of my sleeve as a memory of her flashes through my mind— loud, loyal, and always three steps ahead of me. "Actually, you might be able to meet her. She's coming to stay with Aunt Rose and me."

"Ah, you'll have to bring her by the distillery and show her around."

"I definitely will. Although don't be offended when she tells you she hates whisky," I warn. "Because she really, really hates it."

He tosses me a wink, leaning back a little. "Blasphemy."

I chuckle, shaking my head. "Tell me about it."

I shift gears. "Okay, and what about Callan? I find it fascinating how much you and Lucy resemble each other. Callan is clearly related, but his eyes are so different."

His expression falters for a second. His eyes lose that usual spark, and the playful edge in his voice fades. "Lucy and I look like our mum," he says quietly, his gaze distant. "Callan looks a bit more like my dad. He passed away when we were young. Car accident."

Shit. I didn't mean to go there. My stomach sinks as his expression shifts, and his eyes darken. I swallow, suddenly wishing I asked something less loaded, less personal. "Knox, I'm so sorry. I didn't mean to bring up any unhappy memories."

He gives me a small smile, brushing it off, but I can still sense the weight behind his words. "I appreciate that. I was very young when he passed, only eight."

My heart tugs at the thought. That must've been so hard. It was tough enough losing a parent as an adult. I can't imagine what it would've been like at that age, especially so suddenly.

"That must have been so difficult for you guys."

He nods, his shoulders relaxing a little. "It was. My mum ended up remarrying later. Paul is great. Really stepped up for us. Most folks that know us don't realize we're not his."

I can tell just how deeply this man loves the people who raised him. "It sounds like you have an amazing family."

The pride in his voice is unmistakable as he says, "I really do. They're better than I could've ever hoped for." There's a pause before he continues. "I do know a bit about your family through Rose. I understand your mom was her twin?"

A lump forms in my throat as the memory drifts in. I nod, swallowing down the emotion. "Mmhm. She was. We lost her to cancer when I was twenty-one." I stop, gathering the strength to keep going. Something about his gaze, understanding and patient, makes it easier. "I had a really hard time with it. She was the kindest soul and was all I had. I think about her every day."

"I can't even begin to imagine how hard that must have

been, Juliette." His voice softens, the furrow in his brows deepening as he looks at me with genuine empathy. "Rose always speaks so highly of her, too. I can tell she was incredible just from the things I've heard."

The weight of his words hits me harder than I expect. "Thank you." I pause, swallowing the sudden lump in my throat. "On the other hand, I do have a father. I just have no idea who or where he is. At this point, that ship's sailed."

His face shifts, a mix of amusement and curiosity flickering in his eyes as he laughs. There's something incredibly soothing about the way he takes everything in stride without pushing or prodding. He doesn't look at me with pity, just understanding. "What do you do for work back in the States?"

"I'm a second-grade teacher." I grin, the words coming out faster and full of energy. "Every day is something different. There's never a dull moment. The kids are a handful, but it's so rewarding."

"Sounds like it keeps you on your toes," he says, a playful glint in his eyes. "You've got the summer off, aye? Think you'll stay in Scotland for a while?"

I notice it then. The hesitation in his gaze, that unspoken question hanging between us like a fragile thread. He's trying to figure out how much time we have, how much room there is for whatever might come next. I take a slow breath, knowing that whatever I say next could change everything.

"I think..." I begin, resting my chin on my hand, my gaze meeting his as I let the words form. "I'm going to be staying here a good while longer. As long as I possibly can."

For a moment, I think I can see him exhale, like he's been holding his breath without even realizing it.

"Juliette?" His voice is low and soft, drawing me in.

I tilt my head slightly, instinctively aware that something's about to shift, my pulse quickening as his gaze drops to my lips. The air between us crackles with anticipation.

"I would really like to kiss you." There's no hesitation in his voice, no doubt. Just an honesty that has my heart racing.

Oh. God.

There's something about the way he says it. Not cocky, not rehearsed, just *real*, that absolutely unravels me. Maybe it shouldn't feel so earth-shattering or like something rare and precious, but it does. It feels like standing barefoot on the edge of a cliff, the world spread wide below me. And in that moment, I know that whatever comes next will rewrite everything I thought I knew about myself.

Because I've been kissed before. I've been wanted before.

But this? This feels like being seen. Like I'm being chosen, not for the version of me I've polished up and put on display, but for the messy, heart-on-her-sleeve girl sitting right here in front of him.

I'm pretty sure my heart is somewhere up in my throat, thudding away like it's got no sense of pride left at all. The craziest part is, I don't even care. I *want* him to know. I want him to see every bit of how much I want him, too.

I swallow hard, my voice barely steady. "Yeah?" It comes out a breathless little thing, shaky and small but maybe the bravest word I've ever said.

"Yeah," he says, like it's the simplest truth in the world. "But only if you want me to."

And oh, I *do*.

I take another slow breath. "Then what are you waiting for, Captain?"

He wastes no time pulling my chair closer, the movement so smooth and natural, my thighs slotting perfectly between his. His fingers thread through my hair with a gentle tug, sending a spark that shoots straight to my core.

When his mouth meets mine, it doesn't feel like a first kiss at all.

It feels like every near miss, stolen glance, and what-if finally catching fire.

It's everything I didn't know existed. Tender but sure. Patient but utterly consuming. He kisses me like it's something he's been starving for.

And god, I feel it everywhere.

It's in the way his hands grasp my hair like he can't stand the idea of letting me go. It's in the way his mouth moves over mine, learning me, memorizing me, leaving no doubt in my mind that this isn't just something casual.

This is *the* kiss.

The kind that rewrites every single one before it.

No kiss has ever curled through my body like wildfire and safety all at once, or made me feel so wanted I could cry.

I melt into him without a second thought, my arms wrapping around his neck, pulling him closer. He groans in response, and I feel it all the way down to my bones. His tongue swipes gently at my bottom lip, tasting me and silently asking for more. My lips part instinctively, and in an instant, his tongue slides in, the slow, intoxicating strokes making everything else fall away.

He tilts his head, deepening the kiss, his grip tightening on my hair. Heat floods my skin, and I can feel every inch of him against me, every movement sending a shiver through my body.

I never want to stop. I never want to come back down from this feeling, this heat, this weightless ache, this dizzy, perfect freefall into him.

Into *us*.

seventeen

KNOX

The second my fingers slip into her hair, I'm done for. It's reckless, the way I drag her closer, but she tilts her chin and meets me there like she's been waiting, too.

Christ, her mouth. Soft and warm and right there, splintering whatever careful control I thought I had left.

It's been so long since I've let myself want like this, touch like this. And when she lets out this soft sound caught at the back of her throat, it rips straight through me. That's it. That's my undoing.

Her fingertips skate the back of my neck, and I finally pull back just enough to see her, to ground myself before I forget who I am entirely. And there she is with wide, searching eyes. Kiss-bitten lips. Breathing just as hard as I am. There's nothing but heat and tension lingering in the space between us, something that doesn't just burn but *pulls*. My chest aches with a want that's dangerously close to need.

I didn't see this coming, but now that I've had a taste of her, I don't know how the hell I'm supposed to go back to what life was like before.

And then she looks at me like I've cracked something wide open in her. Like I'm sitting here holding every delicate part of her, and she's still deciding if she's brave enough to let me keep it.

"Juliette, I—"

"No." Her head shakes, quick and pleading. "Knox...please, don't stop."

Her voice is shaky, threaded with something close to desperation. That's all it takes to blow whatever was left of my restraint to hell.

She *wants* this. God help me, I'm already gone.

I haul her against me like I've been needing to do since the second I laid eyes on her. Hands skating down to her hips, gripping tight, selfish and starved, I lift her like it costs me nothing when really it costs me *everything*. Her legs wrap around my waist, and it feels so natural, so goddamn perfect.

Somehow, I find my footing and stand, carrying her across the room. We hit the couch in a tangle of limbs and need, careless in a way I haven't dared to be in years. Her fingers are in my hair, lips tracing the edge of my mouth, and all I can do is hold on and give in. Take. Offer. Match her hunger with mine.

"Juliette," I rasp.

She looks at me. Really looks, and it's not just heat or want in her eyes. There's something wild and raw.

Her heartbeat slams against my chest, right in time with mine. For the first time in a long time, I don't feel empty or lost.

I just feel her.

She shifts in my lap, all soft curves sliding against hard lines. And fuck, when she rocks against me, my cock twitches in response. The friction is maddening, a sweet kind of torture that makes it impossible to think straight. I'm hard as hell, straining against denim that suddenly feels two sizes too tight, and there's no hiding it.

My hands tighten at her waist, holding her there, holding *me* together. She feels too good. Her touch is featherlight as she drags her fingers along the edge of my jaw, and my pulse stutters in my throat.

Before reason or patience or every line I shouldn't cross has a chance to claw its way back into my mind, our mouths crash together again.

Hard. Desperate.

I'm drowning in her.

The taste of her, the heat of her, the soft, broken little sounds she makes—it's all chaos in my veins. My hands roam on instinct, greedy and mapping the curves of her waist, the line of her spine, committing every inch to memory like I might wake up tomorrow and this will all be gone.

Her tongue slides against mine, tentative, then bolder, and I know I'm not walking away from this unchanged.

I *should* stop. I know that. I should pull back, catch my breath, say something that isn't just her name rasped into the space between us like a prayer.

But, hell, she tastes like every good thing I forgot I was allowed to want.

Sweet and wild. Soft and reckless.

I'm never going to get enough

NIGHT HAS SETTLED in without either of us noticing. The fire's low and lazy, painting soft light across her face like even the flames know she's the best thing in the room.

We've melted into the couch, shoulder to shoulder, her thigh brushing mine every time she shifts. I lean back, whisky in hand, but I'm not tasting any of it. My head is still lost in that kiss and whatever the hell comes next.

I can still feel the drag of her lips on mine, slow and sweet and goddamn dangerous. Like she'd been holding that kiss back for years and finally let it loose just to ruin me.

"This evening was perfect," she says, her fingers running absently through Beastie's fur.

I try like hell not to smile but fail miserably. "Does perfect mean I get to ask for a second date?"

She arches an eyebrow. "I don't know. Are you already asking me out again? There are rules, you know."

"Mm. I'm not aware of these rules."

"Well, you're supposed to wait a few days before calling me again. But don't wait too long, or I'll think you're not interested anymore."

I lean in slightly, my gaze locking onto hers. "Screw the rules, lass. I want to see you again."

It's not polished. Hell, I'm bordering on desperate, but it's the truth. She doesn't even flinch.

"Okay." She says it like I didn't just throw every line I swore I wouldn't cross right out the window.

"Okay?" I echo, because apparently I need to hear it twice.

She grins. "Yep. I'm all yours."

Christ. I'm done for, even though I know better. There are things I haven't told her, but right now, she's looking at me like I'm the safest place she's ever been.

I can't help it. I reach for her, tugging her into my chest like maybe if I hold her close enough, I won't screw this up.

She fits. All warm limbs and silky hair. Citrus and sunshine cling to her, and I breathe it in like I'm starving for it.

Then she laughs. Perfectly. Effortlessly.

"I can't tell you the last time I had this much fun on a date, let alone a first date," she confesses.

I'm surprised by that. A simple, laid-back night with just the two of us is everything I could ask for, though I wasn't sure it was her style. "Who the hell have you been dating that this impressed you so much?"

A pained expression flashes across her face. "I guess you haven't heard about my ex."

The second she says it, I know I've poked at something that should've been left alone. I clear my throat. "Ah, no. We don't need to talk about it."

She gives me a small smile, a quiet kind of resignation in her gaze. "No, it's okay," she says softly. "His name was James. We met in college, dated forever, got engaged and moved in together. Did all the things you're supposed to do when you think you've got forever figured out."

I stay quiet and let her have the space to tell it however she needs to. Her eyes drift toward the fire, glassy with the kind of faraway ache I wish like hell I could erase. And then she rests her head on my shoulder.

"We were supposed to get married soon," she says almost in a whisper. "As in...now. But a month ago, I came home early and found him with someone else. Someone who wasn't me."

My gut twists, anger flaring hot and useless in my chest. Beneath it, something heavier lodges itself in my ribs.

I want to protect her from the memories and the way that wince crosses her face like she's trying not to flinch at her own story.

"Needless to say," she adds with a faint, dry laugh, "I moved back into my own place. Been figuring myself out since."

I shake my head, my voice rougher than I mean it to be. "I'm sorry, Juliette. He sounds like a real bastard."

That pulls a genuine huff of a laugh from her.

"That," she says, glancing up at me, "we can definitely agree on."

"I'm okay now, though," she adds. "Better than okay, actually."

I nod slowly. "I've always believed that the wind carries us where we need to go." I glance down and let my fingers brush hers, just enough to feel that spark again. "My old man used to say that, back when life felt like nothing but storms. After a few rough patches of my own, I'm inclined to agree with him."

She goes quiet for a second, eyes on mine like she's tucking my words somewhere safe. Then that smile pulls at her mouth, a little shy, and so damn beautiful it nearly guts me. "I like that a lot," she says, voice barely above a whisper. "Very insightful."

And maybe it's stupid, but I let myself feel that flicker of pride like I've done something right just by making her smile like that. But the feeling's gone as quick as it came, replaced by the press of something heavier because sitting here with her, this close, this good...it's got a cost. There's shit I've buried deep for a reason, and the longer I sit here pretending it's not clawing its way up my throat, the more I wonder how long I can keep it locked down.

What the hell am I doing?

She's already survived the wreckage of a man who promised her forever then torched it all without blinking. And now here I am beside her like I'm not just one more gamble her heart can't afford.

Fuck.

I need to figure out what the hell I'm doing before this goes any further. And yet, I still lean in to press a kiss to her temple as if I have the right.

"I hate to say it, lass," I murmur against her skin, "but your aunt's counting on me to get you home soon. I'd rather not be on her bad side come tomorrow."

She pulls away, her body stiffening as she stands, a look of surprise crossing her face. "Oh, gosh. I didn't realize it had gotten so late. I'm sorry."

I shake my head quickly. "Don't apologize. I've kept you here longer than planned, and I'm the one to blame for that. That's on me, Juliette."

I've been selfish, soaking up every second I've had with her. I can't bring myself to regret it. Not really.

A faint blush colors her cheeks, and I can't help but chuckle. She has this adorable way of getting modest at the strangest times, like it's some kind of reflex. It only makes me want to tease her more just to see that sweet, shy side of her again.

As we get ready to leave, my eyes drift to Juliette who's kneeling by the door as she says goodbye to the cat. Her voice is soft, playful as she talks to him, her fingers gently combing through his fur. The kitten purrs in response, basking in the attention.

I think I might be a little jealous of the damn cat.

She glances up at me, a soft smile playing on her lips when she catches me watching. "He's quite the charmer, isn't he?"

"He's not the only one," I reply.

She raises a brow, clearly trying to suppress a laugh. "Oh, really? What's your game, then?"

I shrug with a grin. "Well, I'm practically irresistible."

"Confidence is key, huh?"

"Something like that," I murmur, my voice rough as I lean against the doorframe, trying to hold onto some sliver of control.

The sight of her on her knees sends a hot rush of blood south so fast I have to grip the doorframe tighter. The curve of her neck, exposed in the low light, pulls my gaze downward to the delicate line of her collarbone peeking from under her sweater where it's slipped just enough to tease. Her lips, still swollen from our kisses, part just slightly as she meets my eyes.

"You ready?"

She doesn't move. Just stays there, her face tilted up and mere inches from where I'm straining against my jeans.

Christ almighty.

Finally, she nods, rising to her feet. "Lead the way, if you must."

"Don't tempt me, lass. I'll lock this door and keep you here, no questions asked."

I regret the words the moment they leave my mouth. That was way too intense. But before I can backpedal, I catch the shiver that runs through her. Her pupils dilate, and her breath catches just slightly.

Her chest rises and falls a little faster, and I watch, transfixed, as she pulls her bottom lip between her teeth.

"Knox," she whispers.

I reach out, tracing my thumb along her jawline. She leans into my touch like she's been waiting for it. Her skin flushes warm under my fingertips, a delicate pink blooming across her cheeks and down her neck.

"I shouldn't have said that," I murmur.

She shakes her head. "No, I..." When she swallows, I watch the delicate ripple of her throat. "I like that you did."

This woman is going to be the death of me.

Without a word, I lean in, pressing a soft kiss to her lips. The urge to stay there overwhelms me, but I pull back and guide her toward the door.

eighteen

KNOX

I 'm distracted during the drive, but I'm not sure Juliette notices. She seems perfectly content sitting beside me, whether we're talking or not. The silence between us is comfortable, yet it's making my thoughts spiral in ways I'm not sure how to manage. We're almost back to Rose's cottage when she breaks it.

"When do I get to see you again?"

I keep my eyes on the road, my hands tightening on the wheel as I try to find the right words. Would I like to see her tomorrow? The day after that? Hell, I'd love to. But the bitter reality is, work eats up most of my time, and there are things I haven't told her.

I can't tell her yet, or I risk losing her before I even have the chance of fully knowing her.

"How about I give you a call tomorrow after I check my work schedule? I might be able to get away during the day this week. If not, my evenings are open," I suggest as we near the winding road that leads us to the cottage.

She hums, pretending to consider it. "Hmm. Not exactly a swoon-worthy response, but I suppose I'll allow it."

That gets a small laugh out of me, the tension in my shoulders loosening a bit.

"I'm kidding, obviously," she adds. "That works for me, but please don't feel obligated. I know you're busy."

I sneak a quick glance at her, just enough to catch the doubt in her eyes before I force myself to focus on the road. It's like she's bracing for rejection, and it guts me.

She's not a burden. Not even close.

"I can assure you, it's not out of obligation, Juliette." The words come out raw and honest, and I don't care how they sound. She needs to hear them.

A hint of pink blooms on her cheeks again. She's got a sharp tongue and clever comebacks, but then there are these moments, quick as a blink, where the armor slips. Where I catch a glimpse of the girl underneath the confidence.

It might be the sexiest thing about her.

Just as fast, she pulls herself together, a small, knowing smile curving her lips. "In that case, I'll be awaiting your call."

I throw the truck into park, fingers already curling around the door handle when her hand lands on my forearm, tentative, but enough to freeze me in place. I turn toward her slowly, raising a brow in silent question.

"Will you say goodnight to me here?" she asks, quieter this time, but there's this glint in her eye now—she's being bold again. "You can still walk me to the door if you want. I just... thought maybe it'd be safer. You know, in case you were planning to ravish me again."

I throw my head back in a laugh, unable to hold it in. This woman. She's perfect, and she doesn't even know it.

I lean over the center console, my voice low and rough. "Are you *asking* to be ravished, lass?"

Her eyes twinkle with mischief as she leans in. "Do I need to ask? I can write out an invitation if you n—"

Before she can finish, I lean closer and claim her mouth. No hesitation. No holding back. She meets me with the same kind of wild, gripping the front of my shirt like she needs me closer. It's frantic and messy and so goddamn good I almost forget where we are.

She pulls back first, just enough to breathe, her lips swollen and eyes shining. "Anyone ever tell you you're a good kisser?"

I laugh, pulling her close over the console to kiss her again. Slower this time, softer, savoring every second. "I'll see you soon," I murmur against her lips. "Let's get you inside before your aunt comes barging out and catches us out here like teenagers up to no good. I haven't had to worry about something like that in at least fifteen years."

She sighs. "Okay. That's fair. Let's go."

After stepping out of the truck, I swing her door open and catch her waist, lifting her down with ease. Her palm lands against my chest in a playful swat, catching me off guard, but damn if it doesn't make me grin.

Our steps fall into sync as her fingers slip into mine. I squeeze her hand gently, grounding myself in the warmth of her touch, not ready to let go just yet.

"Goodnight, Juliette. Make sure you tell Rose I was the perfect gentleman," I jest, hoping to hear her laugh one last time before she goes inside.

She quirks her brow. "If that was a gentleman back in the truck, I can't wait to see you *not be* so gentlemanly."

She throws me one last teasing look that sets something inside me roaring to life. Her fingers wave in a slow goodbye before the door clicks shut behind her, and I stand there, frozen.

Who am I kidding? I've been in too deep since the moment

she walked into my life. I can lie to myself all I want, but the truth is, I'm hooked.

I shift my stance, suddenly painfully aware of the pressure building between my thighs. Damn it. I can lie to myself all I want, but it's too late. She's under my skin, and no amount of distance or logic will ever change that.

Still, there's this gnawing feeling in my gut, warning me that we're barreling toward something that could wreck us if we're not careful. If I had any sense, I'd walk away before it's too late. Step back, take the easy way out.

But right now, I'm not that man. I'm not thinking about easy. I'm thinking about her. And whatever this is, wherever it's going, I'm not letting it slip through my fingers. Not without trying.

I've been dodging this conversation, but I can't keep avoiding it, especially not after tonight.

My house is too quiet compared to just an hour ago. The contrast makes the dread settle heavier in my chest, like I hauled it in with me and dropped it right here on the living room floor.

With a resigned sigh, I tap the familiar number into my phone. He never lets calls go unanswered, no matter how late they are.

"Hey, pal!" Finn's voice is chipper as always.

"Hey, Finn," I greet him, doing my best to sound normal but failing miserably. "What's up?"

There's a loud, chaotic commotion in the background. "Living the dream, as usual. Hey! Don't throw that!" He shuffles around for a second before he's back on the line. "Sorry about that. Kids are still awake somehow. They were supposed to be in bed an hour ago. Elsie's wrangling them. What's going on with you?"

Finn's the kind of friend who knows me better than I know myself sometimes. We've been through it all together, so when I call, he knows it's never a casual chat. There's usually a problem brewing, and more often than not, it's something legal.

"I'm done, Finn. I just want to get this over with," I say, frustration seeping through my words. "Let's give Hallie whatever the hell it is she's demanding and wrap this up."

There's a pause before Finn's voice crackles through. "Woah, hold up, Knox. No way in hell. As your attorney, I gotta tell you that's ill-advised. And as your friend, I have to ask... Are you *fecking* mad?"

I lean back in my chair, running a hand through my hair. "No, I'm not. I'm just done. This has been dragging on for over a year, and I can't keep going like this. I need it over. Now."

I can practically hear Finn's skepticism crackling through the line. His tone shifts, edged with concern. "All right, what's going on? Why the sudden urgency? You know we have to handle this the right way. She doesn't deserve a damn thing, which is exactly why we've been fighting this long."

I drag a hand down my face, exhaling hard. "I can't do it anymore, Finn. I can't keep being tied to her. I need out."

The silence stretches between us for a beat before he asks, "Is this about another woman?"

"It's about moving the hell on," I grit out, rubbing a hand along the back of my neck.

There's another pause, then that dry, knowing scoff of his. "So, that's a yes. When did this happen?"

I take a long, measured breath. "It is and it isn't. There's someone who's made me realize I can't keep living like this."

It sounds like a half truth even to me. And hell, maybe it is.

Because before Juliette, I was fine letting this continue on forever.

"Aye, I don't know, Knox. I mean, I don't disagree with you, but we've worked too long and hard to protect you for it to end like this."

I can't help the laugh that slips out, even though I know this is serious. The absurdity of the situation, and Finn, of all people, talking about long and hard, breaks the tension for a moment.

"Long and hard, aye?" I tease, barely holding it together.

Finn groans on the other end of the line. "Are you serious right now? Are you a child? For God's sake!"

I pinch the bridge of my nose, still chuckling. I probably sound a little insane, but I really needed that moment of humor. "Sorry. I'll grow up now." I take a breath, shifting back to business. "Seriously, though, what are my options? I need to get this over with."

Finn's voice is steady, but I can sense the hesitation. "We're only six months away from the two-year mark. Can't you hang on that long? The court will issue the certificate, and it'll be done."

"And what stops her from coming after me for more after that? Nothing. I could be tied up in a legal mess for years. I can't deal with that, Finn."

"Aye...okay. Let me review everything first thing tomorrow. I'll give you a call after, yeah?"

"I'd really appreciate that."

"Damn you, Knox. We could've won this."

"Aye, I know," I mutter. "But some things are more important."

nineteen

JULIETTE

My aunt's already asleep when Knox drops me off. I'm thanking the stars for that because I am *not* ready for a post-game analysis, especially since tonight involved her boss. But there's one person I do want to debrief.

Inside, I peel off my shoes, swap my outfit for my favorite sweats, the ones so worn they're practically held together by nostalgia, and grab my phone. Bree answers on the first ring because of course she does.

"Bree Smith, expert in all things deliciously wicked, at your service," she announces in that singsong voice that somehow manages to pierce through the background noise of the hospital where she works.

"Are you on your break?" I ask, curling my legs beneath me in the bedroom chair that's become my favorite spot.

"Fifteen sacred minutes of freedom. My feet are killing me." She lowers her voice. "Now spill everything before I die of suspense."

I recount every detail. The way Knox's hand brushed mine at dinner, the stories he told, the way his eyes seemed to see straight through me. Bree gasps and interjects at all the right moments, her energy so contagious that I forget ever being nervous at all.

Then I get to the part about unpacking my baggage, and my words start dragging. "So, yeah. I basically handed him a front-row seat to my baggage claim," I mutter.

She snorts, slicing right through my self-pity. "Okay, first of all? *Everyone* has baggage. Second, you're adorable and honest, so if he's even remotely decent, he's not gonna run for the hills. And third," she pauses, and I can almost see her leaning in for dramatic effect, "you *like* him"

"Maybe," I mumble, biting my lip to smother the grin threatening to take over. "Oh, his house was insane, by the way. Like, actual postcard-worthy views. And he has this tiny kitten..."

She makes a strangled sound. "Are you sure this man is real? Just *Juliette*, casually dating a Scottish god with a kitten, a mountain retreat, and a solid sense of humor." She sighs. "I haven't even seen what he looks like. Send me a picture."

I tug at a loose thread on my sleeve. "I don't have one."

"You don't have one?" she echoes, scandalized.

"You could probably check the distillery's website?" I offer weakly. "Maybe there's a picture there."

"Hold, please," she says, her phone clattering against the counter before I hear the rapid-fire clicking of her nails on the screen.

There's a beat of silence before she inhales sharply. "Are you kidding me right now?" Her voice practically hits a new octave.

My phone buzzes with a notification. Curious, I switch to speaker and check the text. Bree sent a screenshot from the website. A polished, professional shot of Knox standing beside a copper still, looking every bit like he walked off a whisky-themed romance novel cover. Piercing eyes. Lopsided grin. Daring the world not to be completely obsessed with him.

"That's the Knox you're talking about?"

"Yep. That's the one."

"You're telling me you *hesitated* when he asked you out?" Bree's voice is thick with disappointment. "I'm truly let down. Marry that man. Have his babies. Hide yourself away in the mountains and never come back. I wouldn't even blame you."

I laugh, because of course she's being dramatic, but she also has to be joking.

"You're ridiculous," I say, shaking my head even though she can't see me. "This is just...nice. It's casual."

I say it like I believe it. Like my stomach didn't just flip thinking about him. Like my brain isn't already replaying every stolen glance and almost-touch.

"At least tell me your night hit first, second, *and* third base. Maybe even a home run," she says shamelessly.

"You're relentless."

"So?" she presses.

I hesitate for half a second. "Yes to first base. Maybe halfway to second?"

The squeal that follows is loud enough to make me regret telling her.

"Was it amazing? Earth-shattering?"

I laugh. "All of the above? It wasn't like kissing someone because you think you should, or because it's the next logical step. It felt like..."

"Like what?"

"Like coming home to a place I've never been before," I admit, surprising myself. "Does that sound completely insane?"

"Not insane. Romantic as hell," she says. "And exactly what you deserve after wasting years with James's dull ass."

"James wasn't *that* dull," I protest weakly.

"James color-coded his sock drawer and thought cilantro was too spicy."

I half-heartedly roll my eyes, but I can't deny she's right.

"Okay, fine," I concede with a laugh. "But to be fair, Knox's socks are probably color-coded, too. His house is immaculate."

"But does he think pepper is spicy?"

"He makes his own whisky. I'm pretty sure his taste buds can handle more than salt."

She hums approvingly. "Look at you, Jules. Two weeks in and you're kissing hot Scotsmen in their mountain hideaways. I'm proud of you, you know that?"

"It's just one date, Bree."

"It's not just one date. It's you choosing yourself. It's you being brave enough to want something real."

Before I have a second to reflect on that, she continues.

"If you don't marry him and run away into the sunset, I just might."

I snort. "What are you talking about? You have Dillon, who is basically as amazing as they come."

"Yeah..." She falters for just a second before recovering. "But the thing is, he doesn't have an accent. And I'm realizing now, that's totally the missing piece of the puzzle."

This time, we're laughing together. And *god*, I miss her.

I DIDN'T EXPECT to still be smiling about it this morning, but here I am, replaying every word and every glance. There's a kind of lightness in my chest I haven't felt in a while.

Aunt Rose peers at me from her desk, suspicion already written all over her face. "You look dangerously cheerful for someone who's allegedly sworn off men." She swivels in her chair, sipping her coffee like she's not preparing to interrogate me. "I didn't hear you come in last night. How was the date?"

Her smile says *I already know,* but she wants me to say it out loud.

I drop into one of the dining chairs next to her desk with a sigh. "It was really great. I had such a good time."

Her smile widens. "I'm glad. So, what did you two talk about? Other than me, of course."

"Oh, you know," I say with a laugh, "life, family, friends, tragic past relationships. The usual."

She raises a brow, clearly intrigued. "Ah, so James came up in the conversation?"

I groan. "Just a little. I didn't waste too much time on that."

Her eyes flicker with the kind of glimmer that tells me she's picking up on something. "Did Knox tell you much about any of his past relationships?"

"Now that I think about it, no, he didn't," I say thoughtfully. "But I also didn't ask. Honestly, I'm not sure I care all that much about who or what was in his past at this point." I shrug. "Besides, I know you would've warned me if he was a crappy person before I even thought about saying yes to his invite."

It was one date. One ridiculously fun, emotionally irresponsible date. That's it. Not exactly grounds for digging through his past as if I've got a right to it. We laughed, we kissed, we set my entire nervous system on fire, but that doesn't mean it *means* anything.

Right?

Except, I keep thinking about the way his eyes lingered on me when I talked about my mom. How he didn't fill the silence with empty words. How his fingers brushed mine like he'd done it a thousand times and would do it a thousand more.

It did mean something. I know it did.

She offers me a small smile, but there's something off about it. Just like when we were at lunch the other day.

"Is there something I should know?"

She hesitates then shrugs. "I'm just being nosy. Knox would tell you if there was anything you needed to know. Your heart is on hiatus anyway, right?" she teases.

Her words don't do much to ease the knot of skepticism tightening in my stomach. I catch a flicker in her eyes, a shift in her expression, subtle but telling. She's trying to figure out exactly where my head is at. She's not buying my half-hearted reassurance, and I'm not sure I'm buying hers, either.

After a beat, she leans forward, her gaze steady. "Knox is a good guy. I promise he's nothing like James. I wouldn't lie to you about that."

I give her a wary nod, my fingers fidgeting with the hem of my shirt as I try to shake off the weight of her words. I know I've been a little careless, caught up in something that feels too good to question. It's just...so nice to do something for myself with no one else's expectations hanging over me. I got lost in the simplicity of being with someone who wasn't looking for anything but company. And I know I'll do it again because it's too easy to forget all the reasons I shouldn't when everything just...clicks.

KNOX

What a morning. Back-to-back meetings, non-stop calls. It's like the universe decided to pile everything on at once. There's not a moment I can just breathe. Not even a second to glance at my schedule and figure out when I can get some air.

I shot Juliette a quick text earlier, telling her I'd have to call her later.

I glance at the clock, and damn. I've been glued to my damn office chair for almost four hours. My eyes are burning from staring at the screen, and the chair's got a permanent impression of my ass. My muscles are locked up and my body's screaming for a break.

I'm pushing myself up from my desk when I catch a figure in the doorway.

"Mum, hi. I wasn't expecting to see you today."

"I thought maybe I'd stop by and see if you had time for lunch?"

"For you, always." I rub my hand over my neck, trying to

shake off the tension. "Is it okay if we just grab lunch here? Today's been a total mess."

"Sure. Is Callan around today? I haven't seen him."

I let out a quick breath, leaning back against the desk. "Ah, no. He's off in Edinburgh for the next few days, handling some promo stuff. Why? Am I not enough for you?" I raise a teasing eyebrow.

Picking on Mum's too easy. She's a saint, plain and simple. Had to be with all the hell the three of us put her through back when we were kids running wild. No matter how much we got into trouble, she never wavered. Her steady presence was the one constant we could always count on when everything felt like it was falling apart. She was the glue, holding us together. That hasn't changed.

I won't lie, though. She could absolutely kick my arse if she needed to. Tough as nails. I'd never test her on that, even if she's always been the softest spot in the family.

We step into the distillery café, and I motion for Mum to take a seat at the table while I head over to the counter, grabbing our usual. I have the drinks in hand when I make my way back, dropping into the chair across from her.

I take a second to really look at her. She's got that same calm, collected look she always wears, but today there's something in her eyes. Something that makes me pause.

A slight furrow in her brow...yeah, that's the telltale sign. She's got something on her mind, but I don't push it. I take a slow sip of my drink and lean back in my chair, giving her the room to speak when she's ready. Over the years, I've learned it's better to just wait.

"So, what's new in your life, Knoxie?" she asks, her voice teasing but there's that hint of prying beneath.

The nickname still makes me cringe, but I'll always be *Knoxie* to her. "Not too much. Work's been a madhouse with all the festivals coming up. Our tour business is growing like crazy, but I'm not complaining. Dad would've loved it."

I watch her, and for just a second, her eyes flicker with a mix of grief and pride. Grief for Dad, for everything he never got to see. And pride for what we've managed to build without him. I know she's proud of us, but it's clear that part of her still misses him.

"I'm in awe of you and your brother." Her voice is thick with admiration. "The way you both stepped up so young to rebuild this place. It's hard to put into words what it would've meant to your dad. He'd be so damn proud."

Her words hit hard. It's tough hearing her talk about him like this, especially since I never really got the chance to know him the way I wish I had. Twenty-four years, and she still carries that pain like it just happened.

It's not like she hasn't built something beautiful for herself with my stepdad. She has, and I'm grateful for that. I know she's found peace in it, but that doesn't make Dad's absence any easier to cope with.

"I appreciate that, Mum. Really." I give her a small smile, hoping she hears the sincerity in my voice.

She waves it off. "Anyway, tell me what else is new. Like, oh I don't know, the fact that you have a girlfriend?"

I narrow my eyes, suddenly feeling like I'm under the spotlight. *Callan*, that damn snake. We had a deal, didn't we?

"Did Cal tell you that? Well, you should ask him about Jamie."

Mum doesn't flinch. She raises an eyebrow and leans in. "No, Lucy told me she saw you talking with Rose's niece. I was kidding when I called her your girlfriend, but it sounds like there's something you're not sharing? We'll go back to the Cal comment in a minute."

Damn it. Cal's going to murder me.

I shake my head, already working through how I'm going to make this up to him. Mum might be a saint, but she's a meddling one.

"Please, forget I said anything about Cal," I say, holding up my hands. "I want him to tell us in his own time. I really have no idea what's going on with that."

"That's fair enough," she replies, nodding, but there's a gleam in her eye. "But you're not denying anything I've said about you, so..."

I let out a deep sigh, feeling the weight of her gaze. This woman has been waiting for years for one of us to "*make her a Nanna*," and I'm about to burst her bubble.

"Honestly, there's not much to tell." I lean back in my chair, running a hand through my hair. "Her name's Juliette, and we had dinner over the weekend. That's as far as it's going. She's heading back to the States soon."

All of that is mostly true. The date, her leaving. As for how far it'll go? That's still up in the air.

"Besides," I continue, "you know things aren't settled with Hallie. I'm doing my best not to drag anyone else into that mess."

Mum's nose crinkles in disgust at the mention of my ex. Can't say I blame her. Hallie's the worst kind of storm, and Mum's never been a fan of getting caught in it.

The food arrives, giving us a brief distraction. We dig in, but it doesn't take long for the silence to creep back in. I take a moment, napkin pressed to my mouth, then lean back in my chair and give her a pointed look.

"I know you've got something to say, Mum. Don't hold back now."

My words come out snappier than I mean, but this topic's always been a sore spot for both of us.

162

Her gaze sharpens, making it clear she doesn't appreciate my tone. And for a second, I'm back to being a teenager about to have my arse handed to me.

"I just want her out of our lives, Knox," she says, her voice steady. "And I know you feel the same."

"Aye. I'm working on it," I mutter.

She nods. "Okay, then. Well, let me know if there's anything I can do."

"I appreciate that. If anything changes, you'll be the first to know," I reply, knowing damn well there's not a thing she or anyone else can do. Even my attorney can't seem to get me out of this hell.

She pats my arm gently, that sympathetic smile tugging at her lips. "Let's get you back to work. I've heard your phone buzzing on the table since we sat down."

Somehow, I've managed to clear my schedule for Wednesday afternoon. Just as I'm about to dial Juliette's number, my phone rings in my hand. Without even thinking, I swipe to answer.

"Finn, hey. What's going on?"

"No good afternoon? How are you?"

"Finn," I repeat, not in the mood for his bullshit.

I can practically hear him rolling his eyes on the other end. "Killjoy. I have an idea, but I've got some questions for you first."

"Anything. Ask away."

"How often were you travelling in the year before you separated?" There's a hint of suspicion in his voice, like he's trying to piece something together.

"A lot," I admit. "We were in the thick of expanding the distillery. New partnerships, suppliers, distributors, the whole deal."

He doesn't miss a beat. "And where was Hallie when you were gone?"

I can feel a frown forming. Where's he going with this? "She was home, as far as I'm aware." My voice is steady, but the question starts to nag at me.

"Mmhm. And explain to me why you started this whole process."

I take a breath, feeling that old frustration rising again. "She started acting like a different person. One second, she was loving and supportive, and the next, she was cold and cruel. Accused me of cheating while I was working my arse off. Then she started demanding huge amounts of money for reasons I couldn't make sense of and would fly off the handle if I said no."

"Aye," he starts. "So here's the thing. We've had access to her financial records leading up to the application, but we were mainly focused on her financial position, not the details of her expenditures."

Another pause, then he goes on. "Would you be able to send me the dates of all your work trips? The lengths of them, and where you stayed during that year before you submitted the divorce paperwork?"

My stomach drops. Something's not sitting right, but I don't have a choice but to go along with it. I click through my folders and emails to see what I kept track of. "Aye, I'm sure I could. Looks like it's all here in some form or another."

"As we both know, the judge decided your marriage hadn't broken down after the initial application," Finn points out, as if I need the reminder. "But if I can prove adultery, it's a shoo-in."

I lean back in my chair, my brows pulling together. "What are you talking about?"

Initially, I had to prove that the marriage had *irretrievably broken down*. But there are specific grounds for it, and since we weren't separated long enough for desertion or any other claim to hold water, the judge rejected the initial step in the process. Now, Finn's talking about adultery as if it's the magic fix.

"Knox..." He hesitates for a second, trying to find the right words. "I'm almost certain Hallie was cheating on you the entire time you were married."

A wave of emotion crashes over me. Disbelief, confusion, anger, betrayal. My mind races in a dozen different directions, trying to make sense of this new revelation. "How do you know?"

"If my suspicions are correct," he starts, his voice measured, "Hallie was never home while you were away. She was in St. Andrews, and there are numerous transactions at a hotel there. It won't be difficult to obtain concrete proof, not if you're willing to pay for it."

My words come out harsher than I mean for them to, but I can't hold it in. I'm fuming. "How did we miss this, Finn? If that's true, this could've been over years ago."

"I'm sorry, Knox. We just weren't considering this avenue, so we weren't looking. She was painting *you* as the cheater, and she was the forgiving wife who wanted to give you a second chance."

The realization of how much we missed and how much I've been blind to hits hard. My fingers clench, resentment burning inside me, but beneath that, a dull ache stirs. I put everything into making the relationship work, choosing to ignore the red flags because I thought it was my fault.

It's a pattern I've known my whole life. Always stepping in

to lift the burden, playing by certain rules because that's what's expected, being the one to set things straight. It took me too long to realize that some things aren't mine to save.

"What's done is done. I just need it taken care of," I say, my tone firm and final. There's no room for debate here. "Do whatever you need to on your end. I'll get you my travel details."

Finn responds with calm assurance, already having mapped out the next steps. "We might not even have to do much. Get me the particulars, and I'll get something set up with them. There's a chance they don't want this going back to the judge."

"I'll get those over to you before I head home for the day," I promise. "I'll talk to you soon."

I end the call, and I'm...furious. Enraged. Livid. Fuming. *Seething.* There aren't enough words to describe the storm brewing inside me.

Hallie, with her bloody manipulation, fought tooth and nail to drag this out. My only shot at getting the divorce granted was proving that her behavior had ruined our marriage. But she was determined to prolong the fight, and somehow, she came out on top.

After that, I was forced to endure two years of separation before I could try again, unless I gave in to her extortion. I refused to give her a damn thing, so I've had to wait it out.

I curse myself for ever falling for her schemes. It stings knowing she only wanted me for my money, but the real gut punch? Finding out she was unfaithful all along while I stayed loyal. How could I have been so blind?

I shake my head, my dad's voice echoing in my mind. But this? This isn't some light breeze guiding me. It's a full-on tempest. And there better be a damn good reason it brought me here.

I really hope Finn is onto something.

With a sense of urgency, I gather everything he asked for, double-checking I haven't missed a thing. Once I shoot the email off to him, I don't waste any time. I pack up my things, mentally steeling myself for whatever's coming next.

I click the office door shut behind me, and the flicker of light from Rose's office catches my attention. She's still at her desk, eyes glued to her screen, looking just as worn out as I feel.

"Hey, what are you still doing here?"

She glances up, giving me that same look that makes it hard not to notice how much she and her niece share in the eyes department. "Just wrapping up the catering selections."

"Shit, sorry about that. I was supposed to handle that, not dump it on you."

"No worries." She waves it off.

I nod, just about to turn and head out of the office when she calls my name.

"Hey, Knox?"

I stop, shifting back to face her. "What's up?"

"Do you know what you're doing?" Her voice holds an edge of concern, a worry I hear loud and clear.

I pause, letting the weight of what she's asking settle in.

"Aye...I'm working through it," I answer, my tone steady, but not as sure as I want it to be. "I don't plan on sharing much with anyone until I've got some solid answers, and that includes Juliette. I'm sorry if that's not the response you were hoping for, but right now, there's not much to say. She could be leaving in a week and none of this would matter."

She gives a solemn nod, but there's still a trace of apprehension in her eyes. "I understand, and that's fair. I'm just looking out for both of you."

A lump forms in my throat. "I'll be careful with her, Rose. I know how much she means to you," I say.

She offers a half smile. "That's all I can ask for. Now shoo. I've got work to do."

I give her a quick wave and slip out, the soft click of the door behind me doing little to drown out the turmoil stirring inside. I promised I'd be careful, but the truth is, the pull I feel toward Juliette isn't something I can talk myself out of.

JULIETTE

I nstead of braving the outside world today, I stayed in the cottage to get lost in a good book. The stillness is a breath of fresh air, with only the sounds of soft rustling leaves and the occasional chirp of a bird interrupting. It's almost like the world is taking a deep, slow breath with me. This is my happy place.

I have no idea how long I've been curled up like this, limbs half asleep and completely lost in someone else's world, when my phone buzzes against the cushion beside me. The sound startles me enough to jolt me halfway out of my blanket cocoon.

Knox.

His name lighting up my screen has my stomach doing this ridiculous little flip.

I clear my throat, willing myself to sound...not insane. Not like someone who just spent the last five minutes daydreaming about his stupid perfect voice.

"Hey, you!"

Well, that was anything but chill.

His rich voice comes through, smooth like honey. It pulls

me in. "Hi, Juliette. You always answer the phone like that, or am I just special?"

Heat rises in my cheeks. "Maybe a little of both," I reply, trying to keep my tone light. "How was work?"

He lets out a heavy sigh that seems to be laced with a mix of exhaustion and relief. "Busy, but that's not a bad thing. Just leaves me worn out by the end of the day."

"Mm, I know all about that," I reply. "I'm always drained after those busy days, but they're always the most productive and rewarding, too. What did you have going on today?"

A shiver races down my spine as his low, husky laugh filters through the line. Almost like a whisper just for me. "Just the usual. Meetings, calls, and more meetings. I'll spare you the details."

"I'd love to hear about it if you want to tell me. You're not going to bore me if that's what you think."

There's a brief pause, just long enough for me to wonder if he's trying to decide how much to share. "Knox? Are you there?" I ask, glancing at my phone to make sure the call hasn't dropped.

"Aye, sorry. You really want to hear about all the meetings I had today?" His voice carries an edge of surprise. Did he not expect me to ask?

"Of course, I do. I'd love to hear about anything that's important to you."

He doesn't hesitate, launching straight into his day, talking through meetings, new product ideas, a call with Rose about the magazine feature. There's pride in his voice. When he mentions a meeting with the local hotel about tour packages, that's when he really lights up.

He talks about his work like it's all part of something bigger, like every moving piece matters. I find myself hanging onto every word.

"You are definitely a busy guy. How exciting, though. All of it."

"It is," he agrees. "Enough about work, though. I actually called to ask you out again."

"Whatcha got in mind?"

"I was able to snag some time away from the office on Wednesday afternoon. Would that work for you?"

Two days from now. Only two days, and yet, I find myself disappointed that it's not tomorrow...or today. Where are those chill pills again?

"Wednesday works great. What are we doing?"

"It's a surprise. But dress for the weather and wear comfortable shoes."

I smirk, silently guessing what's coming. *Hiking.* I can already sense my legs protesting, but I'm excited nonetheless. "Noted. I'll be looking forward to it."

"Same here, lass," he replies. "I have to go into the office for a bit that morning, but I can pick you up once I'm done there."

"Yep, that works for me." A spark of excitement zips through me at the thought of spending more time with him. Just the two of us, no distractions.

"Great. Well, I'm about to pull up to the house, but I'll talk to you later?"

"Sounds great! Have a good night. Give Beastie some love for me."

I can practically see his grin and the shake of his head when he says, "Aye, I'll do that. Have a good night, Juliette."

"Talk to you later, Captain."

I hang up, letting out a deep sigh. The nagging question of *what the hell am I doing* creeps back into my mind, just as it does every time I finish a conversation with him. I seem to forget that there's no middle ground in this situation. I either

171

stay or I go, and let's be real, abandoning my whole life for the sake of a few moments of bliss doesn't seem reasonable.

Just when I start to settle into my "mature" frame of mind, trying to be all responsible and sensible, my phone buzzes with a text from Knox. I roll my eyes at myself for even trying to act like I've got this figured out.

I open the message and almost die. It's a picture of the kitten, curled up on Knox's chest.

KNOX
Uile-Bhèist says hi.

Are you kidding me?

It's the cutest thing I've ever seen. Before I know it, I'm smiling so hard it feels like my face might split in half. I take a second to collect myself, but it's no use. I'm a goner.

Lord, throw me a lifeline, because I'm in *deep*.

twenty-two

JULIETTE

A couple days later, I'm trying—and mostly failing—at not glancing at the clock every thirty seconds until the sound of a truck rumbling up the drive has every nerve on high alert. I grab my hiking shoes, which are more like sneakers with hiking aspirations, just in case we're not actually scaling any mountains today.

As much as I love my aunt, I don't want to make Knox suffer the awkwardness of running into her again. So, instead of waiting for him to come to the door, I slip outside first.

Knox is stepping out of the truck just as I make my way toward him. "Hey, I would've come to the door," he says, offering me a smile that's enough to make my heart stutter.

"I know you would have," I reply with a grin. "Just call me an eager beaver."

The second the words leave my mouth, I internally facepalm. *Well, that's out in the universe now.* Great. Just great. It's officially a word vomit kind of day.

He quirks a brow, his lips twitching as he tries to hold back a laugh.

"I'm done being weird now, I promise," I say, holding up my hands in mock surrender.

My heart does this traitorous little flip when he hits me with that smirk. Just the slightest curve of his mouth, dimple and all.

"I like your weird," he says, voice all low and rough-edged. Then, with a wink, he says, "Now get your sweet arse in the truck."

My mouth falls open, a laugh bubbling up from deep in my chest. "Did you just say *arse*? That's...wildly superior to *ass*. It's like fancy swearing."

He shakes his head, his hand finding the small of my back like touching me is a habit he's already forming. My skin tingles beneath the light press of his fingers.

"Fancy is one word for it," he murmurs dangerously close to my ear.

I climb into the truck, glancing back at him over my shoulder, feeling daring and maybe just a little reckless. "Feisty. I like it."

I expect him to laugh. Maybe roll his eyes or shake his head.

What I'm *not* expecting is the playful slap on my sweet *arse* before I've even turned around in my seat. I gasp. Actually gasp. My face heats like I've been set on fire, and suddenly, I'm way too aware of him standing there looking far too pleased with himself.

I duck my head, biting back a grin that feels suspiciously giddy. Knox slides into the driver's seat, throwing me a look that's all challenge and amusement.

"Oh no, sweetheart," he drawls. "Don't get shy on me now. You started this."

I turn my head to catch his stare, and we both burst into laughter. The tension melts away, and there's this effortless comfort between us that's too good to be true. This kind of banter, the playful teasing, and genuine compliments are like breathing after holding my breath for too long.

This is so different from what I had with James. I used to think what I had with him was how it was supposed to be—full of sacrifices, those small moments of joy buried under the weight of obligation. But now, it's so clear. *This* is how it's supposed to be. Fun, comfortable, passionate in the best way possible. No heavy expectations, no constant bending of myself into something I'm not.

"You're right," I say. "I'll work on the shy thing. Now, hold my hand and tell me where we're going."

His smirk is immediate, and I swear, I'm already addicted to it.

"That's better," he murmurs, a little bit smug, a little bit pleased.

I glance at him again, and damn, he looks good. His shoulders are relaxed, his grip on the wheel loose but steady. When his other hand finds mine, it's anything but tentative. It's confident, like he's claiming something that's always been his.

"I thought we'd head to one of the paths with incredible views not too far from here," he says, glancing over at me. "It's one of the shorter, easier ones. I wasn't sure how adventurous you wanted to get."

I squeeze his hand. "That sounds awesome. And yeah, I appreciate that. I have a feeling I'm not exactly on your level when it comes to fitness."

He chuckles, turning just enough to catch me with a raised brow and that infuriatingly sexy smirk. "You think I'm fit?"

Cocky.

"Oh, please. You *know* you are."

He squeezes my hand again before shifting the conversation. "The path will take us from Killan to Loch Tay. Have you been in that direction yet?"

I shake my head. "Nope, don't think I have. I can't wait. Long walks and beautiful forests are kind of my thing."

We keep driving, and the village reveals itself slowly, nestled between rolling hills and cradled by the gentle curve of a lazy river. Weathered stone buildings with gabled roofs line the streets. Everything about it looks like it's been shaped by centuries, every cobblestone path a whisper of footsteps that walked before us.

"Wow," I murmur, the word barely skimming the surface of how I feel. "I'm speechless." I glance over at him, still trying to take it all in. "Do you ever get used to this? Everywhere you look, there's something beautiful."

He pauses for a moment, his brow furrowing as he gives my question some thought. "I won't speak for everyone, but I know a lot of us can take it for granted. We get caught up in the everyday stuff. Work, traffic, you know the drill. I haven't been out this way in years, and I wouldn't be if you weren't here."

"Makes sense." I nod. "This is new to me, but I'm loving every second of it. It's like when people ask me what it's like to live in Kentucky and then hear I've never been to the derby. They act like it's some type of crime."

His lips twitch into a smile. "I can see that. You get so caught up in the day-to-day, you forget to explore the stuff right under your nose."

I glance over at him as we pull into a parking lot. "How long is this path?"

"Not sure of the exact distance, but it takes maybe an hour and a half to walk the whole thing. There's also a small detour we can take if you'd like to see some castle ruins."

"Oh, I'd love that. Let's do it."

Our footsteps echo on the wooden planks of the old railway bridge as we fall into a comfortable silence that doesn't need to be filled with words. It's not long before the waters of Loch Tay come into view. The glassy surface stretches out before us, perfectly mirroring the vast blue sky above. It's one of those scenes that's so breathtakingly beautiful, it almost doesn't seem real.

The waves lapping against the shore blend with the soft rustle of leaves in the breeze. Everything feels suspended, the world holding its breath just for us.

"How about we take a seat for a bit?" Knox suggests, nodding toward a quiet spot near the water's edge. "If you don't mind the sand."

"Sounds perfect." I follow and settle onto the ground beside him, legs stretched toward the water, our thighs pressed together. The contact is innocent enough, but my body reacts like it's been waiting for this touch.

I steal a glance at him. His gaze is fixed on the horizon, but something about the way the light catches his face makes it impossible to look away. There's a softness there that pulls at me, drawing me in like the tide itself.

"All right, twenty questions time," I say. "Rapid fire. You ready?"

He lets out a small laugh at my enthusiasm. "As ready as I'll ever be."

"What's your favorite color?"

"Blue," he replies quickly. "Yours?"

"Green," I answer, without thinking. "What's your favorite food?"

"A full Scottish breakfast. Nothing beats it. And you?"

"Mexican. Specifically, tacos, chips, and queso. Okay, your turn to come up with a question."

I watch him for a moment. A smirk creeps across his face as he shifts slightly, locking eyes with me. "If you could choose a superpower, what would it be?"

I laugh, no hesitation in my answer. "Easy. Mind reading.

He raises a brow. "I think I'd hate that. Too much noise. Teleportation is more my speed."

I nod thoughtfully. "Oh, that's a good one. I'll give you that."

Our conversation flows so easily, the words slipping between us like we've been doing this for years. I find myself laughing more than I have in ages. We've long since crossed the twenty-question mark, but I'm not in a hurry to wrap it up.

Knox has this way of weaving little pieces of himself into his words with the small quirks and stories behind the things that make him who he is. It's all so captivating. I can't help but watch him as he talks, the way his eyes light up when he speaks about what matters to him. It's like I'm seeing all these pieces of him, and they're fitting together in a way that makes me want to know more.

I find myself leaning in, hanging on to every word, not just because they're interesting, but because there's something about *him* that pulls me in. The way his lips move when he talks, the deep, rich sound of his voice. I catch myself wanting the weight of his lips against mine again.

And then I'm quickly pulled back to the present, shaking my head to clear away the thoughts, but not before it stirs something low and hot in my stomach. The longer we sit here, the more I realize how easily this could slip into something more... and how badly I'm starting to want that.

twenty-three

KNOX

It's been a while since I've had someone to just sit and talk with for hours with no rush and no agenda. Just rambling about anything and everything.

I take a slow breath before asking my next question. "What's your biggest fear?"

I'm not sure why I ask it. I don't usually open up to people, let alone ask something so personal. It's a question that feels too intimate. And yet, I ask anyway because I want to know her. I want to understand what makes her tick, what keeps her up at night.

Her eyebrows lift, just the slightest hint of uncertainty flashing in her eyes before she smooths it away. She glances out over the loch, eyes tracing the rippling water as if she's deciding whether to take the plunge. "Hm. You mean like creepy clowns or are we talking about life and loss kind of fear?"

"Whatever strikes your fancy."

She nudges me with her elbow. "If I'm being honest, the future scares me right now. More specifically, the thought of giving love another shot. Of letting someone in again. It went so horribly wrong the last time."

The honesty in her voice carries the weight of something not easily put into words. I can see it in the slight tension in her jaw and the way she exhales like she's laid down a burden she's not sure she's ready to release.

I get it more than she probably realizes, and there's this urge to tell her that. To let her know she's not alone in feeling that way. But it's not the right time. Not yet.

She shakes her head, looking a little guilty. "Sorry, I think that was more than you bargained for. I ruined the mood."

"You haven't ruined anything. I asked you because I wanted the truth. Those kinds of things matter."

She studies me, eyes narrowing a fraction. "Okay then. What about you? What are you afraid of?"

I lean back, raising an eyebrow and delivering with a straight face, "People who wear socks with sandals."

Her carefree laughter bursts out, and for a second, the world gets a little brighter. I can't stand that frown I saw on her face earlier, so I nudge her shoulder with mine. "Ready to walk the rest of the way?"

I keep my gaze on her as she stares out at the horizon, her eyes drifting over the view, soaking it all in. Then, with a nod, she lets me know she's ready.

I push to my feet, reaching for her hand. When she takes it, I pull her up gently. Brushing the sand from her clothes, my fingers graze her skin, a fleeting warmth that settles somewhere deeper than it should.

We fall into step next to each other. The wind tugs at her hair, the loch stretching behind us as we leave the shore and step into the woods. The air turns cooler and heavier. The ground softens beneath our feet, muffling each step.

Finlarig Castle appears from the shadows, its crumbling

stone walls extending from the earth. Time has worn it down, but it still stands proud, a ghost of the past watching over the present.

I catch her gaze as she lifts her eyes to the ruins, her expression shifting, mouth parting in awe. The excitement that lights up her face hits me square in the chest, and I can't help but smile, watching her take it all in. There's a wonder in her eyes, like she's looking at magic. It's impossible not to be swept up in the way she admires it.

"Oh, my goodness. It's beautiful."

"Are we looking at the same thing?" I tease.

She rolls her eyes. "Yes, beautiful. Achingly so." Her voice softens. "It's like looking through a window into the past. Like at any moment, you'll hear whispers of history drifting on the breeze. It's remarkable."

She's not just looking at the ruins, she's *feeling* them and the way history seems to bleed through the cracks of stone. Normally, I'd be too caught up in my own head to slow down enough to notice it, but right now, through her eyes, everything is different. The wreckage in front of us isn't only crumbled stone. It's a story waiting to be unraveled. I finally take a real look at it, and I find myself nodding slowly.

"You're right," I admit, glancing over at her. "It is beautiful. In a...chaotic sort of way."

"Sure, we'll go with that," she teases, but her attention shifts back to the ruins as she moves with careful steps, inspecting every nook and cranny. The way she absorbs everything around her, engraving every detail into her memory as if she knows how fleeting it is. Damn. *That* is the most beautiful thing I've seen in a while.

She takes her time with unhurried steps, and I follow her with my eyes. Then, just like that, she's back, her voice floating through the air. "Hey, what's for dinner? I'm starving!"

I laugh and call out, "I'll take you out if you can get back over here in less than ten seconds!"

Her eyes light up, that playful challenge sparking something in her. She's gone before I even finish my sentence, feet kicking up grass as she sprints toward me. I start the countdown, my voice ringing clear across the distance. "Ten...nine... eight..."

I keep my eyes fixed on her as she closes the gap, running faster than I expected. I barely have time to brace myself before she crashes into me, breathless and laughing.

"Seven seconds and a tackle." I let out a low whistle. "Impressive."

She takes a step back, hands on her hips as she catches her breath. That mischievous grin doesn't leave her face. "I try."

That flush on her cheeks? Damn near mesmerizing. Her eyes flicker with some perfect mix of trouble and sheer determination that makes it impossible to look away. And then there's the way she's breathing, short and uneven, her chest rising and falling in a rhythm that lodges itself in my brain and refuses to leave. It's distracting as hell. Addicting.

The air, which was still moments before, shifts as a breeze picks up, tugging at my shirt and carrying the faint scent of the earth. Almost like a sign. A push.

Go on. Do something about it.

Without another thought, I pull her back into my arms, the warmth of her skin sinking into mine. Her breath catches as my eyes lock with hers. I hold her tighter to make sure she's real, that I'm not imagining the way her body fits perfectly against mine.

We're both standing on the edge, inches from falling, but I need to know. I search her face, looking for any sign, any flicker, that she feels the same pull between us. I know she does. I can feel it in the way her hands rest against me, the way her breath quickens, the way she doesn't pull away.

She closes the distance. Her lips are soft, a whisper against mine, but the second they touch, everything else fades. My hands move to her face, cupping her jaw and pulling her closer. She responds with equal urgency, her fingers digging into my shoulders, her lips parting and inviting me in deeper.

Time stretches and compresses all at once. Every brush of her lips against mine is like discovering something I've been searching for my entire life without knowing it. When her fingers thread through my hair, my heart hammers against my ribs like it's trying to break free. To offer itself up to her completely. I can't tell where I end and she begins. There's no past. No doubts.

She sighs against my mouth, a sound that wraps itself around my heart and pulls tight. I want to memorize it, hold it, and never let it slip away.

WE DON'T GO FAR for our early dinner, sticking to the bistro tucked in the heart of the village.

"It's so cute and cozy in here," Juliette says, slipping into one of the corner booths as she places her drink from the bar on the table.

I chuckle. "Aye, and they've got the best food."

As I settle in, my phone buzzes in my pocket, snapping me back into the reality I was hoping to escape. My heart drops when I see Finn's name flashing across the screen. The quiet and easy day we've had starts to unravel, and I'm yanked right back into the mess I've been trying to push away.

I glance at the message. It's exactly what I expect. The

meeting with Hallie's attorney. That damn knot tightens in my gut, the weight of everything unresolved pressing down. I should be used to this by now, but it never gets easier.

My muscles tense, the stress creeping in, but I push it back, burying it as deep as I can. I won't let it touch her.

Juliette's eyes are on me, and I see that subtle shift in her expression as she catches the change in my mood. "Is everything okay?"

I exhale, trying to shake the weight off. I don't want to bring any of that shit into this space. Juliette deserves better than a guy who's got his mind somewhere else, looking over his shoulder at a mess he can't control.

I force a smile. "Aye. Everything's fine." The words come out too easily, like they're rehearsed. I'm not fooling anyone, least of all myself.

She stares at me, those understanding eyes searching mine, and for a moment, I want to confess everything. The whole damn truth that's eating me alive.

Instead, I reach across the table and brush my hand against hers, offering a silent reassurance.

She hesitates for a second, but she doesn't press. Instead, she moves on. "All right then. What's your order?"

I let out a slow breath, thankful for the shift in focus. "Ribeye. No question. And you?"

She laughs, shaking her head. "I should have guessed that. I'm getting the fish and chips."

She shoots me a frisky look, raising a brow. "And don't even think about judging me for how many fries I eat or whatever you call them. I've got absolutely no self-control when it comes to them."

I smirk, leaning back in my chair. "Oh, I don't know, lass. Those chips might just be a deal-breaker."

She narrows her eyes. "Speak now or forever hold your

peace. I could never be with a man who doesn't support my fry habit."

I chuckle, but the lighthearted banter shifts into a heavier weight. Her smile falters. I watch as she realizes what she's said, the tension building between us. We're dangerously close to stumbling over the edge into territory neither of us is ready to name.

And the truth is, I can't be *with* her. Not officially. Not while Hallie's shadow is lingering over everything I do.

"Well," I clear my throat, "I'd never stand between a woman and her chips."

The waitress appears, notepad in hand, saving us from the silence that threatens to swallow us whole. We place our orders, and when she leaves, Juliette takes a long sip of her drink, eyes fixed on a distant spot over my shoulder.

"So," she says finally, setting her glass down with deliberate care, "tell me something about yourself I don't know."

I lean back in my chair, thinking about what to share. There's a lot she doesn't know, but I need to play it safe for now.

"I didn't always want to take over the distillery," I admit. "When I was younger, I wanted to be a marine biologist."

Her eyebrows shoot up, genuine surprise lighting her features. "Really? What happened?"

"Life, I suppose." I shrug. No need to get all emotional about how it was my duty as my father's oldest son to make it work because he was gone. Even at a young age, I understood the importance. I have absolutely no regrets.

She leans forward an inch. "I guess most of us have dreams that change or get set aside."

"What about you? What did young Juliette want to be?"

Her lips curve into a nostalgic smile. "A writer. I used to fill notebooks with stories about magical worlds and brave heroines."

"Do you still write?"

"Sometimes, though it's more of a hobby now." She traces the condensation on her glass with one finger. "Life has a way of redirecting us, doesn't it?"

Her lips curl into a soft, thoughtful smile. There's no way she realizes how breathtaking she is. It's not just because of how she looks, though that alone would be enough to undo a man. It's the way she keeps tucking her hair behind her ear, and the way those eyes never look away too quickly. There's something about the way she talks like she's not trying to be anything other than exactly who she is.

I admire it. I want to know what makes her laugh when no one's watching. What makes her sad when she thinks no one sees. I don't know what I'm supposed to say next. Because, the truth is, I'm already a little lost in the idea of knowing her.

twenty-four

KNOX

I just dropped Juliette off and am easing my truck into Finn's driveway. The front door swings open before I even have a chance to get out. Two little voices ring out, slicing through the quiet neighborhood.

"Uncle Knox!"

They come charging at me like a stampede, tiny feet pounding against the pavement. I drop into a crouch, arms wide, ready for the chaos that's coming. Sure enough, they barrel into me.

"Hey, you wee shites." I grin, letting them take me down with no fight.

Their giggles are enough to make the look of exasperation on Elsie's face worth it. "Sorry, Elsie," I say, standing back up with the two boys still holding on to my hands. "I wouldn't be the cool uncle if I didn't teach them how to swear."

Elsie shoots me a look, but there's a smirk hiding behind it. "Mmhm. You're lucky I like you." She glances toward the house. "Finn's in his study if you want to head in there."

I give her a quick kiss on the cheek before turning to walk

into the house. The study door's cracked open, and Finn's hunched over his desk, fingers flying over the keyboard.

"Hiya, pal," he greets without looking up from his computer. "Go ahead and sit. Give me just a second."

I sink into the tartan-upholstered armchair, kicking back and letting my mind wander while he finishes up whatever he's working on.

"All right, I have some news," Finn finally says. "All of the travel dates you sent me line up with when Hallie was in St. Andrews, so our suspicion is looking pretty damn solid. I made a call to her attorney and asked for a meeting now that we've got this new piece of the puzzle."

Son of a bitch.

"And?" I'm already bracing myself.

"Well..." Finn's voice is calm, but I note the tension in it. "He wasn't thrilled to hear from me. Even less thrilled to hear what I had to say. We do have a meeting set up, though. It's just...not for another month."

I let out a sharp breath, my stomach tightening. "Why so long?"

"They need time to plan, and I need to gather more proof. I've started drafting the application for the writ to obtain the hotel records, but that's also not something that happens overnight."

I let out a long, tired breath, trying to push my frustrations down. "Okay. I appreciate everything you're doing, Finn. I just... I just wish it didn't take so damn long."

"Aye, that's the legal system for you." His tone is flat. He's as fed up with it as I am.

Figuring it's time to shift gears, I start telling him about Juliette. How we met, how much time we've been spending together.

"I mean, I like her, Finn," I add, my voice dropping a bit. "I can't help but wonder if it's fair to bring her into the shitshow that is my life right now. She's been through enough already, you know?" I pause, rubbing the back of my neck. "So, is it wrong of me to keep this from her?"

"Honestly?" Finn doesn't miss a beat. "I don't know. I won't pretend to understand how a woman's brain works. Let's ask Elsie."

"Ah, I don't think that's a good id—"

"Elsie!" he cuts me off, calling out loud enough for her to hear. "Knox has a girly question for you."

A few seconds later, Elsie's blonde head pops around the doorframe, her eyes narrowing as she steps into the room. "Aye?"

"Knox here has a girlfriend that doesn't know he's married," Finn announces.

Elsie looks like she's about to throw something at me. "Knox Cameron MacKenzie, what the hell?!"

"I guess that answers my question," I groan, leaning back in the chair. "We only met a couple weeks ago. She's from the States and here for the summer. We've had a couple dates. I didn't see the point in sharing the drama with her if this isn't going anywhere. But now that we're doing...whatever this is, I'm not sure how to handle it."

Elsie stares at me, eyes wide in disbelief. "Um, you tell her, you *eijit*."

"It's not that simple, Els. I don't want to bring her into this until I know when this shitshow with Hallie is going to end. It could be over in a couple weeks, or this could go on for another six months. Is it so bad to wait until I have an end date to tell her?"

"That's your choice," she says, crossing her arms. "Telling her *soon* is better than not telling her at all, but I also think she deserves to know now, regardless of the outcome. I know I wouldn't take well to being kept in the dark with something like this."

I drag a hand through my hair, trying to shake off the anxiety that's been slowly creeping up my spine. "Aye. Okay. Thanks, Els."

She gives a soft hum in response, and without another word, turns and walks off.

When I throw Finn a glare, he shoots me a sheepish grin.

"Sorry, pal," he says, shrugging like he's got no regrets. "If someone's going to tell you how it is, it'll be my lovely wife."

I'm starting to think I'm damned if I do, and more damned if I don't.

JULIETTE

I can't believe it's been a month and a half since I stepped off that plane. If I didn't know any better, I would say it was just yesterday.

Time has a way of bending here. Days blend together in a haze of easy laughter and late-night talks that stretch until I'm fighting off sleep. I've actually been spending a lot of time with Knox. At first, it was quick lunches at the distillery but then came the impromptu drives to neighboring villages, his fingers drumming against the steering wheel to whatever folk song playing on the radio.

Last night, we sat on his porch watching the sun set over the hills while sharing a bottle of whisky—*the good stuff*, he insisted. We didn't talk about anything important, or maybe we did, in a roundabout kind of way.

The evening air was cool but not cold, and when he draped his jacket around my shoulders, I felt something shift between us. Like the final piece clicking into place.

I've memorized the way his eyes crinkle when he laughs,

how he runs his hand through his hair when he's thinking. I can't seem to let go of the sound of his lilting accent or the way his smile acts as an invitation to something more.

More than anything, it's the way he kisses me that haunts my thoughts. His lips are always gentle at first, but then it's like something snaps and the kiss is the one thing he can't hold back. The way he pulls me against him, the warmth of his body, the taste of whisky lingering on his lips, and his hands, always so careful but never quite able to stay in one place.

It's always just a kiss, though. We haven't let it go any further, but I don't think either of us is fooling ourselves.

I'm leaving soon.

That's what I keep reminding myself when his hand lingers at the small of my back, or when I catch him watching me with that look that makes my insides turn to liquid heat. I remind myself every time our fingers brush, every time he leans in close, and every time his voice drops low in a way that sends a shiver down my spine.

I'm leaving, and that's why I'm holding back, but I can't tell if he's doing the same because he knows the end is coming or if he's forcing himself for some other reason. We haven't talked about it. Haven't even touched the subject. Part of me wonders if it's better that way.

I'm pushing all of it to the back of my mind today. I'm bouncing on my feet as I stand by baggage claim, my gaze darting between weary travelers until I spot Bree, and all sense of composure flies out the window.

A squeal bursts out of me, loud, unrestrained, and *deeply* embarrassing. A few strangers turn to stare, but I don't care. She's here and that's all that matters.

We crash into each other like a scene straight out of a dramatic reunion. Full sprint, zero hesitation, arms locked tight before either of us can get a word out. The miles, the weeks, the texts don't quite capture how much I missed her.

"Juliette, my love!" Bree squeezes the air right out of me. "Oh my god, you look amazing. Scotland has been *so* good to you."

"It has been." I'm grinning so hard my cheeks hurt. "I'm having the best time, but I missed you."

She pulls back just enough to give me a long, knowing once-over, eyes twinkling with pride. "Well, you look happy, Jules. Like you're really back to yourself."

Her words hit me square in the chest, settling in that unguarded place where all the important things live. No one knows me like Bree does. She's seen every version of me, the shattered and the whole, the lost and the found. For her to notice the change means more than I can put into words.

"Thank you," I murmur, my voice faltering just a little. "I really needed to hear that."

Before I can get too emotional in the middle of baggage claim, I loop my arm through hers and steer us toward the carousel. "Come on, let's grab your stuff. Aunt Rose is dying to see you."

By the time we pull up to the cottage, my aunt is already at the door. The second Bree steps out of the car, she throws her arms wide and calls, "Hello, my dear adopted niece!"

They're lost in conversation before I make it inside. I haul Bree's bags to my room, then collapse onto the loveseat beside my aunt, sighing in relief.

"So, what's the plan this week?" Aunt Rose asks.

I stretch my legs out, letting my head tip back against the cushion. "We'll hang out here for a few days," I say. "Then we're heading back to Edinburgh. We've booked a hotel right across from Waverley Station, so we'll have a few more days to explore before Bree has to fly home."

Aunt Rose hums her approval. "Oh, you two are going to love Edinburgh. So much history, so much to see."

"Are you going to the distillery to work tomorrow?" I ask. "I was thinking about popping in with Bree for the official tour. Maybe we could meet you there for lunch?"

"Yep, I'll be there. In fact, I know someone who'd love to meet you, Bree." Her brows inch up, and her smile turns downright sly.

Bree, never one to miss a beat, gasps dramatically. "Oh, *yes!* I am so excited to meet the man himself. Jules has spoken *very* highly of him," she says, shooting me a look so smug I want to shove a pillow in her face. "I can't wait to see if he lives up to the hype."

I tip my head back and groan, because of course they're tag-teaming me. Absolute menaces, both of them. And I must be the world's biggest sucker, because I still love them anyway.

"Yeah, yeah," I grumble, crossing my arms. "Let's just hope he doesn't take one look at you and run for the hills. We're a package deal, after all."

The conversation is cut short when my phone starts ringing. Knox's name flashes across the screen, and before I can so much as react, Bree's eyes light up with pure trouble.

"Eep!" she gasps, hands clasped. "Please, *please* let me answer it."

I sigh, already knowing there's no stopping this. I pass her the phone, bracing myself for whatever chaos is about to unfold.

"Hello, new friend," Bree greets, all sugary sweetness as she puts the call on speakerphone. "How are you on this fine evening?"

A beat of silence, then that familiar, low timbre fills the room. Smooth, rich, and devastatingly calm.

"Ah, hello there. Am I to assume this is Bree?"

She grins, shooting me a look of delight. "Smart man. Juliette said you were, and she usually doesn't lie."

I roll my eyes, but I can't fight the smile pulling at my lips. This is going to either be hilarious or a complete disaster. Maybe both.

"I've heard a lot about you, too. Word is, you're quite the personality," he quips.

She tosses her head back in laughter. "Touché, new friend. Touché. That's a very polite way of putting it." She winks at me, then adds, "Well, I'm positive Juliette is about two seconds from wringing my neck, so I'll let you talk to her. See you tomorrow, whisky boy."

I groan, shaking my head as I grab the phone from her before she can say anything else mortifying. "You're the worst," I mutter, but she just grins, completely unbothered.

Switching off the speaker, I slip into the bedroom, closing the door softly behind me. "Hi there," I murmur.

"I like her already."

I smile, leaning against the doorframe. "It's hard not to. I wasn't sure how busy you'd be tomorrow, but I thought maybe I could swing by with Bree, if you've got some time for us?"

"Always, Juliette." There's an intensity in his tone that makes my chest tighten. "You never have to ask."

I swallow hard, trying to act like I'm totally unaffected, but my pulse is already picking up. It's like he has this magic power that makes everything else fade, leaving only the sound of his voice that does things to me I probably shouldn't let it do.

It's honestly a blessing he's not standing in front of me right now, because if he were? I'd probably be gripping his shirt, whispering something reckless like *take me somewhere, anywhere...just make it private.*

"I appreciate that," I manage to say. "I'm really excited for you to meet her. She's practically my other half. Oh!" I laugh before adding, "You might want to get extra security when Callan's around, though. I don't know what kind of damage those two will do when they're under the same roof."

He huffs a laugh. "It'll be good for someone to give him a run for his money."

It's probably going to be total mayhem, but at least it'll be the best kind.

"Well, I won't keep you," he says after a beat. "Go enjoy your time with the family."

The way he understands that the two women in the other room are my family, one by blood, the other by choice, is everything. The way he accepts that without question means more than I can say.

"Thanks," I reply softly. "I'll see you tomorrow."

"Goodnight, Juliette."

His words curl around me like a slow, lingering touch. It's the way he says my name that makes my pulse stutter. I can't shake the feeling that I'd love to hear him say that to me every night.

I smile when I remember what Mom always told me about soulmates. Having a soulmate is like finding the person who will steal your fries without asking, but you don't even care because they're the only one who gets you.

She always said I was her soulmate, and I thought she was bonkers.

I never felt *destined* to be with James. But I saw Knox just yesterday, got off the phone with him less than a minute ago, and yet, here I am, with this strange feeling that a piece of me is somewhere else. It's like my heart wandered off and decided to stick around with him.

I wish I could talk to Mom about this, ask her what she'd have to say about all of it. But instead, I have to settle for the two wisecrackers I've got.

"Hey," I say, stepping back into the living room, "what's your opinion on soulmates?"

There's a moment of complete silence as two pairs of wide, puzzled eyes flicker toward me. Then they exchange a glance and, simultaneously, burst into laughter.

twenty-six

JULIETTE

The moment Bree and Knox met, there was a flutter of nerves I didn't expect. I wanted so badly for it to go well, for Bree to see him the way I did. But when Knox reached out to shake Bree's hand and she wrapped him up in a hug instead, all the tension in my body evaporated in an instant.

I didn't realize how tightly I was clasping my hands until Bree shot me a knowing glance that said, *relax, we're good.* Watching them together brought on a sense of reassurance, like maybe these pieces of my life could actually fit together, after all.

Now, I'm sitting at one of the high-top barrel tables in the tasting room, Knox's arm casually draped over my shoulders. I'm tucked into his side as we watch Bree and Callan exchange introductions, their banter already heating up.

Bree eyes Callan with a mischievous grin. "So, you're the infamous brother I've heard so much about?"

He tilts his head, sizing her up. "And you must be the troublemaker I was warned about."

"Guilty as charged," she replies without missing a beat.

To anyone else, it would look like they're flirting. But this is Bree. She's like this with everyone. Playful, full of energy, all charm and mischief with a dash of sarcasm. I've seen her light up rooms like it's nothing, breaking down walls with a smile and a wink.

He leans in just a bit. "All right, then. What kind of trouble are we talking about here?"

Bree's smirk deepens, and she lets the words roll off her tongue with a wink. "Oh, you know, the usual. Daring escapades, maybe a little light vandalism here and there."

Callan throws his head back in laughter, the sound warm and rich and echoing through the room. "Light vandalism, huh? Guess we'll have to keep a close eye on you while you're here."

I bite back a laugh as Bree bats her lashes, playing the innocent act. "Please, I'm an angel," she declares, her voice so syrupy sweet it's enough to give someone a cavity.

Angel, my ass.

Bree's more like a hurricane in heels.

"An angel, huh?" he says, his eyebrow raised in skepticism. "Is that before or after the vandalism?"

"Depends. What's the statute of limitations around here?"

Bree's always had a talent for toeing the line without quite stepping over it, and Callan... Well, he seems like the type who enjoys the game as much as she does. But what catches my eye is how he's looking at her, his eyes following her movements, his expression softer and reading her in a way I don't think he's aware of.

Their banter bounces back and forth until Callan's phone buzzes against the table. The spell breaks for just a second as he glances down, a flicker of disappointment crossing his face before he smooths it over.

"Looks like I'm being summoned," he says, pushing back his chair. "Duty calls."

The second Callan is out of earshot, Bree shifts gears. The teasing fades and she turns her attention back to us.

"Knox, mind if I steal you for a minute?" Her lips quirk as she tilts her head toward me. "I promise I'll give him back."

Knox lifts a brow but nods. "Aye, sure."

Bree doesn't do unnecessary conversations, which means this has a purpose. I wave them off, forcing a lighthearted grin. "Go on. I'll just be over here, pretending I don't want to eavesdrop." I say it as a joke, but it's not. I'm dying to know what's being said.

Knox dips his head, lips brushing my temple. Then he follows Bree a few steps away.

Today's been easy. No snags, no second-guessing. But old wounds don't exactly ask permission before they start aching, and that familiar flicker of doubt is tightening its grip.

He isn't James.

Still, the thought creeps in around the edges, nosy and persistent.

I force my attention elsewhere, trying to anchor myself in the sound of conversation, the clinking of glasses, and the rich scent of whisky in the air. I nod and smile absently when someone nearby catches my eye, but my thoughts keep snagging on the sight of Knox with his back to me, broad shoulders blocking any chance of reading either of their expressions.

It's the not knowing that sets my heart fluttering in a way I don't like.

I'm so caught up in trying to decode their conversation that I barely register when Knox turns back to me with that stupidly handsome grin. My god, it's a sight. He doesn't have to say a word. That smile alone tells me I can exhale.

"Everything okay?" I ask.

"More than okay," he replies. "You want to get out of here?"

"Oh, I don't think I can. Bree and I are supposed to go out for dinner tonight."

"Not anymore. Rose's taking her out tonight." He leans in close, his lips brushing my ear. "And you're coming with me."

The words aren't loud, but they land with the weight of a promise.

I remind myself this is just Knox being...Knox. He's decisive. It's one of the things that first drew me to him, that ability to take up space without forcing it, to make a statement feel like a certainty, not just a suggestion.

But the way he says it now, like my answer was never really in question, has me feeling things I probably shouldn't. I find myself caught in a dizzying pull that a reluctant part of me wants to lean into. To let him lead. I *promised* myself I'd never let a man call the shots again after everything with James. Yet, with Knox, I want to believe I can trust again.

Besides, I really do want to go with him.

I glance over at Bree, and her expression is nothing short of triumphant. She shoots me a sly smile, one that makes me roll my eyes.

"Looks like you've got me all to yourself, Captain."

His arms slide around my waist and his mouth finds the curve of my neck in a kiss pressed just below my ear. "Now that's what I like to hear."

My heart doesn't just flutter. It goes rogue.

The low timbre of his voice sends a current through me, pooling low in my stomach. It's maddening how easily he affects me, how a few words from him can leave me breathless. And the worst part...or maybe, the *best* part? I like it.

As we step out, his hand finds the small of my back. A subtle touch, but it sets off sparks below my skin. Overhead, the sky spills into a canvas of blush pinks and molten oranges, the kind of sunset that feels like a held breath before the stars take over.

I glance up at him, and for a heartbeat, the world around us slips away. It's just the two of us, untouched by everything else, and I can't help but wonder if I'll ever be the same after him.

twenty-seven

KNOX

I planned to give Juliette some time with Bree while she's here. As much as I want to keep her all to myself, I know it wouldn't be fair. When Bree suggested I take her place with Juliette tonight, there was no way I was turning that down.

We've mostly spent our time around other people, and I'm craving another moment where it's just the two of us. I'm not usually the type to get all sappy over a quiet night, but right now, that's exactly what I need. No distractions. Nothing grand. Just her and me, and the chance to hear her laugh, to watch her eyes light up when she talks to me.

I glance over at her as we walk to the truck. "What do you feel like doing tonight?"

"Can we just grab some pizza and go to your house? That honestly sounds like heaven."

The wave of relief that rolls through me is almost ridiculous. "That works for me. I know a great pizza joint not far from here. We can pick it up and bring it back to my place."

She flashes that sweet smile at me, and *fuck,* it hits low. It's not the fluttery kind of thing poets ramble on about, but the gut punch that makes you forget how to breathe. She has no idea what she does to me.

"Perfect," she says, her voice light, though I catch the soft hitch in her breath as I lift her into the passenger seat. My hands settle on her waist, fingers brushing against her skin as I secure her seatbelt.

I lean in, just close enough to steal a taste, pressing a slow, lingering kiss to her lips. I let my tongue graze the edge of her lower lip, savoring the softness, the heat, the way she shivers beneath it.

When I pull back, her eyes are heavy, glazed with that perfect mix of want and need. Her lips part slightly, chasing the last of the kiss. I linger, watching her like I might change my mind and pull her back in. Then I turn, every fiber of my being screaming not to, and shut the door behind me.

"What kind of pizza do you like?" I ask as I slide into the driver's seat, giving myself a second before I glance at her again. "I'll call in a takeaway order so it's ready by the time we get there."

She blinks like it takes her a second to remember how to speak. Her brow furrows, still a little breathless. "Hm. I'll eat anything, really. You pick. Oh, except for anything fishy. Fish has absolutely no place on a pizza."

I chuckle. "Now that we can agree on."

Thirty minutes later, we're pulling up to my place with two pizzas in hand. One's simple, something I know she'll like, and the other's a little bolder, a bit of a gamble. I'm curious to see if she'll be up for it.

"Oh my gosh, did you buy Beastie a *cat castle*?" she squeals when she spots the cat perched smugly in the top tier of a brand-new cat tree near the window.

"Aye, but he's still a pain in the arse." I mutter it under my breath, but I'm not as annoyed as I make out to be.

"Stop it," she scolds, shooting me a playful glare. "He is precious and perfect and can do no wrong."

"Hmph. Tell that to the armrest of my chair that has been shredded to smithereens."

She just waves me off without even glancing up, completely absorbed in scratching behind the kitten's ears.

I shake my head. She's got a soft spot for that furball, and it's not hard to see why. I pull plates and glasses from the cupboard, setting up the pizza on the island.

She strolls over, settling onto one of the barstools and making herself at home. I catch myself watching the way she scoops up the cat and arranges him on her lap.

"All right." She leans forward slightly, peering into the box. "I saw you ordered the margherita, which I do love, but what's this other one?"

"That's my personal favorite," I reply. "Black pudding, haggis, and smoked cheese."

I'm not surprised when her face drops into a look of horror. "You don't have to try it. It's not for everyone," I reassure her, though I'm still enjoying her reaction more than I probably should.

"I wouldn't mind trying a bite, but I have a feeling I'll be sticking to the margherita."

I pull a slice from the box and hold it out to her, watching as she inspects it like it's a ticking time bomb. She gives it one last skeptical look before finally taking a cautious bite. Our eyes meet, and I can't help but watch a little too intently, noting the way her throat works when she swallows.

Then, she winces.

She grabs the whiskey bottle like it's the only thing standing between her and death, practically chugging it. "Ugh. Yeah, that's all you," she groans, still trying to avoid choking.

"Can't say I'm a fan," she says, voice a little hoarse, and I just about lose it.

"I figured," I laugh. "But it was entertaining to watch you suffer through it."

She shoots me a look that could melt steel. "Mm. You just wait. I'll think of something equally disgusting for you to try."

I quirk a brow. "I'm *definitely* looking forward to that."

We dig in, plates full, and the conversation rolls easy from there. Nothing forced or fancy, just banter between bites and a few laughs that sneak up on me. We hit everything from dumb childhood stories to movie opinions we'll probably fight about later, and of course, the age-old, controversial topic of pineapple on pizza.

"I thought my fry habit was going to be the deal-breaker, but pineapple on pizza? I don't know if I can get over this, Knox," she says, her voice dripping with feigned disappointment.

I'm having far too much fun pushing her buttons. "It's sweet *and* savory. What's not to love?"

She furrows her brows, her eyes narrowing. "I don't know. The fact that it's a culinary crime scene, a fruit salad gone rogue—take your pick."

We both laugh and it's strange, but there's a subtle tilt, like the world's not quite on the same axis anymore. I'm not sure it'll ever shift back. Is this how it is now? Life split into before and after her?

Before Juliette, everything was simple and predictable. I knew exactly what came next. But now... Now I'm here, savoring moments like this. Laughing over a damn pizza, and somehow, it's the best part of my day.

I glance over at her again. I didn't plan on letting anyone in. Didn't think I could.

But here she is.

She hops off her stool and starts clearing plates. "You sit. Just tell me where your containers are, and I'll put the leftovers in the fridge."

She moves through the kitchen like she's done it a hundred times. No hesitation, no asking twice. Confident. Capable. For a split second, a thought hits me—*she belongs here.*

I try to shove it down to a place where it won't stir up things I'm not ready to name but it sticks. I stand there like a fool, not sure what the hell to do, then finally turn away, grab the bottle, and pour us another round.

I carry the glasses to the living room and set them on the coffee table before sinking into the couch. The cushions give beneath me, but my mind doesn't budge. It's still caught in the space she's filling without even trying.

A minute later, she slides in beside me, tucking herself against my side with a soft, content sigh. Her head settles on my shoulder, and I freeze for a beat, just long enough to feel it.

The calm. The quiet. *Her.*

I didn't know how badly I needed the sound of her laugh filling my kitchen, or the way her body fits against mine so effortlessly. She makes this whole place feel more like home than it ever has.

I swallow hard, chest aching with things I don't know how to say. Too much, too fast. And yet...not enough. She snuggles closer, and my arm moves on instinct. I wrap it around her, pulling her in tighter.

"So," I say, "remind me what you and Bree are up to over the next few days."

She starts talking about their trip to Edinburgh, her words rushing out faster the more she gets into it. The excitement in her voice is contagious, and I find myself hanging on to every word. I could easily lose track of time listening to her.

"You'll have the best time," I tell her. "Edinburgh's a hell of a place. I think I'm gonna miss you, though."

I don't say it lightly. I've gotten so used to seeing her around without even realizing how much it's become a part of my routine. I'm not sure how it'll feel when she's gone.

She lifts her head from my shoulder, her eyes locking with mine with that look I've come to recognize all too well. A small crease forms between her brows, like she's trying to figure out if I'm messing with her or if I actually mean it.

"Really?"

I nod. "Aye, I will."

Her eyes linger on mine for a beat longer than usual. "I think I'm going to miss you, too," she murmurs, her voice barely above a whisper. Suddenly, there's an unspoken confession hanging between us that doesn't need to be shouted to be felt.

I don't know if it's the weight of her words or the way she's looking at me like she sees more than I mean to show, but there's a pull between us that feels too strong to push away this time.

I reach up and brush a loose strand of hair behind her ear, fingers grazing her cheek. Her breath hitches. Mine does, too.

I lean in, pulled to her like gravity and unable to stop myself. The space between us shrinks, and I stop short, close enough to feel her breath on my lips. One more second and I'll lose the thread I'm barely holding onto.

twenty-eight

My mind keeps running over every moment we've shared, each one lingering like an obsession I can't cast aside. His deep laughter fills the space, making everything a little less heavy. The way his green eyes always find mine, drawing me in without even trying. And the way his words wrap around me like someone who already knows me better than I know myself, pulling me in deeper than I thought possible.

I've never felt this before. This...ache that spreads through my chest at the thought of being away from him, even for a few days. It's almost unbearable. But this can't be love, can it? It's too soon.

With the gentlest touch, he presses his lips to mine. The doubt, the uncertainty, and the cracks I've been holding together all fade away, leaving behind something whole, something perfect. My fingers curl into the fabric of Knox's shirt, as if holding on to him is the only thing keeping me tethered to reality.

Everything else falls away. All that's left is the heat of his kiss and the dizzying pull of being lost in him.

When we finally break apart, breathless and flushed, he rests his forehead against mine. My fingers graze the sharp line of his jaw, unshaven and rough beneath my touch. For a moment, everything stills. We both pause, caught in the crackling tension between us. His eyes darken, and the hunger in them is unmistakable.

"Juliette," he murmurs, the sound of my name a breathless plea and a command all at once. "What do you want?"

Every nerve in my body goes on high alert.

Him. I want *him*. I want him in a way I've never wanted anything in my life.

"I want..." I trail off, my voice trembling.

"Don't do that, Juliette," he urges. "Tell me what you want."

I meet his gaze, my heart pounding so loudly I swear he can hear it. The world shrinks to just the two of us, each beat of my pulse acting like a countdown. The words escape me in a whisper. "You," I breathe. "I want you."

The confession hangs in the air between us, a delicate truth that shifts the ground beneath our feet. Knox's eyes blaze with a fierce light. His hands tighten on my waist, the heat of his touch searing through the thin fabric of my shirt.

"Are you sure?" he asks. "Because if we do this, there's no going back. I won't be able to let you go."

The promise in his voice, the raw, unfiltered possessiveness, strikes something deep inside me, igniting a fire that starts in my chest and spreads through every inch of my body. I *need* him. Consequences be damned.

I nod, words evading me as his fingers begin to trace slow, deliberate circles on my hips. Each touch sends a jolt of heat through me. No words could match the rush of sensation flooding my body, every inch of me alive and buzzing with anticipation.

Then, without warning, he lifts me into his arms, and I let out a gasp that quickly morphs into laughter as he strides up the stairs without any trouble at all. I wrap my arms around his neck, pressing my face into the curve of his shoulder, feeling the steady beat of his pulse against mine.

In his arms, everything feels...right. The way he holds me close makes me feel safe and cherished. Like nothing could ever hurt me again.

As we cross the threshold into his room, he gently sets my feet to the floor. I take in the dimly lit space in a glance. The king-size bed, a jacket slung carelessly over the back of a chair, books stacked unevenly on the nightstand. Personal without a ton of effort.

His eyes stay locked on mine as he steps closer, his fingers brushing down my sides just enough to make me pause.

I reach up, my fingers threading through the dark strands of his hair. I pull him toward me, the kiss coming with a desperation that leaves both of us breathless. His mouth is warm, hungry, and every inch of him claims me. A low rumble vibrates through his chest, and his fingers tighten around my waist, holding me steady as my legs brush against the edge of the bed.

With a subtle nudge, I find myself sinking into the soft sheets. He follows, his body angling over mine, his weight pressing me deeper into the mattress.

He hovers above me, his muscled arms caging me in as I arch up, my body seeking the heat of his. He dips his head, his lips grazing the tender curve of my jaw, the light touch sending a tremor rippling through me. It's gentle but so intense, like a spark igniting in the deepest part of me. I tilt my head, exposing the curve of my neck, and his mouth follows the silent invitation, tracing a path of soft, feather-light kisses down to the hollow of my throat.

The warmth of his breath caresses my skin. "You're so beautiful, *mo ghràidh.*"

I tilt my head to meet his gaze. "Mm. Tell me what that means?"

His lips curl into a small smile as he leans closer. "My love."

The deep, husky rumble of his voice resounds through me as he whispers those words. A surge of heat rushes through me, and my hand reaches up, pulling him closer, unable to get enough of the way his body is mere inches from mine.

"My love," I whisper back. Our lips meet in a gentle collision, a whisper of a touch that quickly heightens into something more urgent, more demanding. His hands slide beneath my shirt, his fingers splaying across my stomach, leaving trails of heat in their wake. I press into his touch, a soft moan escaping me as his mouth claims mine, his tongue sweeping inside.

I melt into him, every curve of my body fitting against the hard planes of his, as if we were always meant to be like this. My fingers tremble, the anticipation making me fumble with the buttons of his shirt. But he's already one step ahead, his hands covering mine, stilling them with a silent command before his fingers work the buttons free. In a fluid motion, he sheds his shirt, the fabric slipping to the floor.

The low lighting spills over his chest, catching on the hard ridges of muscle like it's trying to worship him too. God, he's unreal. All broad shoulders and thick arms. My eyes drag lower, drinking in the kind of body that promises the best kind of ruin. Heat flares between my legs before I can even pretend to stop it.

He hasn't even touched me yet, and I'm already aching.

He stands there like he doesn't know what he's doing to me.

Or maybe he does, and that confidence only makes it worse. Makes me want to fall to my knees and worship every inch of him. Makes me want his hands on me, his mouth, his weight. All of it.

"Your turn," he murmurs as his fingers graze the hem of my sweater. I sit up, the world narrowing to only him. I let him pull the fabric over my head, my breath catching as he slowly removes it.

His soft lips brush against my collarbone, a sharp contrast to the roughness of his hands as they slide down my back and skillfully unclasp my bra. The straps slip down my arms like silk, leaving my skin exposed to the heat of his touch.

When the bra falls away, I feel a brief flash of vulnerability, but I force myself to resist the urge to shield myself, sitting exposed in front of him.

"Beautiful..." he whispers. But then he corrects himself, his gaze never wavering from mine. "No. Perfect. So fucking perfect."

His mouth claims mine again. This kiss is demanding, and I lose myself in the slide of his tongue against mine, the firm pressure of his lips, the scrape of his stubble against my sensitive skin.

Knox's hands are everywhere at once, caressing my breasts, my waist, my thighs. Every touch ignites a spark that dances along my spine. I arch into him, craving more, needing to feel his skin against mine.

My hands, eager and trembling, find their way to the button of his jeans. The metal clicks open, and I begin to tug the zipper down. Before I can get very far, his hand wraps around mine, his fingers firm but gentle around my wrist.

"You're sure, Juliette?"

I look up to meet his gaze, my breath shallow. "I've never

been more sure of anything," I whisper, my voice barely more than a breath. "Please, Knox."

His mouth crashes down on mine, fierce and unrelenting, swallowing any lingering hesitation. My fingers graze the outline of his arousal straining against his denim, and he shudders. He pulls away briefly, his eyes burning with a need that mirrors my own, before quickly shedding his jeans and briefs.

His hands move to my skirt, the zipper biting into my skin as he pulls it down, the motion careful and full of promise. He peels it away to reveal my bare skin, then gently slides my panties down, a rush of heat radiating between us.

"I want to feel you first," I say, my voice husky with desire. My hand slips between us, wrapping around his thick length. He's hot and smooth and impossibly hard beneath my touch.

Knox is a vision standing over me, head thrown back, jaw tight, muscles pulled taut. Every inch of him is straining, the cords in his neck standing out as he groans

"Fucking hell, Juliette." His accent thickens with each word. "You're going to be the death of me."

My fingers tighten around him with tentative strokes that grow bolder as I watch the effect I have on him. His eyes are half lidded, burning with a possessive heat that makes my core clench with anticipation.

"I've dreamt of your hands on me," he confesses, his voice dropping to a ragged whisper. "But *nothing* compares to this."

I lean forward from my spot at the edge of the bed to lick his sensitive tip. His hands tangle in my hair, a throaty moan escaping his lips as my tongue circles the velvety head. I glance up through my lashes, savoring the desire etched across his face —pupils blown wide, lips parted, chest heaving.

Just as I part my lips to take him deeper, his fingers tighten in my hair, gently pulling me back.

"Stop," he growls, voice ragged. "I need to be inside you, Juliette."

He lifts me from the edge of the bed and lays me across the sheets. His body covers mine, the delicious weight of him pressing me into the mattress as his mouth claims mine in a desperate kiss that tastes of whisky and want.

My body responds to his words with a flood of heat between my thighs as his fingers come between us, sliding through my slick heat. "Christ, you're soaked."

All I can do is moan in response as he drags his finger over my clit.

"Juliette... Condom," he groans.

I shake my head. "No, we don't need it...unless you want it." My gaze holds his, silently begging. I need him. *All* of him, with nothing between us.

His voice drops, the words a raw rasp, a whisper of control. "Say you're mine."

"I'm yours," I whimper.

He leans down, his tongue tangling with mine, stroking my craving for him. He's hard against my thigh, pressing insistently against my heated skin as he positions himself between my legs.

I reach between us, my fingers wrapping around his length, guiding him to where I need him most.

"Please," I whisper, my voice breaking on the word.

The head of his cock presses against my entrance, and he pauses.

"Look at me," he commands softly.

I open my eyes, meeting his intense gaze. The green of his irises darkens to a deep forest shade, pupils blown wide with desire.

"I want to see your face when I make you mine."

With a slow, controlled thrust, he pushes inside me, filling me completely. A gasp rips from my throat at the exquisite pressure, a delicious burn settling in as my body tries to accommodate his size. My fingers dig into his shoulders, leaving marks on his skin as I adjust.

"Fuck..." he groans, his forehead pressed against mine, breath rugged and uneven. "You feel incredible."

He stays perfectly still, his fading control evident in the trembling of his muscles beneath my fingertips. I roll my hips, taking him deeper, and a strangled sound escapes him.

"Move," I whisper against his lips. "Please, Knox."

"Say it," he demands, biting down on my bottom lip.

I whisper the words that are going to be branded into my soul. "I'm yours."

I wrap my legs high around his waist, and he withdraws almost completely before driving back in, each deliberate thrust sending a fresh wave of sensation spiraling through me. His hands grip my hips, angling me just right, hitting a spot deep inside that makes stars burst behind my eyelids.

"More," I moan, my head thrown back against the bed.

His thrusts quicken, each one deeper and more urgent than the last. I can feel the tension building, my body wound so tight I'm sure I'll shatter at any moment.

Knox's mouth trails hot, open-mouthed kisses down my neck, his teeth grazing my pulse point.

"That's it," he murmurs against my skin. "Let go for me."

His words send me over the edge. I come with a cry, my body clenching around him as waves of pleasure crash over me. Knox's rhythm falters as he watches me unravel beneath him.

"God, you're stunning like this," he rasps.

I'm still trembling with aftershocks when he begins to move again, deeper and more forceful.

"Knox," I gasp, feeling another climax building impossibly fast. "I can't—"

"You can," he insists, his voice rough from exertion. "Again, Juliette. Come for me again."

His hand slides down and starts stroking my clit with devastating precision. The dual sensation is too much. Him inside me as his fingers work their magic. His eyes hold mine captive.

I shatter again, more intensely than before, my vision blurring at the edges. This time, he follows me as he thrusts deep one final time, my name a broken prayer on his lips as he pulses inside me.

We cling to each other as we come down from the high, our bodies slick with sweat and hearts racing in tandem. Knox rolls to the side, pulling me against him. His arm wraps around me, holding me close.

He brushes a strand of hair from my face, his touch impossibly gentle.

"Are you okay?" he murmurs, pressing a kiss to my temple.

I nod, unable to find words that could possibly capture the storm of emotions swirling inside me.

"I didn't hurt you?" His voice is laced with concern.

"No," I whisper, finally finding my voice. "That was... I don't even have words."

I let my fingers trace the lines of his chest, savoring the warmth beneath my touch. "It's never been like that before," I admit.

His hand tightens around my waist, pulling me toward him with a possessive urgency that makes my breath catch. And then his lips claim mine.

Every muscle in his body is taut as he rises over me again. The way he moves, like he's on the verge of breaking, has my heart pounding harder in my chest. God, I *need* more. It's not enough.

His lips brush my ear. "Speak up, lass. If you want more, I need to hear it."

I freeze, realizing I said the words out loud. My cheeks burn with embarrassment, my pulse drumming in my ears. No turning back now.

I loop my legs around his waist again, pulling him closer, grinding my hips against him. My voice falters with desperation. "I need you. I need more of you."

He thrusts in with a devilish grin as his voice dips into a low, wicked murmur. "There she is..."

Well, fuck me.

Literally.

twenty-nine

KNOX

B eing inside her, feeling her heat, is like nothing I've ever felt. Her tight warmth pulls me in, and I get lost in the rhythm and the sweet taste of her skin.

She's so fucking beautiful when she comes with my name on her lips. The way she clenches around me, a tight, pulsing vise drawing me in. I thought I was spent, but the intensity builds, an unrestrained rush that consumes me as I spill into her again. It's the most freeing feeling I've ever known. She's here, and she's mine.

No one has ever gotten under my skin like she has. She's not just another face. She never was. No, this is something deeper, something that's slowly creeping under my skin and changing me. She doesn't demand anything. The way she laughs, the way she challenges me with a simple look, it makes me want to cross the boundaries I've created for myself. With her, I don't feel like I have to be the strong, silent one. For someone who's spent years protecting everyone else, that feels like a goddamn revelation.

I never thought I'd let anyone get this close again, but here she is, pulling me in without even trying. I can't deny it. I love her. She's the calm I didn't know I needed, but she's also the storm that rattles every single thing I thought I knew about myself.

I run my fingers through her hair, the strands slipping between my fingers, her slow, steady breaths falling in sync with mine.

The fire between us hasn't even started to die down. It's still there, simmering just beneath the surface.

I don't want to think beyond now. I can't afford to. The outside world, with its noise and responsibilities, feels so distant right now. It might as well not even exist. The only thing that matters is her, here, in my arms. I just need *this*.

Time is racing, and I'm chasing it, trying to hold on, trying to make every second count. It's too precious to waste. Every moment, every breath, every glance we share is something I want to remember. Something I'll carry with me, because once the world returns, I'll need this to keep me grounded.

"Juliette." My voice is low, just above a whisper, but she hears it. She looks up, the soft fall of her hair brushing her shoulder, her eyes locking on mine.

I open my mouth to speak, but the words get caught somewhere in my chest. I take a long, steady breath, trying to shut down the storm of thoughts raging in my head. I want to tell her everything that's been building up inside me but fear clamps down tight.

Instead, my hand moves on its own, brushing a strand of hair from her face, the simple gesture masking the weight of everything I can't say.

For a split second, there's a flicker of disappointment in her eyes, and it punches straight through me. If I say the words, there's no going back. But I need her to feel what I'm struggling to say.

I pull her into me, holding her like I can keep her here forever. I focus entirely on committing every detail to memory. The curve of her hips, the freckles dusting her nose and cheeks, her full lips that fit so perfectly with mine.

Then she shifts, her voice cutting through the silence. "What are you thinking?"

I don't want to burden her with my worries, but the pressure to be honest is suffocating. I swallow hard, forcing myself to speak, even if it's only a fraction of what's truly on my mind.

"I'm thinking that I want more time with you." My voice is rough around the edges, vulnerable in a way I rarely allow myself to be. "I'm thinking that whatever this is between us, it's not something I want to end."

Her eyes widen, searching mine. I can almost see her processing my admission, weighing it against whatever expectations she's set for herself.

"Knox..." she whispers. My name on her lips makes something in my chest constrict. She shifts beside me, propping herself up on one elbow. The sheet falls away, exposing the curve of her breast, and despite everything we've just done, heat coils in me again.

"I wasn't expecting this," she finally says. "When I came here, I thought... I don't know what I thought. But definitely not this."

"Regrets?" I ask, trying to keep my voice neutral despite the sudden tightness in my throat.

She shakes her head quickly, her eyes never leaving mine. "No. God, no, Knox. No regrets." Her fingers trace a path along my jaw, the gentle touch sending ripples of heat through me. "I just wasn't prepared for how this would feel."

I catch her hand in mine and press a kiss to her palm. The relief is almost staggering. "I'm not great at this," I admit. "The talking part."

Her laugh is soft. "I've noticed."

The weight of reality presses down, and I feel the familiar urge to pull back. The thought of watching her walk away without fighting for this, though? That's worse than any fear.

The meeting with the lawyers is only a few days away. If I can make it through that and walk away with answers, I'll finally be able to stand before her as a man who's earned the right to ask her to stay.

"I don't want to ruin this," I say, my thumb tracing the curve of her cheek. "Not with words that might come out wrong or promises I can't keep yet."

She nods, but I can see the questions swimming in her eyes, the uncertainty that's been building since we first collided. I need to give her something, even if I can't give her everything.

I pull her closer, breathing in her scent. "Let's just...be here. Right now. With each other." I press my lips to her forehead. "I swear we'll talk before you go. Really talk. About what this is."

Her body relaxes against mine, the tension leaving her shoulders. "Promise?"

"I promise." And I mean it. No more hiding behind silence or half truths. "Tonight, I just want to feel you."

She grins up at me, her voice low and teasing. "Well, if you keep talking like that, I might just hold you to it."

I can't help but chuckle, the sound slipping out before I can catch it. It feels good. Too good.

I would move mountains to have her in my life. I would burn bridges, walk through fire, sacrifice everything I've ever known just to make sure she's beside me.

I SLIP OUT OF BED, careful to avoid the soft groan of the floorboards. Juliette's still there, tangled up in the sheets and bathed in soft morning light. Her hair, dark and wild, spills across the pillow, a mess of waves that makes her look even more beautiful than she already is. For a second, I just watch her. She sighs in her sleep, her face peaceful and untouched by anything that might steal her calm.

I can't help the smile that tugs at my lips. This is something I could get used to. Waking up and finding her in my bed. Too damn perfect.

But I can't stay forever, no matter how much I want to.

I make my way down the stairs, and my eyes land on my phone sitting on the kitchen counter. Still exactly where I left it in last night's rush. It's funny how easily Juliette's managed to pull me into her orbit, making everything else feel insignificant in comparison.

A flicker of dread twists in my gut as I grab it, the screen lighting up with a string of missed texts and voicemails.

Finn.

"Shit," I mutter, swiping to call him back without bothering to listen to the messages.

"Where the hell did you disappear to last night?" his groggy voice answers.

I grin, the memory of last night playing out in my mind. "Juliette was here. Well, she's still here."

"You rascal," he says, a laugh in his voice. He knows I don't bring people home, never mind having them stay. "It's getting serious now?"

"It might be," I say, my voice a little more uncertain than I'd like. "She's, uh, upstairs right now. Haven't told her about anything yet. Is that why you called?"

"Aye, it is," Finn confirms. "Apparently, whoever Hallie was having an affair with could face some serious consequences if word got out." I hear the smirk in his voice. He's enjoying this.

I run a hand through my hair. "So let me guess. She'll agree to the divorce if I stay silent."

"You got it. And...she's not paying back anything she took on the way out."

"I don't give a shit about that. That money has been gone for over a year now. She didn't even have access to most of it. She can keep the little she got away with."

"Then it's settled, pal. We won't have anything further to discuss in the meeting later this week. I'll just have everything ready to be signed and get it to the court one last time."

A wave of relief crashes over me. It hits like a freight train, sweeping through my chest and spilling into my limbs until the tight knot of worry that's been coiled around my ribs for what feels like forever unravels, piece by piece.

I close my eyes for a second, letting it sink in. The chance to move on.

"Thanks, Finn. Seriously." The words are almost too small for the gratitude that consumes me. "I couldn't do this without you. Do whatever you have to do to get this expedited. Cost isn't an issue."

"I'm on it. Now, get back to your lass," he says, mischief lacing his words before the line goes dead.

I'm left standing there, my thoughts racing. Only a few more days. That's all it'll take. Once those papers are signed, I'll tell Juliette everything.

The soft creak of the stairs pulls me from my thoughts, and I look up, my heart skipping a beat when I see her. She's coming down slowly, wrapped in nothing but the comfort of my flannel shirt, the edges falling loosely around her petite frame, brushing the tops of her thighs. Her hair is mussed from sleep, tumbling over her shoulders. Eyes heavy, lips parted, she looks so damn soft. Bare. *Mine.*

She's breathtaking.

But it's more than just that. There's a rush of fierce possessiveness I can't brush off. Seeing her like this, in my worn shirt, looking so effortlessly at home, sparks a raw, primal need to keep her close. To shield her. To never let her slip away.

I take in the way the fabric falls off her shoulders, the material draping lazily over her skin and exposing the delicate curve of her neck. There's something unbearably alluring in the way she's claimed it as her own. I can't tear my eyes away.

"Lass, you might want to put more on before you get any closer," I warn.

She pauses at the bottom of the staircase, her eyes flashing with mischief, that wicked smile curling on her lips like she knows exactly what she's doing to me. "Oh? Why's that?"

I swallow hard, my gaze pulling helplessly to her bare legs, the smoothness of her skin. My mind can't quite sync up the innocent, sleep-tousled expression on her face with the sensual curve of her limbs. It's like a game of tug-of-war between desire and restraint.

"Because if you come any closer looking like that," I say. "I can't be held responsible for my actions."

Her laughter rings out. "Maybe that's what I was counting on," she purrs, taking a slow, deliberate step toward me.

I raise an eyebrow. "You're playing with fire, lass."

She stops inches away, the heat of her body lingering in the space between us. Her eyes lock onto mine, the spark between us undeniable. "Prove it."

The challenge in her tone is the final straw. My control snaps, and without a second thought, I close the distance between us, scoop her up, and toss her over my shoulder. Her laughter bubbles up as I head for the stairs.

"Is this proof enough?"

She laughs again, a teasing sound that drives me wild. "I think you can do better," she taunts, her hand landing with a quick slap on my arse.

I smirk, my grip tightening on her as I tilt my head just enough to let her know I'm not playing anymore. "That's it, you minx. You're in for it now."

thirty

KNOX

Juliette's been in Edinburgh for a few days now, and every call and text from her has been full of little details she couldn't wait to share. It's all the kind of stuff I never knew I'd look forward to hearing, like what coffee she tried that morning, the street musician she stopped to listen to, or some shop she stumbled into and immediately thought I'd hate.

I miss her.

I barely have time to dwell on that, because today's the day I have to sit across from Hallie. Maybe that's part of why I'm missing Juliette like this. She's the light in a part of my life that's been nothing but fucking dark.

My stomach churns as I drive through the city. My thoughts are a mess of anxiety and anticipation wrestling for dominance in my mind. All these years of legal back and forth that have drained me more than I ever admitted are about to come to a head.

This is the finish line. No more fighting over a divorce that should have been granted from the start. If all goes to plan, this is over.

I pull into a parking space and cut the engine. For a minute, I just sit there. The office building stands in front of me, its light brown sandstone exterior deceptively calm.

When I step into the lobby, my gaze lands on Finn almost immediately. He's pacing in the hushed space, every step wearing marks into the polished floor.

He notices me the second I walk in and gives me a look. I return it with a small nod. Quiet solidarity. We've been in this trench together long enough to not need words for it.

Finn scrubs a hand over his jaw when I walk up to him, exhaling hard. "You ready for this?"

I want to say no. I want to say I'd rather be anywhere else. Preferably Edinburgh in a warm hotel bed with Juliette curled against me, stealing all the covers and every last thought in my head.

Instead, I square my shoulders and say the only thing there is to say. "Aye. Ready as I'll ever be."

The click of heels cuts through the quiet like a warning shot. It's enough to send a cold ripple down my spine. Funny how after all this time, I still know her by the sound of her entrance.

A moment later, Hallie steps up beside me. She looks every bit the part of the woman who's spent years molding her image. Her long red hair cascades perfectly, the strands impossibly smooth. Her porcelain skin practically glows under the fluorescent lights. That bold scarlet lipstick she wears catches the light, giving her a sharp, predatory edge.

Everything about her screams control. Designer clothes that look more like armor than fashion, manicured nails painted crimson. It's all so...precise.

The familiar coil of irritation pulls tight in my stomach like it always does around her. I take a slow, steadying breath and lock it down tight. She doesn't get to take up that kind of space in me anymore.

Not when the only woman I can't stop thinking about is wandering through cobblestone streets, sending me photos of little bookshops and terrible pints.

I brace myself, clenching my jaw tight enough my teeth ache. On cue, the moment Hallie's gaze cuts to me, I catch the flicker of calculation in her eyes. Her mouth morphs into that razor sharp smirk that never quite reaches her eyes.

"Well, well, well," she drawls, voice thick with disdain, "look who decided to show up on time."

I bite down the first response that claws its way up my throat. *Not today.*

"Let's just get this over with," I say as Richard, her attorney, steps out of one of the offices.

"Ah," he says, his polished voice smoothing over the tension like we're all just old friends catching up. "Everyone's here. Let's head to the conference room."

Without a word, Finn and I follow Richard down the too quiet hallway. By the time we reach the conference room, every muscle in my body is wound tight.

We settle in around the oak table, and Richard takes the lead. "Shall we review the terms? I believe both parties are now on the same page."

God, I hope to hell he's right.

Finn doesn't waste a moment, his response clipped and firm. "We all know that Ms. MacKenzie has not been forthcoming about her actions. We're choosing to overlook the money she withdrew before and during the marriage and separation."

Richard leans back in his chair, exhaling slowly and nodding in agreement. "Right, to clarify," he begins, his tone still calm, "she will be keeping the funds she has withdrawn from the joint account but will not be entitled to any further maintenance or assets."

"Correct. I've drafted the agreement to ensure there is acknowledgment that the money was taken under...less than honorable circumstances," Finn continues. "It's clearly stated she won't be receiving anything else from Mr. MacKenzie. There will also be acknowledgment of the adultery on Ms. MacKenzie's part."

Richard's nod is slow, as if he's mentally checking off every box. "The language is distinct in the agreement. Let's also not forget the confidentiality clause. Ms. MacKenzie's image is at stake here. No one needs to be airing any dirty laundry post-divorce."

Finn's response is immediate. "That goes both ways."

I watch the two attorneys, both lost in their work as they lock down the final details. There's a palpable tension in the room, but then there's also Hallie. She's a different story entirely.

Her posture seems almost fragile now. Her fingers tap out an anxious rhythm on the armrest, a far cry from the practiced stillness she's known for. Her eyes dart between Richard and Finn, a mix of frustration and agitation brewing. If I know Hallie, I'm sure she's having a hard time with the fact that there's no massive payout and no fortune to cushion her landing after all this.

I wouldn't say this feels good, exactly. Just that it's...right. More like a painfully slow, hard-earned justice.

Richard breaks the awkward silence. "We're almost done here."

Hallie's barely listening. She's staring straight ahead with a tight jaw, the smallest fracture spidering across that polished mask she's worn so long that it might as well be permanent.

"I think we need to take a moment," she blurts out, her

voice cracking slightly. A sound I never thought I'd hear from her. "Richard, can we speak privately?"

Richard's gaze flickers over to her, the briefest sigh escaping him. "We've been over this. This is the best deal you're going to get, considering the circumstances."

I can't help but feel a small, almost guilty surge of satisfaction rising up. Watching her squirm and realize the control she once held is slipping from her grasp is like a pressure valve finally releasing.

"You're enjoying this, aren't you?" she sneers in my direction, her eyes narrowing. The challenge is there, but there's desperation, too. She's fighting to keep her last shred of dignity intact.

I don't even flinch because that would mean engaging, and truth be told, I'm too damn tired of this dance to bother.

I've seen Hallie at her most ruthless. I've sat across from her in boardrooms and living rooms and lawyers' offices just like this one, watching her bend situations to her will with a smile on her face while she screws over the people around her. I've watched her lie without so much as a blink and manipulate without hesitation.

But today, her mask has slipped just enough to reveal a woman clutching at whatever scraps of control she can reach for.

When Finn slides the papers toward me, the pen resting neatly on top, there's no stalling. My signature flows across the page, the final mark that seals the end of this chapter. There's nothing ceremonial about it. No flourish or drama. Just a simple, unremarkable end to something that's drained enough from me already.

Without a word, without so much as a glance in Hallie's direction, I push back from the table and walk out the door.

Some endings don't need fireworks.

Some just need to be over.

KNOX

I take a day to breathe and let the dust settle after the meetings with the lawyers, but it doesn't help. Because no matter what I do—walk the grounds, pour a dram, stare at the same numbers I've run a hundred times—I can't shake the thought of her.

Juliette.

She's not just *on* my mind. She's in it, and I need to see her. I won't rest until I'm standing in front of her again, hearing her laugh and watching her light up a room.

Convincing Callan to come with me to Edinburgh wasn't exactly a tough sell. He'd been itching for a reason to get up here, and honestly, I knew he'd be all for surprising the girls.

I step out of my hotel room, and he's already in the hallway, leaning casually against the doorframe with his usual laid-back grin plastered on his face.

"You ready, then?" he asks.

I nod. "Aye, let's get going."

With Juliette keeping me updated on every little thing she's been up to, it's easy enough figuring out where she is tonight.

The pub she mentioned isn't far, and the walk is simple. Strolling through Old Town Edinburgh is like stepping into another era with its cobblestone streets twisting through a labyrinth of narrow alleys and timeworn buildings, the air rich with the scent of whisky and hearty Scottish fare.

As we push through the pub door, warmth spills out to meet us. The place is alive with the sounds of laughter, clinking glasses, and the familiar hum of conversation.

Above the chatter, I catch Juliette's laugh, the sound cutting through all the noise like a melody I know by heart. I could pick it out in a crowd of a thousand voices.

I glance over and find her at a high-top table with Bree, their heads close together and completely lost in conversation.

A grin spreads across my face as I make my way over to them. I creep up behind Juliette, my arms sliding around her waist and pulling her in close. She lets out a soft gasp, and I lean down, my lips brushing against her ear as I whisper, "Fancy seeing you here, lass."

To my delight, she lets out a joyful shriek as she turns in her seat to wrap her arms around me.

"I'd know those arms and that voice anywhere, Captain." She grins. "What are you doing here?"

She sways slightly in her seat, a few loose strands of hair falling over her flushed cheeks. And then it hits me. She's drunk.

Not tipsy. Not a little buzzed. But completely wasted. It's evident in the way she's trying so hard to hold herself steady. Her hands keep drifting like she's in a slow-motion dance with gravity.

Her voice softens, and she slurs when she says, "Bree, look. My hot foreign boyfriend is here."

Callan's laughter rings out from behind me. "Christ, how much has she had to drink?"

Juliette glows, her lips parted in a dazed smile. Even adorable and drunk off her arse, she's sexy as hell.

Bree leans back in her chair as she gestures toward the whirlwind that is her friend. "Knox, Callan, let me introduce you to an inebriated Juliette," she says with a grin. "Prepare yourselves for wildly inaccurate life advice, exaggerated story-telling, and random acts of kindness. The most wholesome type of drunkard, this one."

I shake my head with a smirk as Callan tosses his head back with another laugh. Watching Juliette try to hold it together, her tipsy giggles escaping in bursts, is enough to make anyone's day.

Callan claps me on the shoulder. "I'll grab us some drinks, brother. Seems we have some catching up to do."

Juliette stays draped over me, her arms snug around my shoulders. If she wants to be this close, I'm more than happy to oblige.

But then, just like that, a wave of guilt crashes over me. It hits me in the pit of my stomach, a reminder of all the things I've been putting off saying to her. The things I've been carrying around, pressing down on my chest like a damn weight.

Looking at her now, eyes wide with that alcohol-fueled excitement and her laughter bubbling up... It's not right. Tonight was supposed to be the night I finally said the things I should have said weeks ago. To admit the truth that I was married. And to hopefully move forward with a clean slate. I want to tell her I'm all in, even if it means navigating a long-distance relationship until we figure it out.

I know better than to think she'll remember any of it tomorrow.

Juliette, oblivious to everything but her own joy, belts out a song only she seems to hear, drawing cheers from a nearby table. She sounds awful, the melody hardly resembling anything familiar, but she's lost in the moment and having the time of her life.

Bree, on the other hand, looks like she's about to lose her mind. Her face is a picture of desperation, hands pressed firmly to her ears as she tries to block out the noise. "Knox," she says. "I believe you're the only one with the power to stop this madness. Do something."

I give her a reassuring nod and lean down to press a quick kiss to Juliette's lips, mostly for the sake of everyone else in the pub. The second my lips meet hers, her singing halts.

When she pulls back, she tilts her head, locking eyes with me. "I was killing it, but you're forgiven for the interruption."

Goddamn, I love this woman.

"It was...intriguing. Maybe you can give me a private show later?"

She leans in a bit closer, and her voice drops an octave. "Are we talking about a concert, or like, sex?"

This version of her is a completely new kind of captivating.

"How about this... I'll take whatever you're offering."

She nods, weighing her options. "Okay, I'll think about it. Either way, we'll need glitter."

Well, that's concerning.

I shoot Bree a look of alarm, but she just waves her hand dismissively, as if she's already washing her hands of the entire situation. "Can't help you there, friend. This is your problem now."

I laugh, shaking my head. "I've had worse problems on my hands. I'll go see what's taking Callan so long, and I'm going to get you some water," I tell Juliette.

I turn to head toward the bar, but Juliette catches my sleeve with surprising dexterity for someone three sheets to the wind.

"Wait," she says, tugging me back to her, her dazed eyes

holding mine. She blinks, like she's trying to remember some-thing important before resting both hands on my chest to steady herself.

"You know what I like about you, Knox MacKenzie?" she says, voice low and overly serious. "You're so *nice*. So real. No masks. No secrets. Just Knox, all the time. You're a freaking unicorn, you know that?"

She smiles, lopsided and proud of herself for getting all that out.

Her words come at me like a physical altercation, punching me low in the gut. Then, just as fast, she spins around in her seat to face Bree again.

How am I supposed to look into her eyes, so full of trust, and tell her that I've lived a whole life she doesn't know about? Every part of me recoils at the thought of revealing my past to her.

I've been trying to shield her from anything that might break us before we even got started.

What a fucking mistake.

thirty-two

JULIETTE

I groan, pulling the sheets over my head to block out the relentless light slicing through the curtains. The buzz of the mini fridge in the corner of the hotel room pierces my eardrums. Every inch of me aches, a dull, gnawing pain settling deep in my bones. Did I really drink that much last night? I can't remember, but my body screams that I did.

I roll over, the cool sheets brushing against my skin. My foot bumps into something warm and solid. A leg. One that doesn't feel like Bree's.

I bolt upright. The motion sends a stabbing pain knifing through my skull.

"You all right, lass?" The voice is familiar. Low. Rich.

"Oh, thank god. It's you," I murmur, exhaling my relief. I let my head fall back onto the pillow, closing my eyes. "Give me a second. I need to put this puzzle together."

His velvety laugh wraps around me. The tension in my chest loosens almost immediately. The night starts filtering back in pieces. Me with Bree, Knox and Callan showing up, then...nothing. Just a hazy fog where my memory should be.

"I don't know what got into me. I'm not usually that reckless."

Well, I do know what got into me. I got caught up in not having to worry about being all *prim and proper*. I wish I could say Bree's just a bad influence, but if I'm remembering correctly, she didn't drink much at all.

I turn my head, and there's Knox in all his Greek god glory, his bare chest rising and falling with each steady breath. The faint light from the window highlights the sharp lines of his jaw, the muscles in his shoulders, and the faint dusting of dark hair trailing down his chest.

And then there's me, looking like I lost a fight with a hurricane.

"Reckless, huh?" he teases. "Is that what we're calling it?"

"Oh my gosh, did Bree get back to the room okay?" I blurt.

"Aye, she was in much better shape than you. Callan made sure she got in safely."

"Ugh, you guys are the best. I'm officially the worst for ditching her. No offense to you or anything. I'm sure you were great company."

Another laugh rumbles from him, the sound reverberating through the room. Honestly, it's doing more for my hangover than any painkiller ever could. "It was Bree's idea to have you stay with me, lass. She didn't want to be responsible for you."

"Hmph. Fair enough," I grumble, pulling the blanket up a little higher and pretending it can shield me from the embarrassment that's now crawling up my neck.

"Want me to order some breakfast for the room?" he asks.

"Yes, please. Anything with carbs and sugar," I say quickly, because if I stop to think about it, I might spiral back into embarrassment. Right now, the thought of breakfast is the most appealing thing in the world.

He leans in, pressing a kiss to my forehead. "You got it."

My breath catches, but he's already moving, stretching as he rises from the bed. My eyes follow on instinct, tracing the smooth pull of muscle beneath his skin. I try to look away, but it's impossible. It's like my gaze is magnetized to the way his briefs hug his hips, just tight enough to remind me of what's underneath, but not enough to give it all away.

Bummer.

He reaches for his shirt, and my brain short circuits. Those hands. Those beautiful, strong hands that could probably break me in half but choose to worship me instead. I imagine them trailing over my skin, gripping my hips, teasing the sensitive flesh of my inner thighs...

Nope, not going there. I'm already flushed and squirming just from the sight of them. *Get it together, Juliette.* The man is putting on a shirt, not giving you a private show.

Although, I certainly wouldn't object.

Knox glances over his shoulder, catching me staring. His brow lifts just enough to say *caught you.* I'm too foggy to pretend otherwise.

"You sure you just want carbs and sugar, lass?" he teases, his voice dipping low enough for heat to lick up my spine. "You see something else you like?"

Damn him.

I roll my eyes, yanking the sheet back over my head to hide the traitorous grin stretching across my lips. "You *know* I do," I grumble.

He stays by my side all morning, handling things in that steady, no-nonsense way of his. He doesn't ask me how I'm feeling, probably because it's obvious. Instead, he moves around the room quietly, making sure I have everything I need like it's second nature.

Meanwhile, I do my best impression of a useless lump under the covers, groaning dramatically every time the light shifts, or my headache reminds me why I should never mix cocktails. At one point, I let out an especially pitiful whimper, and without a word, he hands me a glass of water.

But eventually, the inevitable happens.

He has to leave.

At the door, he hesitates with his back to me, his hand braced against the frame.

"Juliette," he says. "Before I go..."

The sudden vulnerability in his voice makes me look up. He spins toward me, the expression on his face catching me completely off guard. His eyes hold an openness I've never seen before.

I sit up straighter, pulling the sheets around me. "Yeah?"

He doesn't answer. He moves in three long strides that eat up the space until his calloused hands are framing my face and tilting it up like I'm something precious.

His mouth crashes against mine, all heat and hunger. He tastes like coffee as his tongue slides against mine, my hands clutching his forearms to hold on while he unravels me piece by piece.

There's nothing careful in the way he kisses me. It's raw. Starved. Like he's spent every second up until now convincing himself not to do this and just lost the fight.

When he finally pulls back, we're both breathing hard. His forehead rests against mine, and there's a question in his eyes.

His thumb traces my bottom lip. "What are we doing here?"

My throat goes dry, and I'm suddenly very aware of my tangled hair, my smudged makeup, and the fact that I'm wearing nothing but his T-shirt.

"What do you mean?" I ask, though I know exactly what he means. I just need a second to prepare for this conversation I've been simultaneously craving and dreading.

His jaw tightens, then relaxes, like he's carefully choosing his words.

"I mean, Juliette, what happens when you go back to Kentucky? I need to know if this is just temporary for you."

I swallow hard, my hangover suddenly the least of my concerns. The sheets feel suffocating now, too hot, too tight around me, like they're closing in.

"Knox, I—"

"Because it's more for me," he continues, his voice dropping to a whisper. "So much more."

So much more.

The weight of those three simple words seems to fill the entire room. I don't know why I thought I would be able to guard myself against this moment. When feelings become real and choices have consequences. I never stood a chance.

"I don't need a solid answer right now," he says, his voice still low. "I just need to know if you see this going further."

I can't deny that he makes me feel alive. That he's become woven into the fabric of my days in a way I never imagined. I wake up thinking of him, lose track of time when we're together, and find myself caught up in the way he looks at me like I'm the only thing that matters.

There's no blueprint for this. No roadmap for what we're doing. We're in uncharted territory with no guarantees, no promises. The thought of leaving this behind, of going back to Kentucky without at least *trying*, feels more and more unbearable. When I look at him, I wonder if I can really go back.

Do I even want to?

The thought of staying isn't something I need to think twice about anymore. There's no hesitation when I look up at him. I want this. I want him.

"I do," I whisper.

The corners of his mouth twitch into a soft smile, but there's a fire in his eyes, a flicker of relief.

"There's a lot I want to talk to you about," he says, his gaze drifting toward the door. "But...will you come home with me after the party at the distillery tonight? We'll talk."

"Okay," I reply, my voice steady, though my heart is still racing. "I'll be there."

His lips brush mine in this softest kiss, and my entire body leans into the sensation, seeking more. He pulls back too soon, leaving me chasing the warmth of his mouth.

"Rest up," he says, standing. "I'll see you tonight."

The door clicks shut behind him and silence rushes in. I exhale, flopping back against the bed, staring at the ceiling as my emotions churn in a tangled mess.

I really need to pull myself together, head back to my actual hotel room, and check on Bree.

But first, I need to find my pants.

When I finally drag myself down the hall, it's like wading through molasses. My body is sluggish, my mind clouded with the remnants of last night's chaos. When I finally push open the door to our room, the sharp zip of a suitcase fills the air. Bree is perched on the edge of the bed, her eyes widening the moment she spots me.

"Well, well, well. Look what the cat dragged in," she says with a smirk. She's entirely too chipper for the state I'm in.

I groan, dropping my purse onto the bed before flopping down beside her. "Please, spare me the jokes. My head is still pounding."

She laughs, patting my leg like I'm some poor, helpless creature before standing up and resuming her mission to cram an alarming number of items into her suitcase. "Sounds like you had an eventful night, though. Ready to rejoin the land of the living? Also, I've got a plane to catch."

I let out a dramatic sigh. "Don't remind me. I can't believe it's already time for you to leave."

She nods. "Ugh, I know. This week went by so fast. Have you thought about when you're coming home?"

That question has been haunting me for weeks now, nagging at the back of my mind. The thought of going back isn't just overwhelming, especially after the conversation I just had with Knox, but *heavy*. I'll need to return at some point, no matter what happens. Just...not yet.

For the first time in years, I'm not trying to twist myself into something more polished or quieter or easier to love. I'm not editing who I am to fit into someone else's version of enough. With Knox, I've never been anything but myself. And he's never flinched. Never asked me to be less. That means something.

I swallow, forcing a small shrug. "I don't know, Bree," I admit. "I think I might stay a few more weeks and see where things go from there."

Her expression doesn't shift right away. She studies me, turning my words over in her mind. And then, after a beat, she smiles. A soft, knowing curve of her lips. "You're not coming home, Jules. I know it. You're so happy here."

Tears burn hot behind my eyes, threatening to spill if I so much as open my mouth. If I actually decide to stay, that means leaving Bree behind. And that scares the hell out of me.

She's been my constant. The one person who's always been there, no matter how many times I've crashed and burned through heartbreak and grief. She's never once made me feel like I had to do it alone, even when I thought I wanted to.

I'm terrified of choosing Knox and losing the person who's been my family when I felt like I had none. But what's the alternative? Going back and pretending that my heart isn't somewhere else?

I squeeze my eyes shut, forcing a slow breath.

"Don't you dare," she warns. "You better not be crying over the idea of staying in a breathtaking country with a man who worships the ground you walk on. Especially when your aunt lives right down the street. You deserve this, Juliette. Every bit of it. I need you to believe that."

The words do nothing to stop the tears slipping down my cheeks. She pulls me into a fierce hug, her arms tight like she's trying to shove all the things we haven't said into this one embrace, willing them into my bones.

She finally pulls away with a soft sigh. "I, on the other hand, need to get to the airport since we all know Dillon has been completely useless without me this week."

It's the kind of thing Bree would normally say with a dramatic eye roll or a smirk, but the look in her eyes gives me pause. There's a flicker of dread, too quick to really pin it down, before she glances away. Whatever it was doesn't match the teasing tone in her voice.

I don't like it, and I want to push, but I don't.

Instead, I take a deep breath and swipe away the tears on my cheeks with the back of my hand. "Well, this isn't goodbye. I'm sure I'll see you soon, no matter what I decide to do."

The Bree I know snaps back into place and rolls her eyes, the smile on her face full of affection. "As if I'd give you a choice."

thirty-three

JULIETTE

Bree's on a plane, and I'm on a train moving in the opposite direction. The world outside is a blur of green and brown, the trees and fields blending into streaks as my questions spin faster than the landscape.

Am I ready for what comes next? Do I know Knox well enough to take that leap, or am I just afraid of what happens if I let go of this? Of him?

Staying means sacrifice, and I've made sacrifices before, only to watch them drain me dry. With James, I gave away parts of myself for reasons that never felt right, then never got back what I put in.

But Knox isn't James.

Knox just wants *me*. Not some refined version he can show off at parties or introduce to business associates.

Relief moves through me at a slow and steady pace, untangling the tight ache of doubt.

What I need is a night with him. No noise. No interruptions. Just the two of us in a room, figuring out whatever *this* is.

However, it'll have to wait.

Tonight is for celebrating Knox and Callan's magazine feature.

Getting ready for a night out used to feel like preparing for battle. I'd agonize over every detail, triple-checking my appearance while worrying about embarrassing James or not measuring up certain expectations. Each curl had to be perfect, each accessory chosen to impress his mother or his colleagues. The ritual was exhausting.

But tonight, I'm getting ready for a man who looks at me like I'm already his favorite thing in the room.

I'm in love with this dress. The sleek, midnight gown wraps around me like it was crafted for my body, hugging every curve. It's luxurious, made to make me feel like the best version of myself. Bree practically forced me into buying it, and I'm glad she did. It's like it was tailor-made for nights like this.

The car glides along winding roads, but there's nothing steady about the way my heart won't sit still. My fingers grip the champagne flute more out of habit than need, its contents forgotten except for the occasional sip that does little to calm the nervous excitement rising to the surface.

"It was so nice for Knox to send a car for us," I say, trying to sound casual, but my voice comes out a little breathier than I'd like.

Aunt Rose leans back in her seat, flashing me a teasing grin. "I'm only getting the perks because I'm stuck with you," she says, poking my arm. "Pretty sure this fancy ride wasn't meant for an old bird like me."

The car begins to slow, rounding the final curve in the road. The distillery's stone façade rises against the dusky sky. My pulse quickens as I spot a familiar figure through the car window, his broad shoulders framed perfectly by the setting sun.

Then he starts walking toward us and smiles. That slow curve of his mouth is aimed straight at me like a dare. My lungs forget their job entirely. I could drown in that smile.

But it's when my gaze drops that I feel the real hit.

He's wearing a kilt.

Oh. *Oh.*

The deep greens and blues of the tartan shift with every unhurried step, pleats rippling, teasing at the strength of his thighs that are built for things I probably shouldn't be thinking about in front of my aunt.

Heat surges up my neck, spilling into my cheeks, my chest, everywhere, really, because Knox MacKenzie in a kilt? Not something I was prepared for. This blessed view should be illegal.

The driver opens the door, and Knox is right there, his hand extended to help me out. His gaze travels from my face, down the length of my dress and back up again, lingering in all the places that make my skin flush hotter.

He leans in, his lips brushing mine in a soft, lingering kiss that leaves a spark in its wake. "You look absolutely stunning."

I'm not sure where to put my hands. Or my eyes. Or how to form a coherent thought.

"Thank you," I manage, my voice barely more than a whisper. "You look...incredible."

That's an understatement. The man is devastating.

His smile deepens at my reaction and damn it, there's that dimple. The one that only shows up when he's genuinely amused or trying to kill me with charm. Without missing a beat, he extends his other hand to help Aunt Rose from the car. "And you look lovely as well, Rose."

"Thank you," she says, her eyes twinkling with mischief as she glances between us. "Though I'm starting to feel like a bit of a third wheel."

Knox laughs, the sound warm and rich. "Never. But I may need to steal your niece away for a bit."

"I'd be disappointed if you didn't," she replies with a wink that makes me want to crawl under the car. Then, she catches sight of a colleague nearby and slips off to leave me standing beside Knox.

I slip my arm through his. "I don't know why, but I wasn't expecting the kilt."

"Aye? We usually wear them to more formal events." He smirks, that mischievous glint dancing in his eyes. "What do you think?"

I tilt my head, letting my gaze trail down and back up, deliberately slow. "I think..." I lean in just a little, dropping my voice to a murmur meant just for him. "That you'll be taking me home later and leaving that on."

My fingers reach out, grazing the tartan pattern. The wool is smooth under my touch, the colors rich. I hold his gaze, feeling the shift in the air between us.

"I think you might be mistaken, lass," he murmurs. "I've a mind to take it off, along with that sinful dress you're wearing."

I fight to keep my composure, but his low, deep laugh rumbles through me, vibrating in my chest and sending a shiver of pure, untamed desire straight through every nerve.

His hand slides to the small of my back, the warmth of his palm seeping through the fabric of my dress as he leads me inside.

The moment we step into the lounge, the sheer grandeur of it draws my attention away from the tension between us. Tartan banners drape from every corner, laughter weaving through the clink of glasses. Somewhere beneath it all, music thrums like a heartbeat. Knox's hand stays firm on my back as we navigate the crowd. He moves with ease, pausing every now and then to introduce me to someone new, his voice a low murmur in the sea of chatter. The room is full of strangers, but with his voice anchoring me, I don't feel lost or out of place. Not with him.

"Knox, there you are." A deep, booming voice cuts through the noise. I turn just as a man with a friendly grin steps toward us, a striking blonde woman at his side.

"Finn, Elsie, I'm so glad you're here." Knox steps forward to greet them, leaning in to place a kiss on Elsie's cheek before he turns back to me. "This is Juliette."

Finn extends his hand. "So nice to finally meet you. I've heard quite a bit about you."

"Oh?" I arch a brow, letting my gaze slide to Knox.

He smirks, but there's something undeniably fond in the way he looks at Finn. "Finn and I grew up together," he says. "I wouldn't be where I am today without him. Or his lovely wife."

Elsie rolls her eyes at the compliment. "Enough with the flattery," she teases. "It's wonderful to meet you, Juliette."

"It's great to meet both of you," I reply. "Hopefully, we'll get a chance to sit and chat later?"

"I'd love that," Elsie says, her hand brushing lightly over my forearm as she leans in closer. "Now, I need a drink."

Finn chuckles, his arm snaking around her waist as he steers her toward the bar. "Excuse us for a bit," he says over his shoulder.

"They seem fantastic."

Knox nods. "Aye, they are. The best, really." Then, as if shaking off whatever thought had momentarily taken hold, his eyes flicker over to the long table where caterers are setting up. "Why don't we get something to eat and drink before it's gone?"

The table is a feast for the senses with heaping platters and fresh seafood, delicate finger foods arranged like art. Everything looks too beautiful to eat, but the moment I pop one in my mouth, the explosion of flavor reminds me that beauty is only half the appeal.

After a quick scan of the room, I spot Callan and his *friend*, Jamie, tucked away in a quiet corner, drinks in hand. Without a word, Knox's hand slides up beneath the curtain of my hair, fingers brushing the back of my neck as he gently steers me toward them.

The night unfolds around us in a blur of laughter and stories. Somehow, I slip right into the fold, like I've always belonged here, like I'm not the new girl still learning everyone's names. But right now, all I need is a glass of water to chase away the dryness in my throat. Knox is mid conversation, and I don't want to interrupt.

Rising onto my tiptoes, I lean in, close enough close enough to breathe in his woodsy scent. "I'm going to grab another drink. You keep talking!" I yell over the noise.

He catches my hand in a quick, reassuring squeeze as he nods and turns back to his conversation, never missing a beat.

I weave through the crowd, dodging a few overenthusiastic hand gestures and sidestepping a server carrying a precarious tower of champagne flutes. Elsie and Finn are at the bar, deep in conversation. Elsie spots me first, lifting her glass in greeting.

"Drink?" she offers, tilting her chin toward the bartender.

I shake my head. "Just water for now."

The bartender hands me a glass, and I settle in beside Elsie. Mid sip something catches my eye. Or rather, *someone*.

A woman moves through the crowd like she owns the room, her presence impossible to ignore. Her hair is a cascade of fire under the dim lighting, and there's a sharpness to the way she carries herself. Graceful, but with an edge. I can tell she's used to getting exactly what she wants.

And right now, she wants Knox.

It's in the way her eyes linger on him, the way she subtly shifts her posture to draw him in, like a cat toying with its prey. Her throaty, teasing laugh slips through the air, just loud enough to reach him. He may not be fully aware of it, but she's already got him in her sights.

My grip tightens around my glass as she nears him. Nothing about the way she moves is coincidental. There's precision to the way she closes the space between them, like a chess piece sliding into place.

Knox glances up just as she reaches him and recognition flashes across his face.

The knot in my stomach pulls tight.

I can tell they're acquainted by the way their bodies align, the ease of their proximity, but Knox's expression is anything but welcoming. His jaw tightens, a muscle ticking beneath his skin. And his eyes, usually so warm when they land on me, are narrow and hard. There's a flash of darkness beneath the surface. Not just tension. Fury. Maybe even something worse.

The air shifts, thickening around them, crackling with an energy I don't understand.

I don't wait for it to make sense. The unease that curls in my stomach turns urgent, and I know I can't stay seated any longer. Without thinking, I stand and head in their direction.

Knox is still. Too still. His body, taut with restraint, doesn't give an inch. The woman, though, is the opposite. Liquid confidence. A slow tilt of her head. A curve of her lips.

A cold shiver slithers across my skin.

Something's wrong.

I slip my hand into his, but the moment our fingers touch,

his entire body goes rigid. Tension coils beneath his skin like he's holding back a surge of emotion too volatile to let loose.

For a fleeting second, I wonder if *I'm* the problem. Then his eyes find mine and there's a shift. Just barely, but enough. The hard edge in his gaze dulls, a silent message passing between us. Whatever this is, he doesn't want me in the crossfire.

The woman in front of me is even more striking up close. Her features are harsh, almost sculpted. High cheekbones and arched eyebrows. It's the way she looks at me—cool, assessing, dismissive—that sends a slow prickle of unease down my spine.

"And who would this be?" Her voice is laced with something sweetly poisonous as her gaze drags over me, unimpressed.

Knox's grip tightens around mine. "Hallie. Don't."

The way Knox says her name carries a weight I can't ignore, a warning laced with cold finality.

She doesn't flinch. If anything, that smirk of hers only becomes more provoking. It's like she knows exactly how to push his buttons, and now, she's just twisting the knife for fun.

I don't pull my hand away, even as his fingers flex like he's fighting with himself.

"Don't what?" she asks, her voice low and silky, the tilt of her head making the innocence sound entirely calculated. "I was just being polite."

With a practiced grace, she extends her hand, the motion almost too smooth.

"Hello," she says, her lips curving into something that barely resembles a smile. "I'm Hallie MacKenzie. Knox's *wife*."

JULIETTE

Wife.

The word slams into me, knocking the air from my lungs, impossible to unhear. It echoes in louder than the music, louder than the blood roaring in my ears. My breath catches and my stomach drops so fast it feels like I've missed a step on solid ground.

I blink, once, twice, as if that might clear it away. As if I didn't just hear what I think I did.

I should say something. Laugh it off. Demand the truth. Scream, maybe.

Or, I could turn around, lose myself in the sea of strangers and noise, and pretend this moment never happened.

Pretend I never cared.

My fingers slip from his and his warmth is gone in an instant, like it was never really mine to hold. A chill slips underneath my skin, curling around my spine, sinking into the hollows of my chest.

I don't take the woman's outstretched hand. I can't.

Hallie's voice still lingers in the space between us, sweet as venom, daring me to react. My heart stutters, then slams into a breakneck speed, each beat rattling through me like a warning.

Something breaks inside me, and it's not a clean snap. No, it's a messy, splintering pain that fractures through my chest, like my ribs are being pried apart, making room for the heartache threatening to consume me.

And still, I stand here shaking as the swell rises, slow and cruel, threatening to drag me under.

Sadness. Anger. Humiliation.

They slam into me in one brutal, tangled wave, scraping me raw from the inside out.

I can't breathe.

Tears sting, hot and fast, but I dig my teeth into the soft flesh of my cheek, hard enough to taste blood. I won't give *her* the satisfaction. I won't fall apart. Not here. Not in front of him.

I need to escape this suffocating space before it swallows me whole.

Knox's eyes find mine, and there's a flicker of panic amidst the storm.

I can't look at him. Not when the ground's cracked open beneath me, not when everything I thought I knew has turned to dust. My body moves before my brain catches up, one shaky step back, just enough to break the invisible thread still tying us together.

I need space. Air. Anything that isn't thick with this wreckage. I don't want an explanation. Don't want excuses or half truths wrapped in pretty words.

His wife.

I was going to leave the life I know behind for him.

I was ready to uproot everything—my routines, my safety, my little corner of the world—because I thought what we were building was real. I gave him the fragile parts of me that should have been kept locked away.

And all this time, he was hiding her.

How many times did he look me in the eye and choose silence? God, I feel stupid. I feel *used*.

I thought he would be the one who wasn't like James. The one who didn't twist the truth into something unrecognizable. Who wouldn't play games with my trust or make me question what was real.

I let myself believe Knox was different. That maybe he was the safe place I've been missing.

But this? This is everything I ran from. The half truths. The secrets. The gut punch betrayal dressed up in charm and gentle touches.

His hand shoots out, desperate to catch what's already slipping through his fingers.

I rip my arm back like it burns. And maybe it does, because that touch feels poisonous now.

"No." The word slips from my lips, low and unwavering. Though inside, I am anything but steady. "You don't get to touch me."

I want it to sound strong. I *need* it to sound like I have control. But even as I say it, more cracks form.

I take another step back. When my gaze finally locks with his, the world tilts. Everything blurs at the edges, all color and sound draining from the room until there's nothing left but the thrum of my heartbeat and the shattered look on Knox's face.

His eyes are locked on mine, wide and desperate, and in that gaze, I see it all. The shock. The regret. The way everything is crumbling between us.

My heart clenches—one last tether straining to hold on— and then...it breaks.

The hurt is too deep to fix with apologies or explanations.

It's not even anger that's taking me under. It's that bone-deep ache of being invisible to someone you bared your soul to. Of realizing you were standing in plain sight and somehow still never *seen*.

My gaze shifts to Hallie, and she's watching me with that smug smile that says she's already won. The icy gleam in her eyes sends a chill crawling up my spine. She's been waiting for this, and I walked straight into it, thinking I was safe.

God, what a mistake.

I turn away so fast I almost trip over my own feet. The weight of their eyes on my back is smothering, but there's nothing left to say.

I shove at the heavy doors, and they fly open with a groan, crashing against the frame. The cold air hits like a slap, forcing its way into my lungs as I stumble out into the dark.

My breath comes in jagged bursts, each inhale more useless than the last. My chest rises, falls, then clenches tight like my heart might actually break free. I press a hand to it, as if I can hold it in. As if I can stop myself from coming apart.

I can't.

The first sob barrels through me, loud and wrecked and desperate. And once it starts, there's no stopping it.

The dam splits wide open, and I shatter right there on the pavement, bent at the waist, fists clenched, knees threatening to give out. My cries come out broken, ripped straight from the center of me, wave after wave of grief and betrayal crashing through every inch of my body.

It's not just heartbreak.

It's devastation.

"Juliette?"

The voice is slightly unfamiliar yet soothing. I turn my

head, everything a blur through the sheen of tears, and there's Elsie.

She crouches beside me, not reaching for me, just there. Her face is etched with worry, her brows pulled tight. "Let us take you home, love."

I nod with a slow, heavy motion. Elsie takes my hand, guiding me toward the car where Finn is already standing by the door waiting for us. She settles in beside me in the back seat.

I barely know her, but right now, she's a lifeline.

"Juliette," she begins, her voice gentle but firm. "I'm not going to defend him. He was warned. But just know, he wouldn't be with you if he wasn't fully committed. That witch hasn't been in his life for a long time now."

Part of me wants to believe her and sink into the comfort of her words. But then there's this other persistent part that won't let go. The truth, whatever version of it this is, feels so far out of reach.

Elsie's looking at me, waiting for a response, but I can't find the right words to match the tangled mess in my chest.

If Knox really cares, if this *us* was as real as he made me believe, then why did he keep this from me? Instead, he let me stumble into this blind, like I was a pawn in some game I wasn't supposed to understand.

Did he think I wouldn't care? Or worse, was this never as real for him as it was for me? He was so sure of us this morning, all those sweet words about how this was *so much more*. Yet here I am, standing in the wreckage of a truth I never saw coming.

I know I'll hear him out. It's the only thing I can do, even though I'm dreading it. I want to believe that maybe he can explain himself. The idea of it turns my stomach, but still, I'll listen. I won't be able to bring myself to walk away without hearing his side. Even if I'm not sure I'll ever look at him the same way again.

The car slows as we near the cottage, the gravel crunching under the tires, each pop marking the end of the ride. When we finally stop, I murmur a quiet thanks, then swing the door open.

I step out, my feet sinking into the earth, and for a second, the wind wraps around me, lifting my hair and stirring an odd mix of freedom and weight inside me, like I'm standing at the edge of a cliff and the world is both holding me up and threatening to drop me at the same time.

Then, I notice the direction of the breeze, blowing eastward, as if the universe itself is trying to guide me back to him. It's a subtle whisper, and I can almost hear it telling me to give in to what's been clawing at me since the moment I left.

I feel the pull, the longing. But it's not enough to change my course.

All I can think of is heading west. Away from it all. Away from him.

I laugh, but it's a bitter, empty sound. It's the laugh of someone who thought they could outrun their own heart. All this fearlessness, this idea that I could handle it all on my own... It's led me right here, back to more heartache.

KNOX

"What the hell is wrong with you?" I spit the words like they're poison.

The anger inside me isn't just a feeling. It's a goddamn wildfire, starting slow, crawling, waiting. But the moment it ignites, it's consuming, burning everything in its path. I've never hated anyone, not even when Hallie pulled me into her mess of lies and dragged me under. But Juliette? That's the line. She should've never been brought into this.

Before I can say anything else, Callan moves in like a shadow, planting himself between us. "Knox. Let's take this to your office, aye?"

I swallow back the fire in my chest. Barely. The taste of it lingers, burning the back of my throat. I give a clipped nod and turn toward the office.

I should be chasing after Juliette and making sure she's all right. Finn's got her though, and she doesn't need me right now. She made that very fucking clear. I can't blame her for it.

I slam my office door shut behind us, the sound reverberating through the room. Callan stays just inside the doorway, arms crossed, every inch of him radiating *don't be a dumb bastard*. His version of damage control.

My eyes snap to Hallie, and there it is. That goddamn smirk. The one that's always been her sharpest weapon. My hands curl into fists at my sides, muscles coiled tight and straining against the need to *do* something.

She wants a reaction, so I don't. Like hell am I giving her that satisfaction.

"Why are you here?"

Hallie tilts her head. "Oh, I just thought I'd stop by the big party is all. There's a paper you forgot to sign the other day, and I thought I'd help you out by bringing it by."

I narrow my eyes, disgust rising in my gut. "Bullshit. If there was anything I forgot, Finn would've handled it."

She laughs, sweet but hollow. She thinks she's untouchable. "Come on. Don't act like you're too busy to deal with a little paperwork."

My jaw tightens. I'm not giving into this.

Her grin widens, and her voice drips with mockery. "Oh, fine. I wanted to congratulate you, Knox. See how you're coping with our *heartbreaking*, hardly finalized divorce and check out the American who's got you all twisted up. She's quite pretty, isn't she? In that...simple sort of way."

My blood runs cold before surging hot again. There it is. The real reason she showed up.

"Oh, struck a nerve, have I?" Her eyes gleam with satisfaction. "I simply wanted to meet the woman who's captured your attention."

Callan steps in then, not a trace of his usual dry humor anywhere. Just cool, unflinching detachment. "That's enough, Hallie."

She blinks, just for a second, like she wasn't expecting *him* to be the one to shut her down.

Callan doesn't so much as flinch. "You've had your moment. Said your piece. Now get the hell out."

She opens her mouth, probably to toss out some parting shot, but Callan cuts her off.

"And just so we're clear?" His brows lift, voice still maddeningly calm. "You show up here again, start lurking around, or pull any of this petty, desperate bullshit, we won't be having another little chat. We'll be filing harassment charges."

The briefest flash of surprise crosses her face before she buries it behind that smug grin again. She knows Callan's not bluffing, but she recovers fast. She's danced this fucking waltz a thousand times before and never once missed a step.

She turns on her heel, but not without twisting the knife one last time. She glances back over her shoulder, eyes glinting with a satisfaction that makes my stomach turn.

"Good luck with *Juliette*."

And then she's gone, the sound of her heels clicking down the hall and echoing long after her shadow disappears.

Without thinking, I slam my fist down on the desk. The crack of bone against wood ricochets through the room. Papers jump. A pen rolls to the edge. My phone clatters to the floor.

"Fuck!"

Callan winces, but he doesn't say anything. He just watches me for a beat before stepping back like he's giving me space to bleed out quietly.

"You can't let her get to you like this, Knox." There's steel threaded through his voice now. "It's exactly what she wants."

Yeah. I know that. I know it in my fucking bones. But knowing it doesn't stop the guilt from churning through me.

The image of Juliette's face—hurt, blindsided, and devastated—replays in my mind over and over. The guilt sinks deeper. I can barely breathe. The air's too thick with everything I've fucked up.

The damage is done.

It's like I'm being torn apart from the inside out. In the dizzying haze of it all, my voice cracks. "I can't lose her, Cal."

The rage that drives me, that fire burning in my chest, fizzles out, leaving behind nothing but the bitter, awful truth.

Callan shifts uncomfortably. "I don't know what to say," he admits. "You need to talk to Juliette."

I don't answer right away. I already know she won't listen to me. Her past is etched with scars. Far too much pain and too many broken promises exist in those planes. I've spent hours, days, *weeks* trying to prove I'm nothing like the ones who've torn her apart. But now? Now I've done something worse. I've shattered her trust. I've become another person she can't rely on.

"You didn't see her face. Hear what she said. I've ruined everything."

His gaze hardens, but his voice stays steady. "You're not the bastard Hallie's trying to paint you as. Yeah, you screwed up by not coming clean sooner, but she deserves to hear the truth from you now."

His words spark the smallest flicker of hope, but it dies almost instantly, smothered by the weight of doubt. I don't see how this can be fixed.

"The truth is that I'm married." The words come out flat. "And I chose not to tell her. I thought I could get my shit together, get things straight before I dragged her into it...but it backfired."

I press on, my voice a little rougher now. "You know why Juliette's single? Her ex-fiancé cheated on her, Cal. Made her feel small. Made her feel *less than*. And now I'm just another goddamn liar in a long line of them."

Cal's face tightens with a wince. He didn't know that part of her story, and the silence that follows scrapes down my spine like sandpaper. My jaw clenches so hard it aches, but it's the resentment toward *myself* that really gets me.

"And now you see the problem," I mutter, my frustrations spilling out as I rub a hand over my face and try to push the fury out of my system. "Thanks for stepping in, Cal. I need to call Finn and figure out where they ended up. You get back to the party. This was supposed to be a good night."

He doesn't argue. Doesn't offer more advice or throw me a tired cliché about how I'll figure it out. He claps a hand on my shoulder before walking out, swinging the door shut behind him.

I stare at it for half a second before dragging in a breath. There's no use standing here like an idiot.

I bend down, scoop my phone off the floor where it landed, and dial Finn's number.

But it's not Finn who answers. It's Elsie.

And shit, she is *furious*.

"What the hell is wrong with you?" she snaps. "I warned you, Knox. I *warned* you what would happen if you kept lying to her."

Her voice is shrewd enough to cut through bone, every word landing like a slap I absolutely deserve. "I know heartbreak when I see it, and what she's going through right now? It's a hundred times worse. I don't even know how you let it get this far, but Christ, you've made an absolute mess."

"I thought I was protecting her."

There's a pause. Then a low, humorless laugh. "Protecting her?" she echoes. "She's already *in* it, Knox. She's been in your mess since the second she let you close enough to matter."

Every word hits dead center. Because she's right.

My throat burns when I finally say it. Raw, real, and too goddamn late.

"I love her, Elsie."

There's a long pause on the other end. "You, what?"

"I love her." I say it again, this time with more conviction. "Neither of us saw it coming. We were just taking it one day at a time, and I don't know, Els. I'm not the type to believe in the whole soulmate thing, but with her...it kind of feels like that."

Her silence lingers a moment longer, but when she speaks again, her biting tone is still there, even if the edge has softened a little. "Loving her doesn't change the fact that you should've been honest about Hallie from the start."

"I know," I mutter. "I was scared that if I told her, she wouldn't give us a chance." Saying it out loud makes it worse. The truth tastes like ash, bitter and dry. "I thought I could handle the divorce quietly and then come clean once everything was sorted."

There's a long sigh from Elsie. It's heavy and filled with frustration, but it also holds that thread of affection for me despite everything. "You're my friend, Knox, and I love you like a brother, but what you did was selfish. You robbed Juliette of the choice to make her own decision."

The weight of her words hits harder than anything else tonight. I've been the one keeping Juliette at arm's length, all in the name of "protecting" her. When, in reality, I've just been guarding my own damn fears.

"I know," I say again. "I fucked up." I'm choking on that simple truth, and somehow, it doesn't seem like enough. It'll never be enough.

"We took her back to her aunt's," Elsie says. "I can't tell you whether she wants to see you, Knox. I don't know her well enough to know that."

I swallow hard. "Thanks, Elsie. Tell Finn thanks, too, even though I know I'm on speaker and he's listening."

Finn's voice comes through the line. "Aye, I'm here. Keep us posted."

The call ends, but I'm left standing here, more lost than ever. I've fucked everything up, and now I have to fix it somehow.

I need air.

My feet carry me out into the night, past the muffled sounds of the party still going on inside. I don't even realize where I'm headed until I'm standing right back at the spot where it all began. Where Juliette came barreling into my world behind the wheel of her aunt's rusted-out car. The place where her panic collided with my bad timing. And somehow, it felt like fate.

I can't help but smile at the memory. Her face a mixture of horror and embarrassment as she rolled down the window. Her dark hair whipped around in the wind, and I was drawn to her even then. Before I knew her name. Before I knew the sound of her laugh. Before I understood how she'd turn my entire life upside down.

If I could rewind time, I'd do it in a heartbeat. Only this time, I'd get it right.

I pull out my phone, my thumb hovering over her number. I have to try, even if it's only to hear her voice one last time. With a deep breath, I dial.

Her voicemail picks up, her lively voice cutting through the silence and making the distance between us that much wider. My heart drops.

Swallowing the lump in my throat, I force the words out. "Juliette... I know you don't want to hear from me right now, but I just... I need to say I'm sorry. I screwed up." My voice cracks, betraying the tightness in my chest as I stare out into the dark road ahead.

"I never meant to hurt you," I continue. "God, that's the last thing I wanted. And I get it, I do, if you don't want to talk to me again. But I'd really appreciate the chance to explain... To make things right."

My heart aches with every word I speak.

"I really hope I hear from you... Bye, Juliette."

I hang up, my fingers clenched tight around the phone. A distant rumble of thunder shakes the air. The storm's coming, just like the fallout from everything I've set in motion. All I can do now is wait and hope she'll give me the chance to make it right.

thirty-six

JULIETTE

I've lost count of how many times I've played his voicemail. It's pathetic, really, the way I cling to every syllable, like maybe if I listen closely enough, I'll hear something that makes all of this hurt a little less.

My heart, the foolish, reckless thing that it is, wants to believe him and trust that he never meant for this to happen. But my mind is louder tonight. It builds walls as fast as my heart tries to tear them down.

And still, it haunts me. The rough scrape of his voice through the speaker, threaded with desperation. *"I never meant to hurt you. God, that's the last thing I wanted."*

Love. Even that word is too simple for what's burning in me when I think of him.

It doesn't scratch the surface, let alone sink down to where the truth of it lives. I used to think I understood love. Thought what I felt for James counted.

But these feelings I possess for *Knox?* It's something else entirely.

It's him in every quiet corner of my day, in the way my heart stumbles at the thought of his stupid, crooked half smile. It's how I see something beautiful or ridiculous or completely mundane and instinctively think, *God, I wish he was here for this.*

Every version of me, every messy, broken, hopeful piece I've ever been, was always waiting for him. I think that's what nobody really tells you about that soulful kind of love.

It's not loud or dramatic or performative. It's not something you talk yourself into or out of.

It's undeniable. When you know, you just *know.*

And I know him in that once in a lifetime, nothing before or after will ever touch this, kind of way. The love I thought I knew before him is a tiny flicker in the dark. Brief little sparks trying their best to catch.

Knox is the wildfire. The thing that consumes everything I thought I knew and leaves me standing in the middle of the wreckage, terrified and more alive than I've ever been. And maybe that's what scares me most. Not that I love him, but that I've been waiting for him my whole life without even realizing it.

I should've known better. I *did* know better, and still, I let myself fall. Wide open, no parachute, heart first into something that felt so impossibly rare.

But he's *married.*

There has to be more to it.

I never saw it coming. No ring. No shadow of another woman in his life. No whispered conversations when he thought I wasn't listening. It was *us.* Lunches that stretched long because neither of us wanted to leave. Late-night calls that wandered past midnight. Easy, everyday intimacy that never felt borrowed or stolen.

It was so real. What hurts most is the thought that I could've been so wrong about someone who felt like home.

Underneath the pain, there's this steady calm that pushes in. I can't keep losing myself in people who don't choose me all the way. I can't keep handing over pieces of my heart to anyone who'll take them.

Maybe that's why this next part feels so natural. Like muscle memory. Like slipping back into something familiar and safe.

I need distance. Space to breathe. To think.

Tomorrow, I'll call him. Tonight, I just need to rest. To let the noise fade. Let my heart be mine again.

I BARELY SLEEP.

I toss and turn, my mind running through every question with no answer. Around one in the morning, Aunt Rose tapped gently at my door, but I knew I couldn't open it without falling apart.

By the time morning comes, I'm wrung out, but there's also this small, stubborn flicker of resolve. I might be *heartbroken*, but I'm not broken.

I reach for my phone, my finger hovering over Knox's name. My pulse stutters. And then, because hiding from this won't make it hurt any less, I press call. It rings once.

"Juliette?"

He sounds relieved but also exhausted. Good. He should be losing sleep over this mess.

I swallow hard. "We need to talk."

There's no pause. Just the scrape of movement on his end,

the shuffle of clothes, the jingle of a belt, like he's already moving, already halfway out the door. "Of course. Please. Can we meet?"

What does it say about me that I still want to see him?

"Yeah," I whisper, the word small but steady. "We can meet."

"Do you want to talk at my sister's café?" he asks. "I can pick you up if you need me to?"

"No." The word slips out faster than I mean for it to, instinct more than intention. "Um, no, but thank you. I'll take my aunt's car."

The thought of sliding into that familiar passenger seat like nothing's changed feels suffocating. That truck has been its own kind of safe place. Quiet drives. Easy laughter. His hand steady on the wheel, close enough to touch. I don't trust myself in that space today.

"Okay," he says. There's a small catch in his voice, barely there, but I hear it. Feel it. Neither of us knows how to do this. Whatever *this* is now.

"I can be there in twenty minutes," I offer, because the silence between us is starting to hurt.

"Yeah," he breathes. "Okay. I'll see you soon."

"Bye, Knox," I whisper.

I end the call and drag in a shaky breath, chest tight with that awful mix of relief and dread. I got through talking to him without completely falling apart, but it doesn't loosen the ache lodged in my ribs.

I'm holding it together for now, but every part of me is balancing on that impossible line between wanting to run to him and needing miles of space.

Quietly, I ease my bedroom door open. The hinges groan loud enough to make me wince. Aunt Rose is a light sleeper, and I don't have it in me to answer worried questions. I pause to listen.

Silence.

The bathroom tiles are freezing against my bare feet as I catch my reflection in the mirror. Pale. Smudged makeup. Sad eyes.

I step into the shower, letting the hot water sting my skin, wishing it could burn away even a fraction of what's knotted up inside me. By the time I towel off and get dressed, barely bothering with my hair, the bathroom door eases open.

Aunt Rose's gentle, almost unsure voice fills the space. "Juliette?"

Her eyes scan over me, widening as they take in my disheveled state. "Oh, sweetheart, are you okay?" Her voice cracks just a bit. "By the time I heard what happened, you were already gone, and you weren't answering your phone. Callan said Finn brought you home."

Before I can summon the strength to speak, she steps forward and wraps me in a hug. As her arms tighten around me, memories of past conversations flicker through my mind. Things I pushed away until now.

I pull back just enough to meet her gaze, searching for the truth in her eyes. My arms fold across my chest, instinctively guarding what little is left of me.

"You knew he was married."

She flinches, the movement so slight it's almost imperceptible. Guilt flashes across her face, too quick to hide.

"I knew he *had* been married," she admits. "That's true. I knew she was...difficult, to put it kindly." She falters for a moment, her gaze shifting away. "But the rest? That wasn't my business, Juliette. He's my boss, and it wasn't my place to get involved in things I don't fully understand."

Her eyes meet mine, searching, almost pleading, and asking for forgiveness I don't know if I'm ready to give.

I should be angry, but the truth is, I'm worn down by the weight of too many unanswered questions. There's no fight left in me. The logical part of my brain is also telling me this isn't her fault. Not really. She didn't make the choices that brought me here. And yet, it still stings.

I give her a subtle nod, my throat tight with things I don't know how to say. This is one more thing I'll have to process later, when I've got the space for it. "I'm heading to meet him now. Is it okay if I take your car?"

"Of course," she says quietly, then pauses for a moment, her gaze softening. "Just...text me when you get there so I know you're okay?"

"Yeah, I will," I promise, slipping on my boots and grabbing the keys.

Knox's truck is parked out front of the café when I pull up. The sight stirs a bittersweet mix of hope and sadness. It's that strange ache of wanting and knowing better all at once.

My heart doesn't seem to care about the mess of things. It just knows he's here and decides that's reason enough to twist tight.

I don't waste any time once I park. If I sit here too long, I'll start overthinking, and I can't afford to lose my nerve now. My hand hesitates over the door handle for just a second...

But then, I see him.

My gaze drifts to the window, and the moment I spot him, my stomach drops. He's sitting at one of the tables, looking like he's been torn apart and stitched back together, only half successfully. His eyes are shadowed, his face drawn. It's a look I know all too well.

I take a steadying breath, forcing my legs to move. The door to the café creaks open, the bell above jingling softly. Knox's head snaps up, his eyes locking with mine with a force that makes me stop in my tracks.

The urge to turn and walk away pulls at me like a current, but I fight it. One step at a time.

When I reach the table, he stands. His movements are stiff, like he's trying to hold himself together. The tension in his shoulders is visible in the way he's bracing himself, like he's expecting me to lash out at any second. He pulls out a chair for me, but it's not the familiar, confident gesture I'm used to. There's something careful about it, almost hesitant. I slide into the seat without meeting his eyes. My heart wants to leap and run into his arms and pretend nothing ever happened, but my mind knows better.

The silence stretches between us. The distance between us is almost too much to bear. Every part of me screams to close it.

"I grabbed you a coffee and one of those muffins you like." His hand comes up, rubbing the back of his neck nervously. "I, uh, wasn't sure if you'd want anything or not."

Damn him.

Damn him for being so sweet, so...*him*.

His words hit me in places I thought were already hollowed out. Another crack splits open in my chest.

I nod, forcing the words out despite the tightness in my throat. "Thank you." It's all I can manage, even though I'm not close to being hungry.

When he sits down across from me, the guilt I expected isn't there. Instead, there's a heaviness in his eyes, deeper than regret. It's the weariness of someone who's already given up on themselves, like he's convinced there's nothing left to fight for.

I almost reach out. *Almost.*

"I'm ready to listen," I say quietly, my voice trembling despite my best effort to sound stable. I need answers, and no matter how much it hurts, I owe it to myself to hear him out.

His chest rises as he takes a slow breath. "I met Hallie through a mutual friend. At the time, I wasn't looking for anything serious. I was married to my work, trying to get the distillery back on its feet. It was casual for a long time."

Before I can pick his words apart, he lifts his mug and takes a slow sip. My eyes follow the movement, tracing the way his throat moves as he swallows, the sharp lines of his neck drawing me in like they always do. It takes me a second too long to realize what I'm doing, and I quickly tear my eyes away, heat creeping up my neck.

Focus. Now is not the time to get distracted by his neck, of all things.

"Eventually," he continues, "she started pushing for more. It had been about a year, and neither of us were seeing anyone else. That's when she started talking about marriage. I didn't hate the idea. She was kind, interested in what I did, and seemed genuinely happy just being with me, even when I was exhausted and running on fumes at the end of the day."

I nod, trying to appear composed, but inside, my chest constricts with every word. Hearing him talk about his...*wife* splits me open from the inside out. Judging by the look on his face, I'm doing a horrible job at hiding it.

His fingers tighten around his mug. "Do you want me to keep going?"

No.

"Yes."

His gaze flickers to mine, then away, as if he's weighing how much of this mess he's willing to let me in on. "Long story short, we eloped, and things changed pretty quickly after that. In the time I'd known her, she'd been putting on a hell of an act. It became clear what she was really after. It wasn't me. It was the money, or more specifically, what she could spend it on."

He shoots me a quick glance, catching the crease in my brow before I can smooth it away. "My family's wealthy," he explains. "The business might've struggled, but I didn't. Personally, I was fine. I chose to rebuild it out of respect for my dad. He never got the chance."

His jaw tightens. A sign that there's more he wants to say. Part of me wonders if he's just not saying it, if it's something he's unwilling to share, or if maybe he's waiting for me to push. Or is this just me imagining things, reading too far into his every move?

"Anyway," he says, clearing his throat. "Turns out she was after the money the whole time. I filed for divorce, and it's been a battle ever since. We've been separated for almost two years now, and I should be getting the certificate next week."

My mind spins, trying to make sense of everything he just laid out. I didn't know what I expected to hear today, but it sure as hell wasn't this.

"That's terrible, Knox. I'm so sorry," I say, and I mean it.

A flare of pain crosses his face. "Don't waste your sympathy on me," he murmurs. "I made a reckless choice, marrying her without thinking it through, and I've been paying for it ever since. What kills me is that you got dragged into it. You deserve better than this."

"Then why didn't you tell me?" The words cut loose before I can rein them in. "What did you think was going to happen? That I'd just keep falling while you held the truth in your back pocket?"

He flinches—barely—but I see it.

And still, even with the anger pulsing through every inch of me, there's a part that leans toward him. That stupid, stubborn part that remembers how safe it felt to be held by him.

I hate that part of me.

Because even now, with my heart cracking wide open, I still want the man who broke it.

He rubs a hand over his jaw, his gaze darting away. "At first, I didn't think it mattered. I wasn't expecting this to turn into anything serious." He swallows hard. "Then it did. I didn't want to bring it up until I knew what was happening with the divorce."

His head drops for a moment before he looks at me again. "I'm sorry, Juliette. For not telling you. For the way you found out. For all of it. This... This is exactly what I was afraid of."

I don't even try to stop the tears that slip down my face. Knowing he hasn't been with anyone else while we were together should bring some relief, but it doesn't undo the damage. The trust we built is in pieces, and I have no idea if it can be put back together.

A hundred questions swirl in my mind. Only one slips free. "Did she live in your house with you?" I wince, bracing myself for the answer to an unspoken question. *Was I in her bed?*

His eyes snap to mine, wide with panic and heartbreak. "*No*, lass. No. She's never even stepped foot in that house. I built it after we separated."

I nod, a small thread of relief weaving through the tight knot in my chest. "I appreciate you telling me everything, but I'll be honest... I don't know where we go from here."

He leans forward, his eyes searching mine and pleading in a way that cuts deeper than I want to admit. "I know I should've said something sooner. Words don't cut it for an apology."

There's sincerity in his voice but doubt still gnaws at me. "I believe you. I do. But the truth is, you hid a huge part of your life from me. And that part of your life *does* affect me."

As much as it hurts, my decision hasn't changed. I need space. Not just a day, not just until this pain dulls, but for however long it takes to find my footing again. Alone. Without leaning on anyone else.

"I'm going back home," I whisper. A sob claws its way up my throat, but I swallow it down.

His expression crumbles. The light in his eyes dims, his lips pressing into a tight line. He holds my gaze, like he's trying to will me to stay with nothing more than sheer desperation. "Juliette, please. Not yet. Not like this."

I shake my head, tears spilling over despite every bit of me trying to hold them back. His hand moves across the table, covering mine. I don't pull away, but I feel like I'm drowning in our connection, and it *hurts*. He tightens his grip, and all I can think about is how much I wish I could hold onto him forever, but I can't.

"Please don't shut me out," he murmurs. "Not completely."

Every word sends another crack through my ribs. I can't breathe, can't think. I want to say something to make it stop hurting, but all I can do is whisper, "I can't make any promises right now. I need space. I still have a life back home."

His fingers slip away from mine, and the space between us is suddenly infinite. His eyes hold his pain, but there's also acceptance, and the smallest hint of hope that I can't bear to see.

"I understand," he says. "I won't push it, but please know I'll be here. Waiting."

I nod, but the lump in my throat is unbearable, making it hard to breathe, let alone speak. My legs are weak as I stand. He rises, too, his movements rigid, like it's taking everything in him to not reach for me, to not hold me again. He doesn't. I don't know if that's a blessing or a curse.

"Take care of yourself, Knox."

I turn away, forcing myself one step forward, then another.

His hand catches my arm, pulling me back, and everything in me stalls. I go still. My breath tangles in my throat. I can't turn around. I can't face him again. Not when I'm about to break.

"Juliette..." His voice scrapes low and close against my ear, each word trembling like it's being dragged from the deepest part of him. "I love you more than I can put into words. It would haunt me if I didn't at least tell you that."

The ache hits before the meaning does. It's everything I ever wanted to hear.

He just made this so much harder.

He's standing so close, the heat of his body presses into me. I feel every inch of it, every ounce of longing and anger tangled in the same knot. Why couldn't he have been this honest when it could've meant something?

His lips brush across the back of my neck, so soft, so gentle, and I close my eyes. For just a second, I allow myself to feel the tenderness, the pull to let go and fall into him. But the grief is there, too, tightening around me like iron bands, refusing to let me.

I can't look at him. If I let myself see him, really see him, I'll lose myself. *Again.*

I already lost myself once, so completely that I forgot who I was. I gave up everything, and it burned me. I promised myself that wouldn't happen again.

Every time I look at Knox, every time he gets close, there's this impulse to surrender, to forget it all and let him in. It's tempting. So damn tempting. But that's the same thing that got me hurt before and had me losing myself in someone else's story.

I won't do that again.

When I step out of his embrace, the space between us turns colder than anything I've ever experienced.

I love him so much it hurts. My heart screams at me to turn around, to fall back into him and let him heal all the cracks I've been pretending weren't there. But I don't. I don't look back, not even for a second. Because I know if I do, I might never leave.

thirty-seven

KNOX

I t's been five days since that conversation with Juliette. Five days of pretending I've got it all under control, burying the misery that's carved itself into me. It doesn't work.

She handled it with a kind of strength I couldn't help but admire, even as it destroyed me.

I should be working today. Technically, I *am* working by going through the motions, clicking through spreadsheets, answering emails, nodding at the right times, but it's all background noise. And then there's Rose, who shot me one of those disappointed looks yesterday. And hell, she was right to give it to me.

I need to fix this, but I've got no clue how to start. I'm giving Juliette space, but part of me wonders if it even matters because, for all I know, she's already gone. *Gone for good.*

And if she is...then I've just let the best damn thing that ever happened to me slip through my fingers.

I never used to believe in the kind of love that snuck up and knocked the breath out of you. Didn't believe one smile could change a man. Juliette is the exception, and she was brave enough to hand me a piece of her heart when she had every reason not to.

It doesn't matter that it was fleeting or that we didn't have years to build it. I didn't need time or logic to know it was real. And now, I've hurt her in a way that makes her look at me like she doesn't even recognize me.

That's a look I don't know how to come back from.

Fuck.

A knock at my office door snaps me out of it. Callan's leaning against the frame, gauging just how much of a disaster I am.

"Hey," he says. "How's it going?"

I exhale as I drop my gaze back to the screen, pretending I'm in the middle of something important instead of spiraling in my own head.

"Mm. Everything's fine. Business as usual."

"Cut the crap."

All right, then. No room for small talk today. He's done with the sidestepping.

I glance up, meeting his stare head-on. He's got *that* look. Arms crossed, shoulders squared, settled into the doorframe like he's in no rush to leave. I'm not getting out of this conversation.

I exhale, long and slow, leaning back in my chair. The ceiling suddenly looks interesting. "What do you want me to say? That I'm a mess? That I royally screwed up and have no damn clue how to fix it?"

Callan's voice is quieter but more dangerous for it. "You can start by being honest with yourself. And quit drinking yourself into oblivion every night when you leave here."

I don't flinch, but he knows he's hit his mark. I've never been one to lean on booze. Never needed or wanted to. I don't know if I'm drinking to remember or to forget. Either way, it's not working.

"You're right," I mutter, dragging a hand through my hair. "I don't know how to face this sober. Don't know if I even *want* to."

He pushes off the doorframe and steps inside, dropping into the chair across from me. "She's still here, you know. Flight leaves tomorrow."

The words land like a punch to the ribs. My heart kicks once, hard. "How do you know that?"

He shrugs, a grin tugging at the corner of his mouth. "I have my sources. Rose, mostly."

Figures.

"Cal, I can't just—"

"You can't just, what?" he cuts in. "Keep sitting here, pretending you don't care? Keep drowning yourself in whisky like that's gonna change anything?"

"I—"

He doesn't let me finish. "You've been sulking around here for days. A mess every night. Hell, even my little fur nephew gave me a call and said his dad hasn't been meeting his usual cuddle quota." He presses his hand to his chest, pouting dramatically. "Heartbreaking, really."

I shoot him a look, but he just grins. "Point is, I know you. If you don't try, you're gonna regret it."

"And what exactly am I supposed to say? Oops, my bad, didn't mean to ruin everything, lie to you, and shatter your heart. Please don't go?"

I drag a hand down my face, running through every scenario in my head. They all end the same way—Juliette walking away more upset than she already is.

Callan leans back, arms crossed. "That's on you, brother. But I'd figure it out fast. Especially before Rose gets her hands on you." He pauses, then adds, "And for what it's worth? I liked her. She was good for you. She made you, I don't know, stop taking yourself so seriously all the time. Made you laugh a little more. I haven't seen you that relaxed in a while."

Before I can get a word in, my phone buzzes against the desk. *Finn.*

"Hell, here we go," I mutter, swiping to answer. "Hey, what's going on?"

"Good news, pal." His voice is downright cheerful, loud enough that Callan raises an eyebrow. "You're officially a divorced man. Signed, sealed, and delivered."

Cal shoots to his feet, throwing a fist in the air. "Hell yeah!" he whoops, clapping me on the back so hard my chair scrapes against the floor. His energy is ridiculous, contagious, and despite everything, the corners of my mouth twitch up.

I've been holding my breath for years and finally get to exhale. The weight pressing on my chest, the tension wound so tight in my shoulders, it all just...leaves.

"Thanks, Finn," I say. "I owe you big."

"For you? Anything," he replies. "Now, go figure out how to stop your girl from leaving, or Elsie's gonna have your arse."

"Aye, I'll figure it out. Talk to you soon."

"Congrats, Knox. You're finally free of her." Callan grins, turning toward the door and pausing just long enough to add, "I'll give you your moment. You've earned it."

I've been counting down the days for this moment, swearing it would be some grand form of relief, like walking out of a prison cell and into fresh air. And for a second, it did feel that way. But now it's almost...futile. The one person I need to talk to is about to board a plane and fly halfway across the world. I can't stop thinking about how wrong that is.

The thought twists in my gut, but I know better than to beg her to stay. That's not what *she* needs. What I can do, though, is make damn sure she never doubts me or questions how I feel, ever again.

I have an idea.

I'm on my feet before I can second guess myself, fingers already finding Rose's number in my contacts. She answers on the second ring.

"Knox, I was wondering when you'd call." Her voice carries that mix of kindness and warning that only Rose can manage. "You've got about fourteen hours before she's gone, you know."

"I know." I pace to my office window, staring out at the hills. "I need a favor."

There's a long silence on the other end. I can practically see her weighing her options, deciding if I deserve this chance. Then, her tone shifts, curiosity replacing the edge. "I'm listening."

"I need you to get something into Juliette's suitcase before she leaves tomorrow. It's..." I pause, running a hand through my hair. "It's important, Rose. Please."

"You're not proposing via luggage, are you? Because that's the worst idea I've ever heard."

I laugh. "No, nothing like that. It's just...something to remind her that she matters. That she's worth holding on to. I want Juliette to have it."

There's a pause on the other end. "All right," she says, her voice gentler now. "I'll get it in her bag, but don't make me regret this, Knox. I can only vouch for you so many times before I can't anymore."

I don't argue. I don't want to screw this up any more than I already have.

"I'll make it right," I promise, the words tasting a lot like hope and desperation.

thirty-eight

JULIETTE

Thick clouds roll in, swallowing the sky whole. They stretch over the hills like an ominous blanket, casting dark shadows that creep over everything in their path. My bags sit packed by the door, a chaotic mess of clothes, mismatched shoes, and random bits of a life that I tried to weave together here.

For a moment, I let myself imagine what it could've been like to call Scotland home, to build a life here. But reality pulls me back with a harsh grip, and the truth stings way too much to ignore. There's nothing left for me here. It's time to let go.

I take one last glance around the bedroom, checking for anything I might have missed as Aunt Rose appears in the doorway. "Ready?"

I nod and follow her to the car. We drive in silence, the passing landscape nothing but a blur, each mile dragging me farther from the life I thought I could have.

The first raindrops splatter against the windshield as we near the airport, light at first, then steady, almost like the sky is mirroring the sadness in my heart. I chuckle darkly. *Perfect.* The weather matches my mood.

Aunt Rose pulls up to the departure lane, and we just sit there. Neither of us moves. Neither of us speaks until she decides to break the silence. "Did your mom ever tell you about your dad?"

The question comes out of nowhere. "No, not really."

She nods like she already knew that answer, her gaze distant and unfocused. She exhales slowly. "Well, given everything... I think it's time I tell you a little about him."

I tilt my head, uncertain whether I want to hear what she's about to say, or if I'm even ready for it.

"Skye was always a dreamer," she continues. "A romantic. You know that about her."

Her words bring a flicker of a memory, of my mom with faraway eyes whenever she used to talk about love, like it was something both magical and fleeting.

She pauses for a moment. "She met your dad one summer. Fell for him hard. Just like someone else I know," she says, her lips curving into a bittersweet smile. It doesn't quite reach her eyes.

I'm not sure I want to hear the rest, but she doesn't wait for me to stop her. "When she got pregnant with you, everything changed. Your mom was imagining a future with him, but he was more interested in doing things his own way. He left and never looked back." She looks down for a second, sorrow in her voice when she picks it up again. "Your mom never stopped loving him. When you came along, she made it her mission to make sure you'd never have to feel that kind of hurt."

I try to process what she says but the ground slips out from under me. My thoughts scatter, struggling to keep up. "Why are you telling me this now?"

"Because, sweetheart," she says softly, "Skye let go of what she thought was the greatest love of her life to make room for the real thing, which was *you*. He never fought for either of you. And now, you've found someone who is. You've got the chance to hold onto something real, and you deserve it, just like your mom did."

Her words hit harder than I expected. They're the kind of truth that crashes over everything I've been holding onto. I don't have an answer yet. I'm not sure I ever will. What I do know is I'm not ready to face whatever it is that's stirring inside me.

"I don't know what to say," I manage, my voice barely above a whisper.

She doesn't say anything at first, just reaches over and squeezes my hand gently. "You don't have to say anything, hun. Just think about it. You still deserve some time to yourself, no matter what. But sometimes the bravest thing we can do is open our hearts again, even when we're afraid."

She speaks like she knows something I don't, but right now, I don't see him fighting for anything.

Knox hasn't tried to reach out. Never once made a move to pull me back in. Some small part of me has been clinging to the idea that maybe he would.

I wanted space. I thought I *needed* space. But now that I've had it, I'm not so sure. Did I want him to fight for me? Or was I just too scared to face the mess? The real truth is, I don't know what I want. I'm so tangled up in what I thought I needed that I don't even know where I end and the hurt begins.

So here I am, waiting for something that might never come. Deep down, I know I need to figure out what *I* want before I can ever hope for him to give me what I need.

I'VE BEEN HOME for a week now, but the solitude I've been craving isn't bringing me the peace I thought it would. The house that used to hum with the comforting noise of familiar things now sits unnervingly quiet. The summer air, thick with humidity, sticks to my skin in a way that's more stifling than soothing. My heart aches for a place that feels more like home than this lonely space. Preferably, a place that holds cool breezes, bright laughter, and, most of all, the man who was a part of it all.

And, just to add insult to injury, my luggage never made it back with me.

I've talked to my aunt a few times since I've been home, both of us carefully skirting around the topic of Knox. It's easier that way, even if it doesn't hurt any less. I've been trying to keep myself busy, throwing myself into anything I can find time for.

Lately, I've been spending more time with Mrs. Boone. She's easy to be around, always humming or chatting while she putters around her garden. We've spent hours trimming rose bushes and planting herbs. All small tasks that fill the silence I can't seem to fill on my own. Her stories are a comfort, a welcome distraction from the things I know I should be facing.

This afternoon, while we're out in her garden, she pauses, leaning on her trowel to wipe the sweat from her forehead. She gives me that sharp, no-nonsense look of hers, lips pressing into a thoughtful line. "You've been awfully quiet lately," she says. "Something on your mind?"

I shrug, trying to brush it off while adjusting a few flowers. "Just tired, I guess."

"Tired, huh? Doesn't quite sound like the whole story. You

can talk to me, you know. Sometimes sharing the burden makes it a little lighter."

For a split second, I consider keeping everything locked up tight. But the weight in my chest wins. "Things have...changed. I thought I had it all under control, but now I feel like I'm clinging to something that's slipping away."

She sets her gardening tools aside and looks at me with an understanding that only comes with age and wisdom. "Heartbreak's a sneaky bugger."

I let out a humorless laugh. I guess I'm not as good at pretending as I thought. "Well, do you have any wise words for someone who fell for a man only to discover he was technically married?"

Her eyes widen just a bit before she lets out a low whistle. "Bless your heart. And welcome to my life."

I blink at her, utterly thrown by her response. "Wait, what? Care to elaborate?"

She pats the bench beside her, inviting me to sit. She adjusts her sunhat, leaning back with a wistful smile. "I was young. Charlie Boone swept me off my feet with that southern charm of his and those baby blues that could talk you into just about anything. We were head over heels, married in a matter of months."

Her voice falters, and a flicker of something bittersweet flashes across her face. "It wasn't until after the honeymoon that I found out about Mary."

"Mary?"

She nods, her gaze distant. "His wife."

My mouth falls open. "Wait. You're telling me Charlie hadn't...?"

"Bothered to divorce Mary before marrying me," she finishes.

Well, doesn't that sound uncomfortably familiar.

290

"What did you do?"

Her lips press together. "At first, I was devastated. Furious. I felt like such a fool," she admits. "But then I realized something. I loved that man, flaws and all, and he loved me, too, even if he had a funny way of showing it."

She rests her hand gently on mine. "Charlie made a terrible mistake, but he owned up to it. He divorced Mary, begged for my forgiveness, and we spent the next fifty years making up for that rocky start."

Fifty years. She says it like it was simple. Like it was just a matter of deciding to move forward. "How did you ever trust him again?" I ask, my voice quieter now, almost afraid of the answer.

"It wasn't easy," she admits. "I learned that love isn't about finding someone perfect. It's about finding someone who's willing to work through the mess with you. Charlie proved himself every single day after that."

I nod slowly, turning her words over in my mind. She's placed a truth I'm not ready to carry right in front of me.

"It's never too late to try, sweetheart," she adds, her tone gentle but certain. "Love takes patience and understanding, not perfection. Take it from someone who's been around the block a time or two."

I try to smile, but I'm not sure if it reaches my eyes.

"And I'll tell you this," she continues. "It's not just the block I've been around. I've ridden it more than a few times, if you know what I mean."

I choke on a laugh, my face going pink. Leave it to her to drop a bombshell of unhinged honesty all while keeping that wicked glint in her eye.

Can I really wipe the slate clean and just...put it behind me? Part of me wants to believe it's possible, but there's this

291

other stubborn, bruised part of me that keeps circling back to the same question.

Can I trust him again?

Maybe love is supposed to be patient, supposed to weather the storm and come out stronger on the other side. But how much patience can one person give before it just...runs out? Before the hurt starts to feel heavier than the hope?

How do I know this time will be different?

thirty-nine

JULIETTE

Bree and I are just sinking into the couch, wine glasses in hand, when a heavy knock at my front door interrupts us.

"Who would that be?" Bree asks, her eyebrows pulling together in confusion as she sets her glass on the coffee table.

I shrug, but my pulse picks up a beat. "No idea."

I push off the couch and make my way to the door, unsure of what to expect. When I open it, I'm met by a grumpy delivery man lugging a large suitcase.

"Is this yours?" he asks flatly.

Relief floods me when I recognize the battered bag. "Yes! Thank you so much," I say, rushing forward to take it from him. "Only took ten days," I mutter to myself, rolling my eyes as the delivery man gives no response and turns back to his truck.

Bree steps up beside me, her smirk fully intact. "Well, look at that. You've been reunited with your worldly possessions. A touching moment, really."

I let out a laugh, nudging her with my elbow as we head back inside.

"Are you unpacking now to check if everything made it?"

she asks, glancing at her phone. Her fingers tighten around it, and a small crease forms between her brows.

I don't get a chance to answer before she lets out a groan. "Shoot, I've gotta check on D—" She stops abruptly, something flashing across her face too fast for me to read. "Uh, I just need to run home and see Dillon before he leaves for work."

The words are normal enough, but the delivery is off. What's going on with her?

I don't like to push. Bree will tell me things when she's ready. That's always been our unspoken rule. But she's dodging my eyes and is fidgety in a way that isn't like her.

Dillon's working tonight. That's what she said. So, why does it sound like she's covering for something?

"No problem..." I say slowly, studying her.

If something was *really* wrong, she'd say it.

Wouldn't she?

I hesitate for half a second, debating whether to let it go. The way she's acting doesn't sit right.

"Bree." I soften my voice, hoping she won't shut down the second I ask. "What's going on?"

"Nothing's going on," she says too quickly, her voice pitched slightly higher than normal. There's something about the way her shoulders tense that makes me absolutely certain she's hiding something. I've known her long enough to recognize when she's putting on a brave face.

The logical part of me knows people deal with things in their own time, in their own way. But I thought I was the one person she didn't have to pretend with.

"You know you can talk to me about anything, right?"

She meets my eyes for just a second before looking away, her usual sparkle dimmed. "Of course. It's just...relationship stuff."

That's vague. Way too vague. And I could press, but something tells me I won't get much more than that. Whatever's going on, she's not ready to talk about it.

I force a small smile, nodding even though the unease in my gut doesn't go away. "Okay," I say, letting her have the out she clearly wants. For now.

She grabs her purse from the counter and pauses on her way out, turning back to give me a quick hug. "You're gonna be okay, right?" she asks, her voice softening enough to let me know she's genuinely worried.

"Yeah, I'll be fine."

"All right. Call me if you need anything."

With that, she dashes out the door, and I shut it behind her with a sigh. The suitcase sits in the center of the foyer, glaring at me like a reminder that I've been avoiding something. I guess it's finally time to unpack.

I pull the suitcase into the bedroom, tossing it onto the bed with a soft thud that echoes in the otherwise quiet room. This bag isn't just holding my clothes and shoes. It's also carrying all the things I've been running from. My emotional baggage, literally and figuratively. The irony isn't lost on me, and I let out a small, almost bitter laugh.

Shit. I'm definitely losing it.

I tug at the zipper a little too aggressively until it finally gives. The scent of sea air and rain rushes in, making me pause for a second. It's a bittersweet pull tugging me back to a place that feels both impossibly distant and achingly close.

My hands are shaking as I continue pulling clothes from the suitcase. Then, I feel something tucked beneath everything else.

I pause, brushing my fingers over the worn leather pouch. It's small but sturdy, aged by time and handling. It's deep brown with creases that whisper of years gone by. My stomach twists. I don't recognize it.

My hand lingers there, suspended midair. Like it's bracing. I suck in a breath that doesn't quite make it all the way down and pull the flap open.

There's something solid inside. My fingers close around cool metal, and I pull out a compass, brass and old, dulled by time and touch. My heart stutters. Along with it is an envelope. It's addressed to me, and the handwriting... It's his.

Everything I've been running from is tucked inside, all neat and contained, like my entire world hasn't already been flipped upside down. I try to calm the wild thumping in my chest, but it's useless. I slide my finger under the seal, the paper resisting for a split second before tearing.

As it unfolds in my hands, my mind races ahead, too fast, too frantic, a thousand questions colliding all at once. There's only one that really matters.

Do I want answers?

Juliette,

If you're reading this, it means you left. God, I'm sorry. I'm sorry it got that far. You mean the world to me, and I hate that it took losing you to finally say this.

The truth is, I was scared. Scared of losing you once you saw the mess. After my dad passed, I started guarding everything I cared about too tightly. Especially the people I loved. I thought if I kept my past locked down, I was protecting you from the worst parts of me. But all I really did was keep you out. You deserved better than that.

In the bag, there's a compass that belonged to my great-grandfather. It's been passed down from one stubborn man to the next. He used to say it wasn't for finding places, it was for finding your way when you felt lost. I hope it helps you do just that.

You made me want to be better, just by being you. I love you. I should've told you that a hell of a lot sooner and every damn day, in every way I knew how.

You're worth every risk, and if you'll let me, I'll spend the rest of my life proving that I can be the man you need. No more excuses.

I love you, Juliette. Always will.
-Knox

A SOB BREAKS FREE. I've been so consumed by my own pain, so terrified of facing it, that I couldn't see past it. But this letter... It's a glimpse into his heart, and I just walked away. I left.

Oh god, he's going to think I didn't care. He's going to think I didn't even try. This letter has been sitting in my suitcase for almost two weeks, and he has no idea. He's going to think I just gave up, that I didn't even think twice.

My hand is shaking as I pick up the compass, my fingers grazing over its smooth surface. With a slow inhale, I flip it open. The glass is cracked, thin fractures spiderwebbing across the surface, but it doesn't obscure the needle's steady sway, always finding its way north. My breath catches when I see the words etched inside the case.

Come home to me.

Four words. Four simple words and a whole lifetime of things left unsaid. An entire story I didn't let him finish.

My mind goes back to all the quiet moments we shared that spoke louder than words ever could. The way he held me, the way we never needed to say anything to understand each other. How could I have doubted him? How could I have walked away, so wrapped up in my own fears, without even seeing *him*? Without understanding what he was going through?

What does that say about me?

I need to call him. Explain. Apologize. I need to make sure he knows that I never meant to shut him out.

My thumb hovers over his name on my phone screen.

This is *wrong*.

Saying, "I love you," over the phone isn't enough. He deserves more than a quick, desperate confession through a screen.

He deserves to hear it from me, face-to-face.

I *always* run. When emotions get too big, too loud, too tangled, my instinct is to put distance between myself and whatever is threatening to swallow me whole.

I ran when we got the news about my mom's diagnosis. I ran when I caught James cheating. And when I found out about Knox's wife? I ran then, too.

But where has running ever gotten me?

Nowhere.

Running didn't save my mom. Running didn't stop James from being a liar. And running from Knox... That was a mistake. One I need to fix.

Before I can talk myself out of it, I spring into action. Clothes are shoved back into the suitcase, my hands moving with a frantic energy that almost feels like I'm watching myself from the outside. Just weeks ago, I was running from Scotland, desperate to escape. Now, here I am, rushing back.

I slip the compass and letter back into the pouch, tucking them safely into my purse. I won't risk losing them again.

My heart races as I drag the suitcase back to the front door, the sound of the wheels scraping against the hardwood floor echoing in my ears. My mind's a storm of chaotic thoughts, swirling in every direction. I don't know exactly what I'm doing, but it feels like the only thing I *can* do.

I need to get on a plane.

KNOX

It's been eleven days since she left. Not that I'm counting or anything. I swear I felt the moment her plane left the ground. Like something ripped loose inside me and never stitched back together. It was silent, but brutal.

I still feel her kiss, like it's burned into me. Still taste the goodbye on my lips. I see her wide eyes, trying not to break, and the way she looked at me one last time before she turned around. Like she was already halfway gone.

That look's been haunting me ever since. Playing on a loop in my head, refusing to fade. I keep trying to push it aside, trying to pretend I didn't let the best damn thing in my life slip through my fingers. But wishing doesn't change a damn thing, and it sure as hell doesn't bring her back.

The day before she left, I tore through the front door like the world was on fire. Heart in my throat, hands shaking, desperation burning holes through my chest. I sat down at the kitchen table and scrawled out a letter that probably sounded like a mess of regret and hope.

Then I dug through the old cedar box tucked away in the closet. The one with the heirlooms. I knew exactly what I was looking for. That compass had been in my family for generations, but in that moment, it only belonged to her.

Rose didn't owe me a damn thing, but when I asked, she promised she'd slip it into Juliette's suitcase.

I couldn't go after her, but I needed her to know I *saw* it now. At the same time, I didn't want to suffocate her with more of my bullshit. She needed space. She *deserved* space. Even if not hearing from her all this time has been eating away at me.

I thought I'd hear from her by now. Anything to let me know she got it. It's been nothing but silence. My hope diminishes, that little light that's been keeping me going flickering, with every day that passes without a word.

Today, I'm at home, even though I should be at work. Callan told me I was about as useful as a whisky barrel with a hole in it and that my moping around like a sad Highland cow was putting everyone on edge.

He wasn't wrong.

I'm pacing the length of my living room, running my hands through my hair for the hundredth time. The silence is suffocating, the only noise cutting through the occasional click of the cat's claws skittering across the hardwood.

My eyes fall to the bottle of whisky sitting on the island. It's tempting, but I know damn well that drowning my sorrows won't bring her back. I might feel better for a minute, but it won't fix anything. Instead, I head for the porch. Maybe a walk will clear my head or, at the very least, give me something else to focus on.

I start down the path toward the loch, boots crunching against the gravel with every step. I barely make it a few paces before the sound of tires on the drive stops me cold.

Who would be showing up in the middle of the day? If it's Callan, checking up on me like some bloody nanny, I swear to everything holy, I'll toss him in the loch myself.

I turn back toward the house, squinting against the sun, expecting to see Callan trudging down the drive. I spot a taxi pulling up and freeze.

I take a step forward, my eyes locked on the vehicle as the door swings open. It can't be...

But it is.

Juliette.

She's slightly disheveled, her clothes wrinkled from hours of travel, her hair a wild mess. And yet, without a doubt, she's still the most beautiful woman I've ever laid eyes on. For a moment, I'm rooted to the spot, my heart stuttering as I stare at her like I'm seeing a damn ghost.

Then, everything inside me snaps into motion, and I'm moving, eating up the distance between us with a few long strides. Before I even realize what's happening, she's running toward me, her bags forgotten on the gravel, and we collide.

Her face presses against my chest, her arms wrapped tight around my waist. I hold her just as hard, burying my face in her hair. The scent of citrus and sunshine floods my senses, and for the first time in what feels like forever, I'm breathing again.

I press a kiss to the top of her head as the sobs that wrack her body shake me to my core. "I'm so sorry," she murmurs, her voice cracking. "I didn't get your letter until yesterday. My luggage was lost, and I..." she trails off, her breath hitching.

I pull back just enough to frame her face with my hands, wiping away the tears that spill down her cheeks. Her hazel eyes are swollen with emotion, exhaustion written all over her. "It's all right, lass," I murmur. "You're here now."

Her grip tightens on my shirt, her fingers digging into the fabric as she tries to steady herself and take a deep breath. "I read your letter...and the compass..." Her voice cracks again, and she buries her face back into my chest, the words swallowed by a broken sob.

I swallow hard, fighting to find the right words. "I wanted you to understand. I know I messed up, keeping things from you like that—"

Her breathless words spill out in a rush. "I'm in love with you," she says. "I love you so much. Leaving was the worst mistake I've ever made."

God, I've been dying to hear her say that.

A broken sound of relief escapes me as I pull her closer. My pulse hammers in my ears, and then her mouth is on mine.

It's not soft. Not even close.

It's fire licking at every raw edge I've been carrying since the day she left. It's silence burning off our tongues. Desperation. Hunger.

She fists my shirt, and I grip her hips like a man who's done being careful. There's nothing but heat and heartache and a kiss that says *you're mine and I'm not letting go again.*

It feels like home. Like maybe we were never really apart. Like maybe we never will be again.

The past, the mistakes, the misunderstandings, the distance... It all fades away. All that's left is us, standing here, with the promise of a second chance.

I drag my thumb across her cheek, chasing away the last of her tears. "I love you, too. More than I ever thought possible. I've been losing my damn mind without you."

Her lips part on a shaky breath, her eyes shining with relief and hope. "I'm sorry I didn't listen."

I shake my head, tilting her chin up so she has no choice but to see just how serious I am. "You have nothing to apologize for. But I swear to god, I'm never letting you go again."

A slow smile spreads across her face, and it hits me straight in the chest. "Take me inside, Captain."

Fuck, I missed hearing her say that.

I grab her bags in a rush, my fingers instinctively finding hers as we head for the door. The moment we step inside, I drop the bags.

She looks perfect here. She's finally *home*.

A low groan rumbles in my chest, because fuck, I've gone too long without her. My hands skim the curve of her waist, greedy for contact. "You have no idea how much I've missed you."

She tilts her head, her lips grazing my throat. My hands flex against her, torn between holding her steady and losing all restraint. Then she drags her hand down the center of my chest until it hovers just an inch above the waistband of my jeans.

"Juliette..."

"I need you," she whispers, her words like fire against my skin.

I fight to keep my head on straight, but the grip I have on my control is slipping fast. "What happened to my shy lass?"

I can feel her grin against my neck. "Being shy isn't going to get me what I want."

"And this is what you want?"

She pulls back to meet my eyes. Then, in a voice so quiet I almost miss it, she breathes, "Desperately."

That's it. That's all I need.

Fuck it.

I don't need a second invitation.

I don't think. I just move. Scoop her into my arms like I've been longing to do since the second she left. Her breath catches, then spills into a stunned little laugh that shoots straight through me like lightning.

She wraps herself around me, arms around my neck, her

lips brushing kisses across my jaw as I take the stairs two at a time. I don't slow down. I can't. Not when she's here and whispering everything I've been dying to hear into my skin.

By the time we reach the bedroom, my heart's damn near punching its way out of my ribs. Adrenaline crashes into need, and still, I somehow manage to set her down with a reverence I didn't know I was capable of.

It's hard to believe this is real, but the flush in her cheeks, the rise and fall of her chest, the trust in her eyes—none of it lies. She's here. She's mine. And this time, I'm not letting her go.

I lean in, capturing her lips in a searing kiss that steals my breath and sets my blood on fire. I can't get enough of her, can't touch her enough, taste her enough.

My hands slide under her shirt, skimming along the warm, silky skin of her back. She arches into me with a soft moan as her fingers work at the buttons of my shirt, her movements growing more frantic with each one.

I break the kiss long enough to pull her shirt over her head, revealing the delicate lace of her bra. My mouth goes dry at the sight of her. I want to map every inch of her with my hands, my lips, my tongue.

The rest of our clothes fall away in a rush, discarded in a heap on the floor, crumpled at our feet. I lay her down on the bed, taking a second to just look at her. *Really* look at her.

Her hair is wild and tangled across the pillow, her eyes dark with need, lips swollen from our kisses. She reaches up for me, her hands gliding over my shoulders and pulling me down to her. As our bodies meet, skin against skin, a shudder rolls through me. I can feel every point of contact, every soft curve and dip of her body fitting perfectly against mine.

I trail my lips along the column of her throat, savoring the taste of her skin and the scent that's uniquely her. She gasps as

I nip at her collarbone, her nails digging into my back. The small sting only spurs me on.

Christ, I'm harder than I've ever been in my life. My cock is practically throbbing against her thigh, so stiff it almost hurts. The kind of ache that borders on sweet agony. Her smooth skin sliding against mine is pure torture, making me want to take my time even when every cell in my body is screaming to bury myself inside her. It's like my body knows exactly what it's been missing for the last two weeks.

And now she's here, her thighs parting for me, her body offering everything I've been craving.

"You're so beautiful," I whisper.

"Knox..." she breathes, her nails raking down my back.

With deliberate slowness, I trail my hand down her body. She bows into my touch, her breath coming faster now. "Please," she whimpers. The desperate edge in her voice nearly ruins me in the best goddamn way.

"I dreamed of you every night," I murmur against her skin. "Of holding you, touching you." I hook my arm under her knee, spreading her wider as I align our bodies. Our eyes lock, a thousand unspoken words passing between us. And then I'm sinking into her, feeling her body stretch to accommodate me. For a moment, we're both still. It's like coming up for air after being underwater. The first breath of spring after a long, cold winter.

Home.

Her eyes flutter closed, her lips parting on a soft moan as I begin to move. I don't waste a second, capturing her mouth with mine, swallowing every single sound she makes. I thrust harder, faster, driven by the way her body responds to mine.

"God, I missed you," I groan against her mouth.

She arches again beneath me, her head tipping back.

"Don't stop," she gasps, her voice trembling with desperation. "Please don't stop."

As if I could. As if I would ever want to.

I feel her tightening around me, every pulse of her body drawing me in deeper. Her breath is shallow now, erratic. She's so damn close, right on the edge of breaking. I slip my hand between us, finding that spot I know drives her wild.

I circle my thumb in time with my thrusts, and she cries out, her back bowing off the bed.

"Let go," I murmur against her ear. "I've got you."

A few more strokes and she shatters, my name a broken sob on her lips as she comes apart in my arms. The sight of her, the feel of her slick heat clenching around me, it's too much. Too fucking beautiful.

Tension coils tight at the base of my spine. "Juliette," I groan. "Fuck..."

And then, everything shatters. My hips stutter, and the first surge of release floods through me. I pulse inside her, filling her with each desperate thrust.

I barely hear the raw sounds tearing from my throat. My hands grip her hips, holding her tightly against me as I ride out wave after wave, each one more intense than the last. The pleasure is so fierce it radiates out from the center of me until every muscle in my body is shaking with it.

I collapse onto her, careful not to crush her with my weight, my forehead pressed against hers as we both struggle to catch our breath. I press gentle kisses to her shoulder, her cheek, her temple. Anywhere I can reach. She hums softly in contentment, her fingers tracing lazy, soothing patterns on my back.

"So," she whispers, a smile in her voice. "Does this mean you missed me, too?"

A laugh rumbles through me. "Just a wee bit," I tease, rolling onto my side and pulling her with me. I tuck a strand of hair behind her ear, letting my thumb trace the curve of her cheek.

"I love you," I murmur.

Her eyes lift to mine, glassy with emotion, brimming with trust and so much hope it steals my breath. "I love you, too."

Hearing her say that, tangled in my sheets, curled up against me?

Pure fucking heaven.

forty-one

JULIETTE

Wrapped in the strength of Knox's arms, every jagged, splintered piece of me feels like it's been carefully gathered and placed back where it belongs. I didn't know what true safety felt like until this very moment.

His chest rises and falls beneath my cheek, each breath lulling the last of my racing thoughts into silence.

I forgave him the second I read that letter and realized he was trying to love me the only way he knew how. And maybe that love was messy and imperfect, but it was real.

I tip my head, listening to the steady beat of his heart as his fingers move slowly through my hair. I'm not searching anymore. I'm home.

After a few minutes, his voice breaks through the silence. "How long are you here? Are you staying with Rose?"

I pull back to meet his eyes and realize...I haven't thought this through. Not even a little.

"Honestly? I have no idea," I admit. "I just booked the first flight out and came straight here. Didn't even tell my aunt I was coming."

"Stay with me."

It's not a question. I take a second to process it. "Really?"

He nods with no hesitation. His brow is relaxed, but his eyes are determined. He's already made up his mind, and he's just waiting for me to catch up.

"I just got you back, Juliette." His voice drops lower, threading through my ribs and wrapping around the fragile parts of me. "If you don't have other plans, I want you here. Every night when I go to sleep and every morning when I open my eyes."

I swear, if my heart beats any harder, it's going to break right out of my chest and throw itself at him in surrender. Suddenly, I'm not thinking about anything else. Not the past, not what-ifs, not how terrified I used to be of needing someone this much.

I only know that I want what he's offering more than I've ever wanted anything.

Every night. Every morning.

God, *yes*.

I want his sleepy smile and his scratchy morning stubble. I want his bare feet on the kitchen floor and his arms reaching for me in the dark. I want this messy, beautiful life with him, in all its imperfect glory.

I feel chosen. Not tolerated. Not settled for. Loved— completely, recklessly, tenderly loved.

So I nod, and I smile, and I press my hand to his chest like I'm making a vow. Because I already know I'm not going anywhere. "There's nowhere else I'd rather be."

Knox is just about to say something that, judging by the look in his eyes, would probably wreck me in the best possible way, when a sudden knock at the front door snaps the moment in half.

He exhales sharply. "That's got to be Callan."

Before either of us can move, the front door creaks open.

"Damn it, Cal! Go away!" Knox shouts, already sounding exhausted.

"No chance, brother. You've spent enough time alone now." Callan's voice carries up the stairs, all smug amusement and zero self-preservation. "Hey, whose shite is in your front hall? Is that a purse? Knox, what the—"

In a flash, Knox is *gone*. Out of bed, fully naked, and practically throwing himself in front of me like he's about to face down an army. Arms wide, stance ready—the very picture of a man ready to fight his own brother to protect my dignity.

I lose it. Completely.

Laughter bursts out of me before I realize it's happening. The second it escapes, Callan's voice rings through the hall.

"No feckin' way! I know that American laugh when I hear it! So glad you're back, Jules!" His tone is pure joy, like this is the best thing that's ever happened for his brother.

"Callan, I swear to god, if you don't leave right now..." Knox growls, poised for defense.

I'm still giggling, half from the absurdity and half from the adorable way Knox is doing his best to shield me like some kind of knight with absolutely no armor. "It's okay," I assure him, holding the sheet higher over myself. "I'm covered now."

Knox's broad shoulders flex as he turns, the muscles in his back shifting. His jaw is tight, and his eyes pin me in place... Which is sitting here, covered just enough to be decent but not nearly enough to cool the heat pooling in my stomach.

His voice is rough, edged with frustration and something far more dangerous. "No, Juliette, not okay. I'm not even close to being done with you."

Oh.

My breath stutters. My cheeks flame. Not from shame, but

from the way his words slide under my skin and spread through my limbs like liquid fire. And then, of course, *Callan.*

His laughter rings out. "Sorry to interrupt, carry on!"

Knox exhales, murder flashing in his eyes. He strides across the room and shuts the door. The lock clicks into place, the sound loaded and leaving a ripple of anticipation crackling between us.

When he turns back to me, his voice is commanding in a way that curls through me like a whispered sin. "Drop that sheet, *mo ghràidh.* Now."

God help me. When he speaks like that, it doesn't matter what he's asking. I'll do it.

My fingers tremble as I let go, the sheet slipping from my grip and pooling at my waist. Knox's gaze darkens, trailing over every newly exposed inch of me, slow and reverent, taking his time memorizing all of it.

"Juliette," he murmurs. His eyes drag over me. "The rest of it. I want it gone."

With a swift motion, I kick the sheet from my legs and lie back, vulnerability and power tangling inside me. My heart pounds as he moves forward, every inch of him radiating purpose, control, and *possession.*

His gaze never leaves mine, that wildfire still burning hot in his eyes. When he reaches me, the warmth of his hands against my thighs sends a pulse of need straight to my core.

His grip is firm, claiming, and then his lips trace a slow, searing path down my stomach, each kiss branding and unraveling me piece by piece.

I dig my fingers into the sheets as his mouth moves lower, my breath coming in shallow gasps.

"You have no idea how much I've missed the taste of you," he murmurs against my inner thigh, his breath hot against my skin. "The sounds you make when I touch you just right."

As if to prove his point, his fingers drift higher. When they graze where I'm already wet and aching for him, I can't help the desperate sound that escapes me. My hips jerk in response, seeking more pressure, more friction, more of him.

"Knox," I whisper, my voice unrecognizable, strained, and needy.

His eyes flicker with dark amusement at my plea, a smirk playing at the corner of his mouth. "Patience," he whispers, his breath ghosting over my sensitive flesh.

Then his mouth is on me, his tongue tracing a slow and torturous path along my center. I gasp, my back arching off the bed as the sensation ripples through me. He takes his time, each languid stroke of his tongue building the pressure low in my stomach.

"Knox," I moan, one hand leaving the sheets to tangle in his hair. I'm not sure if I'm trying to pull him closer or push him away.

He answers with a low, satisfied sound, his grip tightening around my thighs as if he can feel me unraveling and has no intention of letting me go. His mouth is merciless, every flick of his tongue sending sparks straight through me. I'm suspended in this beautiful, unbearable high, and he's not giving me a single second to catch my breath.

Through half-lidded eyes, I catch him watching me from between my thighs, taking in every reaction, every tremor that courses through my body.

Suddenly, he pulls away. The loss of his mouth has me keening, my body arching instinctively, chasing the heat he stole away. A tremble ripples through me as he rises over me, eyes wild and dark and so full of need

"I need to fuck you, and I don't think I can be gentle this time."

My thighs clench. My breath stutters.

I nod, because *yes*. "I don't want it to be."

The shift in him is instant.

His fingers fist my hair, yanking my head back just enough to bare my throat. I barely have time to gasp before his mouth crashes into mine. It's all teeth and tongue and unspoken need. Like he's starving and I'm the only thing that's ever come close to satisfying him.

He bites down on my bottom lip, dragging it between his teeth before his tongue slides in, claiming, consuming. My spine bows, a desperate sound clawing its way out of my throat as I clutch at his shoulders.

He's not just kissing me. He's taking, and I want to give him everything.

His other hand finds my breast, fingers digging in with a possessiveness that makes my skin heat. Every press of his palm, every slow, bruising knead sends fire licking through my veins, winding me tighter, pulling me under.

He breaks the kiss, his lips trailing down my jaw, his breath hot against my ear. "I'm going to make you feel every fucking inch of me."

His hands find my hips with a brutal kind of precision, flipping me onto my stomach. A sharp gasp slips from me as the sheets tangle around my limbs, my pulse hammering in my throat.

The only sound is the rush of my breath, the soft scrape of fabric as he shifts behind me. He doesn't speak, but his hands are on my body, pulling me to my knees, positioning me exactly how he wants.

His palm presses into my back, holding me in place. His thick length teases me, but he doesn't go any farther.

Every nerve feels lit, like someone struck a match inside me. I'm suspended in the pause, burning with desperation.

"Please, Knox," I whimper, pushing back against him.

"Tell me exactly what you want, Juliette," he growls.

"I want you inside me," I gasp, my voice barely above a whisper. "I need to feel you. All of you."

He rewards me with a powerful thrust, burying himself to the hilt. A sharp cry rips from my throat at the sudden fullness, the stretch of him overwhelming in the most exquisite way.

Knox groans, his chest pressed against my back as he sets a punishing pace. Each snap of his hips drives me higher, pleasure coiling tighter and tighter in my core. His hands are everywhere, gripping, kneading, igniting sparks across my sensitive skin.

"Knox...I'm so close."

His teeth scrape the curve of my shoulder, sending a shiver straight to my core. The sharp bite mingles with the heady rush of pleasure flooding my veins. My grip tightens in the sheets, knuckles white as I cling to my control. Knox has no intention of letting me keep it.

One hand slides around my hip, his fingers circling my clit, matching the intensity of his thrusts. It's too much, the sensations overwhelming me from every angle. I can barely breathe, can barely think beyond the desperate need consuming me.

"Come for me, Juliette."

His words undo me, permission and command all in one. The coil inside me snaps, ripping through me. Through the haze of my release, he tenses, his movements faltering before he buries himself deep and pulses inside me with a guttural moan.

We catch our breath, and he eases out slowly before pulling me against him. His arms wrap around me, strong and steady, and I sink into the warmth of his skin, the rise and fall of his chest lulling me. His wild heartbeat slows beneath my cheek.

"Oh...my...god," I whisper, still reeling. "Apparently, I don't need much time at all when you talk to me like that."

If we're being honest, I might orgasm on the spot the next time he uses that tone with me.

His laughter vibrates against my cheek. I tilt my head up, catching the mischievous glint in his eyes and the dimple in his cheek that *knows* I'm weak for it.

"Aye," he says. "Same over here, obviously."

I turn into his side, both of us caught in another wave of laughter.

"Let's get you cleaned up," he murmurs, pressing a soft kiss to my temple.

This man. I swear he stepped right out of a dream. Effortlessly charming, impossibly real, and somehow, all mine.

forty-two

JULIETTE

It's the end of October, and I can hardly believe it. Three months have slipped through my fingers without a second to spare. I'm lying in Knox's bed, basking in the autumn light spilling through the window. The Highlands outside are a canvas of color. Reds, oranges, and golds swirling through the trees, like little fires catching in the wind.

I've been back to the States a few times. Just quick trips to tie up loose ends, really. Enough time to make sure my house is ready to sell and to squeeze in some much needed catch-up with Bree. As much as I love Scotland, it's always good to be reminded of the life I created before.

I didn't rush back in August to work. Instead, I made the choice to test the waters here, in a place that feels more and more like home every day. I'm planning to apply for my visa soon. I'm making it my mission to settle in. For good.

Life has been nothing short of perfect. I'm not waiting for

something to go wrong, not looking for hidden curveballs or loose ends lurking around the corner.

I'm happy. Truly, genuinely happy.

As I stretch, Beastie slinks into the room, his sleek form weaving through the golden morning light. He hops onto the bed with a soft meow, curling against my side. I scratch behind his ears, earning a deep, satisfied purr.

Beside me, Knox stirs, his arm instinctively tightening around my waist and pulling me closer. That sleepy smile of his tugs makes my heart flutter in a way I can't explain.

"Good morning, beautiful." He presses a lazy kiss to my shoulder, his lips lingering on my skin. "What's got you up so early?"

I snuggle closer. "It's definitely not early."

His arm tenses around me. I lift my head to find his gaze. "Is something wrong?"

He shakes it off. "Nothing to worry about. Just didn't mean to sleep this late." His lips curve into that familiar, teasing grin. "Some lass thought it'd be fun to keep me up half the night."

I nudge him with my elbow. "Oh, hush. You love it."

He hums in response. "I do love it. In fact, I can think of a few more things I'd love to do to you right now."

"Is that so? Care to enlighten me?"

Knox's grin turns positively wicked. He leans in close, his lips grazing the shell of my ear as he speaks. "I'd start by tasting every inch of your skin until you're trembling beneath me. Then I'd bury my face between your thighs, licking and sucking until you're dripping for me."

I whimper, heat pooling low in my stomach. "Knox..."

"I'd slide my fingers inside you," he continues, "stroking that sweet spot until you're begging for more. And just when you're there..."

His laughter rumbles low in his chest as he pulls away,

stretching onto his back, muscles flexing under smooth, bare skin.

"You're cruel," I breathe, reaching for him.

But Knox is already untangling himself from the sheets, that infuriating smirk still in place. "Sorry, love. I've got a few errands to run today, but I won't be too long."

I pout, resisting the urge to drag him back into bed. "Fine. But you owe me. Elsie asked me to meet her at the café in a little while, anyway."

"Oh, I fully intend to make it up to you." He leans down, pressing a lingering kiss to my lips. "I'm going to go get ready."

He disappears into the en suite, and I let out huff, trying to ignore the ache between my thighs.

Beastie gives me a sympathetic look, butting his head against my hand.

"Your dad is a tease."

I'm at the café with Elsie when a familiar truck drives past.

"Pretty sure that was Knox," I say, leaning forward to get a better look through the big front window. "Yeah, definitely him."

Across from me, Elsie doesn't glance up from her tea. "No, it wasn't."

I blink, taken aback.

"I'd recognize that truck anywhere. Not to mention the man behind the wheel." I smirk.

She rolls her eyes, but I catch the faintest twitch at the corner of her mouth. "Aye, I'm sure you would. You two were made for each other, no doubt about that." Her expression shifts, something gentler working its way in. "Do you know what he's up to today?"

Something about the way she asks makes me pause. "He just said he had some errands. Didn't go into details," I say with a shrug. "He usually pops by the distillery on Saturdays, so it's probably something to do with that."

She hums, finally looking at me. "Interesting."

I narrow my eyes. "Why do you say it like that?"

She takes an infuriatingly slow sip of her tea. "No reason."

Suspicion prickles down my spine. "Elsie."

She presses her lips together in an attempt to conceal her smile. "Oh, would you look at that? Time's gotten away from me. I better run. The boys have football games today."

I arch a brow. "Uh-huh. Convenient. And it's called *soccer.*"

She laughs, slipping on her coat. "They *do* have games. They've been asking when Auntie J is going to show up again."

I remember the first time I saw Knox with Elsie's and Finn's boys. It was like watching a man who had been born to be a father, even if he hadn't known it yet. He scooped them up so effortlessly, spinning them around in the air like they weighed nothing, their giggles filling the air around us. Then, at the loch's edge, he crouched down beside them, showing them how to skip stones with such patience and focus. But it was the way his eyes softened when they spoke that stuck with me. Like everything they said mattered, like their worlds were his to protect.

I smile, tucking the memory away. "Tell them I'll be there next weekend. I wouldn't miss it for the world."

Her expression shifts. "You guys are going to make wonderful parents someday."

The words are unexpected but...not unwelcome. My stomach flutters, and for a heartbeat, I picture Knox holding a baby in his arms, his green eyes filled with the same quiet devotion he has when he's with her boys.

"Maybe someday," I murmur.

"I really do need to run. The boys will be waiting." She leans down, giving me a quick squeeze. Then, with a smirk that tells me she's enjoying this far too much, she adds, "Enjoy the rest of your day, Juliette. I have a feeling it's going to be... *special*."

"What in the world are you talking about?"

She just grins, tossing a wink over her shoulder as she heads for the door.

What is going on today? Did the universe decide it was time for a full-on chaos fest? I roll my eyes, half convinced I'm imagining things, when Lucy strolls over to collect Elsie's mug from the table.

"Hey, love!" she greets. "Don't you look radiant today."

Okay, now I'm starting to think I've accidentally wandered into some alternate dimension. I glance around, half expecting confetti to fall from the ceiling.

"And so do you. Did you discover how to bottle sunshine while I wasn't looking?"

"Maybe I did! Or maybe it's just the coffee." She spins away with a flourish, leaving me wondering if I've somehow missed the memo on what everyone's been drinking this morning—or if the entire world has collectively lost its mind.

With Knox still out, it's the perfect time to call Aunt Rose. It's been a few days since I've seen her. The phone rings a couple of times before it goes straight to voicemail.

I feel that little pinch of disappointment, but before it settles, my phone buzzes in my hand.

AUNT ROSE

Sorry, darling. I'm in the middle of a very
important situation. I'll call you later!

Okay... Looks like it's back home for me.

I'm back at Knox's, sprawled out on the couch when I hear the front door creak open. Knox comes into view, his broad shoulders filling the doorway, the air shifting with him. My heart does that little flutter it always does when I see him.

When he leans down to greet me, his kiss is soft but sure, leaving its mark after he pulls away.

"Hey, you," I say. "You were out longer than I thought you'd be."

He settles beside me, his arm easily slipping around my shoulders as I lean into him. "Aye, turned into a busy day," he mumbles. "I'd like to make it up to you, though."

My eyebrow arches. "Mm, finally. What do you have in mind?"

His voice drops low as he chuckles. "Save *that* for later. We have plans tonight, and you need to get ready. We leave in an hour."

"Oh, fun! Where are we going?"

"It's a secret, lass." His voice softens just a touch, that teasing warmth that's become so familiar to me seeping through. "A wee birdy told me you found quite the dress the other day. You should wear it."

The memory of that afternoon with Elsie and Lucy a couple weeks ago flashes through my mind. We bounced from boutique to boutique, trying on anything that caught our eye. And then I found this emerald-green, floor-length dress that clung to me like it had been sewn with my name stitched into the hem. The off-the-shoulder neckline skimmed my collarbones, giving it an elegant, classic vibe, and the bodice sparkled with delicate beads that caught the light in a way that made me feel like royalty.

Total impulse buy. But with Elsie clutching her chest and Lucy fanning her face, how was I supposed to say no?

"Aye aye, Captain," I tease, giving him a playful salute. "Where could we possibly be going that requires me to dress fancy?"

"You'll see."

I raise an eyebrow, giving him a look that says, "Seriously?" He doesn't give anything away. His lips curl into that half smile of his, the one that's equal parts infuriating and charming.

An hour later, I'm standing at the top of the stairs, smoothing the fabric of the dress as I take a breath. When I step down, Knox is already waiting at the bottom dressed in that damn kilt.

I should be immune by now. I've seen him in everything from oil-streaked jeans to nothing at all, but somehow, this? This is a whole different kind of lethal.

He looks up. "You're..." His voice catches, jaw flexing as he swallows hard. His eyes sweep down the length of me, and when they return to mine, he bites down on his lip. Then he finally murmurs, "Perfect."

As I reach the last step, he stretches his hand out. He smiles at me, faint crinkles appearing at the corners of his eyes.

"Hello, handsome," I say, reaching for him and pulling him close to steal a kiss. "I require a taste," I whisper against his mouth.

The groan that rumbles out of him is low and sinful, a vibration that starts in his chest and ripples straight through mine. His hands slide over my hips, palming every curve like he's reacquainting himself with what's his.

Our bodies speak their own language, one we've written in stolen nights and whispered mornings. I melt into him, the heat between us flaring when his tongue strokes against mine. A dizzy rush spreads through me, liquid and warm, pooling low and fast.

But just as quickly, it's gone.

Knox pulls back with a ragged exhale through gritted teeth. And when his eyes find mine again, they're stormy with want and laced with restraint that looks like it's about to snap.

"As much as I'd love to continue this," he says, "we have somewhere to be."

I push my bottom lip out in a pout. "Fine, but once again, you owe me later."

He chuckles, pressing a quick kiss to my forehead. "Trust me, lass. I plan to make it worth the wait."

forty-three

JULIETTE

The drive through the Scottish countryside is so peaceful. Knox's hand rests casually on my thigh, but as the minutes tick by, there's a subtle shift in his energy. His fingers tap a restless beat on the steering wheel, a pattern that matches the beat of my racing heart.

"Everything okay?" I ask, sliding my hand over his in an attempt to ease the tension that's suddenly there, though I'm not sure why. Unless I think back to Elsie and Lucy's odd behavior from earlier today.

He looks over at me, offering a tight smile. "Aye, we're almost there."

I don't want to press, but a small knot forms in my stomach, wondering what's going on with him. Just as I open my mouth to ask again, the truck rounds a bend, and I stop mid sentence.

Up ahead, the view opens to a massive castle perched against the fading light of the setting sun. It looks like something out of a history book, all stone and towers, standing tall and steady against the sky.

"Is that where we're going?" I ask, leaning forward to get a better look.

"It is," he replies, a grin spreading across his face as he glances at me from the corner of his eye.

The closer we get, the more the castle reveals its rugged beauty. The gray stone walls rise, weathered with time and wrapped in thick ivy that's been there for centuries. A winding gravel path leads up to iron-studded, wooden doors that act as an entrance.

My mind races. What in the world are we doing here?

"Do we get to go inside?" I ask, trying to keep my curiosity from bubbling over.

He nods when he answers, "We do."

There's a group of cars already parked near the entrance, and it clicks—this is some kind of event. Knox parks and rounds the truck, offering his hand to help me out. I take it, that familiar spark spreading over my skin when his fingers curl around mine. He tugs me gently, guiding me up the walkway.

We reach the door, and Knox pushes it open, the creaking of the hinges echoing in the quiet. We step into a stone corridor, the faint sounds of laughter and music drifting along the walls. It grows louder the farther we walk. When we emerge into a courtyard, my heart skips a beat. It's filled with people I recognize. His friends, his family, all chatting and laughing. And then I see Bree.

What is she doing here?

I freeze, trying to make sense of what I'm seeing. The rush of excitement hits me almost immediately, but it's tangled with a layer of disbelief. I scan the crowd, my mind racing as I search for more familiar faces and try to fit all these pieces together.

Then everything falls silent, and we're the center of attention. A flush creeps up my neck and spreads across my cheeks, my hand rising to my chest to steady the thumping of my heart.

"What's going on?" I whisper, turning to Knox.

His gaze locks with mine, and for a moment, everything else falls away. The world blurs, leaving just the two of us. He's looking right through me—or maybe *into* me—in a way that makes everything else irrelevant.

He steps closer, never breaking that connection. My breath catches in my throat, waiting for him to say something.

"I'll never forget the day we met," he starts, his voice smooth, but there's a spark of mischief in his eyes. "I was just driving along, minding my own business, when out of nowhere, a car came barreling toward me. I swear, my life flashed before my eyes. Our tires screeched and coffee flew everywhere. I looked over and found you, hands gripping the wheel like your life depended on it."

The crowd bursts into laughter, and I can't help but join in, even as my cheeks turn bright red. Of course, *he* would tell the story like that. It's funny, but it's also mortifying.

Still caught in my laughter, I throw him a glare, pretending to be outraged. His innocent smile cuts through, and all my frustrations melt away. He knows exactly how to make me forget about why I was annoyed in the first place.

I'm a sucker for that smile.

"Instead of being angry, I found myself captivated by the person in the car," he goes on. "It's funny how things work out. Just like that, everything shifted. You came into my life like a storm, shaking everything up in the best way."

I blink as his words weave through my mind. Suddenly, I'm remembering all the small moments we've shared. The way his smile makes the world lighter. The way he holds me close. And, even when I'm confused and frustrated, how he never lets me drift too far. It's not the big gestures that have stuck with me.

Despite all the chaos and messiness, the way everything turned upside down, the storm wasn't destructive. It was a storm, yes, but a beautiful, life-altering one. And somewhere in the middle of that, I found a home. *Him.*

I take a deep breath, watching as he reaches into the sporran at his waist. He pulls out a small box and drops to one knee.

"Juliette," he says. "From the moment you crashed into my life, everything changed. You've brought light into my world, challenged me, and made me a better man. I can't imagine spending another day without you by my side."

He opens the box, revealing a stunning diamond ring that sparkles in the fading light. "Will you marry me?"

There's no stopping the tears that stream down my face. I don't even want to try. My heart has already made its choice, loud and clear, and my hands shake as I reach for him.

"Yes," I whisper, then louder, "Yes, yes, a thousand times yes!"

With the tenderness of a man who has all the patience in the world, he slides the most beautiful vintage ring onto my left hand.

I can't stand not having his lips on mine any longer. I tug him to his feet, pulling him toward me with a need I can't hold back.

The moment his arms wrap around me, it's just the press of his body against mine and the kiss that explodes between us. The urgency is there, but he's gentle in the way he cradles my face, in the way his lips move against mine like he's memorizing me.

I kiss him back with everything I have.

This is it. This is forever.

The noise comes rushing back as we pull apart, the world snapping into focus. My breath is shaky, my heart thumping wildly in my chest as I glance down at the ring resting on my finger.

"It's perfect," I say, meeting Knox's gaze. "You're perfect. I can't believe you did all this."

His smile stretches wide, genuine and full of everything I've ever wanted. He pulls me close, his arm slipping around my waist. "Anything and everything for you, *mo ghràidh*," he murmurs, his Scottish lilt sending a surge of longing straight through my chest.

This is so surreal, and just as I'm trying to absorb it all, Bree is in front of me, practically tackling me with a hug that nearly knocks me off balance. Her squeals of excitement make me laugh as she holds me tight.

"I can't believe you kept this a secret!" I exclaim, still too stunned to fully comprehend everything happening around me.

She pulls back, grinning ear to ear. "Girl, I had the hardest time of my life keeping this from you. So worth it, though."

I laugh, feeling lighter than ever. And then Aunt Rose's arms are around us, pulling us both into a big, tight hug.

"I obviously couldn't be happier about this," she says, her voice brimming with joy. "But are we going to talk about the tire-screeching, coffee-flying incident?"

Knox and I exchange a look, and a laugh bursts free before I can stop it. Knox's hand runs through his hair. "Aye, you mean the day you trusted your niece to drive in a foreign country for the first time?"

She quirks a brow. "I didn't know it was going to be *that* eventful."

Her embrace lingers after she pulls away. I take a moment to let my gaze wander over the courtyard. It's like time slows down, the soft golden lights casting long shadows while stars twinkle overhead. Everything really is...perfect.

By the time the night winds down, we've shared laughter, good food, drinks, and the kind of company that fills the heart up, but my mind's already a few steps ahead. I want to take my *fiancé* home.

I lean over, my lips brushing against his. "Take me home. Your fiancée has plans for you...and that kilt."

Knox throws his head back with a deep, hearty laugh. He grabs my hand, pulling me to my feet with an easy grin. "As much as we love and appreciate you all being here tonight," he calls out to the group, "the future Mrs. MacKenzie has plans to ravish me."

I gasp, my face flaming as I quickly cover it with my hands in a burst of embarrassment. "Knox!" I shout, half laughing, half scolding. "Your whole family is here, for Christ's sake!"

His grin only widens. "Aye, but they'll understand. It's not every day a man gets engaged to the love of his life."

"I can't believe you said that in front of everyone," I admonish, though my smile betrays me.

He pulls me into him, his hands settling gently on my hips. "Aye, well," he says, dipping his head until his mouth brushes my ear, his voice low and wicked. "The thought of you ravishing me is too tempting. Can you blame a man?"

I never imagined this would be my life. Not in a million years. But here I am. With a man in a kilt, grinning like he won the lottery and can't wait to take me home.

JULIETTE

The drive back home is thick with the kind of anticipation that crackles in the silence between words. My hand rests in his over the center console, and he's tracing slow circles on my skin, memorizing every inch. Like letting go isn't an option.

Outside the window, the countryside rushes by in a blur of moonlight and shadows, but all I can focus on is the ring on my finger.

"You keep looking at it like it might vanish," Knox says.

"I'm still trying to believe this is real," I murmur.

He doesn't say anything. Just glances at me, his eyes catching the light and holding me hostage in that slow-burn way of his.

By the time we get home, I'm already halfway undone. And he knows it.

Knox kills the engine, climbs out, and meets me at my side. He doesn't rush. Doesn't speak. Just laces our fingers again like he's grounding himself with me. When the front door clicks shut behind us, though...it's a different story.

He backs me into the wall, and then his mouth crashes into mine before I even suck in a breath. It's messy and hungry, all teeth and tongue and need, like he's trying to memorize the shape of my mouth with his own.

His hands cradle my face like I'm breakable, but his kiss is reckless, consuming, desperate. His thumbs sweep across my cheeks as he tilts my head and dives deeper.

And just like that, the world falls away. Time, names, dates, reasons—gone. All I know is him. This. The way he kisses me like I'm the only thing that's ever made sense.

"I've been wanting to do this all damn night," he growls, his breath ragged against my lips. "Watching you smile, laugh... knowing you're going to be my wife."

"And you're going to be my *husband*," I whisper, and the words ignite something primal in his eyes.

His hands slide down my sides, bunching the fabric of my dress as he lifts me with ease. My legs wrap around his waist, and I can feel the rough wool of his kilt against my inner thighs, a delicious friction that makes me gasp.

He nips at my lower lip as he carries me toward the living room. Neither of us has the patience to go upstairs. Knox lowers me onto the sofa, my back against the cushions as he stands before me, towering and magnificent.

"Don't you dare take that kilt off."

His eyebrow arches. "Enjoying the view, are you?"

"You have *no* idea."

I reach for him, fingers trailing up his thigh. The realization hits me...there's nothing underneath his kilt. Just Knox, hard and ready for me.

I gasp, my hand sliding higher beneath the wool. "So the rumors about Scotsmen are true."

Knox's smile is pure sin as he moves with deliberate slowness, kneeling between my spread legs. His hands push my dress up my thighs, bunching the fabric around my waist. When his fingers hook into my panties, I lift my hips without hesitation, allowing him to slide them down my legs.

"Beautiful." His voice is rough, laced with that thick accent.

His hands coax my thighs farther apart. I should feel shy... but all I feel is the heat building low and wild as his eyes drink me in like I'm something sacred.

I reach for him, desperate to feel him against me. "I need you, Knox. Now."

He leans forward, claiming my mouth in a kiss that steals my breath. "Patience. I want to savor my fiancée."

"Patience is overrated," I breathe, reaching between us. When my fingers wrap around his length, he hisses, his forehead dropping to mine.

"Christ, Juliette," he groans, his hips jerking forward instinctively.

I stroke him slowly, feeling him throb against my palm. "I want to feel you inside me. *Please*, Knox."

In one swift motion, he grips my waist and lifts me off the couch.

"You're going to get exactly what you want," he says, his voice husky with need as he carries me toward the kitchen.

My legs wrap around him instinctively, my arms looped around his neck as he walks with determined strides. When we reach the kitchen, he sets me on my feet, his fingers finding the zipper of my dress. The fabric slides over my skin, pooling at my feet, leaving me bare. The cool raises goosebumps across my exposed flesh.

"You're perfect," he murmurs as he lifts me again, this time setting me on the edge of the kitchen table.

The polished wood is cool against my thighs as I lean back on my elbows, watching as Knox stands between my legs, his hands caressing up my calves to my knees. His hands slide higher, pushing my thighs apart as he leans forward, his mouth leaving a trail of hot kisses up my inner thigh. But then he straightens, his eyes burning with hunger as they lock on my breasts.

He dips his head, capturing one nipple between his lips, and the wet heat of his mouth makes me cry out. His tongue circles the sensitive peak, then he sucks hard enough to make my back arch off the table.

"Knox," I gasp, my fingers threading through his hair, holding him to me as he moves to my other breast, giving it the same attention.

The sensation shoots straight between my legs, and I'm writhing beneath him, desperate for more. His teeth graze my sensitive skin, and I tug at his shirt, needing to feel his bare chest against mine.

Knox tears himself away just long enough to grip the collar of his dress shirt, his muscles flexing as he yanks it free. The buttons pop off with a satisfying snap, scattering across the kitchen floor. He stands there, chest heaving, his kilt still perfectly in place, the sight of him stripped to the waist leaving me breathless.

His hands grip my hips, pulling me to the edge of the table until I'm perfectly aligned with him. He lifts the front of his kilt, and my breath catches in my throat as I take in the sight before me.

His cock juts out from between his legs, thick and heavy, the tip flushed deep red with need. He's gorgeous everywhere. It's impossible not to take in his broad shoulders, the taper of his waist, his abs defined and ridged beneath taut skin that I want to taste.

"Is this what you wanted?" he asks.

"Yes," I breathe. I reach out, wrapping my fingers around

him. He's like steel wrapped in velvet, throbbing with heat in my palm. Moisture beads at the tip, and I swipe my thumb across it, spreading it over his sensitive head.

Knox hisses, his muscles tensing beneath his skin, the cords in his neck standing out as he restrains himself. The power I have over this magnificent man makes my head spin. I'm just about to stroke him again when his control snaps.

His hands grip my shoulders, shoving me back until I'm flat against the cold table. In one forceful thrust, he buries himself inside me. I cry out, my back arching off the table as he stretches me, the rough wool of his kilt grazing my thighs, sending a shiver through my body.

"Fuck, Juliette," he groans, his fingers digging into my hips.

"You feel so good," I whisper, my voice breaking as he fills me completely. Between the cold table below me and the scorching heat of his body above, the sensations are over-whelming.

Knox withdraws slowly, almost completely, before driving back into me with a force that sends me sliding up the table. His hands tighten on my hips, holding me in place as he sets a rhythm that has me gasping.

"My fiancée," he growls, the possessive edge in his voice sending a shiver down my spine. "Mine."

"Yours," I agree breathlessly, my hands reaching for purchase on the smooth surface of the table. "Always yours."

The sight of him above me, chest gleaming with a light sheen of sweat, muscles rippling with each powerful move-ment, his kilt bunched around his waist is nearly more than I can take. His eyes never leave mine, that intense green gaze searing into me.

I feel the familiar tension building low in my stomach, that pressure that signals I'm close. Knox must sense it, too, because one hand leaves my hip to slide between us, his thumb finding the sensitive bundle of nerves. He circles it with expert precision, his rhythm never faltering as he drives into me.

"Oh god, Knox!" I cry out as the first waves of pleasure crash through me. I clench around him, pulsing with each surge of my orgasm.

Knox slows his movements, watching me with dark eyes as I come apart. When the final tremors subside, he starts to withdraw, but I catch his wrist.

"Wait," I say, my voice husky with satisfaction. A new desire forms, wicked and urgent. "I want to watch you."

His brow furrows slightly. "Watch me what, *mo ghràidh?*"

I push myself up on my elbows, feeling deliciously languid. "I want to watch you finish yourself off."

His eyes widen, then darken with fresh arousal. "Christ, Juliette."

He steps back, his hand wrapping around his thick length. "Like this?" he asks, his voice a rough whisper as his large hand moves deliberately up and down his shaft.

I nod, mesmerized by the sight. "God, yes."

He stands between my spread legs, his kilt bunched around his waist, revealing the powerful muscles of his thighs as he works himself with increasing urgency. His eyes drink me in, roaming over my exposed body splayed before him, my heaving breasts, the ring glinting on my finger, the slick evidence of my pleasure still visible between my thighs.

"You're going to be the death of me," Knox groans, his pace quickening, muscles tensing across his abdomen. I can see the exact moment his control fractures, his jaw clenching tight.

"Look at me," he commands, his voice strained with the effort of holding back.

I meet his gaze, my pulse racing. His hand moves faster, his breathing ragged. Then, with a guttural groan, one that seems torn from the deepest part of him, Knox erupts. The first hot pulse lands on my stomach, then another across my breasts. I gasp at the sensation, watching as his release paints my skin where it pools in the hollow of my throat, more streaking across my trembling thighs.

"Fuck." He shudders as the last of his release fades, leaving him spent. Cum glistens on my flushed skin, marking me as thoroughly his, just like the ring on my finger.

Knox braces himself against the table, his chest heaving as he catches his breath. When his eyes meet mine, they're filled with a mix of satisfaction and reverence. "Look at you," he rasps, voice wrecked. "You're a fucking vision."

My cheeks flush, but it's not embarrassment. I feel claimed in the best way. Worshipped and wild. The heat between us hasn't eased. If anything, it's intensified. I trail my finger through the wetness on my stomach, bringing it to my lips. His eyes track the movement, pupils dilating as I taste him.

"You're going to kill me," he groans, leaning down to capture my mouth in a bruising kiss.

When he pulls away, his expression shifts to something tender. He disappears for a second, returning with a warm, damp cloth. With gentle strokes, he wipes the evidence of us from my skin.

His touch doesn't spark lust this time. Instead, it sparks something deeper that whispers, *you're safe here.*

Without a word, he scoops me up like I'm light as air. No big deal. Just a six-foot-something Highlander hauling around his emotionally overwhelmed fiancée.

I bury my face in his shoulder, completely boneless. It's the only way to survive the whiplash of being worshipped and ruined in the same breath.

If this is what love feels like when it's good and real and wrapped in trust...then he can have all of me. Tomorrow, the next day, and every single one after that.

forty-five

JULIETTE

SIX MONTHS LATER

The world outside Knox's house—*our* house—is finally waking up to spring. The air is lighter, almost like it's celebrating the start of something new along with me.

I catch a glimpse of myself in the mirror and can't help but pause. The woman looking back at me is almost a stranger, but in the best possible way. There's a spark in my eyes now, brighter and clearer. Gone is the doubt and uncertainty that used to cling to me like a shadow. And my smile... It's fuller, more at ease.

If there's any mascara streaming down my face today, it's only for the best reasons.

I run my hand down the delicate lace sleeves of my dress, the soft fabric tickling my skin as I trace the intricate patterns that extend all the way to my wrists. The dress is timeless and elegant with a skirt that cascades to the floor.

I'm not nervous, only excited.

My gaze shifts to my aunt in the mirror, and I catch her eyes. A wave of emotion hits me so hard, it's almost overwhelming. All the love she's poured into me, all the ways she's stood by my side... It means more than I could ever put into words.

"Skye would..." She pauses, her voice catching as she tries to keep the tears at bay. "She would have been riddled with joy over this."

I can't help but notice the gap where my mom should be. The one person who should be here beside me, holding my hand through every step of this moment, but isn't. Aunt Rose is the best person to stand in her place.

She steps closer, placing her hand on mine. "I have a letter for you from your mom," she continues. "I wasn't sure if I should give it to you now or later. She would've killed me if I did anything to ruin your makeup right now."

The hint of a smile forms on my lips, but it doesn't stop the tears that gather in my eyes. *Damn it.*

Do I want to read it now? Yes. The thought of having a piece of her with me on my wedding day would be the most precious gift.

"I'd like to read it," I whisper. "Will you stay here, though?"

Her eyes catch mine, full of understanding as she nods. "Of course."

I take it with trembling hands, my breath catching in my throat as I look at the familiar script of Mom's handwriting. Just the sight of it is enough to break me wide open.

The lump in my throat rises as I imagine her writing these words to me, knowing she wouldn't be able to see this. Her final days, her love, all condensed into this envelope.

I take a deep breath, trying to steady myself. This letter, her words, they're the closest I'll get to having her by my side today.

My Sweet Juliette,

As you walk down the aisle, know that I'm right there with you. Just like I always have been. You're marrying the love of your life (I'm pretty sure Rose would've made sure of that) and I couldn't be prouder of the woman you've become.

I hope you've found the kind of love that lives in the quiet moments. The belly laughs at the end of a long day. The hands that hold yours steady when the world tilts a little sideways. You deserve all of it and more.

I love you more than I've ever known how to say. I'll be walking with you every step, in every moment, for all the days to come.

With all my love, and then a little more,
-Mom

I can't tear my eyes away from the words on the page. I've shed so many tears for my mom over the years, but right now, there's an unexpected calm that settles over me. I can feel her here. Not in some ghostly, dramatic way, but in the grounding feeling in my feet, in the deep breath I just took.

With trembling hands, I carefully fold the letter, tucking it into the pocket of my wedding dress. Yes, a dress with pockets. Whoever thought of it is a genius.

"Maid of honor is here and reporting for duty!" Bree bursts in, a vision in her stunning, forest-green bridesmaid dress. She pauses for a moment, taking me in with wide eyes. "Oh my god, Juliette. Jesus. You're the most beautiful bride I've ever seen in my life."

I laugh at her entrance. She's exactly what I need right now, her energy and humor cutting through all the heavy emotions.

"Let's get you down that aisle," she says. "But I do have something for you from Knox first."

As she steps closer, I catch the weight in her eyes. It's subtle, but it's there...nothing like sadness or regret, but something wistful.

Dillon's name hasn't come up since she told me she ended things months ago. She walked away for a reason, but sometimes I wonder if part of her misses what almost was.

She holds out a familiar leather pouch. I take it from her, my breath catching as I pull out the compass and a small note tucked underneath.

To place around your bouquet as you come home to me.

My heart is doing cartwheels, and my mascara is fighting for its life. Damn him and his perfect words. I'm gonna kiss him stupid later.

Bree leans in to read the note, a mischievous smirk spreading across her face. "Damn, that's romantic. You sure you don't want to share? I could be a really supportive sister wife."

I can't help but laugh, the sound bubbling up easily. "Absolutely not. This one's mine."

She shakes her head as she fastens the little compass to my bouquet. "Yeah, I get it. I wouldn't share, either. Man writes like that, I'd chain him to the porch swing."

Right then, Lucy pops her head around the doorframe. "Hello, my dear future sister-in-law! We're ready for you."

I take a deep breath. It's happening. It's really happening.

I can feel the eyes of everyone in the room on me, waiting for a sign of nerves or second thoughts. But nope, that's not happening. Instead, I flash them a big, determined smile.

"Let's go, ladies. I've got a man waiting for me at the end of the aisle."

KNOX

I stand at the edge of the loch in my backyard, watching the stillness of the water. The air's thick with people chatting and buzzing with excitement. Juliette's about to walk down the aisle, and I swear, my chest might explode. It's been one hell of a ride to get here but all of it led to this moment. And damn if I'm not grateful for every bit of it.

I haven't laid eyes on Juliette in two days. She insisted on that old tradition of not seeing the bride before the wedding, so she's been staying with Rose. I got kicked out of my own house this morning so the girls had a place to get ready. Something about better lighting, more space, and "the right energy."

Cal's next to me as we wait for the ceremony to kick off. He looks over at me, his mouth stretched wide. "You ready, brother?"

I crack a grin of my own. "I've never been more ready for anything in my life."

I catch a quick look at the front of the aisle. Bree's over there, messing with her bouquet and shooting Cal a look that's all kinds of trouble. Cal pulls the same stuff when she's none the wiser, but the guy's about as subtle as a wrecking ball.

And then I see Juliette. She's coming down the path from the house, arm tucked into her aunt's, sunlight catching the edge of her dress. My lungs forget what they're supposed to do. Everything else fades out—every voice, every sound—until it's just her. Radiant. Untouchable. Mine.

God, she's breathtaking.

And not just because she looks like something out of a dream in that dress, but because it's her. The woman who loves harder than anyone I've ever met.

Every step she takes toward me feels like gravity shifting.

I don't even bother pretending I'm holding it together. The tears come, and I let them. How could I not? She's everything, and somehow, she's walking straight to *me*.

When they reach the end of the aisle, Juliette's hand slips into mine. Just like that, the universe lines everything up. All the mistakes, all the missed chances, were just pieces of a puzzle that led to this exact moment.

"You are stunning, *mo ghràidh*," I whisper as she looks up at me, her eyes shining with tears of her own. I want this moment burned into my memory.

The chatter of the small crowd fades into the background, the rustling of clothes and the shuffle of feet all muffled by the sound of my heartbeat. My stepdad starts the ceremony, his voice a familiar rumble in the air. I catch bits of what he's saying, but my focus stays on Juliette.

When it's time for the vows, I take a breath to steady myself. "Juliette, from the moment I met you, I knew my life was about to get a lot more interesting. You've made me better in ways I didn't know I needed. Even when we're chasing after your wild ideas or you're squeezing another pair of shoes into a closet that's already full, I'm totally and completely enamored by you."

A pause. A breath.

"I promise to laugh with you, to listen when the days get quiet, to be your home no matter where life takes us. I'll choose you, over and over. Not just today, but every day after this, for as long as I'm lucky enough to have you."

I slide the diamond wedding band onto her finger, and my heart swells in my chest. Seeing it on her, knowing she's mine not just in name, but in every way that counts, undoes me. She's everything I've ever wanted, wrapped in lace and wild grace.

My stepdad gives a slight nod toward Juliette, signaling her turn for the vows. She looks up at me with those eyes, and I swear, the rest of the world just blurs.

"Knox. *Captain*," she teases. "You've brought laughter, adventure, and a few extra pounds from your cooking into my life, and I wouldn't change a thing. You are my safe haven, and the home I've always dreamed of. I promise to make you laugh when you're taking life too seriously, and I'll always find a way to keep things interesting. I'm so lucky that forever gets to be with you."

She slips the titanium band onto my finger, and my last thread of restraint snaps clean in two.

I can't wait a second longer.

I pull her into me, one hand at the small of her back, the other buried in her hair, and kiss her like everything that's ever mattered begins and ends right here.

The world spins back into motion when Bree's voice cuts through the air like a firecracker. "Not yet, you savage!"

Laughter erupts around us, and I force myself to break away. My forehead rests against hers, both of us grinning like fools.

"By the power vested in me, and with great joy, I now pronounce you husband and wife. Knox, you may kiss your bride!"

I pull Juliette into my arms, dipping her low in a move that feels natural. This time, when I kiss her, it's slower. Reverent. Like a promise sealed in skin and breath and heartbeats. The crowd erupts in applause around us, but I only hear the sounds of her breathless laughter on my lips. Nothing else matters.

When I pull away, she's glowing, radiant in a way that steals my breath. My voice is rough with emotion as I whisper, "I love you, Mrs. MacKenzie. More than anything."

She looks up at me with that smile that says I'm either about to get kissed or roped into something that's going to change my whole life.

"You're gonna have to share some of that love." Her hand drifts to rest over her stomach.

I glance down at her hand, then back up to her eyes. "What?"

She nods, lips trembling around the smile she's trying to hold onto. It's the tears slipping down her cheeks that undo me. She laughs and cries at the same time.

"I'm pregnant."

I thought I knew what it meant to love her. I thought my heart had already reached its limit, as full as it could possibly get.

I couldn't have been more wrong. She's not just my wife. She's the mother of our *child*.

I've never wanted to fall to my knees for anything more than this.

I don't think. I don't even process it. I just move. One second, I've got her hand in mine, and the next, I'm sweeping her off her feet and spinning her around. Her laughter, that light, wild sound that slips straight into my soul, makes me feel like the luckiest bastard who's ever lived.

When I finally set her down, I can't bring myself to let go. My hands stay firm at her waist, grounding me to this new reality.

I press my forehead to hers, trying to absorb every second, every heartbeat.

"I don't know what I did to deserve this," I whisper. "But I swear, I'll never take a single second of it for granted."

JULIETTE

ONE YEAR LATER

I've never seen a more perfect sight.

Knox lies on our bed, a baby in each arm. One tiny head nestled against his bicep, the other resting right over his heart. Both of them sleeping because they already know they're in the safest place in the world.

Yep, two babies.

Our identical twin girls are four months old now, and I'm still not over it. Still not used to the sight of double bassinets or the fact that our laundry now includes ruffles.

They're this perfect little blend of the two of us with his grin and my nose. But their eyes? I've got a feeling they'll be all him. That wild, bright green. Like spring leaves after the rain.

And if I'm being honest, I'm thrilled. Because those eyes are my favorite part of him. Well...that and the part of him that helped make these two in the first place.

I lean against the doorframe, arms folded over my chest,

trying to memorize the way the morning light kisses all three of them. My whole world, right there in one frame.

Knox cracks one eye open as Keira starts to fuss. No wait, Maisie? Hell, this isn't the first time I've gotten them mixed up. I pick her up from the bed, checking the colored dot on the bottom of her sock. Okay, yep, green dot. *Keira.*

"I've got her," I assure him, smiling at how relaxed he looks with Maisie in his arms. "You rest with her as long as she'll let you."

I settle into the chair by the window with her, the soft creak of the rocking chair blending with the peaceful sounds of her tiny breaths. She's curled up against me, all warmth and sweetness.

"You know," I whisper to my husband, "you really need to stop looking so hot while you're holding the kids. You might make me want fifteen more."

That definitely gets his attention. His head snaps up, eyes flashing with a mix of amusement and that oh-so-familiar warning. "Don't tempt me, lass," he mutters. "I'll put the girls in their room and have you stripped down in ten seconds flat."

I raise an eyebrow and fight back a smile that threatens to break my resolve. "Dare you."

His smirk is pure trouble, but it's the look in his eyes that gets me. That tenderness. That soul-deep kind of love that's just for me. For us. For this wild, beautiful life we've made together.

I see plenty of babies in our future, and a whole lifetime of loving him right beside them.

acknowledgments

I don't even know where to start, but here goes.

In April of 2024, I took a trip to the UK with my husband to celebrate our tenth anniversary. While I was there, I fell in love with Scotland. I'm talking completely, irrevocably, head over heels in love. Scotland sank its wild, romantic claws into me and never let go. I left a part of my soul somewhere over there, and I haven't been the same since. Apparently, neither has my brain because in October of 2024, I started writing and couldn't stop.

Writing has lived in the back of my brain for as long as I can remember, and then one random day, I woke up and decided to do the damn thing. This book was born from that spark and that version of me who stood on a hill in the Highlands and thought... *This. I want more of this.* And now, here we are.

My first thanks goes to YOU, dear reader. Thank you for finding this story and sticking around. You helped turn a dream into something real, and I hope these pages made you laugh, swoon, or maybe even believe in love again. I hope you felt like you were right there in the Scottish Highlands with wind in your hair, mist on your skin, and magic in the air. I can't wait to share more with you, because this is just the beginning.

To my husband—this book would not exist without your endless support. Thank you for nodding patiently through my rambling and for pretending to understand character arcs at 11 pm. You let me chase this wild dream with your whole heart (and wallet) behind it, and that means everything. I love you, I love you, I love you.

To my kids—who better not pick up this book any time soon. Seriously. If you're reading this and you're not at least thirty-five, *put it down.* Thank you for being the little lights of my life and for occasionally giving me the silence to write. You'll probably never remember the afternoons I whispered, "just one more paragraph," or the snacks I tossed your way so I could squeeze out another scene, but I will.

To my mom, Lynda, and sister, Taylor—my original hype squad, who told everyone I was writing a book before I even had a plot. Thanks for cheering louder than anyone else and for sticking around even after reading the spicy scenes. Somehow managing to make eye contact with me afterward? That's not just love, that's straight up MVP level courage.

To my best friend, Ashlee—over twenty years of being my sounding board and you're still here. Thank you for reading my messy drafts and letting me spiral once a month (okay, sometimes twice) about packing up my life, booking a one-way ticket to Europe, and dragging my family across the Atlantic. You never flinch. You just listen and gently remind me that perhaps what I really need is a nap.

A final thanks goes to everyone who poured their hearts and souls into bringing this story into the world. My editor, Sara, who took my chaos and made it shine. The artists who helped me bring these characters to life. And to Emily, who handled all my graphics and content requests so I could keep my sanity. There's no way I could have done it without you all.

If you made it to the end of this, you officially own a piece of my heart (no returns, sorry not sorry). I'll see you in the next one!

about the author

Alexandra Ayres is a Canadian romance author living in Kentucky with her husband and two kids. She writes steamy, emotional stories about bold women discovering themselves and the love they deserve. When she's not writing, she's either planning her next travel adventure or sipping on iced coffee, always chasing inspiration one love story at a time.

AlexandraAyres.com

instagram.com/authoralexayres

tiktok.com/@authoralexayres

amazon.com/author/alexandraayres

goodreads.com/alexandraayres

www.ingramcontent.com/pod-product-compliance
Lightning Source LLC
Chambersburg PA
CBHW030237120726
47903CB00005B/1519